ENTICE

A NOVEL

AVA HARRISON

Cover Design: Hang Le

Line Edit: Lawrence Editing, www.lawrenceediting.com, Editing4Indies
Proofreader: Marla Selkow Esposito, My Brother's Editor
Formatting: Champagne Book Design

Dedicated to my crazy, unconventional family.
A home isn't a place; it's the people.

"There is a charm about the forbidden that makes it unspeakably desirable."
—Mark Twain

CHAPTER ONE

Grayson

"**W**HAT DO YOU MEAN I HAVE TO GO TO MALAGA?" I HISS through the phone. It's eight a.m. on a Friday morning after a long week. The last thing on my mind is travel, let alone traveling to Spain.

"Jeez, Gray. You act as though I'm telling you you're going to prison. It's Malaga, for crying out loud. A beautiful city on the Iberian coast," Addison, my sister, retorts. Easy for her to say. She hasn't worked in weeks.

Speaking of . . .

"Aren't you back to work yet?" I say through the phone.

"Nope," she responds.

A deep breath escapes my lungs, and I pivot my chair to look toward the city. The view from Price Enterprise is perfect. Standing tall on Park and 50th, my office faces downtown. It's a beautiful morning, and I have been looking forward to some much-needed solitude for days. Having to leave on such short notice and head to meetings my sister should be attending is not how I want to spend my weekend.

Don't get me wrong. I love my sister, but she needs to come back already.

"You know, because of work, I didn't get to take a real honeymoon last fall," she says, cutting into my inner rant. I turn back to my desk and pull up the calendar on the computer.

"And you've been gone for longer than most on your 'second' honeymoon. Isn't it customary to only take two weeks off work?"

"Well, I'm taking more." She laughs through the phone line. "Addy."

"Don't Addy me. I got married, and I'm taking time to be with my husband. Don't pretend this is a huge inconvenience. Don't pretend you even care. You're just trying to drive me crazy."

With that, I finally smile. It's true. I don't really care if she's away from the office. I just miss her. After our father passed away, the three of us stepped in to run things. And I enjoy giving her a hard time. Always have. Always will.

"That's what older brothers are for."

I can hear her inhale through the line, and then she speaks. "What's this really about?"

"I miss you," I admit on a sigh. "And I don't know how much more of Jaxson I can take. You're the buffer between us."

"Was that so hard to say?" She chuckles. Obviously, she's enjoying my moment of weakness.

"Yes. But now that I have, I do miss you, and things don't run the same without you here." I don't like to show my emotions, but when it comes to her, she's the only exception.

"Now aren't you glad you get to go to Spain?"

Not really. "Why would I be glad to be going to Spain?"

"One, it's a beautiful country. Two—"

I cut her off. "Addison, you're the one who travels, not me."

"Well, unfortunately, sometimes things have to change. Adapt or die, Gray. With me out of the office, I need you to step in and handle both our positions," she says sternly. Like I need to be scolded by my younger sister on my responsibilities. "Or do you want me to send Jax? I'm pretty sure he'll do . . . okay as my replacement."

"Fine." My kid brother is great, but he is not the one to close any deals. "When are your meetings?"

"Tomorrow," she says as if that doesn't completely fuck up my schedule.

"You owe me."

"Always. Thanks. Love you." She sends me invisible air-kisses before hanging up.

When I place the phone down, I shake my head on a chuckle. My little sister is the only person who can make me do something I don't want to do.

I have a soft spot for her, and the truth is, after everything she's been through, I understand her wanting some time away.

As if summoned, Jaxson walks into my office. I look at him and then at the door. The door that was closed, and he didn't bother to knock before opening.

"A knock is common courtesy," I say, lifting a brow.

"What's got your panties in a twist?" He saunters farther into the room, ignoring my comment completely as though he doesn't have a care in the world, and the truth is, he doesn't. He's much younger than me. I'm supposed to see him as a man, as the COO of this company, but when he walks into my office wearing a white tee, ripped jeans, and a hat, it's pretty damn hard.

"I don't have panties, and if I did, they would be perfectly ironed," I grunt back.

He holds up a hand to relish the mental image before proceeding. "Then why does it look like you have to take a shit? Unless—"

"Do you ever not say exactly what you're thinking?" The

words come out loud enough that if anyone was in the office next door, they would hear. Lucky for me, it's Addison's office, so it's vacant.

"Eh." He shrugs. "Pretty much. So what's troubling you, bro?"

"I wish you'd grow up and work harder," I fire back.

"I work hard."

"Hacking girls on social media is hardly work."

"First of all, you should've specified. Second, how else am I going to find out if they are psycho before dating them?" He poses the question seriously, and it makes me shake my head at him.

My brother is insane.

"Try like the rest of us."

"Yes, and look how that turned out for you. Your last relationship got an F, and not for fucking."

"That's not because I didn't cyber-stalk her, but I digress. When are you going to grow up and take on more responsibility . . . here? As in this office, as in Price Enterprise."

"I'm the COO." His voice is serious, as if he runs the place, as if he comes into work on time and is the last person here.

"In name only. I don't see you having to take over all Addison's meetings."

"Ahhh. Now I see."

"See what?"

"You're envious of our sister." The smug shit smirks.

"Of course, I'm envious. She's off vacationing, and I'm taking over all her work."

"Where is she sending you off to this time?" he asks.

It's obvious Addison has me jet-setting somewhere. Three days ago, I was in Tennessee, then before that, France, and before that . . . how many places have I been since my sister's wedding? Too many to even recollect.

"Spain."

"Spain is a wonderful country. The women—"

I lift my hand to shut my brother up. "I don't care about the women."

"Maybe that's your problem. Maybe if you fucked someone . . ." He trails off for emphasis.

"Not that it's any of your business, but I don't need any pointers on when, where, or who to fuck." My voice rises, and if I wasn't sure the whole floor heard our conversation before, I'm pretty certain they have now. "I'm just sick of traveling." And I am. I like routine. I like order. I like to be in control, and Addison calling me every day breaks all that to shit. My father always wanted his company to be passed down from generation to generation, to succeed, and although I'm doing that by traveling, I feel my time is better spent making sure this company is profitable. The time it takes for me to go to this meeting could be better spent here.

Maybe the meeting isn't that important, and someone else can go . . .

I pick up my phone and call Addison back.

"So soon. No. You can't renege."

"I'm not reneging. I just wanted to know who I'm meeting with."

"Oh, did I forget to tell you?" Her voice lowers, and I wonder what's going on? "You're meeting with Tyler." She pauses, and I know she wants to say more. I don't know how I feel about this revelation.

I haven't spoken to him in years.

"Fuck."

Okay, now I am sure how I feel about it.

"You have a few other appointments too"—she says quickly—"but the big one is Tyler."

"I'm not sure that's a good idea."

"I just feel like I owe him." She sighs through the phone.

"What do you mean?" My shoulders tense from this exchange.

"Here's the thing, Gray. I'm the one who convinced Dad to pass on Tyler . . ."

"It's not the point, Addison. It was business, and Tyler Reed was my best friend. He threw that away over a job," I hiss back.

"I know, but with everything in my life, I have started to think about all the people I have harmed in the past, and Tyler is one of them. I want to do right by him."

"Okay. . ." I trail off for her to continue. "Why now?"

"I heard a rumor that his business is doing bad. Having him work on the renderings for the property might not be a huge job, but it's the least I can do to help."

I let out a long-drawn-out sigh. "I'll meet with him. But so help me, Addison . . . if he's still a six-inch dick, I'm walking."

"He won't be. From what I could tell on the phone when I set up the meeting, he seems genuinely remorseful for his behavior."

"Fine, if that's all, I'll talk to you later. Unless there's another person from the past you want to spring on me?"

"Not at the moment, but let me think harder," she jokes softly. "Love you."

"Love you, too," I respond before hanging up the phone.

I don't know how to feel about meeting with Tyler Reed. There was once a time when he was like an older brother to me, but I haven't seen him in years. He and I were friends in high school. Every summer, I would stay with my grandparents at their Hamptons house, and Tyler's family had a house up the beach. Tyler was older than me by two years, but seeing as no one else was around, we became fast friends.

I don't like to go out east anymore, so we've fallen out of touch and haven't spoken in forever.

Not since the fight.

Wonder what he's been up to?

CHAPTER TWO

River

THE EARLY MORNING SUNLIGHT STREAMS IN THROUGH THE window of the apartment where I'm staying. I have just pulled an all-nighter to finish this term paper, and luckily for me, I'm finally done. It was my last paper for my semester abroad.

Talk about waiting until the last minute. Cutting it close is a problem I have with school assignments.

Even though I knew this paper was due, I couldn't bring myself to even start it until last night. Yeah, not my finest moment, but I was up for the challenge. Equipped with an endless supply of coffee, I spent yesterday and all through the night typing.

Now that it's done, and I have sent it over to my professor, I stretch my hand over my head, then flex my hands and let out a massive yawn.

I'm beat. Drained. My only plan now is to sleep for a week.

Standing, I make my way across the room and climb into my bed. It's warm and inviting. Enormous goose feather pillows beg for me to crash on. After being up for over twenty-four hours, a cot on the side of the road would be welcome.

My eyes start to shut of their own accord when I hear my phone vibrating on the bedside table.

Reluctantly, I reach my hand out and grab it.

It's Kim, my stepmother. A small smile grows on my face. "Kim, is everything okay?" I answer with a yawn.

"Did I wake you?" she asks, her voice more energetic than I'm used to.

"Actually, no." I pull the comforter back and slide under the sheet. "But I was trying to go to bed."

"Ahh, to be young." She laughs. "Late night with friends?"

"Late night with schoolwork."

"Last minute, I see."

"I like to live dangerously, but now, thankfully, it's done, and I can sleep for days."

"So, does that mean you don't want to join your father and me in Malaga?"

I sit up in the bed, realizing Kim doesn't plan to get off the phone soon.

"What's in Malaga?" I ask.

"Business."

I should've known better. Dad is always working. However, as much as he works, it's always a better option than my Lily Pad.

Where most kids were told to call their mothers Mom or Mommy, I was told to call mine Lily Pad. She was a flower child. Born to save the world from corruption, she rejected one conventional society after the other. She was all about peace and love.

Yet, I have no idea where she is right now.

At least I'll find out next week when we meet up in Portugal. I'm sure she'll tell me about all her exploits, including and regardless of how much I protest all the men she met.

Mom's a free spirit like that. Hence my name.

River.

Who names their child River anyway, other than celebs, and more so, who names their girl River? I'm pretty sure River is typically a boy's name.

My mom, however, was apparently born in the wrong generation. She should have been born in the 70s instead of the 80s, a natural hippy.

Case in point, the reason she chose my name. Apparently, that's where I was conceived.

By a river.

She must have thought it symbolic. That I was meant to be free and never trapped, always moving.

Who actually tells their child where they had sex? I'm just happy I wasn't conceived in a Coachella restroom. Oh, and the story just got better—it was a one-night stand.

Yep.

So not only did my mom get knocked up next to a river, but she didn't even know the guy. Which is so cool by me. Yup. Not scarred by this at all.

"So how about it?" Kim says, pulling me out of my thoughts.

"What?"

"Do you want to come meet us in Malaga?" she asks again.

"I have to meet Lily," I say, using my mom's name since I have never seen her as much of a "mom."

I shake my head at the ridiculousness of my life.

One parent who is flighty and wants to be my best friend, and a father who was never around. But in truth, I don't really blame him for that. My mother didn't even know him, and he was young and in high school when he found out. Then one summer when I was twelve years old, she just dropped me off with him. He had no idea what to do with me. So it turned out I had two shitty parents. But at least he had the decency to hire someone to spend time with me. Basically, he hired a nanny for a twelve-year-old.

A hired friend.

Kim.

My nanny eventually married my dad, and to be honest, it's the best thing that ever happened to me.

"You aren't seeing her for a week. I'll book you a flight today, and you can be here tonight. And I'll arrange a room so you can sleep the night away."

"I don't know if I can."

"It'll be fun. Your father has to work, but I'd like to spend time with you."

"I'm not sure."

"Come on. You can come early, nap, and then meet us for dinner. Tomorrow, we can go shopping."

"I doubt I could make dinner," I respond, already knowing if Kim wants to see me, I'll be there, but dinner is another story.

"Oh, that's too bad. I'm sure Gray would love to see you."

"Gray?" I ask, my voice low. She couldn't mean Grayson Price, could she?

"I won't lie and tell you it's not business. You'd be crashing a business dinner, but I'm sure you remember Grayson Price from when you were younger."

I did.

I do.

How could I not?

I have loved that man since I was twelve . . . well, maybe not love but certainly infatuated.

Been following him on social media ever since.

After what he did for me all those years ago, the first thing I did when my father bought me my first phone was google him.

He was easy to find. Even years later, Google and TMZ have fed my habit.

"I'll be there," I say, trying my best not to sound eager.

"And dinner?" she questions.

"I'll be there, too." I hang up the phone, and all of a sudden, I have a new burst of energy. Without another thought, I pop out of my bed and head toward the closet, rummaging through it to pick out my outfits for the weekend.

If I'm going to see Grayson Price, I have to look my best.

Although it's not like he'd look at you. You're young enough to be his daughter.

I chide myself, but it doesn't stop me from packing my clothes and placing it in my carry-on. I don't have much. I have learned to travel light over the years.

A lesson Lily taught me.

CHAPTER THREE

Grayson

TEN MINUTES.

I check my Rolex for the second time. Tyler is ten minutes late. Normally, I'd leave at this point, even if it's business. I'm meticulous about time and being punctual.

I'm meticulous about everything, to be honest.

If this were anyone else, the deal would be off, and I'd take the contract from him. But Addison was adamant that he's remorseful, and if what she said about his business is true, I'd like to help. What I have learned since Tyler and I fell out is life can be fleeting. You don't know how much time you have here, so there is no reason to hold a grudge. If he wants to bury the hatchet, then I'm down as well. So instead of getting up and walking, I shake it off. Lifting my hand, I signal for the bartender.

"I will be having that drink after all. Glenlivet neat."

Tonight, I'm meeting with him to go over the details on the property we have in Malaga. Addison should be here. I don't give two shits about what we do with the land, who leases it, who we sell to, or what is built. I'm a numbers guy. All I care about is that we make money.

The bartender comes over a few seconds later and places a tumbler down in front of me. I lift the glass to my mouth, and as I'm about to swallow, I sense a presence beside me. I turn, take the swig, and look at who's there.

A woman.

She's beautiful.

Exquisite, really.

Young.

With long, sun-kissed locks that fall below her breasts, I lift my gaze to study her features. She's too young for me, that's for certain. She appears to be in her mid to early twenties with big blue eyes and freckled skin as though she's just left the beach. Her hair flows in waves that look tousled by the wind.

If I thought she was lovely before, she smiles, and my pulse begins to race. How long has it been since I've gotten laid? Too long, if I have to ask.

I watch as she nibbles on her lower lip as if she's waiting for me to say something. When I don't, she pulls her shoulders back and then flashes me a smirk.

"Mind if I join you?" But she doesn't wait for me to answer before she takes the seat beside me. In this position, I can see she's wearing a dress, and from where she's perched, it's short.

"Not at all," I say. "What would you like?"

"A glass of champagne, please," she responds. Her voice is soft like an angel.

Fuck.

What is wrong with me?

I turn to the bartender again. "A glass of champagne for the lady."

A second later, the flute is placed in front of her, and she tips it back, her full lips touching the glass, her tongue sweeping out to lick a drop that missed her mouth.

I wonder what her lips would feel like on mine.

"So what brings you to Malaga?" I ask, needing to know more about this woman. "Business or pleasure?"

A seductive smirk spreads across her face as if she's up to no good, and the idea of bringing her back to my room later and sinking inside her becomes more and more promising.

"What?"

"Pleasure," she finally draws out, and I know if I want her, I can have her. I take a swig of my drink and then sear her with my gaze.

"I'm supposed to be meeting a buddy for dinner, but it appears he's not showing. Are you free tonight?"

Since Tyler isn't here, I might as well make the best of my trip.

Her eyes widen, and she opens to her mouth to speak, hopefully, to say yes, but then I hear it.

"Grayson," the voice calls out from behind me, and I turn to find Tyler approaching. I want to curse him for coming now. I know, at first, I hated that he was late, but now that he's here, I want him to leave.

He turns to the lady on my right and smiles. "I see you found him," he says to her, and I narrow my brows . . .

Found him?

He knows her.

"Yes, he was kind enough to buy me a drink." She lifts the glass at him and winks.

"You're not old enough to drink," Tyler adds, and I swear it's like I'm watching a ping-pong game, and I can't figure out what's going on.

"I am in Spain," she chides.

And that makes me look from him to her.

What am I missing?

Tyler . . . Is he cheating on Kim?

"So, Grayson, does she look the same?"

"Does who look the same?"

"River, of course." He points at the stunning beauty beside me.

She looks familiar. Why do her eyes look familiar, and why is Tyler looking down adoringly at this woman? And then it hits me in the gut.

This is no woman. She's a girl. A very beautiful one but a girl, nonetheless.

Young.

Very. Fucking. Young. How did I not see it before?

A girl so young, she could be my daughter. She's *his* daughter.

I look up at the ceiling and take a deep breath.

My chest feels tight at the thoughts running through my mind only minutes before Tyler walked over because this girl isn't just some girl.

This girl is my old friend's daughter.

The little girl I met at my friend's party.

I haven't seen her since she was what . . . twelve, but now that I am equipped with that knowledge, all I see is the little girl I once knew.

The sad little girl I met at Tyler's house on the beach.

Shit.

———— ◆ ————

It's hard to concentrate.

I need to, though. We haven't talked about the past, but I can tell Tyler is anxious about the issues he's having with work. Word around town—aka Addison and then Jaxson—is that Tyler's company is in debt. Hence, why Addison hired him to do the rendering for the Lancaster proposal. We are paying him to make mock-ups on the land.

Right now, he's going over his idea, but instead of paying attention, I keep hazarding a glance at the girl in front of me.

She's way too young for the thoughts that skated across my mind only a short while ago.

I'm probably fifteen or sixteen years older than then her. Tyler hooked up with her mother back when we were in high school.

I remember when it happened. I had gone to the Catskills with Tyler and his family for Halloween. The party out by the river. I remember him and the local girl from town.

Lily Pad.

We didn't know her name then.

No, it was months later when she showed up asking to speak to Tyler.

It was a scandal.

Only a senior in high school, he was about to be a father.

As horrible as it is to say, that was the best sex-ed class everyone had.

Everyone either abstained or practiced very safe sex after that.

Pulling my gaze away, I study my friend. He looks drawn. Large circles rim underneath his eyes, and I wonder when he last slept through the night. He mentioned earlier that Kim wouldn't be coming to dinner because she didn't feel well, maybe he's getting sick too?

The waitress sets our plates down in front of us.

The smell of the food wafts up through the air, filtering in through my nose. My mouth instantly waters. I worked so hard today and didn't take the time to eat.

Lifting my fork, I take a bite, but then from across the table, she moans.

It's soft but still loud enough to stab me in the gut for the thoughts it brings to my head.

A cough or more like a choke escapes my mouth.

Fuck.

Her eyes are closed. Lost in the passion of the delicious bite.

No. Don't look at her. You can't.

Is she even legal?

If I'm thirty-six, that makes her twenty.

Thank fuck.

I don't know if I'd ever be able to live with myself if she was still in her teens.

Twenty, although young, is way better than nineteen.

I'd never be able to look Tyler in the eye again if she was.

"When do you want to head over to the property?" I ask to stop my train of thought.

"The sooner, the better," he responds. I don't know how bad his financial situation is, but a sobering feeling spreads through me. Here I am, lusting after a stranger who turns out to be his daughter when his business might be going under.

I really am a bastard.

I continue to stab at my entrée. It's not that I don't like his company, but I'm still out of sorts from what happened at the bar. As soon as I'm done, I'm going to excuse myself and drink. Alone.

"What are your plans this summer?" Tyler asks.

"Nothing as of yet."

"Good. I'll be in New York, too. I'd like to start as soon as we're back."

"Sure. No problem."

"Should I call your assistant—"

"No. Call me directly," I say, cutting him off. "After our

meeting tomorrow, I'll be here for a few more days, but then I'll be back in the city."

"Great. Thank you. You don't know how much I appreciate it."

As the rest of the meal progresses, the tension is thick in the air between Tyler and me. We discuss sports. We talk briefly about the property, and then we speak about River's school.

She's just finished up a semester abroad studying in Spain.

"So where are you off to now that you're done in Spain?" When the table goes silent, I'm grasping at straws for something to talk about.

She worries her lip before righting herself.

"To see my mother," she responds.

"How is your mother?"

"Flighty," she deadpans.

To that, Tyler chuckles. When he stops, he cocks his head at his daughter.

"Riv—"

"Well, she is. If we didn't have company"—she gestures to me—"I'd regale you with all the dirty details of my youth before you got custody and all the details of the limited time I've spent with her as of recently. But alas, I won't. So yes, Dad . . . she's flighty."

"I'm sorry," her dad starts, and she lifts a hand.

"It's fine," she responds, but even to my untrained ear, it's not. This is a sore spot.

I expect someone to say something, but instead, River pushes up from her chair.

I move to stand, and she shakes her head.

"Just need air."

I feel like an ass. Lesson learned. Don't ask about her mom.

I'm not sure why I catalog that in my thoughts because I won't see her again.

When she comes back, she stands beside the table, looking down at me with those big blue eyes, eyes that one could surely get lost in, ones that I almost did get lost in. I pull my gaze away only to lock onto her swollen lips. She's nibbling on the lower one as she stares at me, and I let out a strangled cough before looking away. Luckily, with the bill paid, I can stand to leave.

"I'll see you tomorrow," I say to Tyler.

Turning to River, I step in, and when I do this time, the soap on her hands infiltrates me. I shouldn't want to inhale her, but I do. And with a lame mumble of an excuse under my breath, I walk away.

No goodbye.

No nothing.

The faster I'm out of here, the faster I can forget I almost hit on a girl young enough to be my daughter.

Thank God I didn't, though.

Even if she smells divine. Even if she is exquisite, it doesn't matter. Leaving is the best decision I've made all night. It's just what I need to get myself in check.

Just as I think I'm in the clear and can escape to the solitude in my room, I hear my name being called from behind.

"Gray," Tyler's voice rings through the air.

I turn around and see him walking briskly over to me. "If you have a minute . . ." he starts, and he looks down at the floor, and I know he's feeling awkward and uncomfortable. "I'd like to speak with you. Alone."

"Sure," I respond, not really wanting to do this, but I'm not one to back down, so I will.

"Let's go to the bar and grab a drink."

I lead the way. This time, we take a seat at a small table in the corner.

Once we both have tumblers of scotch in our hands, he speaks.

"I'm sorry."

His words take me off guard. I wasn't expecting an apology. When I don't respond, he continues. "I have had a lot of time to think over the mistakes I have made in the past. And the biggest mistake I've made is the way I acted with you."

"It's water under the—"

"No, it's not," he cuts me off. "I threw away a friendship over something that wasn't your fault. Addison told me she was responsible . . . but the truth is, it doesn't matter. It was business, and it shouldn't have had anything to do with our friendship. I'm sorry," he says, his voice thick with emotions.

"It's okay."

"But it shouldn't be. After what I did, you giving me this opportunity . . ." He trails. "You don't know how much it means to me. How much I need this."

"What's going on?"

"It's bad. Business is bad. There isn't enough money to cover expenses. This job . . ." His voice cracks. "Thank you for helping me."

"Will it be enough?" I ask, but I don't need him to answer. I can tell by the hollow look in his eyes that it might not be.

"For now, yes. But after . . . ?" He lifts his hands and buries his head in it. "I just don't know."

An idea pops into my head. "But what if it's not just a sample rendering?"

"What do you mean?"

"What if I can convince Lancaster to use you as the architect for the project?"

"You would do that for me?"

I nod.

"I was a dick, and you are still willing to help me."

Again, I incline my head.

"Thank you. I don't deserve it, but thank you."

After that, we don't talk about the past. Instead, he fills me in on what's going on in his life. It might have been years, but it feels like old times.

CHAPTER FOUR

River

"ARE YOU SURE WE CAN'T CONVINCE YOU TO STAY?" KIM says from beside me on the couch.

"I really can't. I'm supposed to meet Lily tomorrow."

"So I only have you today?" Her voice is sad.

"I'm sorry. It's just . . ."

"I know. I'm just giving you a hard time. Don't worry about it. But can you please consider coming to New York this summer? I know you hadn't planned on it, but we would love to have you."

Her lips turn up, but it's tight. Almost a grimace. I know I should forget about Portugal, but my mother . . .

Kim is your mom.

Lily Pad is not a mom.

She is the woman who abandoned you. The woman who only thinks you were worth a summer trip and nothing more.

Kim has my back. She's the one who's always been here, the one I can talk to and cry to.

"So if I only have today, how do you want to spend it?"

"It's just us, right?" I ask, and Kim's eyebrow lifts.

"Were you expecting someone else?"

My tongue feels heavy in my mouth as I try to come up with a plausible answer. I'm dying to see Grayson again, but I can't say that.

"Umm, Dad." My answer comes out all wrong, and I want to cringe as I wait for her to call me out. I never told Kim about my insane crush on my dad's friend, nor do I plan to now. No. My feelings for Grayson are solely for me to know.

"Are you telling me or asking me?" She chuckles.

"Telling," I mutter back, and she leans into me, cocking her head.

"See, and here I thought maybe you were talking about Grayson Price."

"W-W-What? Who? No," I stutter. "No. No. No."

"Really . . . ?"

"Of course not." My words aren't convincing, and my cheeks warm with heat.

"Why not? He's rather easy on the eyes. Has a great job. Stern. Not sure if he smiles, but he is nice to look at."

"He smiles," I say before I can stop myself.

"Is that so?" Her lips purse. "And how do you know this?"

"Jeez, Kim. You're like a dog with a bone."

"That's some bone, though. He's cute."

Cute wouldn't be the word I would use. Handsome, brooding, pure delicious perfection, now those are all better ways to describe the man who plays a recurring role in my daydreams.

"He's also old enough to be my dad."

"First, not really."

"He's Dad's age."

"No, he's not. He's actually two years younger than your father. And you have to remember your dad was super young when he had you," she says matter-of-factly, which is true. Dad was only seventeen when he became a dad. He didn't even know.

"That would still make him fifteen years older than me."

Technically sixteen years until my birthday next month. *But who's counting?*

"Your dad is older than me, and we make it work. Besides, you've always been very mature for your age, River. You have an old soul. An older man may be exactly what you're looking for."

"My dad is only seven years older than you. That's hardly an age gap." As the words pass through my lips, I think about them for a second and realize maybe she's right. Maybe it isn't so bad. He really isn't that much older. Sure, fifteen years is a lot right now, but in the grand scheme of life, it isn't.

"Fine." She throws up her hands. "You're no fun."

What she doesn't know is that I won't even admit to myself how much I want him, and even though the age really isn't the issue for me, I know it would be for him. That and the fact Tyler is my dad doesn't help. So since it's never going to happen, I shouldn't give myself false hope. I can't humor my stepmom's ridiculous fantasy for my life. It's just not in the cards for me.

"Let's go shopping," I say as I stand from the couch, basically shutting down all discussion of Grayson Price and of my lack of a social life.

Maybe in my next city. Maybe with Mom, I can meet someone who can make me stop thinking of a man I can't have.

Mom does make a great wingman. As much as I hate to admit it's true, Mom—aka Lily Pad—is always the life of the party. In the time I have spent with her, I have raised her and not vice versa. She lives as if every breath is her last. Traveling like a nomad, she teaches yoga to make just enough money to have food and a place to eat. She's never in a place long enough to place roots down.

I shake all the thoughts of my mom away and grab my bag. Kim stands from the sofa. She looks tired. I raise an eyebrow. "Are you sure you want to go?"

"Of course." She grabs her purse off the table and heads for the door. "Maybe we can even find some material for you to make me a necklace."

Together, we walk out of the room into the hall and ride down the elevator. In just a few minutes, we're exiting the hotel. The warm summer air slaps across my face as we make it into the roundabout drive in front of the hotel.

The hotel we've chosen is only a few minutes away from the city, so we head that way, walking down roads and beautiful overgrown parks until we get to the main square.

We're surrounded by buildings with ancient architecture and beautiful churches adorned with mosaic tiles. It's lovely and like a dream come true. I'm happy to be here experiencing it with Kim.

We continue our trek to where the clothing stores are, and once inside, we peek around and I try some clothes on.

Small bikinis Dad would kill me if he saw me in.

However, they're perfect for Portugal.

We walk around for about an hour; I find a few pieces that I might be able to use to make a necklace for Kim. Once we're done, we head back to lie by the pool. I drink a glass of sangria while Kim sips on lemon water under a big floppy hat and umbrella.

And although we do nothing, it's perfect. A perfect way to start my summer adventure.

———— ◦◦◦ ————

The next evening, I arrive in Portugal. There are not enough words in the English language to describe my level of exhaustion.

As soon as I land in Lisbon, I find a cab and make my way to the hotel. I had made a reservation at the same one where my mother would be at. While I check in, I can barely keep my eyes open, but I manage to make it to my room. I tried to call my mother when her train arrived, but she didn't answer. Now that I'm settled, I reach for my phone. Nothing again. Like me, she's probably exhausted, so I put my phone down on the pillow and get under the covers to get warm. Before I know it, I'm opening my eyes, and it's the next day. I stretch my arms over my head, letting out a yawn.

Once I wring the sleep from my body, I reach across the bed and find my phone. There is one missed call from my dad and one missed text from Kim.

Kim: Hope you arrived safely. Text your father and me to let us know.

I smile to myself because although my mom hasn't called, both Kim and Dad have.

———◦———

Two days pass.

Two long days.

Two long days with no word from Lily Pad.

I refuse to mentally acknowledge her as my mom at this point because no mother would leave her daughter alone in Portugal without a word.

I've spent the past two days sporting my new bikinis alone at the pool.

But I can't put off my other parents much longer.

Seeing as I only texted them once.

Kim keeps calling, so I'll have to call her back.

But I know myself. If Kim asks, I'll lose it. I won't be able to hold down the hurt I've been feeling about Lily Pad forgetting about me.

But I have no choice.

When the phone rings, I answer. "Hey," I say in a soft voice.

"River?"

"Yeah, I'm here."

"A-Are you okay?"

Although I expected her questions, it still makes me feel like back when I was a little girl and my mother abandoned me for one of many times.

Tears prick my eyes, and I lift a finger to swipe them.

"I'm fine."

"Are you really?"

They fall harder now. So hard that it's like a broken dam.

My breathing becomes labored, filled heavy with choked sobs.

"Oh, River. What happened? What did she do?"

I can barely speak through the sounds coming from me. I know I'm being overdramatic. This isn't the first, and it certainly won't be the last time my mom forgets about me.

Why do I even care?

"S-She forgot," I hiccup and stutter out. How I manage to even say that is beyond me.

"I'm so sorry," she coos.

"Why do I care?" I sob. "Just tell me why the fuck I still give a shit?"

I don't know if I'm asking myself or her at this point.

"Because no matter what, she's your mother, and you love her."

"But why do I?"

"'Cause you're a good person. The best I know."

"Thank you."

"It's the truth. Now here is what we are going to do. I expect you on the next plane to New York . . ."

"But—"

"No. No buts. You were supposed to spend the summer with her, but now, you'll spend it with me."

"Are you sure?"

"Am I sure? Yes, I'm sure. The Hamptons house is quiet when your dad is working. I'd love to have you here. It will be like that first summer . . ."

The first summer my mom dropped me off. My chest feels heavy, and I can't believe this is happening. After that summer, I had sworn I wouldn't allow her to let me down again. I'd sworn that I would keep my expectations low and place a wall around my heart where my mom was concerned. But unfortunately, I had failed.

"We'll watch movies by the pool. Eat ice cream all the time. It will be great."

"Okay. I'll come home, but I'm not sure if I'll come to the Hamptons yet."

"Oh, well, either way, I can't tell you how happy this makes me." She lets out a sigh of relief, and I know she's happy. I'm happy, too.

They're my family. Why am I reaching for someone who doesn't want me? I stand from my bed and make my way to the cabinet and start repacking my bag.

It's time to go home.

CHAPTER FIVE

Grayson

I'T'S GOOD TO BE BACK IN NEW YORK. IT'S NOT THAT I DON'T like traveling; it's just I like to be home more. I like my apartment. I like my stuff. I like my solitude.

I'm different from my siblings in that manner.

Addison loves to see the world, and Jax . . . well, he loves people.

I hate both.

Not my siblings, but the world. And people.

Quiet. That's what I like. That, and a glass of scotch.

The need for solitude started when I was young when I realized how fleeting life could be.

That's what happens when your grandfather dies in your arms.

Having your father die when he was only fifty-seven doesn't help either.

Now I like to be alone. I just don't want anyone attached to me.

Just in case.

So, now, I enjoy those two things other than my family—quiet and scotch—and depending on Jaxson's antics, the latter is debatable.

I'm happy to be home, and now in my office, things are right in the world.

There is plenty to do. Addison should be arriving shortly, and I need all the sales figures in order.

That way, she's prepared for wherever she needs to go next because I certainly am not going in her place. I'd much prefer to spend my summer in the city, working.

The intercom on my desk phone starts to ring, pulling me out of my haze. I look down to see it's Nicole, my assistant.

I hit the speaker button.

"Yes."

"Addison is here."

"Can you tell her to go to the conference room?"

"No problem."

"Also, call Jax and see where his ass is."

She laughs into the line.

Jax, unlike every other employee in this company, makes his own schedule. Regardless of what I say to him, he comes and goes as he pleases.

Who knows what he's doing half the time. The only reason Addison and I are not on his case is because, at the end of the day, he gets his shit done. Who cares if he's doing it here or from his apartment? He could do it from Bora Bora, for all I care, as long as it got done.

He might do, actually.

"Yes, boss."

I press the intercom button to disconnect and then lift my coffee to my mouth. I'm happy my sister is back because I have no desire to travel again. The only good thing that came out of my trip to Malaga was seeing Tyler, but that only led to a bigger problem . . . hitting on his daughter.

When I saw her at the bar, I obviously didn't recognize her, but how could I really? She had grown up.

She wasn't the little girl I met once, a long time ago.

No, she certainly had changed.

Perfectly straight teeth replaced crooked ones. Disheveled, wavy hair was now long gone.

Her skin was flawless like the porcelain of a doll, her lips full and kissable.

Jeez, what is wrong with me?

At least I didn't think of her body . . . and now I'm thinking of it. I let out a groan. Why did she have to be Tyler's daughter? Although young, she would have been the perfect distraction for my trip. A nameless beauty to sink into.

Then I would have come home and forgotten her.

Instead, I'm home, and I can't get the damn girl out of my head.

Her body, her smell, her eyes.

I lift my mug and take a swig, forgetting how warm it is and burning my tongue. But I welcome the feeling. Anything to make me forget River and all the things I wanted to do to her.

My friend would have me by my balls if he knew.

Hell, Addison alone would murder me.

Jax would find it funny.

But luckily for me, none of that will happen.

Her father mentioned she was traveling to Portugal, so I'll never have to see her again. Which is a good thing because she deserves more than a fuck, and I can't give her or anyone more than that.

My phone rings yet again, and again, it's Nicole. Before I can even speak, she says, "They're ready for you in conference room one."

"Thank you."

With one last chug of my coffee, I set off to see my siblings.

The hallways are quiet as I make my approach. It's after eight now. I'm surprised we were able to get everyone together this early. Addison is most certainly jet-lagged, and Jax . . . knowing him, he probably slept in the apartment in the building. I open the door and my normally present scowl instantly drops when I see her.

My sister looks beautiful. Happy. Nothing like the way she used to look.

"You look good," I echo my thoughts.

"Thanks, you look tired," she responds with a shrug.

"Thanks, I've been working." The sarcasm in my voice is not lost on her as she rolls her eyes playfully.

"I worked."

"Yeah . . . on what?" Jax pipes in.

"On my tan, of course."

"What did Olly do with our sister?" Jax says, turning his head toward me.

I shrug.

"So how was your honeymoon?" I ask.

"It was amazing actually." She's practically beaming as she says this.

"But it's good to be back . . ." I lead because it better be. I'm never letting her leave again.

"Yeah, it really is. I missed this place."

"Well, we missed you. New York isn't the same without you," Jax says, and I nod.

It's not.

"About that . . ." She bites her lower lip.

Fuck. Here it comes. The moment my baby sister tells me she's moving to England.

"Please don't say you're not here for good." I groan, lifting my hand to my hair and pulling on my roots at the thought. She hasn't even told me the news yet, and I already have a headache thinking about what I'll do without Addison here.

"Well . . ." she starts and then stops.

"Addy. You can't."

"I won't be moving there full time. I'm going to be doing three months here and three months there, and so on."

"Seriously?" Jax says.

"Yes. His life is there, and well, I can work from anywhere. I'm usually traveling anyway."

"That's not the point," I huff out. I'm not sure why I'm so angry. My sister is happy. Isn't that what I should be concerned about? But for some unknown reason, I am.

I'm angry she's moving. Angry everything is changing. I'm just plain angry right now.

"Gray . . ." Addison lifts her hand to touch mine. "It won't change anything. I'll still be around constantly annoying you."

"You were never an annoyance," I mumble.

"Yep. Only I am, right?" Jax jokes.

"I just don't like—"

"I know. You like control. And so do I. But I'm telling you, Gray. You should try living . . . it's so much better."

"I do live."

"Live for what, work?"

"Don't start, Ad. It wasn't too long ago that you were right here with me."

"I know, which gives me the perfect way of saying I know, and trust me, this is so much better. You should try to back off a bit this summer."

"I am," I say before I can stop myself.

"You are?"

"Well . . . I'm going to be taking some time to work on some other matters. I won't be able to do your job for you anymore."

"Oh, well, what are you doing?"

"I'm helping Tyler with the Lancaster specs."

Addison cocks her head. "Is that so? Should I be worried? Is he trying to poach you from our company?"

"No, it's nothing like that. The truth is, I want to help him. His company is in a lot of trouble, and while the job we gave him is helping him tremendously right now, he needs to land the job as the architect on the Lancaster job."

Addison's face grows somber, and she worries her lips. "Good. Do what you have to."

Jaxson leans forward in his chair. "So I'm the boss? You're away, you're away . . ."

"NO," we both shout in unison and then burst into laughter.

CHAPTER SIX

River

ONCE I REALIZED MY MOM WAS A NO-SHOW ONCE AGAIN, I got on the first flight back to Valencia, packed up my belongings, and headed to New York.

Now home, in my parents' apartment, I can finally relax. Or unwind or, to be honest, breathe.

My mother's actions have been resting heavily on me while in Europe, but now I'm starting to feel better.

"You're here?" Kim says as she steps into my room, her footsteps lightly tapping on the floor as she makes her approach. I lift my head and take her in.

She looks tired again.

"I am," I answer with a smile.

"How does it feel?" she asks tentatively.

I lie back dramatically on my bed, allowing my body to flop down, which elicits a laugh from her.

"It feels so damn good."

The bed dips, and I sit up to find her sitting beside me.

"Do you have plans now that you're back in town?" she asks. "Are you seeing any of your friends from school?" Her head inclines with curiosity. This is why I love Kim so much. Unlike my mother, the woman who should care, Kim truly cares.

Even before, when she was hired to take care of me, she loved me more than anyone else.

"I haven't thought about it really. Plus, none of my friends are in town this summer."

"The city is hot in the summer." She smiles, and I already know where she is going with this.

"It is."

"There's no pool," she says next.

"There's not," I agree.

"It's smelly, too."

I laugh at that. "I'd hardly say it's smelly."

"Well, maybe not here, in our apartment, but in other areas . . ." She trails off.

"Areas I won't go."

"Don't make me beg."

"I can't just sit around the pool all summer."

"Why not? You were supposed to sit around all summer in Portugal."

"That was different," I mutter, looking down at my hands.

She takes my hand in hers, and I lift my gaze. "How was it different? You were supposed to spend your summer with your mom. I have always considered you my daughter, Riv. Spend the summer with me. Hang with me. It will help." She pauses, swallowing. "It will help me keep busy when your dad is in the city working."

"Okay," I answer. I owe it to Kim to be there for her since she's done so much for me. Plus, what could be better than spending every day with her, hanging out, watching movies, and drinking rosé by the pool?

Not that I think Kim will be drinking with me, but she'll let me drink even though I won't be twenty-one until next month.

Sounds like a perfect plan.

"When do we leave?"

"Your dad has a meeting tomorrow, and then we'll leave after."

"So this weekend."

"Yeah."

"Didn't expect to go so soon . . ."

She gives me a tight smile. "You can always come down later."

"No. Don't be ridiculous. Tomorrow is fine."

I have so much to do before I'm ready to go, but I don't say anything. Instead, I watch her smile spread, and I know that no matter what I have to do, I'll do it. Just so I can see her smile like that. I'd do anything for her.

The day passed with a series of errands, and by the time I hit the bed last night, I was out.

Now I'm packed, in the car, and we're driving out east to the Hamptons.

The low volume of the music in the car provides a nice backdrop for the drive. Low enough that if anyone chooses to speak, they can be heard.

"Do we have any plans this week?" my father asks Kim.

She shakes her head. "No. Why?"

"Just asking. I might have an appointment, but nothing is set in stone."

"Oh, really?" she asks.

And I yawn. We still have about an hour drive, so I might as well get some sleep. Between traveling, packing, unpacking, repacking . . . from Valencia, to Malaga, to Portugal and eventually back to New York, I'm exhausted.

I look down at my cell and realize my mom still hasn't reached out.

It's odd, but I'm too drained to think about it.

There is no way I can keep my eyes open another minute, not with the lull of the car moving and the faint music in the background. My eyes start to flutter shut. Then I hear it . . .

The one name that has my eyelids opening.

"Gray might come to the house, if that's okay?" he says to Kim.

My heart starts to hammer heavily in my chest.

Gray.

Grayson.

Mr. Price.

In the Hamptons house.

With me.

Suddenly, I am no longer sleepy.

Energy now courses through my body at the thought of him being in my house. This weekend has suddenly become a lot more interesting.

So, instead of sleeping, I think of the man who has haunted my dreams since I saw him at twelve years old. The green eyes I can't shake. The scruffy face I long to touch, to feel scratching against me.

The man who saved me without knowing, and who I have loved ever since.

Yes.

This should be interesting.

I hope.

———◦O◦———

It doesn't take us long to get to the Hamptons. Either that or I spent the whole time thinking about Grayson. Sooner or later, we make the turn and travel up the long driveway covered by trees nestled along the beach. The coverage of the leaves opens to the sprawling estate owned by my father.

A large gray Nantucket sits along the coast. My father pulls the car into the driveway, then into the garage. When we walk into the house, it smells like fresh lilacs. This is the first time we're using the house this summer, and I welcome the solitude it brings.

Soon, the house will be hustling and bustling because my family likes to entertain and throw parties. I wonder if we're still having the summer soiree. The truth is, I wasn't supposed to be home, but I'm happy I am. Being here reminds me of the summers of my youth.

Stepping into the house, I walk up the stairs that lead to my room and find it just as I left it. Large bay windows open to a terrace that overlooks the Atlantic Ocean. I start to unpack, getting lost in the chore until I hear footsteps outside my room.

"Dinner will be served in thirty minutes," my father says from behind the door.

"Okay, I'll be right down." I put the final piece of clothing away and walk to the en suite.

I don't need to freshen up or make myself presentable because it's just us tonight. We're here a few days early, so there are no cocktail parties or dinners, and there are no nights out and no drinks. But still, I know my father, and I know when he looks at me, he sees so much of my mother, since I'm her spitting image, so I always like to be put together at least in front of him so he doesn't think I'm like her other than in looks.

I run a brush through my hair, making sure to tame my normally rambunctious locks. Once I'm satisfied, I head downstairs.

The table is set. A few seats are free, but I choose the one directly beside Kim. Once I sit down, I reach for a glass of wine, and my dad lowers his head to look at me. "Jeez. I'm almost twenty-one."

"But not yet," he says.

"Tyler . . . let the girl have a drink," Kim says.

Reluctantly, my father pours me a glass. Without waiting, I pull the glass into my hand and take a sip. The robust taste hits my nostrils before I swallow. It's exactly what I needed. I drink my glass faster than everyone else, and my stepmom doesn't stop laughing. My father doesn't look impressed.

"When will Gray be here?"

"I'm not sure."

"Will he be staying?" Kim asks, and I look down at my plate and start to play with my food. I'm scared they will see my reaction to him. I can feel my cheeks warming, and I'm sure my face is beet red.

Not good, River. Not good at all.

"Well, I assume not. But you never know."

Is it too much to beg?

Or at least I can do a silent rain dance that Grayson Price will stay the night.

That would be unreal.

No.

Stop that train of thought before it crashes and burns midride. It's one thing for Grayson Price to be my fantasy or my dream, but it's another thing to pursue him.

As much as I want to.

As much as I want to throw caution to the wind and try, I know I can't. He's my dad's friend. He's my dad's business associate, and even I know that's crossing a line I don't dare cross.

That would be something my mom would do.
And I am not my mother.
But I can flirt, right?
There's never harm in flirting.

CHAPTER SEVEN

Grayson

WAKING UP AT MY USUAL FOUR A.M. ON FRIDAY MORNING, I go for a run before work. As soon as I finish getting ready, I'll stop by the office and then head out east.

Running every morning keeps me grounded. I lose track of everything, and it helps me release all the tension I hold inside. As the wind hits my face, it feels as if all my troubles fade away for a moment.

As if for a moment, my time isn't limited.

After my run, I'll go meet with Tyler.

I thought I'd be meeting him at his office in the city, but apparently, he's already out east with Kim.

That's what he told me when he scheduled. Although we were supposed to meet in his office to discuss the project, Kim wanted to go out east sooner rather than later.

The truth is, I'm dreading going. Too many bad memories out there. I try never to go. But helping Tyler means something to me, so I have no choice but to push the feelings inside me down.

The early morning traffic shouldn't be bad, but I decide to take the company helicopter instead. I can fly in and then fly out later today.

Once I'm dressed and showered from the gym, I head to the garage in my building and get in my car.

Grabbing my phone, I call my assistant. "Nicole, do me a favor. I'm flying out to East Hampton. Can you get a car to meet me to go to Tyler's?"

"Sure. No problem, Mr. Price."

The woman has been with me for years, but no matter how often I tell her, she refuses to call me anything but Mr. Price. It's quite funny too, seeing as she is significantly older than I am.

I should be calling her Mrs. and not the other way around.

When I make it to the helipad on the Price Enterprise building, the pilot is there and ready for me.

Clear skies and a high in the 70s means today is perfect for a flight. It'll be a perfect weekend for the beach.

But you aren't here for fun, nor would you go there for that.

You're going to help a friend, and then you're going to leave.

Once we are airborne, I close my eyes and thank the heavens that at least I know River won't be there.

She mentioned at dinner that she was off to Portugal. I was thankful for that piece of information. No way would I tempt fate by being in the same room with her again.

But being in his house with her . . .

No. That would be too much.

I never would have agreed to meet him there if there was even a chance. Closing my eyes, I allow myself to rest, and before long, I feel the jerk of the helicopter landing.

I must have fallen asleep.

I reach my hands above my head and wring out any remaining sleep.

Once the blades have come to a stop and the doors are opened, I unbuckle and head out. On the ground, the car and driver Nicole arranged for me are waiting.

I should have driven.

Relying on anyone isn't for me. I prefer control over everything, including when I come, when I go, and how I get there and don't like to let anyone have any control over me. The driver opens the door of the Mercedes, and I step into the car and take a seat in the back. Pulling out my cell, I check to see if I missed any texts.

Just the usual business, nothing I'm needed for.

Jaxson is his usual self and chose not to come in today. Apparently, he went out last night.

Must be nice to be him.

Not that I can talk. I'm not in the office either. But unlike him, I am working today, just not in the same capacity.

No, what I'm doing is more important than nursing a hangover.

Soon, we're pulling along the large Nantucket in the circular driveway.

"You don't need to open the door," I say as I fling it open. "I'll call you when it's time to pick me up."

The lunch meeting should take a little over an hour. We'll be able to square off the details, I'll give him some insight on what Spencer likes, and then I'll leave. I imagine I'll be back in the city in no time. Maybe even soon enough to have an early dinner and then call it a night.

The gravel beneath my feet crunches as I walk toward the large white door. There is a heavy knocker in the center, but instead, I opt to press the doorbell once and then wait.

"Coming," someone says from inside. It sounds like a female voice. The door flings open, and I expect to see Kim, but the vision in front of me has my mouth gaping open and floundering like a fish out of water.

She must be shocked to see me too because she drops

whatever is in her hands. I follow the movement of the phone falling. I bend to grab it, and as I move to stand, I allow my gaze to sweep across the sight of her in front of me, starting from the floor.

Trailing up her long legs, leading to jean shorts . . . Why does she have to be so damn enticing?

My head tilts farther up. A cropped tee showcasing a trim waist and the outline of well-defined abs.

This is too much. I'm in my own personal hell right now as I realize that River is standing in front of me. River Reed, who should be in Europe.

But she's not.

Of course, she's not.

Instead, she's standing there looking like a high school boy's wet dream.

Or college, for that matter. Oh, who am I trying to kid, she looks like every man's fantasy, including mine.

This is bad.

"Here," I grit out as she peers up at me, her sunglasses covering her eyes.

"Hey, Mr. Price." She smiles. A coy smile. One that tells me she not only knows I was gawking at her, but she enjoyed it, too. There's something about her that drives me mad. She is almost fully ripe, but not quite. Dancing on the fringe of fully blossomed. It's like watching a rose opening its petals one by one in slow motion.

No one is opening anything, Grayson Price. Look the fuck away.

A cough escapes my mouth, and I pull my gaze from her. "Thank you."

I need to look at something else, anything else. Instead of

staring at her, I take in the suntan lotion in her hand, and I swear the visual taking root in my brain should be illegal.

If there is a God, Kim will not be serving lunch outside. If there is a God, River will leave this house and not come back until I'm in the air hovering over Manhattan.

She opens the door wider. "Aren't you going to come in?"

"I thought you were in Portugal," I hiss. I shouldn't be angry with her, but I am. She can't be here.

Her smile deepens, little lines forming beside her lips. "Ahhhh . . ." She bites her lip. "Were you thinking about me, Mr. Price?"

"No. I'm here to see your dad." I step past her and into the foyer.

The sound of the door closing behind me makes me turn back around to look at her.

At the temptress placed here to drive me crazy.

"He's not back yet. He went to grab something a minute ago." She shrugs and starts to walk past me, leaving me alone in the foyer with no other choice but to follow her.

So I do. Hating, yet not hating the view at all.

"Grayson, you're here," Kim says as we step into the kitchen, and River turns and leaves.

"That I am." I look around the room but find it's just her. "But apparently, Tyler isn't," I respond.

"No fear. He'll be here soon. He just ran out to grab something. We decided to grill shrimp for lunch, and we have a salad as well. Is that okay?"

"That's heavenly."

"And easy." She laughs apologetically. "Come, let's go outside. We'll dine al fresco." Her face lights up to a big smile as she leads us out the French doors to the patio.

In typical Hamptons fashion, the backyard opens to a well-manicured lawn with a pool set among the grass to blend.

It looks refreshing. Even though it's not terribly hot out yet, I wouldn't mind unwinding and taking a dip.

I'm not here for that, though.

The table is set, and I notice that this time, there are only three places. I guess River won't be joining us.

I let out a sigh.

Thank fuck.

Lunch would not have been productive if I had to stare at her the whole meal. At least now, I can work and then be gone before she returns.

"Grayson," Tyler's voice rings through the summer air, and I turn my head back toward the house. Standing, I walk toward him, where he meets me and pulls me into a one-arm hug. "Great to have you here. I really appreciate you coming."

"Of course," I answer.

"Well, it's not like you were in the neighborhood," he jokes.

"It's not a bad commute."

"Are you staying in the Hamptons this weekend?" he asks. I see Kim walk over to him, and he leans down and places a kiss on her lips.

"No, I'll head back to the city once we're done with lunch." There is no way I'll be staying at the home my family owns here. It might be only a mile away, right up the beach, but it holds far too many bad memories for me to ever stay there.

The chair scrapes against the stone floor, jarring in the quiet, and Kim sits down next to me.

"You're not going back to the city tonight. The traffic will kill you," she says.

"Sweetie . . ."

She looks over at him. "I'm pretty sure Gray didn't drive." He gives me a smug look. "Did you?"

I shake my head.

"What do you mean?" she asks, completely clueless as to how else I would get here. "Did you take the train?"

That has Tyler laughing. "Lord no. No way is Grayson taking a train."

"Then . . . ?"

"He took a helicopter."

"Well, I don't think you should go back, regardless. Stay with us," she says, turning her biggest and brightest smile toward me.

I shake my head. "I couldn't impose."

"Impose?" Tyler says. "Please. We still have work to go over."

I look over at the man who used to be my best friend, the one I haven't seen in years all due to a bruised ego. But now, his company is bleeding money and landing Lancaster is the key to keeping his company afloat. He needs me here.

"Yeah, okay. I'll stay."

"Oh, great," Kim exclaims, clapping her hands excitedly.

"Here . . . or will you be staying at—" Tyler starts to say, but I cut him off.

"I'll stay here."

"I'll have your room made up," Kim singsongs.

"I don't have any clothes," I think out loud.

"We do have a washing machine," she says in a mocking voice.

"So you want me to what, sleep naked? While you do my wash?" I laugh.

"It wouldn't be the strangest thing we've ever done," Tyler quips.

And it's my turn to laugh because he's right. It's not. We were friends growing up. Compared to the things we did, an impromptu trip out east with only the clothes on my back is nothing.

I shake my head at him, and then as I'm about to say something else, the sound of the door opening has us all turning in its direction.

And the reason I shouldn't stay struts out.

Wearing nothing but a bikini.

Shit. I really didn't think this through.

How it would be so easy to have her, to just taste the forbidden fruit one time.

But as much as I want to take a bite, I know I can't. I know I shouldn't.

But Lord do I want to.

Fuck.

Having lunch here is much harder than I thought. Tyler rambles on about God knows what, and luckily for me, I have sunglasses on, or it would be painfully obvious to everyone in a twenty-mile radius that I am, in fact, not looking at him as he speaks.

No.

I'm not.

Instead, my gaze is fixated to the spot directly above and to the right of his face.

To the spot in the distance occupied by his barely legal daughter. Right now, as Tyler talks about logistics, she's applying sunblock. Her hands reach down to apply the lotion to her long and already tanned legs. Legs that span the distance of the chair.

How tall is this girl?

I'm six foot three, and wearing heels, she was only a few inches shorter than me.

That'd put her at about five foot nine.

"Grayson?"

The sound of my name has me shaking my head.

"Hmm?" I answer.

"What do you think?" he asks.

And that's when I realize I have no idea what I think of his question because I wasn't listening at all. "Sorry, can you repeat that? My mind was elsewhere."

Not a lie.

It was elsewhere. It was thinking about what your daughter's legs looked like and what they would feel like wrapped around my waist as I thrust inside her.

Goddamn.

This line of thought is not okay.

"I asked about possible dates to have the meeting with Lancaster. Are there any dates when you're not available?"

I respond, "No," before I even pull out my calendar.

The truth is, I have no idea when I'm not booked. But for him, I'll make it work.

But what I won't make work is coming back to the Hamptons.

This is way too much even for a saint.

After the longest lunch of my life, Kim stands and then I stand as well.

"Come on, Grayson, I'll show you to the guest room." She turns to show me the way around. She's slow to walk, and I wonder if she's still under the weather, but she never lets her smile falter. Instead, she lets out a yawn.

"Tired?" I ask.

"Yeah, but nothing a nap won't fix."

"Okay, as long as I'm not putting you out."

She halts her steps and turns to me, her hand reaching out and taking mine in hers.

"He missed you," she whispers, and I know she's talking about Tyler.

I nod, not knowing what to say. "I've missed him too."

"Then you'll spend time with him tonight." She turns back around. "Come this way to your room."

She leads me down a long hall, and she gestures back behind us. "That door at the end is Tyler's and my room. The other rooms are this way."

We pass a door, and I expect us to stop, but we pass one more and then a third. "This is the guest suite. It has its own bathroom, so you should be very comfortable. It also has a balcony."

"I'm sure it's perfect."

She opens the door, and I place my own hand on it to allow her to enter first. The cozy room is decorated in white furniture and white linens. Along the wall are large glass doors with a perfect view of the ocean.

"Just as I suspected. Perfect."

"Great. I'm so happy you decided to stay."

"Me too."

With that, she leaves, and I walk over to the doors and swing them open.

The sea breeze wafts into my nose. The summer air and rays of sunlight beat down on my face. I inhale deeply, allowing my shoulders to uncoil. I haven't relaxed in a long time, so this might actually be a welcome visit. I can spend time with my friend, work, and then relax.

What can possibly go wrong?

The sound of a splash has me looking down, and then I see her surfacing from the depth of the pool. She reminds me of one of those old romantic comedy movies where the girl lifts off the water . . .

Cue the music.

She's going to be a problem.

One I won't be able to solve by putting in the extra hours.

CHAPTER EIGHT

River

I KNEW HE WAS COMING, BUT I WASN'T PREPARED FOR IT. Seeing him does wicked things to my body.

I hate it.

I feel as though I'm reckless when he's around.

Led by my hormones I can't control.

I feel like I'm my mom.

How she must have felt the summer she met my dad. When she was desperate to touch him.

No matter the consequences.

My head pops through the water, and I breathe out the oxygen I was holding.

Then I dive back in yet again to swim the length of the pool.

I've always loved to swim. It's almost a strange irony on how cathartic it is to be in the water, seeing as my name is River.

Beneath the water with the force of my legs pushing me forward, diving into the depths of the unknown is where I feel most at home. I must get that from my mother. My father doesn't like the unpredictable life, but my mother loves the murky abysses where you can't see the future.

Once I'm done with my lap, I look up.

Out of the corner of my eye, I see I'm being watched.

A figure stands on the balcony. The balcony next to mine.

Grayson Price.

He stares at me, not moving, just watching, but his perusal invigorates me. It lights me on fire. I dive back in to break the connection and concentrate on something else. Despite knowing that I don't want to be my mother, I couldn't resist teasing him and flirting with him. I guess no matter how hard I try, I'm destined to be like her after all.

Maybe I shouldn't care.

Maybe I should embrace those parts of me.

Not wanting to think about what this line of thought means, I swim harder. I swim and swim.

Back and forth until all thoughts of Grayson Price vanish beneath the surface of the waters, and then when I emerge, thankfully he's gone.

If there is any tiny bit of resolve left in me to stay away from Grayson, it's lost when I see him sitting at the kitchen counter with my dad. He has a glass in his hand, and he throws his head back.

Suddenly, with just one look at him, all my good intentions fly out the window.

He looks so relaxed right now.

With my dad, it's like he's drunk from the fountain of youth. He looks younger than usual, and his shoulders are no longer tense. My father looks the same way. It brings a smile to my face to see them together like this.

Grayson starts to laugh.

A sound I have never heard.

The man is so serious all the time, but here, with my father, when no one else is around, he seems so different.

This side of him is intoxicating. What it must feel like to be on the other end of that laughter? To make him smile. To make him lose himself.

That's what I want. I want to be on the receiving end of that laughter.

"What's so funny?" I say, making my presence known.

They both turn and look in my direction. The shadow of Grayson Price falls back down. His relaxed features fade away right in front of my eyes as his shoulders tense, and he schools his features.

Small lines crease his face. Instantly, he looks his age.

Older.

Angry.

But why is he angry?

Then it hits me like a ton of bricks. Me. He's angry with me, but I have no idea what I've done.

I know he was mad that I approached him in Spain knowing who he was, but I thought we had gotten over that.

He accepted my apology, so what did I do now?

"Any wine for me?" I ask, pulling out the chair beside my father.

He shakes his head. "No."

"There is a full bottle in front of you," I deadpan.

"And on your birthday, you can have some."

"Dad . . ."

"Yes." He lifts his chin.

"Give the girl wine, her birthday is in a few weeks," Kim says as she walks into the kitchen and smiles at me.

"Jeez, Dad, if we're going to do this every time we sit down for dinner, I'm eating out."

"When's your birthday?" Grayson grits out.

"Fourth of July," I respond, and he stares at me. As if he's taking in what I just said. I watch as he lifts the glass to his mouth and takes a long swig of it.

"And you'll be twenty-one?"

"Yes. Legal." My throat bobs with a swallow. I don't know why it unnerves me to talk to him.

I watch as he lifts the drink yet again, chasing my words with more wine. Without another word, he turns his attention away from me, and even though he's gruff, I miss his attention.

So instead, I stand and make my way to the cabinet and grab another glass. Then I pick up the bottle and serve myself some.

Lifting it to my mouth, I first smell, inhaling the aromas wafting off the glass. If I can say one thing about my mother, it's that she taught me about wine.

Last summer, she met me in France, and we drank Burgundy.

Instinctively, I touch my wrist, to the memory of that trip.

That trip went better than this year's. Well, of course, it did. She actually showed up for that trip.

I take my sip and enjoy the way the liquid pours down my throat and pools in my belly, making me warm.

Once done, I set my glass down. "What's for dinner?"

"We ordered in."

"Oh . . ." I was hoping for a home-cooked meal. I'm not sure how long I'll be here, but I also understand Kim cooked lunch. "That sounds great."

"Come on, food's on the table."

We each grab our glasses, and together, we follow Kim into the dining room. The table is set with lemon chicken and orzo on each plate.

It's quiet at first, and then my dad turns to me. "So, Riv, now that we have you back, what are your plans?"

I look at Kim. I figured she had mentioned to him I was staying here.

"I thought she could stay with me."

"And work on her tan?" He lifts a brow.

"I thought—"

"You'll come back to the city with me during the week, and I'll put you to work at my office. It's high time you start getting work experience. No more gallivanting around the world."

His meaning reads loud and clear, and I know he's saying he doesn't want me to be like my mom.

I don't want that either.

The truth is, I'd be bored lying out here every day. I only travel with Mom because it's the only time I'd see her.

Now that this trip is canceled, I'm not sure when I'll see her again.

"Okay," I answer. "I'd like that." And I would. It's not a lie. I'd love to spend time with him as well.

"Have you spoken to her?"

"No," I say, looking down at my wrist. My fingers caress the charm from last summer on my bracelet. One for each city I have been to. The only one I'm missing is Lisbon. Without Mom there, it felt hollow to buy a charm.

Lifting my head, I mindlessly flick at the piece that feels like it's strangling my wrist as I meet Kim's gaze. She bites her lip and gives me a tight smile. She knows about my bracelet. She knows its significance.

The air feels heavy and still around me, so instead of looking at Kim or Grayson, I focus on my dad.

He's shaking his head at my answer, so I look down at my plate because I don't want to look at him. I don't want to look at anyone, but especially not him. I don't want to see the disappointment there. Or worse, see the sadness reflected back at me. My father might not have always been there for me, but ever since he took me in when my mom abandoned me, he's made up for it in spades.

I stab my fork into my plate, silence thickening around us until Kim cuts it off.

"So, Grayson, do you have any plans for the Fourth?"

"Nothing yet."

"Then I insist you stay with us again. We're throwing a party for River's twenty-first birthday. You must come."

Tentatively, I look up from the plate and catch Grayson staring at me. He looks from me to Kim, and I watch as his Adam's apple bobs as his jaw tightens. It's a slight movement, and one most wouldn't notice, but I notice everything about this man.

I know he's about to say no.

Then he does something I don't expect when he answers.

"I'll try to be there."

Conversation is tight throughout dinner. Grayson is exceptionally quiet. I don't know him well, but I know the man I saw with my father.

The carefree man with his head thrown back in laughter. This man sitting across the table is not that man.

This one's walls are up.

More like walls and gates.

I know I'm the reason. My presence has him wound up tight. I feel the same way, completely unhinged by his.

But where mine is from desire, his appears to be from hatred.

Kim stands from the table, signaling the meal is over, and I stand as well.

"I'll clear," I say before she can object.

"No, actually, Mary is still here for the night. No need for either of us to clean."

Grayson and my father stand then as well.

I watch from a few feet away as he fixes his shirt, smoothing away the wrinkles that have creased his pink button-down.

"I have a great idea for tonight," Kim says.

"And what would that be?" I ask, turning toward her. Her lips part into a large smile.

"Do you remember when you first came here?" she asks, her voice low. Thick with emotions. Her eyes seem lost in time, and I know why . . .

How could I not?

How could I ever forget the summer my mother abandoned me?

How could I ever forget the summer my mom brought me to a man's house that I didn't know, a man who would be my father? I was scared at first, but at least he had the insight to hire someone to help.

My father wasn't around much that summer or the summer after that, but Kim was and all the escapades we got into. So I'm not sure what she means when she asked me if I remember because that summer has so many memories.

"I remember. There are just too many things to remember."

"Movie night."

I lift my eyebrow and study her, seeing if she's telling the truth, and she is.

"I thought the TV . . ." I start to say, and she smiles, shaking her head.

"I had a new one set up." She smirks. "Come on."

We all follow Kim right outside to the patio. Set up among the night sky directly next to the pool is a giant inflatable TV.

I'm instantly transported back to being twelve. I remember it like it was just yesterday. She put on a movie that was one hundred percent not appropriate for a child my age. But she knew better. She knew I was far above my age.

So when she put on the scary psychological thriller in black and white, the one a twelve-year-old shouldn't watch, I sat back and enjoyed being taken seriously for the first time. I reveled in the knowledge that she knew I wasn't as young as I appeared. After that, we ate ice cream, and I wonder, looking over around the deck, if that's what we're doing tonight also.

"I don't think I'll be joining you." Grayson's voice cuts through the silence. I turn to him, and his cool, calm, and collected facade is still present. "I have work to do."

"Oh, come on, Gray . . ." my dad implores, and Gray, in turn, lets out a sigh.

"Fine, but I can't stay long. I do have work to do."

"Come on, take a seat. I'll grab the popcorn. No ice cream tonight." She winks at me.

"Ice cream?" Grayson asks.

"Yes, movie night is a night for ice cream sundaes, but alas, I'm all out of supplies, so popcorn it is."

"Popcorn is enough," I say, and she shakes her head.

"I promise this summer, we'll have an ice cream social like we used to."

"Okay." I laugh. "Deal."

Ice cream socials, as Kim called them, were the best.

She would set up a table with a red and white umbrella and the whole shebang. There she would have multiple flavors and toppings all served in an authentic glass ice cream bowl.

The memory of all the things Kim did for me that summer to make me feel welcome in my dad's home return.

I look over to where Kim is bouncing out of the house with two bowls of popcorn in her hands has me smiling.

"Here, guys, sharing is caring," she says, pointing at the couch.

I swear I think I hear Gray groan, but when I turn in his direction, his handsome face is completely stoic.

Without knowing what to say, I take a seat on the outdoor couch and tuck my feet under my legs. He sits at the farthest point from me, but even I know he has to move closer if he plans on sharing the popcorn with me.

But knowing him, he won't.

He is not into sharing, and he is most definitely not into caring.

"I'm not going to bite, you know." I pat the couch closer to me. "I grew out of that phase as a toddler. You can come closer."

He stares blankly at the place my hand rests.

"Kim will think you don't like her popcorn," I try another tactic, lifting my brow, and he furrows his. "Don't wanna insult the host."

Actually, Grayson Price *is* here because he cares.

He cares about my dad and cares about Kim. My comment is a low blow. Manipulation at its finest.

An ugly thought pops in my brain, but I shoo it away and reach my hand out for the popcorn.

From the corner of my eye, I can see him glance over at the popcorn.

Jeez, is this man stubborn.

I move my body closer to him but just barely.

Not enough that he notices, or if he does, he doesn't turn away from the screen. With each breath I take, I close the gap. It's slow, but eventually, the only thing separating our bodies is the bowl of popcorn.

Now he looks over.

His eyes are stormy.

A harsh look reflects in them. The green is replaced with black pupils searching for light in this dark night. His gaze meets mine, and he clenches his jaw as he watches. As though he's giving me a warning look. So I shrug my shoulders and let my lip lift up.

"It's just popcorn, Mr. Price. You can have some. Sometimes, it's okay to indulge in something you know you shouldn't."

My words hang in the air, the double entendre bouncing between us.

Whatever he's thinking, he must push it away with a shake of his head, and then he watches the screen again.

I keep my face toward the screen. We're watching a scary Hitchcock movie, the type Kim always loved to watch.

I have seen it so many times that I'm barely watching. Instead, I'm watching him from the corner of my eye.

Wondering if he'll move closer.

Wondering if he'll look over at me.

Wishing he would.

Hating myself for praying for that.

Needing something to distract myself with, I reach my hand into the popcorn. That's when I feel it.

He's reaching in too.

Our fingers touch.

Hovering above the bowl.

Skin to skin.

An electric current zings through my flesh, almost jolting me upright.

I know I should pull my hand away, but I can't. His hand is touching mine, and I don't want to pull away, so instead, against all better judgment, I move my fingers.

Allowing the tips to trail over his rough knuckles.

My eyes are still aimed forward, but I'm watching him. I watch his Adam's apple bob as I caress the skin.

I watch him swallow.

His chest rising and falling with each pass of my hand.

He looks torn, provoked, on the verge of something.

Something I'm not sure I can decode.

But I do see something I recognize very well. Loneliness. It bursts from him, alive and raw and pulsing like an injured animal. I can smell it. I can almost *taste* it. We are the same, yet we are nothing alike.

As if allowing himself this minute of indulgence, he closes his eyes. But then as quickly as the moment starts, his eyes pop open and his face contorts into a scowl.

He pulls his hand away quickly.

"What are you doing here?" he hisses in complete disdain.

"It's my dad's house."

"Don't play dumb with me, River. We both know you are a bright girl."

"Break it down for me." I sit back, cornering him into spitting it out.

I feel the full measure of his scrutiny under his steady gaze. "On this couch. Next to me. What are you doing?"

"I'm just sharing an innocent popcorn with you."

The popcorn is innocent. Me? Not so much . . .

He stands abruptly.

"Grayson . . ." I hear Kim say, but his sudden movement and the way he glares down on me makes me feel small, weak, abandoned.

"I'm going to bed," he announces, and Kim looks from him to me and then back to him.

"Is everything okay?"

"Peachy. Thanks for the popcorn. It was delicious. And innocent. Wasn't it, River?"

"Yup. The court of justice would agree," I deadpan without missing a beat.

"Enjoy your movie." He stomps away.

I dump the popcorn to the side and wait until Kim looks away before I let out the breath I've been holding.

Jerk.

CHAPTER NINE

Grayson

I CAN HEAR THEM LAUGHING AND TALKING, SO I ASSUME THE movie is over. I couldn't stay any longer. Instead of watching the movie, I worked. Answering emails I didn't need to answer all to get her out of my mind.

She stunned me when she touched me.

And even more so when she softly caressed my knuckles.

I was frozen in place, dead in the water like a fat seal in front of an angry shark. Even an hour later, I can't get the thoughts of her hands, fingers, of her touch out of my mind.

Snap out of it, idiot.

This isn't good.

There will be no thinking about her like this.

It's not natural. Or okay. Or anywhere on the morality spectrum I live by.

But it's not like she's a minor.

Well, she is your friend's daughter. A friend you haven't seen in years. A friend you never speak to.

It's still wrong.

You're here as his guest.

I can't think about what it would feel like to have her . . .

A sound pulls me out of my sordid thoughts. I turn from where I'm sitting on the balcony.

It was the sound of the door for the adjacent balcony.

In the dark of the night, I can see the light filter through the space.

Someone is coming out.

I hear the scratch of the chair.

"I'm sorry," I hear. And my back goes ramrod straight.

It's her.

And I'm not sure who she's talking to.

Should I tell her I'm out here? Should I make myself known?

"I'm sorry I did that to you, Mr. Price." Her words have me sucking in air.

She's talking to me. She's out here to speak with me. I shouldn't answer, but I do.

Even if it's wrong.

"You're right."

"What?"

"You shouldn't have," I say. My voice is flat, my words monotonous.

"I-I," she stutters, taken aback by my voice. "I'm not sure why you are so angry."

"Then why apologize?" I scold. "If you don't mean it, why the pretense?"

"Why are you so tense? You weren't this tense when you asked me if I was free to spend the evening with you in Malaga," she huffs.

"I didn't know you then," I answer truthfully. In the dark, I feel I can be more honest.

"And now that you do? What's changed?"

"Don't go there," I grunt back. My voice is still low enough that no one else will hear us.

"I just don't understand the problem."

"Seriously?" I ask in complete disbelief. How does she not see the issue here?

"Seriously," she retorts.

"You are young enough to be my daughter."

"Not really. You're only fifteen years older than me."

"Sixteen."

"No. Not really. My birthday is in a few weeks. So by my math, if I was forty and you were fifty-five, age wouldn't be an issue." Her words turn my blood to ice. She has no idea how wrong she is. With my luck, I'll probably be knocking on death's door when she's forty. "That night in Malaga, you wanted me. Why are you denying me now?"

"How about the fact that you're my friend's daughter?"

That shuts her up. I can hear inhaling and exhaling, trying to think of a response, but what can she say to that?

She is my friend's daughter, and it doesn't matter if we haven't spoken in years. This is a subject you don't breach, a forbidden fruit you don't taste. Not now. Not ever.

It doesn't matter how decadent you know it will taste. You don't.

It's not on the menu and never will be.

⚬

The early morning sunlight wakes me. I feel like I got hit by a train. I didn't sleep well at all last night. How could I? How can I sleep at all? Not after last night. Not after the way she made me feel. Because that's the truth.

That's the goddamn fucking truth.

I'm so controlled I don't allow my emotions to get the better of me. I only allow myself to feel for my family, and that's it. My life . . . is work. Nothing more, nothing less.

Just work. Sure, I get laid, but there's no connection. No relationships.

I have an empire to run.

Yes, I run it with my siblings, but as the oldest, the burden falls on me. It's my responsibility to make sure our family name stays intact. It's my responsibility to make sure Addison is happy. My mother is happy. And that Jaxson stays out of trouble. I am the patriarch of this family now, and I have to make my father proud.

The lack of sleep has me reaching my arms up and stretching. I need coffee. Stat. I pull back the sheets and step onto the wood floors. Luckily for me, there's a bathroom in this room. Because that would be awful to bump into my neighbor in the bathroom. Now the thought is in my brain. River in the shower.

I brush my teeth quickly, throw some water on my face, and then open the door and grab the pile of my freshly washed clothes placed outside. Stepping back inside, I put on my jeans. I can't believe I'm wearing the same outfit. Oh well, at least it was washed.

Once dressed, I pad down the stairs and into the kitchen, hoping, praying there's a coffeepot. What meets me has my steps faltering.

River is standing there. Her feet bare, her long legs just as naked.

All she's wearing is a T-shirt that falls right below her ass.

If she were to bend over . . .

I groan, which makes her stop what she's doing and turn around.

She cocks her hip when she sees me.

Her lips twitch until she's smirking at me.

Fuck.

Why does she have to look at me like that? And an even better question is why do I have to like it?

"Are pants not hip anymore?" I grit out. Her lips part and she sweeps her tongue out, wetting her lips. This girl is trouble. She oozes sexuality without even trying.

"The word hip is no longer hip, Mr. Price."

"That may be, but you are still not wearing any pants. Why?" I ask again. This time, the anger in my voice is palpable.

"Jeez, Gray. Calm down." She lowers her arms and places her hands on the hem of her barely-there T-shirt.

She lifts it.

"River," I whisper-shout because at this point, I can't have anyone else hearing what's going on. "Do not take off your shirt."

Instead of heeding my warning, River lifts the shirt to reveal not only a pair of tight biker shorts but also her navel.

"Pants are not hip, but these sure are." She winks. "See?"

"Yes, I see. But your shorts are making their name proud. They're pretty darn short."

"I like to excel." She shrugs. "You should meet my pea coat. It keeps me warm in New York's December even with just a bra underneath."

And now I think about her in nothing but a bra and a coat. River is God's way of giving me a heart attack.

She turns around, and with her shirt still lifted, I can see the perfect shape of her ass.

Like a peach. Perfectly shaped like one you'd want to sink your teeth into. "Want coffee?"

"What?" Did she say something? I pull my gaze up and see her watching me, watching her.

"I asked if you would like some coffee."

"Yes."

"Yes, please. Where are your manners, Mr. Price?"

Where the rest of your so-called shorts are, I'm tempted to whip back.

I narrow my eyes at her. If she wasn't my friend's daughter, I'd bend her over that counter and show her how polite I can be.

Just when I think it can't get any worse, it does.

Because that's when she decides to lean over said counter and reach for God knows what. I can't concentrate on anything past the view in front of me.

"I can feel you staring," she says, her voice low and sultry.

I shake my head and try to conjure up an answer, any answer for why I'm staring at her ass.

"As I said, me and the shorts have a problem."

"So it seems. Should I just take them off?"

"No."

She drops her hands and starts to pull them off.

"No means no. Didn't they teach you that at your private girls' school?"

Then she shimmies out of them. *Fuck.*

"River!"

She shrugs as if it's no big deal and smiles. "Bikini bottom." And then her phone chirps, and she leaves.

Leaves me there in the kitchen, rock-hard and hating myself and hating her for the way my body reacts.

CHAPTER TEN

River

I'M NOT SURPRISED TO FIND OUT THAT GRAYSON LEFT RIGHT after our run-in this morning. They don't know I saw him. I was already outside by the time my father and Kim woke.

I went outside for my morning laps, and when I was finished, I found out he had returned to the city.

I'm sure I'm the reason.

Despite what I tell myself, I continue to tease him.

Taunt him, really.

I know I should stop, but it makes me feel alive to see him stare at me. I feel invigorated when, despite his internal protests, he has no control over his body's reaction.

I love to watch the scowl on his face because I can see right past it. I can see the way his pupils dilate, and I can see the way he inhales and swallows.

He wants me.

He wants me bad.

He just doesn't want to.

I should stop.

But to be honest, it's too much to feel his stare.

Like a bright ray of sunlight, even though it makes you feel sweltering hot, it feels so good to be burned, nonetheless.

"What are you up to for the rest of the day?" my father asks as he walks out onto the deck where I'm sunbathing.

"You're looking at it." I shrug.

"So is this how you actually plan to spend the whole summer?"

"I told you I'd work."

"Okay, good. I wanted to make sure."

"Jeez, Dad. I'm not Mom," I hiss back.

Regardless of my imperious actions with Grayson Price, I'm not Mom.

"Sweetheart . . ."

I shake my head.

"You know I didn't mean it like that."

"Didn't you?"

He walks over, sitting on the edge of my lounge chair. Reaching his hand out, he takes mine in his and gives it a little squeeze. "Riv . . . I know you aren't your mom. I—"

"It's fine. No harm done." I stand from the chair and leave him there.

Because, in the end, no matter what he says, not being like Mom is a constant struggle.

The need to march to the beat of my own drum scares me sometimes. Like when I up and decided to move to Spain—that was something Mom would do. The only difference is, I studied. She would have just slept with half the city.

Every day, I see myself becoming more like the things I hated about her, and the things that made her abandon me. So although my dad didn't mean it, he has no idea how hard I have tried to distance myself from anything like that.

To be more.

Be better.

As I step inside the house, the cold air hits me like a ton of bricks, causing goose bumps to break out across my skin.

Now that I am officially shivering, I calm down.

How can I not? I'm now a frozen icicle in the house dripping on the marble floor because I acted rashly and didn't grab a towel.

I inhale.

And then right my thoughts. Squaring my shoulders, I turn around.

I find my dad where I left him.

But this time, he has his head cradled in his hands.

"Dad."

That makes him look up.

"I'm sorry, Dad. I didn't mean it," I whisper, embarrassed by my earlier behavior.

"I didn't either," he says, his voice low.

"I know."

"Please sit. I'd like to talk to you."

My head bobs, and I sit down beside him. "I'm sorry I acted that way. Sometimes, I'm so concerned that I will be viewed like her."

"I understand."

"Thank you. And yes, I'd like to work with you," I say. That will give me purpose and maybe a better direction on what I want to do after I graduate next year. I have no clue where the future will take me, but I know I need to work and get experience with different jobs to meet new people and figure out my life.

Working with my dad will hopefully be exactly what I need.

"Great." He pats my knee and stands. "We'll go back on Tuesday. That way we miss the traffic, and we'll return Thursday."

"Fabulous."

Tuesday comes before I know it. I'm excited to start my job, but mainly because Dad has been working with Grayson, and I'm hoping that I too will get a chance to work with him. I'm not sure if I will, though, since the job is more of an internship. Maybe I'll get lucky and be able to shadow him at his meetings.

My dad's office is on the seventh floor of a building situated three blocks south of Canal Street. It's an older building without a ton of bells and whistles, but it serves its purpose. He used to have a bigger space in midtown, but apparently, business hasn't been doing so hot, so he had to downsize.

I'm not sure what the problem is, as Dad is the best, but I know he's been stressed about money recently.

He doesn't know I know, but I overheard him on the phone saying how much he needed to impress the Lancasters.

Once we exit the elevator, my father shows me to my desk, which is located directly beside his assistant's.

"As an intern, I expect you to help Rose with her day-to-day work, and I want you to shadow me as well. I will also have you work with Larry in accounting. Since you are a business major and you're not sure what you plan to do, working with a little bit of everything might help you get some direction for the future." He lifts a brow as he says this, and my cheeks warm. Without realizing it, he basically just scolded me in front of Rose about the lack of direction in my life.

I'd be lying if I said I wasn't embarrassed. But instead, I square my shoulders and nod. He's not wrong. I certainly share some of my mom's carefree personality, which is one of the main reasons I want to go into a field in business.

The morning is spent watching Rose go over correspondence. An hour before lunch, Rose stops typing and turns toward where my chair is pushed up against her desk, so I can watch her.

"Why don't you head over to Larry now? That way you can grab lunch from there and come back to me."

"Sure." I nod, wanting to make it easier for everyone. "Where's his office?"

Rose lifts her hand and points down the hallway in the opposite direction of my dad's. "Last door on the left. Past the bookcases."

Standing, I make my way down the hall. Just as I'm about to enter, I hear whispering. I stop my movements when the voice sounds angry.

"I'm trying to fix the problem." The voice, who I assume is Larry, sounds anxious. I'm not sure what the problem is that he needs to fix, but it sounds serious. "Now is not a good time . . ."

I hear the phone crashing down into the cradle and wait for a minute before letting my presence be known. Whatever that was, it didn't sound too good.

"Hey, I'm River," I say as walk into the office. The first thing I notice is the room is a mess. The second is that Larry obviously doesn't appreciate me being here. Larry is older than my father, balding and sporting a comb-over of brown hair speckled with gray. His lips are pulled tightly together in a scowl.

"Tyler's daughter," he sneers, obviously not into small talk. "Time to babysit," he mutters under his breath, so low he probably thinks I didn't hear. But I did. Apparently, he isn't thrilled about me being here.

"The one and only, and excited to be here to learn," I respond sugary sweet before walking into his office and pulling out a chair.

He shakes his head, lets out a sigh, and then hands me a file.

No direction. No nothing.

This should be fun.

The next two days fly by, and before I know it, it's Thursday. So far working here is different from what I expected. Rose is sweet, and Larry is a dick, but it's fascinating, nonetheless.

Especially my dad.

I've never seen this side of him before. He's incredibly smart. His ideas inspire everyone around him.

His designs are truly one of a kind.

Spanning distances, and time, and merging them to make a cohesive structure that marries multiple concepts and cultures.

He's in his element as he shows his idea for a state-of-the-art office space for a new tech company. This is where he thrives, and it inspires me to find something that makes me this passionate.

I lift my hand and touch the necklace sitting on my skin. It feels cool to the touch. The metal and glass feel heavy. With a shake of the head, I let it go and focus on the papers in front of me instead.

When the meeting concludes, my dad walks over to me.

"Grab your bag, sweetheart."

"We're going back out east?"

"Yes, but first I have one more meeting."

"And you want me to come?"

"I do."

"I'd love to." I step away and go back to my desk and grab my purse. I don't need clothes as I have a set at both my parents' houses. I find him in the hallway in front of the elevator, waiting for me.

"This will be quick. I just have to drop off some paperwork."

The elevator door opens, and we step in.

A low humming song plays in the backdrop.

"I have to stop at Price Enterprise, and then we're off."

"Price Enterprise?"

"Yes, you know, Grayson's company."

My skin starts to warm at his name. "Of course," I say, but as I say the words, butterflies start to swarm in my belly.

I'm too excited to say more.

I never thought I'd see him again.

Not after my childish behavior.

But now that I know, it's like a spark rekindles my attraction.

And I'm excited.

———✦———

I knew the Prices were wealthy, but the level of opulence when I walk into the building makes me froth at the mouth. It's not like I didn't grow up with money. I mean, for the first twelve years of my life, I didn't, but then I met my father. When I moved in with him, I've had money since, but not at this level.

Floor-to-ceiling windows, stainless steel furniture, marble floors. Sleek elevators leading to the upper floors. My father and I walk past security, giving our names, but we must be on a list because he nods for us to continue. We walk past the first set of elevators until we make it to a glass hallway that leads to another set. There's only one elevator here.

"This is the elevator."

I want to say duh, but seeing as I'm supposed to act professionally, I don't.

Together, we step inside. There are no buttons, I notice

right off the bat. My dad laughs. He obviously knows what I'm thinking. "Yep. There are no buttons because this elevator only goes to the Price's floor."

"They have their own floor?"

"They have their own building. But yes, the penthouse is their floor. The only people up there are Grayson, Addison, and Jackson."

"What are you building for them?"

"Actually, I'm not building anything for them."

"I don't understand. Then why are we here? What were you doing with him in Spain and at the house? I thought you got the contract?"

"They're planning on either selling or leasing the land to the Lancaster hotels chain."

"And what does this have to do with you?"

"I was brought on to show the buyer potentials for the property. I was hired to produce renderings."

I nod with understanding. "Seems like a lot of work for something that won't even be built probably."

"They pay well." He laughs.

"I'll say."

"But the goal is to impress the Lancasters so much they hire me for the actual project."

Now it makes sense. All the hours working in the Hamptons with Grayson on this.

He wants to land the job.

Bad.

The elevator comes to a stop, and a beautiful girl not much older than me greets us.

"Hello, I am Jasmine, and I am one of the project managers here. Follow me."

"Pleasure to meet you, Jasmine. I'm Tyler. And this is my daughter, River."

"The pleasure is all mine, sir." Her heels click on the marble as we make it down the long hallway. She shows us to a glass room and inside it's empty.

"They will be in shortly. Is there anything I can get for you while you wait?"

"Nothing for me, Jasmine. River?"

"I am fine, thank you."

My father and I walk into the space, and we both take a seat. While we wait, he opens up his briefcase and places the papers in front of him. I know he's emailed them over, but Dad is old-fashioned like that, and he likes to bring renderings.

I'm staring into space, thinking about nothing in particular, when I hear the creak of the door. Two men I have never seen walk in, and then they are followed by a beautiful tall brunette in a pantsuit.

"Tyler. It's so good to see you," she says.

"Likewise. I hear congratulations are in order."

She looks down at her hands and then smiles up at him.

"Yes. Thank you."

She's practically glowing with happiness.

For a moment, although brief, I'm slightly jealous of the way she beams.

I want that. My problem is no one ever makes me feel like that. Warm from the inside out.

Well, that's not true.

One man makes me feel like I'm sweltering inside. But that's never going to happen. Not when he sees me as a petulant, flirtatious child.

Speak of the devil.

He's next to enter. Dressed nothing like he was in Spain or in the Hamptons. I almost fall over to the floor when I see him.

A dark gray three-piece suit. Charcoal, actually. With a matching vest and crisp white button-down and black tie.

If I thought this man was gorgeous before, this is when he really shines.

He commands attention.

He commands all eyes on him.

He also happens to command my goddamn panties.

I can't look away.

He meets my stare, widening his eyes in surprise. But then before anyone else can catch the look in his eyes, he schools his features and lets his stone-cold facade fall back down.

This isn't the man I found laughing in the kitchen. And this certainly isn't the man who asked with concern about Kim.

No, this man is cold and serious.

This man rules a boardroom.

A business.

And to be honest, this man in my deepest, darkest fantasies would rule me.

My father stands, but unlike in the Hamptons, Grayson doesn't offer him a one-arm hug. No. All professional here. Instead, he extends his hand and firmly shakes it.

"Grayson."

"Tyler."

"I hope you don't mind I brought River. I thought this could be a good experience for her."

He barely looks at me or acknowledges me. Instead, he nods and turns his back to take his seat.

I feel cold and berated.

No one else seems to notice his icy demeanor toward me, though.

Maybe I'm reading too much into it.

Maybe I'm not.

Maybe he just hates me.

I want to say something to him, but I don't. Instead, I suck in my cheeks, biting hard enough to hold my tongue, and let them speak.

But I never take my eyes off him the whole time.

Not once.

I stare until I have memorized every line on his face.

Before I know it, everyone stands, and apparently, the meeting is over. I'm supposed to have learned something, but I didn't.

The only thing I learned is that I have it bad for a man who wants me gone.

And it sucks.

When the meeting is over, my father lags behind as everyone else leaves, and so do I. The presentation was a big success, and the client actually wants to use Dad's plans for the hotel.

My dad busted his ass to make it perfect, and it paid off. I'm so happy it went the way my father hoped. This is a game-changer for him. Although he's a renowned architect, this is a whole other level, and I'm proud of him.

"Thank you for thinking of me," my father says to Grayson.

"Of course. We've been following your work even though we haven't spoken, and we've been impressed, so when this job came up, we thought you would be the perfect person to show the schematics of the potential for this property. I'm just so happy it worked out."

"Me too. We need to celebrate."

Grayson looks at me and then back at my father.

"Okay." His response is reluctant. Although he wants to celebrate with my dad, it's obvious he doesn't want to celebrate with me.

"Don't worry, I know you're busy right now. Plus, we're heading back to the Hamptons. But if you find that you're free, we'd love to have you."

I feel my heart beating faster. I desperately want him to come, but something tells me he won't.

Then he surprises me. "I'll celebrate. However, I'm busy tonight."

"Tomorrow then?"

"Tomorrow works. I can fly in for the evening."

"Should I have the guest room made up?"

"No," he quips a little too fast. "This time, I have to get home."

"It could be a late night."

"Won't be a problem."

My father bobs his head, and I remember Grayson has a helicopter. Coming and going from the city won't be an issue for him.

"See you tomorrow," my father says, and then Grayson turns and leaves without so much as a goodbye.

No acknowledgment that I was even in the room.

My father collects his belongings and we head back to the private elevator.

"How are we going to celebrate?" I ask.

"We can go out to dinner."

"Sounds like a plan."

"Is there anyone you'd like to invite?" he asks.

I turn my attention to him. His eyebrow lifts with his curiosity.

"No."

"I mean, if you have any friends . . ."

"I don't."

He looks at me, and I feel small.

Like a little girl again.

"I don't really have friends." I shrug, refusing to let this fact embarrass me.

He waits for me to continue.

"Before I came to live with you, I never had a home base. It's hard to make friends when you don't know where you're going to be. Then I came to live with you . . . but I wasn't like those girls. After the way I lived with Mom, I didn't fit in. I have a few friends from college, I guess, but they aren't around."

I think about the Prices. About how they are brothers and a sister and they have each other's back. I think about how much I'd give to have a fraction of what they take for granted.

He looks down at the floor and then back up at me. Sorrow meets my gaze. "I'm so sorry she did that to you, and I'm so sorry it took me so long to realize you needed me."

I shrug. "It's all in the past now." But in truth, it's not. I wish it were, but I'm still a nomad. Moving from place to place with no real home.

It's not as if I have a place in the city. I'm staying with my father. I got rid of my apartment when I moved to Spain, so I don't have a place of my own yet. I know I could, but the truth is, I have no idea what I want to do with my life, so why settle? I need to find something I'm passionate about, and then I need to move on with my life.

But for now, I'll concentrate on where we're going to celebrate my father's amazing job. On the ride back to the Hamptons, I scroll through every social media site for the hippest, coolest restaurant I can find that has an attached lounge. That way, we can have drinks if the night decides to keep going. It's hit or miss, though. We could sit in the bar and have drinks and dinner to celebrate him, and I'll still feel like I'm going out, minus the going out. I mean, my parents will be there, but Grayson will be there too.

I still can't believe I opened up and told my father what I did.

I don't want him feeling sorry for me, but the words came out before I could stop them.

I need to start making jewelry again as an outlet for these feelings I'm having. It keeps me busy when my thoughts turn dark. But ever since I have been home from abroad, I haven't been inspired. But I need something to keep me busy.

Maybe I'll find some inspiration when I'm in the Hamptons.

By the time we make it home, I've booked us a restaurant that turns into a lounge around ten p.m. Apparently, the music turns up, the lights dim, and waiters even dance on the tables on some nights. The atmosphere is perfect.

Enough ambiance to have a good time, but select enough for Grayson Price.

Not that I should care what he thinks.

He might be hot as shit, but he's sporting either a serious chip on his shoulder or a stick up his ass.

I'll do my best to avoid him tomorrow because as much I am attracted to him, I don't chase men who so obviously hate me.

Nor do I pine over them. No. Tomorrow, I'll drink, dance, and have a good time.

No matter what Mr. Grumpy has to say about it.

I'll wear my cutest dress, high heels, and who knows, maybe I'll meet someone.

One can hope at least.

CHAPTER ELEVEN

Grayson

I CAN'T REMEMBER THE LAST TIME I HAVE NEEDED A FUCKING drink as badly as I need one right now.

When I said yes to this celebration, I obviously wasn't thinking clearly.

I was imagining a drink or two, maybe a quiet dinner. But this is everything but that.

Here I am, at a restaurant that doubles as a trendy lounge. Equipped with white furniture and Lucite tables, it resembles a modernistic space—cold and sterile.

On the outside walls of the room are banquettes. The room is dim and pulled back along the edges are white chiffon drapes that hang from metal wires.

I imagine when the lights dim further and dinner is no longer served, the drapes are pulled out to enclose the space for "private" parties.

I twirl the ice around my glass before taking a large swig.

The need for something to help me relax is all-encompassing. So I take another swig and look across the table.

That's when I see her looking at me. I'd hoped she wouldn't be here. I'd hoped that maybe she'd be out on her own, but that was not how tonight played out at all.

Instead, she is here, and she is barely dressed.

Her dress should be illegal.

Her beauty even more so.

The thing about River is she doesn't even know how gorgeous she is. It's not that I know this firsthand, but I can tell by the way she lowers her eyes when I look at her. Or by the way she bites her lip. She's uncomfortable with the attention.

The past few times I have seen her, it's as though she's battling her own demons. Or she is torn on how to act.

One minute, she comes across as confident and self-aware, and then at other times, she looks unsure, second-guessing herself.

Yes, asshole, like a teenager would.

You're here for your friend. Just ignore her.

But that proves impossible as our eyes lock in a stare down. She refuses to look away, and I can't.

I'm not sure what it is about her, but I'm completely transfixed.

Her long, blond hair falls loosely over her shoulders, and her bright eyes stare at me as if she's imagining a million ways I can fuck her at this lounge.

Shit.

Now I'm thinking of all the ways and places I can do that too.

I shouldn't have said yes.

No, definitely not.

From across the banquette, I watch her.

And I know this was the dumbest mistake I have ever made.

To make matters worse, she's leaning forward, giving me a perfect view of her cleavage in the joke of a dress she's wearing. This dress is shorter than the T-shirt she was wearing the other week.

Black and form-fitting, it leaves nothing to the imagination.

I'm not even sure how Tyler hasn't pulled her out of the lounge and made her put something else on.

Fuck.

A napkin. Anything. If it isn't bad enough that it's short, it also dips low to show her cleavage.

No joke, from the dip to the hem can't be more than ten inches.

I groan to myself and readjust my pants under the table.

Why is it so warm in here?

And why are my pants so damn tight?

The answer screams in my brain, but I refuse to admit the reason. I'm happier thinking the air is broken.

Yeah, that's it.

No air conditioner.

"It's cold in here. Can I have your coat, Ty?" Kim asks her husband, crushing the illusion I have conjured in my brain.

Grabbing my drink, I swallow again, slow but purposeful. To make my anger ebb, to make the visions disappear.

The music around us has risen in volume and a soft glow now illuminates the room. I look around, and multiple patrons are now dancing on the benches of the banquettes.

Please don't let River dance.

I don't think I can handle the sight.

She cocks her head at me as if she's trying to discern what I'm thinking, and then she does the one thing I don't want. She stands and starts to sway her hips.

Kim looks up and apparently loves the show. She doesn't get up, but she cheers as her stepdaughter starts to sway to the music.

I look over at Tyler, hoping he puts a stop to the madness, but he merely shrugs his shoulders.

"Are you going to let her dance like that?" I ask him.

"Not much choice in the matter," he says, lifting his own drink to his mouth. "Better here than with people I don't know. Plus, I guess you'll figure it out once you have a kid—they're not hot on being told what to do."

Oh, I know. Your daughter made that perfectly clear.

He thinks she's safe here. But what he doesn't know is I'm more dangerous than the rest because I know she's off-limits, and I want her anyway.

Not wanting to watch anymore, I stand and make my way to the bathroom.

I need to splash water on my face or something. The visual is too much to bear. Normally, if she were any other girl, I'd take her home and fuck her out of my system.

That, however, is not an option. So instead, I stalk past the throngs of people who are now making the center of the restaurant into a makeshift dance floor and walk down the hallway.

Once I'm standing in front of the mirror, I look at myself.

I look older.

Drained.

Angry.

I splash water on my face.

Unfortunately, it does nothing to calm me. Instead, I'm more pissed.

I feel like a dirty old man for wanting her.

And no amount of water will change this. I just have to leave.

I step outside the bathroom and bump right into someone.

My hands reach out to steady the person, and when I look down, I suck in a breath.

It's her.

My hand is wrapped around her hip. She's a breath away.

"What are you doing here?" I grit out.

"My dad wanted me to check if you were okay."

Of course, Tyler. Of fucking course.

"I'm fine."

"Doesn't look that way from where I'm standing."

She reaches out and her hand touches my face, where the little droplets of water still cling to my skin.

"Are you sure you're okay?" She lifts her hands to show me the liquid.

"It's just water."

"Exactly. Why do you have water on your face? Are you not feeling well?"

"No, River. That's not it." I try to sidestep her, but she follows my movements.

"Then what is it? What's wrong?"

"You," I shout. "You're what's wrong."

As soon as the words leave my mouth, I realize what I've done. But it's too late. The expression on her face falls. Her eyes are wide, staring at me. It's almost as though she's stopped breathing as she comprehends what I've just said.

"Me?" she whispers. Tears fill her eyes. One lone drop escapes, trailing down her cheek. I want to swipe it away, but that would make everything approximately a thousand times worse.

"River, I didn't—"

"It's fine," she cuts me off, and now that I've calmed, I realize what a dick move that comment was.

But this girl makes me crazy.

"River," I start again. But she just shakes her head.

91

"I understand. Really, I'm not as stupid as you suspect I am."

She turns her back to me and starts to walk back to the table.

I start off after her. I might not be able to broach this topic with her, but I also don't want her to be upset, especially if her father sees.

That would be lower than lower.

When I get back to the table, River is by herself, and I look around but can't find anyone.

"Where are Tyler and Kim?" I ask.

"I don't know," she responds.

"I'll look for them," I say, but as I start to move to look, my phone vibrates in my pocket.

Tyler: Kim wasn't feeling well, so I took her home. Can you give River a ride back, please?

I look down at my phone.

He left abruptly because Kim wasn't feeling well. River is staring at me, waiting for me to go look.

"That was your father . . ."

Concern washes over River's face. "And?" she whispers, and among the bass of the music I can't hear her, but I read that word on her lips anyway.

"He took her home."

"What?" she shouts. I grab her by her hand and pull her back through the crowd and into the hallway.

"He took her home," I say now that we're away from the noise.

"Why?" Her voice is so soft I can still barely hear her, so I squeeze her hand, giving her the only comfort I can.

"She wasn't feeling well," I admit on a sigh. "I'm going to take you home, okay?"

"They left me," she whispers. She looks up at me; she looks younger than ever now. Lost, almost. I pull her to my body, a move I shouldn't make, but at this moment, I don't care. She needs me, and regardless of how wrong it is, I want to give her my strength and support.

She allows me to hold her, and with my arm around her, I lead her back to the driver I have waiting for me outside.

She doesn't speak as I guide her into the car.

And once inside, I hold her next to me. She feels so natural in my arms, tucked away for me to care for.

I shouldn't think this right now, but I like the way she feels. I like the way it feels to have her in my arms, with me protecting her.

She breathes in and out, and the sound is soft. I stroke her shoulder, cooing it will be okay. Other than the soft words I whisper, nothing is said, and before long, I help her out of the car.

Once out, I turn to my driver. "I'll call you tomorrow."

He nods.

I won't be needing the helicopter, after all. Or if I do, it won't be for a while. I need to make sure Kim is okay, and that Tyler is as well.

But for the present, my concern is the girl in my arms.

Together, we walk to the front door. I expect the lights to be off at this time of night, but everything is on.

I pull River with me and look around, but I don't find anyone.

"Let me take you to your room," I say, and she nods.

With my hand wrapped around her still, I walk her up the stairs, and then through the door to her room. When she sits on the bed, I hear her mumble to herself, "They left me," *but then she must remember* I'm there because she shakes her head and then she looks up at me.

"Thank you." Her voice is barely a whisper. "Can you find out—"

I lift my hand, not wanting her to utter it out loud.

"Yeah. I'll keep you posted as soon as I get any info. Do you want me to come back?"

"Yes, please."

"And if you're sleeping?"

"I won't be."

I incline my head and then set off to find Tyler.

It doesn't take me long.

He's sitting in his office; tumbler in hand with three fingers' worth of amber liquid.

When I step into the room, he raises his glass and takes a swig.

"She got dizzy and was so tired. She couldn't keep her eyes open," he says. "I think something is wrong. She almost passed out at the bar . . . and then she threw up."

"She threw up?" I ask. "Did she drink too much?"

Slowly, I enter farther, and then I take a seat in the chair adjacent to him.

"She didn't drink at all. Kim doesn't drink. I'm just not sure what's wrong with her. She's been so tired and dizzy, and now vomiting."

"Do you think she's—"

I'm about to say pregnant, but he shakes his head. "She's on the pill."

"Could be the flu," I respond. He nods again, but he doesn't look too sure.

"Have a drink with me," Tyler says.

I reach across to the decanter filled with scotch and give myself two fingers' worth. It's going to be a long night.

Lifting the glass, I take a swig. I allow the liquid to pour down my throat. Tonight was supposed to be a night of celebration, and now it's anything but that.

"I hope it's nothing serious," he whispers after a while, breaking the silence. "River's real mom was once . . ." He trails off.

"What?" I ask.

"Nothing." He lifts his drink.

"She'll be fine," I respond.

He goes quiet for a second and then turns back to me. "Thank you for being here."

"There's nowhere else I would be."

"And thank you for giving me the opportunity with Lancaster . . . I really needed—"

"Stop, there's no need to thank me. You got that gig on your own with your own talent."

"Thank you."

And then we both go quiet.

CHAPTER TWELVE

River

THEY LEFT ME.

I never thought they would leave me.

I know Kim isn't feeling well, but I never expected her to forget me.

No. Kim wouldn't abandon me.

She's just sick. She's been tired for weeks and complaining of feeling dizzy. I need to stop projecting every fucked-up insecurity in my crazy basket on my relationship with my dad and Kim.

I'm lying in bed now with an endless loop playing in my head. It's not rational to think they will leave me or abandon me all because she got sick and had to go home early. She's tired, so maybe she's fine. But my fears have me going crazy.

Fear of them abandoning me.

My back muscles begin to tighten, and it feels difficult to inhale oxygen. I need air. I'm suffocating.

Each pull of oxygen burns my lungs.

I inhale.

Faster.

Faster.

Faster.

It reminds of the beach. When my mom left me. My chest constricts. It feels like everything is closing in.

I try to concentrate on something else. I try to hear his voice. Even though it's been nine years, I listen for it. I hear it in my head.

The grandfather clock.

Through each inhale I take, I feel myself becoming more grounded as I listen to the sound.

Tick.

Tock.

Tick.

Tock.

Creak . . .

Someone's coming.

I can hear the sound of footsteps making their way toward my room.

The door squeaks as it's opened, the hinges protesting against the silence of the night.

A hissing sound. Is it as loud as I think?

Or does my fear intensify the sound?

I know when it's fully open because the footsteps that were once feet away are now closing in to where I'm lying.

The bed dips.

I don't look up. I don't move.

"River." I hear his voice and my heart starts to hammer recklessly in my chest.

It's not my dad.

It's Grayson Price.

In my bedroom.

On my bed.

I stop breathing. If this is a dream, I don't want to wake up.

"River," he repeats. "Can you look at me?"

I shake my head. If there is anything worse than having a panic attack the way I just did, it's having someone witness it.

I know he saw me in the car.

But this is different. I basically had a nervous breakdown for no apparent reason.

I don't even know if anything is wrong.

He will take one look at me and think I'm an overdramatic child.

"Please," he pleads. His normally gruff voice is soft, and the implication makes a tear fall down my cheek.

If he's tiptoeing around me, things must be bad.

When I don't speak or move, I hear him sigh.

Yep.

I'm the petulant little girl hiding under the bed from the monsters.

But in my case, the monsters are all the fears I have hidden inside me for so long.

What if she leaves me?

My mother left me.

As if hearing my inner struggles, I feel his hand touch the blanket covering me and then it's lifted off.

His hand finds my back that's exposed to him.

"Everything will be okay," he coos as he starts to run his fingers on my skin. As if I'm a wounded animal he needs to calm. "Everything will be okay."

"How will it?" I finally croak.

His movement on my back stops, and then I feel his hand reach around to my face nestled in the pillow. His warm hand turns my jaw, forcing me to look in his direction.

It tilts me up so our eyes meet.

His gaze is unwavering.

It's disarming.

No one has ever looked at me as intently as Grayson Price looks at me now.

"Because I know." His voice is strong as if he's trying to convince me. His words should make me feel better. It doesn't. What does this man know about anything anyway?

He's barely spoken to me.

Barely looked at me.

So what does he know?

"You don't even know me, so how can you even say that?" I fire back. My voice might be low, but my feelings for his hatred are obvious.

I lift my hand to swat his fingers away, but his opposite hand stops my movement. Instead, his right hand is still on my jaw, and now his left holds my wrist in his hand.

"River," he says sternly. "You need to calm down."

"Why? Why do I need to calm down?"

"Because you're stronger than this. I know you are."

I know you are.

Does he? A thousand little sharp, brilliant shards of memory, like broken glass, dance in my mind at that moment.

I let out a deep sigh. "I can't."

Still not letting me go, he runs his fingers up and down my jaw. "I might not know you well, but I know what I've heard and what I've seen."

"And what is that?"

"You are as hard as a diamond and tough as nails. You have lived through so much, and you have always held your head high. Even though life was uncertain, you didn't let that define you, so right now, when nothing is certain, you need to find that strength again."

His words stun me, but what has me completely out of sorts is the way he never breaks eye contact and how he continues to touch me, caress me. Comfort me.

Time stands still in his arms, and then when I'm not sure what he will do next, time comes to a screeching halt as he realizes what he almost did.

He pulls back abruptly, shaking his head viciously.

"I—" he starts, but I turn away from him.

He did his job; he calmed me, but Lord knows I will not look at him long enough to see the rejection there.

So I dismiss him instead.

"You can go," I mumble under my breath. "I'm going to bed."

I can feel him stand from the bed, and then I hear him take a step and stop. "Go, please." And with that, he doesn't object. He continues to walk out the door, and then and only then do I let out a frustrated breath.

I can feel the heat of the early morning sunlight streaming in through my window. I can't see anything, though.

My lids feel like they're glued shut. All the tears I have cried made my face and eyes swollen this morning.

Last night.

All the events that transpired come back to me.

The lounge.

The rejection.

The phone call . . .

Kim.

She's fine.

You're letting your own issues of abandonment drive you crazy.

She isn't going anywhere.

You don't know that.

My heart starts to beat rapidly in my chest as I realize I never did speak to my dad or stepmom yesterday.

No, instead I cried myself to bed, all after the fact Grayson Price made me feel like a silly little girl.

Again.

I push the thought aside and wipe at my tired eyes.

When they finally open, lights glisten across my bed, making my room fuzzy. I want to shut my eyes again, dive back into my sheets, and pretend the past few days haven't happened. I want to pretend I was ignorant of everything but drinks by the pool, popcorn, and a movie.

But I can't.

So I kick my legs out from the sheets and move to stand.

The floor is cold beneath my feet. I take a few steps before throwing on my robe, then swing my door open and head to find my parents.

The door to their room is closed, so either they're sleeping or they're downstairs.

Taking the stairs, I head down to the kitchen.

No one is there either. I make my way back into the kitchen and then see a note.

River,

Kim is feeling better, but we went back to the city. I'll call you soon.

Love you.

Dad.

They left.

He says Kim is okay, but then why did they leave me . . . ?

Again.

Without a goodbye.

Like Mom.

My nerves are shot.

I'm alone in the house, and I'm not sure what to do now as I wait.

I reach for the phone. I'm not even sure who I want to call, but as I stand in the kitchen all alone, I press send on a contact I don't expect.

Mom.

She still hasn't called. Or checked in. But right now, I need someone, and she is my mom.

I don't have many people.

So even if she's not perfect, I hope she answers.

I need her.

The phone rings and rings, but no one answers.

Eventually, her voicemail picks up. And I hang up. Throwing my phone on the counter, I stalk over to the espresso machine and brew up a coffee.

I'll just sit here and wait.

I wait and wait. I make it through three cups of coffee before I hear the sound of footsteps.

I turn toward the entrance of the room and am shocked by who greets me.

He's still here.

"What are you doing here?" I say.

He walks farther into the room and grabs himself a mug. Once he fills it with coffee, he takes a sip.

"Please help yourself to my coffee," I deadpan.

"Don't mind if I do," he retorts.

"You haven't answered my question."

"And what question is that?" His voice is smug.

Condescending.

It's a good thing he's so good-looking because he certainly lacks personality.

I'm not sure why Dad was ever friends with him. But then I remember the way he laughed. There must be more to this man than he shows me.

Shame I'll never see it.

"Why are you here?" I ask, again.

"Your father asked me to stay."

"Well, I'm not a little girl. I don't need a babysitter."

"Apparently, your father doesn't share the sentiment. After seeing you last night, I'm Team Daddy," he says under his breath.

"Asshole," I fire back.

"Whoops. A tantrum. Where's your time-out zone? In your room? On the stairs?"

I shake my head. "You know what? Just leave."

"No can do. I made a promise to a friend."

"I relieve you of said promise. I'm twenty, about to be twenty-one. Go. I don't need you here, nor do I want you here." I narrow my eyes at him.

My anger is misplaced, but I don't need this arrogant ass keeping me company today. I'd rather be alone.

He lets out a sigh.

"Listen, I'd like to stay. Your father asked me to, and I want to do that for him."

He looks me in the eye, and I can tell he's being sincere.

"I want to give him peace of mind," he adds. Small frown lines form and crease his forehead.

I can tell right away that he does, and that he's not lying. The truth is, I don't want to be alone. Even if I said I did, I don't.

And at least with Grayson here, I have a distraction.

Not that I expect him to speak to me at all, nor do I think he'll spend time with me.

Knowing him, he'll probably avoid me like the plague.

I stand from my seat and walk over to the sink, placing my mug down, and start to leave.

"Where are you going?" he asks.

I turn around and look back at him. His beard is a bit longer than normal today. Like he hasn't trimmed this week. He looks worn out too.

But even with both those facts, he's too handsome for his own good.

"Somewhere else."

"Please don't leave the house. If they call, I want to be with you."

I let out a long-drawn-out sigh. "I won't leave."

"Thank you," he responds. "Where can I find you? If I need you . . ." he confirms.

"I'll be working out." With nothing more to say, I turn my back to him and head up to my bedroom to throw on workout clothes.

I have way too much pent-up energy to do anything productive, so to calm my mind, I'll do yoga.

My mother taught me yoga as a child—that and many holistic things that a man like Grayson Price would probably laugh at—since everyone does yoga, so I grab a mat from the gym and head out to the deck. The view of the beach and the sound of the waves lapping against the shore are sure to relax me.

CHAPTER THIRTEEN

Grayson

THAT DIDN'T GO WELL.

I imagine when Tyler asked me to stay here, he had no idea of the sparring war River and I are now engaged in.

Except that's what we're in, a full-out war.

River is pissed. She wants nothing to do with me and pretty much wishes I would disappear at the moment.

Is that such a bad thing?

It would certainly make today easier. She can stay out of my way, and I can stay out of hers. Once we know what's going on with Kim, I can fly back to the city and move on with my damn life.

Walking back into my room, I throw on the clothes that Tyler let me borrow today. This is becoming an occurrence I'm not comfortable with. But what can you do?

My friend needed me, so I'm here. Making up for old times' sake.

By wearing his clothes. Living in his house. Hanging out with his daughter.

This is so fucked up.

Grabbing my sunglasses, I head down the stairs to go outside. River said she'd be in the gym, so I'll be able to rest without worrying about seeing her for a while.

I step out onto the patio and make it a few feet before I'm stopped in my tracks.

God-fucking-dammit.

Great. Just freaking great.

She's not in the gym.

Nope.

Why would she be where she's supposed to be?

No, instead River is on the patio, wearing nothing but tight boy shorts and a sports bra. And if that wasn't enough, it's actually worse than the tiny scrap of material covering her body.

Because her outfit isn't the problem at all . . .

The fucking problem is, from where I'm standing—actually, to be honest, there is no safe location on the patio for the view that greets me . . . River in downward dog.

Goddamn, I can't even look away, no matter how hard I try, because there she is in full glory. Her ass is in the air, and the view is spectacular.

Regardless of who she is, I can appreciate how exotic she is in that position.

She moves in a fluid motion, graceful and flexible, a lethal combination.

I groan to myself. I need to get out of here before she sees me.

Fuck, because as soon as I think that, she looks up and our gazes meet. Shit. Now it's too late to escape. She continues to move, pivot, and stretch as if she doesn't have an audience, or maybe she moves because of the audience, because as she does, she never takes her eyes off me.

We're engaged in a silent battle of which one of us will break the connection first.

I refuse to back down. Showing she affects me isn't an option. So as she moves through her routine, I watch.

Like a voyeur, like a predator stalking its prey, but in this case, I can't even tell who is who.

She's enjoying me watching.

I'm enjoying the show.

Finally, she moves into her final position and stops.

"How did you like the performance?" She grins.

"I liked it fine," I respond, trying to keep my voice level, but it's no use. The bite of annoyance is there. "You could use a few pointers."

"From a yoga instructor?"

"Or from an actual dog. Really, not the best form I've seen." I'm annoyed.

I'm fucking annoyed and not necessarily with her, but more with myself. I shouldn't be staring at her like that.

"What are you doing out here?" I ask. I tend to ask her what she is doing in places a lot. Maybe because she is always fucking everywhere.

"I could ask you the same question," she fires back.

"Well, I think it's quite obvious."

She lifts a brow. "What is obvious is what I'm doing here . . . yoga."

"And I'm here to enjoy . . ." I look around and up at the sky. "The sun."

Glancing back at her, I see her lip is slightly tipped up, and then she nods. She has a strange look on her face, one of mischief, and I wonder why, but then she lowers her shorts, and I know why.

I should leave. I should go right back inside and sequester myself to the guest room until I know what's wrong with Kim, but I'm apparently a glutton for punishment. Because now she's standing in a bikini bottom and that damn sports bra.

The view will never get old. She is absolute perfection. As I watch her, she turns away from me and dives into the pool. The splash echoes around me, and then she resurfaces.

"Needed to cool off." She smirks as she begins to tread water, and suddenly it becomes sweltering. I feel hot. The outside air is too hot.

Maybe it's her. Her in the pool. Her wet.

All I want to do is dive in as well.

I shake my head and try to look elsewhere, but from the corner of my eye, I can tell she is watching me. Her head is cocked as if she can hear my internal struggle and is figuring out a way to put the final nail in the coffin.

"It wouldn't kill you to relax," she says from where she now treads water in the pool.

"I am relaxed," I answer back.

"Says the guy whose back is so straight I swear there's a stick shoved up your—"

I glare at her, and she halts her words. She's gone too far, and she knows it. "I'm sorry," she whispers. "I shouldn't have. You're not here by choice. I shouldn't be such a bitch."

My mouth opens to respond and shuts, but before I can find the right words, she dives back under the water, breaking away from a conversation she doesn't want to have.

With nothing more to say, I have two choices—get in the pool or lie out.

River is already in the water, so I opt to relax in the sun.

I lift my shirt and recline, sunglasses covering my eyes, that way she can't see me watching, but I am.

I watch her swim. She's completely in her element as she does her laps. She swims with such ease. She's a natural.

She's on the fourth lap when my phone rings. I look down

to see that it is Tyler. Lifting up the phone, I show her the screen, and then I nod to her, signaling it's him. She stops her laps and begins to tread water again.

"Tyler. You okay, man?" I answer.

"Yeah. Sorry about that. We're back in the city. Kim is resting," he responds.

"And the doctors?"

"Unfortunately, they can't schedule any tests until after the weekend." His voice sounds tired, and I know that he's upset her doctor can't see her early.

"That's bullshit. They just expect you to wait?"

"They said it could be the heat or dehydration that is making her sick. Apparently, it could make her dizzy, vomit, and feel faint too."

"Let me call—" I start to say, but he cuts me off.

"No," Tyler says.

"But—"

"Grayson, you've already done enough. I don't need you calling in favors for me."

"You sure?"

"Positive. How's River?"

"She's in the pool. Do you want to speak to her?"

"Yes, please."

I stand from where I'm sitting and walk over to the pool. She swims over, and I place the phone on speaker.

"Hey, Dad. Is Kim okay?" she asks from the edge of the pool. But I can tell from the way her cheeks pinch in, she's trying hard to rein in her emotions. She cares about Kim, loves her, but she's not happy they just left her.

"We won't know anything until Monday. I'm sure she's going to be fine."

"Should I come back to the city, or will you both be return-ing?" she asks, and I can hear the hope in her voice.

"Stay. I'm not sure what we'll do but don't rush back. We probably won't find out anything until Monday."

"Okay." If Tyler could see the look on her face, he would tell her to come. She looks crestfallen that they don't want her there.

"See you later . . ." he responds before hanging up.

Normally flawless, now a small line is knitted between her brows. She's still beautiful, but it's apparent she's not handling this well.

She's trying to put on a strong front, and I imagine it's be-cause of yesterday. And that she doesn't want me to see her weak again. I don't know what to say to her, how to reassure her, so instead, I think of my own sister and think of what I would do in a similar situation.

Distraction.

If this were Addison, I'd distract her. I'd keep her mind occupied.

But . . .

I look at her from where I'm perched at the end of the pool. She's not your sister.

Is it a good idea to spend more time with her?

Even if Tyler asked me to, that was yesterday. I was only supposed to make sure she got home okay. He never told me to stay. Then I did, and he didn't tell me to wait any longer.

Now I'm still here and have this desire to take care of her.

Before I can stop myself, I lean forward and reach my hand out.

"Come on, out of the pool," I say, and she looks genuinely confused by the movement. Can't say that I blame her. My be-havior has been erratic at best.

"We're leaving," I announce.

"We are?" she asks.

"Yep. We can't stay around here all day waiting, especially since it will drive us both crazy. So come on."

"Where are we going?"

"That's a surprise." I have no idea where we are going, but I have until she's showered and dressed to decide.

That can't be too hard.

I have everything at my disposal, car, plane; fuck, I even have a helicopter. Now to think of what would make River happy?

That's when I realize what an asshole I have been. I have spent days with this girl, eaten multiple dinners with her, and I still don't know anything about her at all. I'll take us to lunch and find out what makes her tick, and then I'll plan an epic night to keep her distracted until Tyler calls with more information.

It's a perfect plan.

Now if only I didn't feel like something will go epically wrong.

Rather than call my driver, I find the keys to Tyler's second car. He won't mind if I borrow it. It only takes thirty minutes before River descends the stairs, ready to go. She looks gorgeous as always. Her wavy blond hair falls past her shoulders, but as beautiful as she looks, it's her blue eyes that give her away. They are still hollow from nerves, but hopefully by the time we're done with lunch, and I devise a plan, that look will be gone.

I allow my gaze to linger for too long, taking her in to completion. She's dressed in a short yellow dress that flows up with every step she takes. As always, she is sin and temptation, all wrapped up in an innocent bow.

She's too beautiful for her own good and certainly for mine.

I'm really going to need to get back to the city stat and find a woman to fuck. Either that or find a repeat I wouldn't mind sleeping with again.

That's the problem; it's been so long since I've gotten laid that I'm fantasizing about this girl.

A girl I can't have.

"Come on," I say and start walking toward the garage, needing space.

Behind me, I hear her sandals slapping against the marble floor. She's trying to catch up.

I don't let her; I keep walking at a fast clip until I'm sitting in the car. The passenger door opens, and she slips inside, slightly out of breath from her attempts.

"Where to in such a rush, boss?" she says sarcastically.

"Lunch."

"Great. And here I thought we had a deadline since you're walking so fast." Her voice is laced with annoyance, but then her stomach grumbles from beside me in her dad's Porsche. "Well, apparently there is a rush. I'm famished." She laughs.

We pull out of the garage, and with the top down, her hair blows with the wind, making her look free.

I take the main road and drive into East Hampton. Once there, I pull over and find a parking spot. I'm not much of a Hamptons guy. I actually despise it, but when I do come, I know this great French café.

I park the car and then throw my door open and exit. She follows suit.

"Right there," I say, pointing at the bistro. Together, we make our way to the café, and when we step inside, the hostess smiles brightly at us.

"We have a reservation for two," I say. "Under the name Price."

She looks down at the piece of paper in front of her and then grabs two menus.

"Fantastic, Mr. Price. I have your table ready. If you would both follow me." She steps forward and leads us to the table I requested. A small table tucked away in a private alcove.

Once seated, River looks over the menu, then looks up at me.

"You haven't opened your menu," she states.

"I've been here before. I always order the same thing."

"And what is that?" she asks, putting her own menu down. Challenging me yet again.

"Croque Madame."

Her eyes widen, and then she smiles. "I didn't see that coming."

"Is that so?" I ask.

"You seem to be so healthy." Her cheeks turn red, and I wonder what she is thinking. "You are in such good shape," she adds, and now she is fully blushing. The color looks beautiful on her skin, and I wonder if the warmth spreads everywhere? "I didn't expect you to have a sandwich bathed in butter and béchamel sauce."

"I'm a lot of things, and healthy is just one of them, but I always make an exception for this when I'm in the Hamptons."

"What else do you make an exception for?" she asks.

"Lobster rolls. What about you? What's your favorite?"

She closes her eyes and then pops them open. "Lobster rolls too, high tea, real sushi from Japan, oh, and authentic Cuban food." She nods to herself.

"Anything else?" I say, a slight chuckle leaving my mouth. This girl talks about food like she loves to eat.

"How much time do you have?" She laughs, and the sound does strange things to me. My shoulders loosen at the sound.

"You like to eat," I state.

"I do, but I also like to eat regional favorites."

"So eating a Croque Madame not in France is a no-go for you?" I say.

"I wouldn't say that necessarily . . ."

"So then what would you say?"

"I'd say you can get that where it's their specialty, but here in the Hamptons, why not find something they're famous for, here?"

"Such as?" I pipe up.

"Farm to table. Fresh ingredients."

I nod, and as she speaks of food and produce, I can see parts of her that I assume she gets from her mother. She might live in the Hamptons and work for her father, but she hasn't always been this girl.

No. Before, I remember hearing she traveled.

"How do you know so much about local favorites?" I ask, vaguely knowing the answer but wanting to know more.

"I have had extensive travel experience."

I lean back in my chair. Maybe this will give me a better insight.

"Where have you been?" I ask.

"Where haven't I been?" She smirks.

"Seriously, though, tell me about it."

She rolls her eyes as if she's shocked I want to know this. "You don't really want me to tell you," she says.

"Sure, I do. I'm fascinated by where all you have been at such a young age." At the word young, she grimaces.

"Why?" she asks.

"I just am. So how about you help me out here?" I joke, and for the first time in forever, I feel different. Lighter. I want to joke and laugh and tease her too.

Her gaze is intense as she watches me, and then she balances her weight on her forearm and looks up at the ceiling.

"My mother, do you know my mom?"

"Only met her once," I respond, and she inhales before swallowing.

"She's kind of a free spirit, hence the name River . . ."

I nod for her to keep going.

"Growing up, I traveled everywhere, and then . . . eventually, I came to live with my dad, but every summer, well, every summer since my dad got custody, my mom and I would take a trip, and we traveled like nomads, meeting people, eating with the locals. Immersing ourselves in the culture." She stops and looks back at the ceiling above, lost in her own thoughts.

This isn't what I wanted to do. I didn't want to hurt her by my question, but it seems that's exactly what I've done.

She looks far away. Her eyes lost. Like a child dropped in the forest with no breadcrumbs to lead her home.

"Are you okay?" I ask.

She shakes her head and rights herself. "Of course." She allows the facade that she has obviously constructed around herself to drop back down.

I don't like it.

She doesn't resemble the River I've seen with Kim or her dad. She reminds me of me.

Cold.

Collected.

And I hate it.

I grab her arm and stand.

"Come on, let's go." I start to pull her out of the restaurant.

"We haven't even ordered," she responds.

"I know."

"Where are we going?"

"Somewhere a little far afield, but suitable nonetheless." I keep it vague as we walk back to the car. I fire off a text. The plane will be waiting for us in twenty minutes.

CHAPTER FOURTEEN

River

WHEN HE GRABS MY ARM AND STARTS PULLING ME through the restaurant, I have no idea what's happening. His face looks different. I mean, obviously, it looks the same, but there is a lightness to his features.

A soft look I have never seen before.

"Where are you taking me?" I say, quickening my pace so I can keep up with him.

"To lunch," he responds over his shoulder as he pushes open the door, and we leave the restaurant.

Before I know it, he's ushering me back into Dad's car, and we're speeding off to an unknown destination.

I have no idea where we are going.

But as my hair gets swept away by the wind, I can't help but be happy for this excursion.

With each swoosh of the breeze, I feel free. Like I can spread my arms and fly away. It's exactly how I need to feel right now.

So much is buried inside me. So much fear. So much doubt.

I know the ideas in my brain are completely irrational, and that my parents aren't going anywhere, but after my mom leaving, not showing up, and in the most recent case, disappearing altogether, the idea of people leaving me . . .

Yeah, I'm completely irrational.

But luckily, here in this car, it's almost as if I'm in a movie reel, and nothing bad can happen.

The car zooms through traffic, weaving in and out of lanes, until we finally pull into a private airfield sometime later.

He brings the car to a stop directly beside a private jet.

"I thought we were going to lunch?" I ask, confusion evident in my voice.

"We are." A smile stretches on his beautiful face, so foreign and unnatural, and yet, painfully beautiful. This is the first time I've ever seen him smirk, and my body feels weak from its effect. It's a good thing I'm sitting because as cliché as it sounds, I would have for sure swooned or stumbled or something of that nature. Instead, I smile as the butterflies begin to take flight in my belly. "Okay."

"Let's go," he says as he shuts the car off.

Reaching out, I place my hand on him to stop him from his exit. He looks down at where my hand is, and his jaw tightens at my touch. Quickly, I remove it. "I didn't bring anything."

"You don't need anything." The door pops open, and he begins to step out, but not before turning over his shoulder, and saying, "We'll be back before dinner."

"Oh. Okay." I swing my own door open and step out of the car.

Grayson walks in front of me, and I fall into step with him. When we approach the jet, he lets me pass and walk up the tiny metal steps first, and then follows me.

"Hello, Mr. Price," the flight attendant says and turns to me. "Hello, I'm Molly, and if you need anything, I'm at your service."

"Thank you," I answer.

"Come." Grayson walks me to a seat and then sits in the seat facing me. His chair is backward, and I'm happy he let me face the right direction.

"So are you going to tell me now where we are going?"

"No." This man is infuriating.

"This is kidnapping, you know."

"No, it's not. Your father knows you're with me."

"You're taking me out of the state."

"Technically, you're an adult."

"Oh, now I'm old enough." I smirk. "Oh, come on," I press as I buckle my seat belt and look out the window as if there will be a clue on the ground.

"It's more fun this way," he says, and I turn my attention back to him.

"Fun?" I lift my eyebrow. "I didn't even know that word was in your vocabulary," I muse.

"Well, I'll have you know it is. Not often," he retorts, "but on occasion, I'm quite funny."

I think back to him and my dad, and I know it must be true.

"I'd like to see that," I say, my voice low and steady. I try to control the tremble, but having him look at me and be so normal is doing crazy things to me.

What I say must rattle him, or how I say it because once the words slip out, I see his back tense and that damn wall fall back down.

As the plane starts to taxi, a nervous energy starts to run through me. My fingers start to tap the armrest the faster the plane goes. I think we're taking off, but I can't be sure, because as the plane lifts off, I'm basically bouncing in my seat. Once in the clouds, my brain starts to run a million miles a minute, wondering where we are going and why?

"River," I hear from somewhere. But my mind is still off in the clouds.

"River?" he says again. I reach my hand up to scrub my face back to awareness.

The plane is no longer moving. I lift my lids until they are open and peer into Grayson's green eyes.

I feel asleep.

"We're here," he says, and I stretch my arms over my head and look out the window.

Unfortunately, there is nothing to see. Just a hangar in an unknown airport.

"Where did you take me?" I ask.

"Soon . . ." He trails off mysteriously.

"Oh, come on," I plead.

"You said you wanted to see that side, so consider this your one ticket for admission into the Grayson Price show," he deadpans as if the comment from before still bothers him.

"Do I get candy with my purchase?" I joke, and my comment makes his lip twitch.

Please smile.

And he does, and when he does, it's like the sun has finally come out after a long storm.

"Maybe," he retorts, still smiling.

Cue the butterflies.

"I'd better be a good girl then," I chide. His pupils dilate at the reference, and then his mask falls back down.

Damn.

We both go quiet now that I have ruined the mood. The door to the plane opens, and I stand and start to walk out. I take the three steps down and find yet another car waiting for us.

"Must be nice," I mutter under my breath.

"What?"

"To be a Price." I gesture to the car and back to the plane.

"It certainly has its perks," he says, but then he looks away. "And pitfalls."

By the sound of his voice, I'm sure that like all things in life where there are ups, there are also downs. With Grayson now looking out the window, I turn my body to look out my window. There's not much I can tell. It's a highway.

"If you keep looking, you'll ruin the surprise."

"Fine," I huff out, pretending to be upset. But in truth, I'm anything but. I'm actually the complete opposite. I never expected Grayson to treat me like this. To treat as more than a nuisance.

And I don't want to ruin a moment of this. Not one second.

Because I'm pretty sure when we return home that this will all be a mirage. Quick to fade the closer you get.

The driver weaves through traffic, and I still have no clue where we're going.

I look over at Grayson, but his usual mask is pushed down over his features.

"Come on, just tell me," I say, touching his arm. I watch as his shoulders tighten, and his eyes widen, and it makes me want to be brazen. It makes me want to touch him more.

He shrugs as he pushes farther away from me in the car. "You'll realize soon enough."

Before I realize what's happening, we make a series of turns, and then I see the ocean on my right. We're at the beach?

But the better question is, which beach and where?

"Maine," he says, answering the unspoken question.

"We're in Maine." My voice sounds shocked.

"Yep." His one-word answer annoys me. I want him to tell me more.

"Why are we in Maine?" I ask, not letting it go.

"Because you wanted lobster." He says this like it's the simplest notion in the world. As if everyone could hop on a private jet to eat lobster for lunch. I burst out laughing, and he scrunches his nose in confusion.

"You are a strange man," I say, shaking my head.

He doesn't respond to my comment. Instead, he watches out the window at the scenery passing by as we drive to our location.

Eventually, we're pulling off the road and turning on what looks like a dirt path.

We continue our trek; the SUV bumping over the gravel, until we pull up to a run-down looking shack overlooking the Atlantic Ocean.

"The best lobster roll in the country . . . maybe even the world." He shrugs.

I look at the beat-down shack on the beach. It looks like it's been here for years. The wood is discolored from the salt air. He must notice my confusion because he explains.

"It may look like shit, but it's the best, a hidden gem."

I smile at that because this is what I was saying earlier today. My mom might have been a lot of things, but this place reminds me of the fun we had. Traveling the world and finding hidden gems.

"I can't wait."

"Come on." He opens his car door and steps outside. I slide out his side as well, and he reaches out his hand to help pull me out. I'm taken aback by the gesture.

I didn't expect him to do this.

I let him take my hand in his, and when our skin touches, I feel warm inside. It feels like shivers run up my body at the touch, but I hold back any reaction, scared if I move or act in a way that Grayson deems inappropriate, he will shut down. And I'm enjoying this far too much to allow that to happen.

My shoes hit the ground beneath me, and together, we start to walk. He drops my hand, and I miss the warmth, but I don't dwell on that.

No, I can't.

I know what Grayson is trying to do. He's trying to distract me. And even though he's been a jerk half the time, he hasn't been today, and I welcome the change.

We walk around the building, and it's literally a shack on a beach. There isn't even anywhere to sit.

Actually, that's not true; in the distance a few feet away, I can see an old picnic table.

"Go sit, I'll grab us lunch," he says.

I do.

I make my way up to a rickety old wood table. The wood is almost gray from wear and I'll probably get a splinter in my ass, but I love it. The salty air wafts in through my nose. It reminds me of summer with Mom *when she would show up for me.*

I smile. No matter how many times she bails and abandons me, I still love her.

She just gets too distracted by life, by adventure. I can feel the calling in my blood as well. So as my hair drifts around me, I lean back onto to the table—splinters and all—and close my eyes.

The brilliant rays of sun stream down against my skin, and I inhale and then I expel all the stress inside me. I know life has no guarantees. Anything can happen, so as I wait to see the next hurdle in my path, I let go of the fear and enjoy the world around me.

With my eyes closed, my other senses pick up, and I can hear the footsteps, I can smell the butter and lobster, and I know he is here, standing in front of me. I pop open my eyes and see him staring down at me.

A peculiar look marring his face.

His head is tilted, and there are no lines on his face from this angle. No, it's as if he's just watching me. Deep in thought. Studying me.

But where in the past disdain filled his green eyes, now they are soft.

I lift my hand to cover my eyes, the sunlight bright and not allowing me to fully take him in. But my movement must wake him from his trance because he coughs and rights himself.

"I have our lunch," he states, placing the white paper bowls down. Inside them is probably the most mouth-watering lobster roll I have ever seen.

He then takes a seat across from me.

His back facing the ocean.

"Eat," he says.

I reach out and lift the butter hoagie to my mouth. My taste buds come alive at the first bite.

It's decadent.

Smooth and buttery in my mouth.

I let out a groan or moan; I'm not even sure at this moment because it's that damn good.

That's when I hear a sound beside me and look over to see Grayson Price choking, or coughing, or something.

"Oh my God, are you okay?" I ask, placing my roll down and reaching across to touch him.

He shakes his head, eyes wide, and then pulls away from my touch.

"Do you have to moan like that? It's just a lobster roll."

"No. It's not just a lobster roll. It's the best lobster roll I've ever had," I say, and then I take another bite, moan included, again.

"Yeah, just great," he growls.

So much for the change in personality . . .

Mr. Grumpy is back, and I'm not even wearing those sinister shorts.

CHAPTER FIFTEEN

Grayson

I DON'T KNOW WHAT TO DO AT THE SOUND THAT COMES OUT of her mouth. Record and make it a Billboard hit? The shit's addictive.

My mouth hangs open in complete shock as I imagine endless possibilities with that sound. I imagine what the look on her face would be if I drove her crazy. Feasting on her. Thrusting in her.

Having my way with her.

She stares at me, and she realizes I'm angry. But I don't even know why I'm so angry. She didn't do anything wrong. It's me. I'm the problem.

Big fucking problem.

Today was a mistake. I know why I did it, and now that I'm here, it's too late to do anything more. I'll just be careful and rein in my emotions. I won't let her drive me mad.

I stand abruptly, and she quirks an eyebrow.

"Where are you going?" she asks.

Great, just great, where *am* I going? I don't fucking know. I look toward the building.

"Napkin," I say as I storm off in the opposite direction. With every step I take away from her, my lungs start to fill with more air.

I can breathe again.

Thank fuck.

For a moment there, it felt like a vise was tightening around my lungs. Watching someone eat shouldn't invoke that reaction, but the way she licked her lips and the way she groaned around the food . . . Her tongue slipping out of her mouth when she was done and licking her plump lower lip. I can't help but wonder what that same tongue would feel like on me.

"Grayson," River probes from where she is still sitting on the bench of the picnic table.

I turn my head and look at her, but seeing as I still don't trust myself with words, I just stare.

Glower is more like it.

"I need a napkin too," she shouts, and I give a curt nod.

As soon as I'm back at the shack, I grab a stack of napkins and then head back.

Now that the sound of her moans has faded away, I'm ready to get on with today and then head back to the city. And back to my life.

I shake my head to myself.

"So tell me about studying in Valencia?" I ask because at this point, we need to talk about something. Anything that isn't her moans or shorts or yoga poses.

"I loved it."

"What college do you go to?"

I know she said she studies abroad in Spain, but she never said where she went to undergrad.

"NYU," she says, and I quirk a brow.

"Great school," I respond.

"Surprised?"

"Hardly. You're a smart girl," I say, and she crinkles her nose.

"Girl?" She rolls her eyes.

"Yes," I say firmly. Reminding her, and me,

"I'm hardly a little girl," she says in a clipped tone. "I'm turning twenty-one in a few weeks."

For some reason, that news has my shoulders loosening. She's turning twenty-one soon.

Legal.

Well, she's already legal, but for some reason, twenty-one sounds so much better than twenty.

I'm only fifteen years older, and I don't feel like a dirty, disgusting old man.

And for some reason, it makes all the indecent thoughts I have been having seem a little less sordid.

But she's still Tyler's kid.

I had almost forgotten that fact.

A fact that it's imperative I don't.

"So you go to NYU." I change the topic back to something safer. "What are you studying?"

"I'm studying business."

"Really? I would have never guessed that."

"Why? Do I not seem the serious type?" she bites out, and I hold my hand up.

"No. I didn't mean it like that," I answer, lifting my hand in peace.

"Then how did you mean it?" she fires back, obviously upset by my assessment.

I let out a sigh and try to think of Addison. I'm being such a dick to this girl, and she really doesn't deserve it. So I think of my sister and try to answer the best way I can. "Truth. No. You don't look like the type. I don't know you, but you don't look like someone who would be happy doing that."

"And what do I look like I'd be happy doing?" she asks, her voice low.

I incline my head and stare at her. Really look.

Her golden blond locks are flowing with the breeze; they are sun-kissed and wavy. She looks like she belongs on a beach, lapping in the sun. Free.

She looks like she would do anything better than sitting behind a desk.

"Something creative. Somewhere you can feel free," I say, and her eyes widen. "Something that gives you passion."

At my words, she lifts her hand to the hollow of her neck and touches her necklace. The necklace is unlike anything I have ever seen. It looks like it's glass, surrounded by strings of metal protecting it.

Then I remember the piece she wore to the lounge and her stepmom's comment.

"Did you make that?" I ask, and she nods and pulls her hand away from her neck; the sound of her charm bracelet jingling makes me ask my next question. "And this too?" I lift my own hand up to touch the bracelet. She inhales when my finger touches her skin. I'm holding the metal, touching the charms, but the pad of my thumb is trailing a pattern on her.

Now it's her turn to watch me. And watch me she does, but I watch her right back.

She doesn't blink. Her large blue eyes peer into mine. They are full of emotions; emotions I have no knowledge about, but I want to.

I want to delve inside her and find it all out. But I can't, and I won't. So I'll settle for the here and now, instead.

Touching her lightly, I hope she doesn't pull away yet because I'm not ready to break the connection.

"I-I don't think you know what you're talking about." She then turns her head away from me, looking back at her roll and taking another bite. But this time, she doesn't groan. Actually, no sound leaves her mouth for the rest of lunch.

I'm not sure what I said, but there is no doubt a story there. It's not my place to find out, though. No matter how much I want to, I won't broach that subject again.

The less I know, the better.

Once we're both done, I throw out our trash, and we head back to the car. River is still quiet, but I chalk it up to nerves.

We are silent for the entire car ride back to the airport, and then we board the plane.

I'm sitting across from her.

"Thank you for lunch," she finally speaks.

"My pleasure."

"I know you didn't want to, so I appreciate it."

"Why would you say that?" I ask.

"Let's not pretend here. You don't like me. I know this. You know this. Fuck, I'm sure Molly"—she points at the flight attendant—"knows this. It's no big secret. Yet, you still did this."

"Your father—"

She holds her hand up. "My father told you to bring me home last night. He never told you to stay, and he never told you to distract me. That was all you, and you didn't have to, so I appreciate it."

She's right.

I can tell myself I did this for Tyler all I want, but I didn't. I did this for me. Because no matter what I've told myself, I wanted to get a glimpse into who she is.

I could have just left, and then today, I could have just

gone to the bistro, but instead, for some sick and twisted reason, I wanted more.

So here we are, about to take off from a lunch that never should've happened. A lunch date I should never have gone on because instead of quenching my thirst for knowledge on her, it actually made me more parched.

Now I want to know everything.

And that thought alone makes my back muscles tighten.

Because I can't.

I turn to look out the window, essentially silencing the conversation. The plane starts to move, and sooner than later, it's taking off.

Once we have reached altitude, I stand and walk up to where the flight attendant is.

She looks startled, and I smile to calm her.

"Is there something I can help you with, Mr. Price?"

"You're fine. I was just going to get myself a drink."

She unbuckles her seat belt and stands. "Please let me, sir."

I nod and then head back to my seat.

River hasn't moved. Instead, she just looks up from where she is as I sit.

"Drink?" I say, and she nods. "What do you want?"

"Water."

"You can have a drink if you want."

"Are you sure? I am just a . . . girl."

"Just have a drink, okay?"

I sit down with a huff. This girl is driving me crazy with her new attitude.

For the first time, I'm trying not to be a dick, and it's thrown back in my face.

Molly walks over at that. "What can I get you, Ms. Reed?"

"I'll have a vodka soda."

"My usual," I say before she goes to get our drinks.

"What's your usual?"

"Scotch."

"Creature of habit."

"Yes."

"Why does that fact not surprise me?"

"I'm not sure," I deadpan.

"And Mr. Grumpy is back," she says sarcastically under her breath.

"Excuse me?"

"Oh, nothing." She smirks.

"Did you just call me Mr. Grumpy?"

She shrugs. "Well, if it walks like a duck and it quacks like a duck, it's usually a duck."

"So now you're calling me a duck?"

"Basically." Her chide still holds the sarcastic tone.

Molly comes back, and I take a swig. "I am grumpy. So it's actually a good nickname. I'll have to tell Addison."

Her face tightens. "Addison?"

"My sister." And I watch as she does something I don't expect. She exhales.

"You have a sister?"

"I do. And a brother too." Now I'm the one being an ass.

She takes her own sip and then inclines her head.

"Oh . . ." she says as if it's all coming together. "Tell me about them."

Her question surprises me. "You want to know about my family?"

"Well, I don't have a family . . . well, you know what I mean, so yes, I want to know what it's like not being an only child."

I lean back, placing my drink down on the table, and think about the best answer for that.

"Good. Bad. A little bit of both. I work with them. You actually met Addison."

"I did?" she asks.

"Yes, at the meeting. The one where your father pitched Lancaster."

"Ahh, yes. I remember her. The one who looks like a model?"

"I'll have to tell her you think so. So Addison is my younger sister, and Jax is my kid brother."

"How old is he?"

"Twenty-seven."

"Well, that's hardly a kid," she chides, and I realize that I've yet again referred to her age and pissed her off. The reason slaps me in the face. It's because as young as Jax is, this girl is even younger.

"He's trouble. Which makes him a kid."

"How is he trouble?" She leans forward, and from where I'm sitting and my height compared to hers, I now have a perfect view of her ample chest.

"He just is. He barely works, does things he shouldn't, etcetera, etcetera."

"I'd like to know the etcetera." She laughs.

But I have no intention of telling her about Jaxson's extra-curricular activities.

"Let's just say it's better for you and me if you don't know."

"Well, now I'm thoroughly intrigued."

I lift my drink, take a swig, and then place it back down. "Your mom never had more kids?"

"No."

"I remember that summer," I say.

"Lucky you."

"What do you mean?" I ask, not understanding this line of conversation.

"You're lucky you stayed clear of her. She brought loads of trouble too. My dad wasn't as lucky."

"I hardly think he thinks that."

She shrugs, then lifts her drink and takes a large sip.

I watch her from where I'm sitting, trying to remember that summer. I remember that she was quiet and shy, but now I see a different side of her. It's as if when no one is looking, she's desperate to run free.

It's as if she's changed her personality to appease people.

I have now seen both sides of River and I wonder which is the real one.

CHAPTER SIXTEEN

River

NOW THAT WE ARE BACK IN THE HAMPTONS AT MY father's house, I'm not sure what Grayson's plan is.

I can only assume he'll leave now.

But I don't want him to. I don't want to be alone.

Other than Kim, I don't have many friends, and I hardly think you can call your stepmom a friend.

I let out a sigh; I can't even call Grayson Price a friend. He's basically an unpaid babysitter.

When will I meet someone who likes me for me and who wants to be my friend or boyfriend?

Sure, I've hooked up, and I'm certainly not a virgin. Just like Mom, I have never lacked the attention of men. But I've never lived anywhere long enough to have a real relationship.

Who am I trying to kid?

I've lived places long enough to have one, but I've just chosen not to.

I have consciously held everyone at bay and not allowed anyone in.

If you allow them in, they can leave.

I shake my head at how pathetic I sound.

Most girls my age have daddy issues. I have daddy and mommy issues in spades.

God, I'm cliché.

I'm standing in the kitchen grabbing water when I hear the steps behind me.

"Your dad is on the way back," he says, and I stop my movements and turn to face Grayson.

His hands are in his jean pockets.

"He is?"

"Yes. Apparently, he took her to an urgent care, and now they are coming back."

"Is Kim okay?"

"He didn't say much, but it appears she's fine."

"Then why is she so tired and why does she keep feeling light-headed?" I ask, more to myself than to him. "Are you going to leave?" My voice is low and uncertain.

"I'll probably wait for him to get here," he says. I wonder why. He doesn't have to. But then again, he's trying to rekindle his friendship with Dad, that much is apparent, so maybe that's why he's staying.

At this point, he's already gone above and beyond for Dad for being my "nanny." A grumpy nanny, but a nanny, nonetheless.

I'm grateful for him, though.

My reaction to people leaving me, in general, is over the top on a good day, and Kim and Dad know this. So the fact that my dad asked him to stay means a lot, and the fact that he did means even more.

"You don't have to. I'll be fine." The man must think I'm a basket case, and maybe I am. I have unresolved issues I have never addressed, and maybe my reaction to things isn't normal.

"I know I don't have to, River, but I want to." Upon hearing the finality in his voice, I don't bother to object or say anything else on the matter. There's no point, so I go about my business, grabbing a bottle of water from the fridge and then making my way to the sliding glass doors.

The summer air hits my face, and I'm thankful I had the foresight to grab water. It's way too hot not to stay hydrated.

I sit outside for a while; time seems to stand still as I wait. Eventually, I can feel his presence.

He sits in the recliner next to me.

I expect him to talk, but he doesn't. Instead, we relax in comfortable silence.

Soon, I hear the door sliding open. My whole body turns toward the sound, and I see Kim and my father walking out onto the patio.

They both walk over . . .

Kim has a bandage covering the crook of her arm where they obviously drew blood.

My heart starts to beat rapidly in my chest. And the plaguing voice inside me tells me something is wrong with her, but the other voice, the one that sounds a bit similar to Grayson Price, tells me everything is going to be okay, and that there is a perfectly rational reason for her dizzy spells.

They walk over to where we sit. They both look exhausted but not sad, so that has to mean something.

I know I'm being completely crazy and irrational. But I have always had a doomsday personality when it comes to people leaving me.

I'm sure it stems back to my youth, but right now, I wish I could control my thoughts and fears.

"Hey, River." Kim smiles. My dad does, too. There's something off, though.

"Hey," I respond, and Grayson nods.

"Would you like to go inside so we can talk?"

"Umm, sure," I say before standing. Together, we all walk toward the doors and then into the house. My father leads us into the living room.

"Any traffic getting here?" Gray asks as if that's a conversation we should be having, but I guess he wants to end the uncomfortable silence.

My dad shakes his head as we continue into the room. Our footsteps sound loud to my ears, but then we sit and quiet descends.

I want to shout spit it out and tell me what's happening, but my tongue is heavy with my own fears.

"I guess we should tell you what the doctor said," my dad starts.

"Umm, yeah, that would be nice."

He takes Kim's hand in his and lifts it to his mouth before pressing a kiss to her knuckles.

"Well, it seems that even though we weren't trying, we're going to have a baby."

My ears start to ring.

Baby.

The sound of my heart thudding in my chest is all I can hear now. He continues to talk, but I feel like I'm submerged in a pool after diving in. Only certain words are breaking through to my conscience.

"It seems that her dizzy spells, headaches, and lightheadedness were all due to the influx of hormones. Although rare, some women experience these side effects."

Pregnant.

Kim is pregnant with a baby with my dad.

I know I'm supposed to say something, but I can't.

There are no words that I can form, and my mouth feels like it's glued shut, and it won't open.

A strange feeling of dread washes over me. What does this mean for me? Kim is all I had for so long.

She always put me first.

She was the only person who had my back.

What does it mean if she has her own family? Where does that leave me in this family?

"Isn't that exciting?" my dad says, and Kim's eyes are on me, staring at me intently.

"This won't change anything," Kim whispers to me because she knows me too well.

But how can it not? How can my life ever be the same now?

The baby will come first for her.

And once again, I'll be abandoned.

I know these thoughts are selfish and far from honorable, but the knowledge does nothing to dim them.

Scattered thoughts of my past hit me like a ton of bricks. I'm well aware that these thoughts are not rational, but as they start to invade my mind, I can't turn off the voices.

All I can feel is the pain of losing my mother when I was twelve. The pain of my father leaving me to Kim and not spending time with me, and the pain from only weeks ago when my mother forgot about me.

The pain from when Kim and Dad left me at the restaurant without a second glance.

That was the beginning.

There was already no place for me in their thoughts and they didn't even know about the baby then.

I don't know what I'm doing, but my brain feels cloudy as my emotions swirl inside me.

Pain.

Anger.

But most importantly, fear.

Fear of the unknown and what this means for me.

"River—" my father starts, but I stand. "Nothing will change. We both love you—"

Nothing will be the same.

I place a giant smile on my face. Plaster it on. Drop my well-painted facade down. The one that doesn't allow people to know how I feel.

"That's amazing news. I'm so happy for you."

I need to leave.

I need air.

I need to breathe.

Lifting my arm, I look at my watch. "I actually am meeting a friend, so I have to go." I start to walk. "Congrats again," I say over my shoulder as I head out the front door. I have no destination in sight. I just start down the path that will lead me into town. I don't have a bag or a phone. Hell, I don't have anything at all.

I didn't think this through. I wasn't thinking at all.

Now halfway up the road, I know I made a poor decision, but I refuse to turn back. My pride smothers me, reminding me that once again, I acted impulsively.

Like her.

Like the first of many people to abandon me. I guess now I can add Kim to the list.

It's inevitable.

A baby changes everything. They changed everything. I have no place now.

I continue to walk, tears filling my eyes. I hate how I'm acting. I hate that I allow myself to be impetuous, but sometimes, I can't control the impulse. I've always been like this, and I blame her.

It only takes a few more minutes before I realize I'm not alone on my trek.

"Are you following me?" I ask, knowing the answer.

"Yes."

I stop at the voice. I thought it would be my dad, but I was wrong. It's not. It's Grayson.

And the fact he's following me makes no sense. None at all.

"Why?" I ask.

"I honestly don't know." He sighs.

There on his handsome face is the scowl I have gotten used to. The one that tells me he hates me, or at least, he hates the way I act. Which makes even less sense to why he is here with me.

"Then do yourself a favor and walk back," I hiss.

"I don't think so."

"Despite what you think, I'm an adult."

"You certainly act like one," he deadpans.

"Seriously, leave."

"No."

I shrug. "Fine. Stay. Go. I don't care."

I continue to walk, and now he walks beside me slowly to keep pace with me. I ignore him, paying him no mind as I walk the half mile into town.

"Now what?" he asks.

"Oh, you're still here." I look over at him and meet his stare. He inclines his brow, and I huff. "Fine. But I'm going for a drink."

I watch as his head shakes in disapproval, and then he smirks. "You don't have a wallet."

"I'm sure I can get someone to buy me one," I say back. At this, his eyes widen.

"I'm coming. And I'll be buying." The tone of his voice makes energy course inside me. Grayson Price is sexy, but angry Grayson is even hotter.

"Fine, come. But I'm not a cheap date."

"I'm sure I can handle it."

"Have it your way." I lift my hand in the direction we have to go in. "Lead the way."

CHAPTER SEVENTEEN

Grayson

I HAVE NO IDEA WHAT THE FUCK IS GOING ON.

I am in way over my head on this one. Tyler might have used to be my best friend, but we haven't spoken in years, and somehow, I have been thrown headfirst into his family drama.

I don't need this shit.

I could be back in the city, drinking scotch. I could be with a woman . . .

Instead, I'm following this child in the midst of some sort of tantrum. She might hate when I refer to her as a child, but right now, she's acting like one.

Like a child having a meltdown in the middle of a department store.

I hate it.

I'm way too old for this shit.

Yet . . . here I am, following her.

It's like despite my better judgment, I'm an idiot when it comes to this girl.

Sure, she's hot. But am I really that hard up that I can't walk away?

River stirs a primitive need inside me, and I couldn't let her leave like that.

Tyler did stand to go after her and so did Kim. But I told them with the mood River was in, someone other than them would be better.

Knowing she has no one else, I found myself stalking out after her.

Of course, my friend had no idea why. But I know the reason I trailed her is because in the little time I have spent with her and the walls I had built, I couldn't let anything happen to her. Despite my attempts to shield myself from the desires I knew I had, I also couldn't let her be alone.

So here I am.

Following an under-aged girl into a bar.

To have a drink. An illegal one.

I'm not a stranger to bending the law . . . Usually, however, it's through Jaxson by proxy.

But this time, minor in hand, I'm walking her up to the bar and ordering us a round of tequila shots. I'm not surprised when they don't card her. Why would they? She's here with me. The bartender comes back with our shots, and I lift mine in the air and so does River.

"To new families," she grits out. Her voice is strained along the words.

"To change being okay," I counter, and she rolls her eyes at me, before taking the shot and drinking it.

I take my own, and the chilled shot trails down my throat.

"Just what I need," she says as she places the empty shot glass on the bar counter. "Another." She smiles at the bartender, and he turns to look at me. I nod.

Before I know it, we've had more shots than I can count. I'm happy we walked because even though I'm not drunk yet, something tells me I will be before River is done.

We are currently between rounds and she is dancing along to the music playing overhead.

There isn't a man in the room not looking at her. Including me.

She's swaying her hips seductively just as she did the other night at the lounge. There is something so exotic about her. Her sun-kissed hair combined with her eyes gives the appeal of the girl next door, but when she looks at you, she's much more than that. She looks like she comes from a universe away, new and tempting and brand-new.

I watch as a man approaches her. He places his arm around her and swings her back so her ass presses against his groin. She doesn't even seem to mind. Her gaze is hazy from too many drinks, and I'm thankful I came with her.

This dick is getting handsy, and she's too drunk to care.

Without another thought, I stalk over to them, grab her by the arms, and pull her toward me.

"We got a problem here, bro?" he asks. "We were dancing, weren't we, sweetheart?"

"Yeah, Grayson, we were dancing." She slips back like the smart-ass she is. At least in her drunken state, she still has her winning personality. Even with her sarcastic bite, I like her, and I don't want this dick to touch her, so I do something I shouldn't. Something I know is wrong, but I do anyway.

Maybe it's because I'm drunk.

Or maybe it's because I'm stupid, but either way, once I do it, I regret the move instantly. I pull her toward me, throwing my arm around her until she's flush against my chest.

My dick hardens in my pants against her ass, and I know she feels it when she squeaks.

Yep. Big mistake.

Now she knows.

Now she knows despite what a giant ass I am to her, I want her.

The only question is, what is she going to do with that info?

"She's mine," I grunt out.

"That true, sweetheart?" the man asks, and I basically growl at him.

I feel River trembling. I'm not sure if it's out of fear or lust, but I hold her tighter, running my hands up and down her sides. She moves her ass against me slowly.

Her breathing is heavy, and I know it's lust.

She's not afraid, she's turned on, and fuck if that doesn't turn me on more than it should. I bracket my hands around her hips and hold her tighter, allowing her movements and ministrations to tease and taunt me.

Goddamn, she is temptation. She is a piece of decadent candy, begging to be licked. I want a taste, but if I'm not careful, I'll eat the whole damn thing.

The man looks at me and then at her. Whatever he sees in her, he finally nods. "Sorry about that, man." Then he walks off.

I continue to hold her until I know he's gone, but when he finally walks to the back of the room, I drop my hands and pull her out of the bar.

"Where are we going? I wasn't done drinking," she whines.

"Party is over."

"Why are you grumpy again?"

"I don't know. Why am I so grumpy? Let's think," I hiss. "Maybe it's because I almost just got into a fistfight at a bar."

"I'm not sure why," she says as she stumbles on the gravel. She almost falls, but I'm quick to catch her. I put my arm around her. I'm looking down at her plump, kissable lips and trail my gaze to her beautiful body while she looks up with those big blue eyes. *Are you done staring at her?* I allow myself to gaze at where her pulse beats erratically at her neck.

It would be so easy to kiss her. To feel her lips upon mine as she opens to me, allowing me to give in to my temptations.

We are locked in a silent battle. She's exhaling, and I'm inhaling her breath.

Our bodies are tightly entwined.

If she fell, I'd fall.

I lean in, and now we are a breath apart.

When she exhales, her minty breath wafts in through my nostrils.

She must have just eaten a mint. I want to taste it.

Taste her.

I feel my resolve faltering. Lost in a battle of wills with myself. If I move an inch, I'll finally know what she tastes like. Her lids flutter shut, and my body moves of its own accord until I'm hovering. She lets out a breath, and I breathe it in.

"Just do it . . ." she pleads, and like ice-cold water being dumped on me, I realize what I almost did.

I push back, and her eyes open.

Confused.

Hazy.

Drunk.

"Come on," I huff. "I'm taking you home."

She doesn't fight me on this. It's obvious that the alcohol is having its desired effect on her.

She's drunk.

And now I have to get her home.

What a shitshow.

Today started off bad, and it turns out, it never got much better. My only hope is that I can get her home and be done with today already.

Unfortunately, due to her drunken state, getting home

takes longer than it took to get to town. And if that wasn't bad enough, I have to bracket my arm around her and guide her the whole way. Eventually, the house comes into focus. I'm ready to take her home and be done.

She holds her steps. It's like she's anchored into the ground. I give her arm a tug, but she refuses to budge. Then she starts dramatically shaking her head back and forth.

"What's wrong?"

"I can't go in there."

I let out a sigh. "Well, you're going to have to," I grit.

She tugs my hand.

I look back down at her, at her wild hair flowing, and her hazy eyes, unable to focus.

And then she sways, confirming she's way too drunk for me to bring to her father.

He'd kill me.

Fuck, he'd kill me if he found out half the shit I did or thought.

"Fine," I huff. "Follow me."

When she doesn't follow right away, I take her hand in mine and lead her down the path to the beach.

Although the beach is in their backyard, it's far enough away that she won't be seen unless they know to look.

"We'll stay here while you sober up."

"I don't want to go in," she whines.

"You're going to have to eventually."

"Do I, though?" She is thinking aloud. Not good.

"This is your home. Where do you plan to stay?"

"With you . . ." She smiles, half-hopeful, half-seductive. Drunk River is way too flirtatious for me to be alone with.

"Yeah, that's never going to happen."

"Why?" She bats her lashes innocently.

"Other than the obvious."

"And what would that be? Because I know you want me." Her voice is low and breathy. Making me imagine what she would sound like in the throes of passion.

Yep. This version of River is going to be a problem.

"Stop acting like a child," I scold.

"How am I acting like a child? I'm asking you a question. I don't see the correlation."

"Of course, you don't. You're drunk and acting like a child."

She leans forward from where she is sitting in the sand, and her movements are wobbly. "And you're acting like a dick."

"That might be the case." I shrug.

"So you admit you're an ass?"

"I believe the word was dick, but yes, I'll admit it. But I don't want to be here."

"So why are you?"

"Because you need babysitting, obviously."

"And you're the one to do it." She rolls her eyes. "'Cause they don't care anymore."

"What are you talking about?"

She throws her hands up in the air and then leans back and covers her face with a groan.

"You don't get it. You'll never get it. No one gets it."

"Maybe I don't get it . . ." I start. She lowers her hand, and I see the tears in her eyes. The sight makes my heart tighten inside my chest. "But I want to."

Her eyes widen, and she inclines her head to see if I'm being sincere.

I am.

I really do want to understand what this tantrum is about.

Because for as much as I don't know her, I know she doesn't act like this normally. Something has her upset and clearly acting irrational, and I want to know what it is.

She won't find anything but the truth when she looks into my eyes.

I reach my hand out. A move I know I shouldn't do. I need to stop touching her, but I can't.

It's like a gravitational pull between us. My need to feel her takes over all my rational thoughts right now.

Another tear trails down her face, and this time, I reach out and stroke it.

She looks so lost, and I just want to help her be found.

"Talk to me, River."

"What if they don't want me?" she whispers. Her voice is so low that I almost don't hear her over the sound of the waves crashing on the sand beneath us.

"What if who doesn't want you?" I ask.

"My dad. Kim."

My fingers continue to stroke beneath her eyes, swiping the tears that fall.

"Why wouldn't they want you?"

"You wouldn't understand." She moves to push my hand off hers and turn away, but I don't let her. Instead, I pull her closer.

She's so close I can feel her body move from her heavy breathing.

Reaching my hand under her chin, I tilt her face up.

"Talk to me."

"My mom left me."

I don't speak. She's talking, and I don't want to stop her.

"My dad didn't want me." She inhales. "Kim did."

"She still does."

"You don't know that. Once the baby comes, things will be different. Where will I belong then?"

She starts to cry now, fully and in earnest. My heart twists into River-shaped knots.

I hold her. I hold her as she sobs. As her body shakes. I hold her until her body is wrung of all emotions, and she's limp in my arms. I hold her, and she is the perfect weight for me to carry. Forever.

I cradle her against my chest.

She looks so young now. Not at all like the temptress before.

No, now she looks like a broken child, and it kills me.

It shouldn't, but this woman does things to me. She makes me want to care. She makes me want to feel. To turn on the emotions I have pushed down for so long and just be.

And that thought alone makes one thing clear . . .

I have to leave.

I have to stay far away from River Reed.

CHAPTER EIGHTEEN

River

MY BACK IS STIFF, AND IT FEELS LIKE I CHEWED ON CHALK the entire night. I try to blink my eyes open, but it's as if glue has permanently sealed them.

What is wrong with me?

That's when the headache begins. If I can even call it a headache. It's so much worse than that. It's like my body was placed in a meat grinder. I have never been this hungover in my whole life.

I look around to see where I am. It's dark, but tiny rays of the early morning sunlight stream in from the window. Enough so they illuminate the room.

My room.

How did I get here?

Last I remember, I was walking away from the house. No. I shake my head. That's not it.

The bar.

The shots.

Grayson pressed up against my body, hard and wanting.

A pounding starts to ring through my head as more images from my night come back to me.

His hand on my jaw, trailing circles on my skin.

He wants me.

He was going to kiss me.

Then he stopped.

My eyelids hurt, and I rub them furiously as I try to remember more.

He stopped. He didn't kiss me.

No.

Instead, we walked home, but what else happened? I rub my hands through my hair, trying to pull the memory out, and that's when I notice something grainy in my hand. I pull my hand away and look down.

Sand.

The beach.

Shit.

The beach.

My breakdown.

I fell apart in front of Grayson and he held me.

Now that I remember everything, my cheeks warm with embarrassment. Especially when I realize I'm here, and he's gone.

God, I'm an idiot.

Not only did I make an ass of myself, but I told him everything.

Will he tell my father? Or worse, Kim?

No. He wouldn't do that.

A groan escapes my mouth as I realize I'll have to speak to them eventually.

I didn't handle the news well. Sure, I put on a smile to their face, but they know me. Behind my smile, she always sees the truth.

Kim will see through my shit and my facade.

Even today, I feel sick to my stomach about what the future holds. I'm not sure I can fake it today.

I'll have to leave for a few days. Go back to the city.

But my dad will be there with me.

It's fine.

He's been so busy with work he has barely noticed anything recently. I pack quickly, needing to breathe and think.

I walk down the stairs sometime later with my bag in hand. Unfortunately, I find them in the kitchen. They both look up.

"Hi," Kim says softly.

I place a fake smile on my face. I know I should be happy, and I'm sure I will be, but right now, all my deep-seated insecurities are rearing their ugly head.

Between Mom not showing up in Portugal and now this, I feel vulnerable. Like my nerves are exposed and everything burns inside me to recede into myself.

I just need to get out of here.

"Hey," I respond, sugary sweet. "I'm heading back into the city."

"Are you okay?" she asks.

"Yeah, sure. Why wouldn't I be?" My voice is way too cheerful for this time of day and for this conversation.

"You know that a baby won't—"

I let my smile widen and hope she doesn't see the lie there.

"It's fine. I'm happy for you," I lie. "But I just heard of a party . . ." I trail off.

"Oh, okay. I just didn't want you to think—"

"I know. Will one of you take me to the train?"

My dad stands. "Of course."

"Great. Thanks," I say before turning to walk out the door.

The drive to the station is quiet. My dad isn't good with emotions or me. Never has been. Kim is the one who bridges the gap.

"I'll see you on Tuesday?" he asks, and I nod. "Yep." And then I'm out of the car, bag in hand, to wait for the train back to the city.

It feels like a huge lump is in my throat.

Change is not something I deal with well. Never has been.

It reminds me of the instability of my life. Those first twelve years.

Of not having a home of my own.

Of living out of suitcase and changing locations as often as I changed clothes.

Of not feeling like I truly had a family and then I feel the bile collect. Dad and Kim will have a family . . .

The sound of the train hissing along the tracks pulls me out of my thoughts. It's pulling up before I know it, and with a loud screech, it stops.

I step inside the car. The seat beside the window is empty, so I take it.

Scenery passes. Fields of green, and then new construction, towns, and highways.

Eventually, we pass through Queens and into the city. And it's not long before I'm back in the city in my dad and Kim's apartment.

Once I'm situated and my bag is in my room, I head into the bathroom and run a bath. Sometime later, I'm submerged in the warm water, trying to right my thoughts.

Maybe everything will be okay.

Or maybe it won't.

But one thing is clear. I need to start living my life. I need to be independent. I need to start thinking about my future and what will make me happy.

The first thing I need to do is rent an apartment. I can't live here anymore. I need to talk to Dad about money and rent.

Maybe I can ask about a long-term position or working more hours.

But it's not even in the field I'm supposed to be getting a job in.

Grayson's words ring in my ear. *You don't want to go into business. You don't want to sit behind a desk.*

Or do I?

With so many uncertainties in my life and future, I need to think long and hard about what I want before I do anything.

No need to think about it now, though. Instead, I close my eyes and relax. I'll go to bed early and then think about what happens next when I wake tomorrow.

Tuesday comes sooner than I thought it would, and since my dad is coming from the Hamptons, I go to the office alone.

We have a ton to work on, so I'm not sure I'll have time to speak to him. Normally, I get in with him, but since he's not here, I head into the coffee room alone. A bunch of my coworkers are there.

"Morning," I say to Alana, and she looks confused.

I have always kept to myself here, but not today.

"Oh, hi, River." The rest of the group looks at us, and then they all smile too.

"How was your weekend?" I ask them. They might be surprised by my sudden interest in them, but they let it go quickly. Alana tells me all about the summerhouse she's renting with a bunch of friends in the Hamptons.

Todd, our other coworker, is also sharing a house.

Apparently, this is a thing. Groups of twentysomethings renting and sharing a house out east. They pack four people into a room, and the house has five rooms. So it's a party of twenty singles for the summer.

It sounds like something Mom would do.

Speaking of Mom, she *still* hasn't called.

It's been weeks since we were supposed to see each other, and to be honest, I'm getting kind of worried.

As flighty as Mom is, I've never gone this long without hearing from her.

And that thought scares me. What if something happened? What if she's not okay?

I tried to call her, but she didn't answer.

I'm not even sure where to find her at this point. I close my eyes for a minute.

"River, you okay?" Todd asks me, and I give my head a little nod.

"I'm good. Just tired."

"Rough night?" He laughs.

"If rough night includes searching listings for a studio apartment, then I guess, yes."

"Are you looking for a place?" Alana asks.

"I am."

"Would you live with a roommate? My friend is looking for a roommate."

"Really?" I respond, turning to look at her.

"Yep."

"When?"

"Now." Her words have my mouth dropping open. It could be perfect. "It's an amazing pad too. Her roommate moved out because of her boyfriend."

"Do you have a boyfriend?" Todd asks.

"Nope," I answer.

"And you are back at NYU in the fall, right?"

"I am."

"See, it's meant to be. She's doing her master's at NYU. You'll love her. If you want, I can put you in touch with her."

"Sounds great."

"See what place?" I hear from behind me, and suddenly, my newfound friends are quiet.

I turn around to see my dad staring at me.

"Hopefully my new place," I say before walking past him to my desk.

He follows me. "You're moving out?"

"I think it's about time, don't you think?"

"Why do you say that?"

"Well, with the new baby . . ." I cringe at how petty I sound since it really has nothing to do with the baby, but for some reason, I'm lashing out and want to hurt him the way I'm hurting.

CHAPTER NINETEEN

Grayson

"WHAT'S GOING ON WITH YOU?"

I lift my head from my computer to see Jax standing in my doorframe.

"I have no idea what you're talking about," I respond.

"The stick up your ass . . . it's shoved up higher than usual."

I lift my brow. "If that's all, Jax, get the fuck out of my office."

"See." He points his finger at me. "Grumpy."

His words make my hands clench. It makes me think of her, and I've been trying not to since last week. After she cried, she passed out, and I carried her up to her room.

Seeing as she was drunk, I stayed for a while to make sure she was okay. But eventually, when it was obvious she was fine, I snuck out like a high school boy.

This girl. She's driving me insane.

Not just because she's young enough to be my kid . . . but also because I can't stop thinking about her.

Or wanting her.

And my only desire is to stay as far away from her as possible, but seeing as Tyler got the Lancaster deal, I highly doubt that will happen.

"Maybe you need to get laid," my brother grumbles.

"My sex life is none of your business," I hiss back.

"Sex life. That implies you have one, and if you do, I feel bad for whoever you're banging if you're still this stiff. Pun intended."

"Will you just shut up?"

"See, just as I thought. How long has it been?"

Too long.

Too goddamn long.

Before my trip to Malaga, that's for sure.

Since I've been home, I've been too busy working.

Who am I trying to kid? I've been too busy having a hard-on for my friend's kid.

"Just get laid," he says as his parting comment.

If only it were that easy.

The only person I want is off-limits to me.

I'm fucked.

And not in a good way.

The rest of my day proceeds in the same manner.

I'm a bastard to everyone and no one chooses to disturb me.

The phone on my desk rings at about four p.m., and I grab it.

"Mr. Price, Tyler is on the phone."

"Put him through, Nicole."

"Hello, Gray," he says through the line.

"Hey, man, what are you doing calling my office? You could have called my cell . . ." I trail off.

"Well, it's work-related, so I figured."

His voice is serious, making my back straighten.

"Got it. What can I do for you?"

"I have the new sketches, and I wanted to show them to you before I submit them to Lancaster."

"Oh, great," I respond. "I'll have a messenger come pick it up."

"No need. I've sent them with River."

River.

Is coming here?

Shit.

I hang up the phone and reach over to grab the bottle of scotch I keep in my office. Just in case of emergencies.

I pour myself a small glass and lift it to my mouth just as Jax walks into the room.

"Interesting," he says, and I place the now empty glass down with a thud.

"Get out."

"No chance . . ."

"I said leave, Jax," I scold.

"I want to know what has you so worked up." He has a damn smirk on his face. I need to ask Addison if we can fire him.

"Nothing," I clip. "Get out."

As if the fates were laughing, security chooses that moment to buzz me.

I press the button.

"Yes," I answer.

"I have a Ms. Reed here, sir."

"Send her up," I say before hanging up.

Then I look back at Jax.

"Leave." My anger is rising, and I need him out of this office now.

"Who was that?"

"God, man, do you ever listen? Fuck! Do you ever work? Or do you spend your whole day harassing me?" I scream across the room.

"It's good to see I'm not the only person you're grumpy to," a soft voice says, and that's when I know I'm royally fucked now.

Jaxson has yet to meet River, and now that he will, my ass of a brother will most certainly figure out that she is the source of my stress.

He's too damn perceptive not to. And what he'll do with this information is entirely unknown. He looks from her to me and then back at her. His lips tip up into a smirk. Bastard.

"I don't believe we've met." He saunters over to her, extending a hand. "I'm Jaxson Price, this asshole's brother." He points at me.

"I'm River Reed, the bane of this guy's existence," she quips, pointing at me as well.

That makes Jax smile even wider.

"I like this girl." He laughs.

"Don't like her too much. She's Tyler's daughter," I huff, and then I realize my mistake. Because Jax looks from her to me, and then his eyes widen with understanding.

Fuck.

"Even more fun," he says.

"Do you have the plans?" I say to River, cutting off Jax. I need to end this right now.

"Yep, here they are."

"Why these architects refuse to go strictly digital shocks me, but I can't say I'm not happy to have you as the messenger, so I won't complain," Jax says—well, more like flirts—and I can feel my anger rising within me.

"Well, if that is all, River . . ."

"Lord, my brother is a jerk. I'd say he doesn't mean to be rude, but that's a lie." He snickers, and I have an overwhelming desire to punch him. But since I'm not one for violence, especially at the office, I grit my teeth. "If you're done with him"—he points at me—"how about we go out for happy hour?"

I look over at River now. Her eyes have gone wide with surprise.

"You want to go out with me?"

"Yeah, why not?"

"I'm not twenty-one yet," she says under her breath.

"The plot thickens," Jax whispers under his breath. River is too far away to hear, but I'm not.

I narrow my eyes at him, but he's having way too much fun with this.

"Not to worry."

"Okay." River smiles. "I'll just freshen up in the bathroom, real fast." She walks out the door.

"What are you doing?" I snarl at him.

He turns from me to head out the door, but right as he's leaving, he turns to look over his shoulder. "Forcing your hand." And then he's out the door, and I'm left alone. Fists clenched and thoroughly pissed.

CHAPTER TWENTY

River

I HAVE NO IDEA WHAT I'M DOING. NONE AT ALL. OBVIOUSLY, I offered to go to see Grayson to gauge his level of contempt for me.

Answer: A lot

The man clearly hates me, which sucks.

But another thing that was also apparent was that his brother was the polar opposite of him.

Watching their exchange was not only entertaining as all hell but also enlightening.

So here I am now, walking toward the elevator with Jaxson Price.

He presses the button and it instantly opens to the private elevator.

"After you." He lifts his arm chivalrously. I step in, and once he does, the door closes.

"That was pleasant." He laughs. I move my mouth to answer, but before I can, he speaks again. "Good thing I came around and saved the day."

"You certainly are my knight in shining armor."

"You jest, but Grayson was being pretty awful." He inclines his head and looks into my eyes. His gaze has changed. It's no longer soft and lighthearted.

No.

Now his green eyes look colder, more serious.

As handsome as he is all sullen, I like him better when he smiles. I can only handle so much asshole for the day. My stomach tightens as I wait, or maybe it's just the elevator.

"He's not always like that," he says. His words shock me. The seriousness in his tone even more so.

"I know."

"You do?"

"Yeah," I respond with one word as I don't want to divulge more details. I'm still not sure about Jaxson.

He nods. The elevator stops.

"Where to?" I ask.

"A bar."

I follow him in.

It's a dive bar in the middle of a trendy area. Once inside, I realize it's not a dive at all. It actually appears to be an old-fashioned speakeasy.

"This place is cool."

"It is, right? My buddy owns it."

He takes my hand in his. I'm surprised that, at his touch, I feel zero reaction.

It's not that he's not hot. He is. He's just as gorgeous as Grayson, just in a different way.

"What do you want?" he asks me.

"What are you getting?" I counter.

"Dirty martini."

"I'll have the same."

"Oh, I bet."

A waitress comes over, and Jax leans back in the booth as he orders.

Once we are alone again, I wonder if I can breach the conversation of Grayson without tipping him off.

I open my mouth to speak, but he beats me to it.

"So," he starts, lifting a brow, "tell me what's going on with you and Grayson."

His question knocks the wind out of me, and I swear I start to choke.

"Easy there," he says as I try to catch my breath.

He hands me a glass of water, and when he does, our fingers connect. I hope and pray I feel something because being with Jax would be easier than wanting Gray, but unfortunately, as his skin touches mine, I feel nothing.

Damn.

As good-looking as he is, I have no desire to be with him. At all.

Sure, I find him fun enough, and he's by all means closer in age to me, but nope.

Nothing.

Not one spark.

I take the water, and he pulls back. The cold of the liquid helps me to swallow and cools me down as well.

Although I have no attraction to Jax, I'm sweltering from the line of questions.

"I don't know what you mean."

"Sure you do, Riv . . . Can I call you Riv?" he asks as if we are old friends and we haven't just met.

"Sure, why the hell not."

"Here's the thing. I don't mince words. I'm great at reading people, and I know everything."

"Wow. Cocky much?"

"Yes. And I already can tell you and I are going to be friends. So how about we just cut the bullshit and talk?"

As pushy and obnoxious as Jaxson Price is, I can already

tell I'm going to like him, and even though I have just met him, I know he's right. I do want to be friends with him. For some reason unbeknownst to me, I trust him, which is odd because I honestly don't trust anyone.

You trust Grayson.

I shake my head at that thought and concentrate on the here and now instead.

"Okay," I say. "We can talk."

"Fantastic." He lifts his hand and gets the waitress' attention. "Another round for both of us. Also, we'd love to have a food menu."

I lift my brow.

"It's going to be a long night." He smiles, and I roll my eyes.

"Lucky for me, I'm good at breaking curfews."

The waitress walks away, and I finish the remainder of my drink in one swig.

When she returns with our fresh cocktails and a menu, Jax takes the liberty of ordering us half the menu to share off the small plates. I have no idea what half the shit he says is, but it sounds good to me. I do have work tomorrow, so I probably shouldn't be too hungover. Eating will help.

As we wait for the food, we drink. We're both quiet. But I know that this reprieve is only temporary.

And just as I suspected, with a large grin on his face, Jaxson leans back into a comfortable reclined position and opens his mouth.

"How long have you wanted my brother?"

His question is shocking, and I shouldn't answer truthfully, but I do.

"Too long to even mention."

"Months?"

"Years."

His eyes go wide at the answer. "I didn't realize you've known him for years. I was under the assumption your father and Gray haven't spoken in—"

"Years," I answer for him.

He nods. "Yeah."

"The first time I saw your brother, I fell in love."

"How old were you?"

"Too young for your brother to notice me, but he did." Now his face scrunches, so I reach out my hand. "No. Not like that. Jesus."

"Then how?"

Since I don't know him well enough to tell him very much, I shake my head. "Let's just put it this way, up until that point, my upbringing wasn't your typical story. My mother dropped me off at my father's; mind you, I had never met my father before. That was when I met your brother. I was sad, and Grayson found me."

"So since then . . . ?" he leads me.

"Since then, I was intrigued by him, and it was pretty easy to get a glimpse into his life. His name is often mentioned in the papers."

"Gray is a pretty low-key guy," he says.

"Yes, maybe for his personal life, but your family is anything but low-key. You have helped so many people over the years, and it wasn't hard to see pictures and remember the man who helped me once."

"So then what happened?"

"He helped me twice." I shrug.

"So do you see him as a savior?"

"No." A part of me does, but I also see him as a man who

intrigues me, as a man I want desperately, and as a man who makes me not focus on the bad.

"And what does Gray think of all this?"

"He doesn't," I whisper.

"Oh . . . he does," he responds.

"He hardly knows I'm alive, and when he does, he's yelling at me for being a little girl."

"Yeah, that sounds like Grayson. Always lecturing. Always stern and collected."

"Why is he like that?" I ask, wanting to know everything about him.

And Jax just shakes his head. "Not sure. Besides, it wouldn't be my story to tell. Trust me when I say I want to help you with your cause, but even if I knew, I wouldn't divulge secrets."

"With my cause?" I ask. "What cause?"

"Why, landing Gray, of course," he responds smugly.

"What makes you think one, that I want that, and two, that I have any chance?"

"First of all, don't ask dumb questions. You want that. It's clearly written all over your face. Plus, you practically just told me you are in love with my brother. Two, have you looked at yourself? He'd want you."

"It's not always about looks."

"You're right, it's not, but, Riv . . . I know my brother and I have never seen him worked up over anyone the way he's been worked up over you."

"Why, because of what you saw in the office today?" I ask.

"No, not just because of the office. I know he took you to Maine."

The fact he knows that shocks me.

"That was because my stepmom—"

He shakes his head at my words.

"Don't sell yourself short. I know you think he did all those things out of the kindness of his heart for his friend Tyler, but let me tell you something. Bullshit. He didn't do any of this for your dad." He pauses for emphasis. "It's all been for you. He hasn't seen your father in years. My brother doesn't do anything for anyone unless it's me or my sister. An aged friendship isn't going to make him fly to the Hamptons or go to Maine."

"You would know better," I say, and he inclines his head.

"Yes, I would, and what I know is Gray wants you and hates himself for wanting you all at the same time."

"Then why do you want us together?"

"Because, at least with you, Grayson feels something," he mutters under his breath, making me look up at him.

"What do you mean?"

"Not my story to tell." He lifts his glass and takes a swig, then places it back down. "So are you in?"

"In?"

"Do what it takes to get him?"

"I'm not going to trick him into liking me," I huff out. Although I am tempted for half a second.

"No, but you can help speed it along."

I take a breath. "What did you have in mind?"

And then his lips spread into a wicked smile, and I know, without a doubt, he's up to no good.

The next day is spent thinking about what Jaxson said. When we parted ways, he gave me his phone number. I'm not sure I'll take him up on his crazy plan to make Grayson jealous, but

I heard him out anyway. Seems a bit excessive, like something my mother would do, so I doubt I'll call him . . .

But I have the number just in case I change my mind.

Today, I'm leaving work early to check out the apartment Alana told me about. Her friend Sadie is meeting me there to show me the place, so I can see if I want to move in. Although I have pretended everything is okay with my dad and Kim, I still feel strongly about moving out. They will have a new baby, after all.

Once I find the address of the building, I walk in the door, and the first person I see is the doorman. It doesn't take long for a pretty girl to walk over to me with a giant smile on her face.

"You must be River," she says.

"Sadie?" I question, and she gives me a little finger-wave.

"Also known as your future roommate." She smirks, and even though I haven't seen the place, I know I'm going to move in.

"Come on, let me show you the apartment."

———◦———

The rest of the week flies by. Dad has been giving me space and so has Kim. I should appreciate the move, but if anything, it actually bothers me more.

I have decided to move into the apartment because it really is perfect. Located on 32nd Street and Park, it's only two blocks away from the subway and is centrally located to everything. I should probably live downtown to go to NYU in the fall, but the truth is, I hated living in the dorms and rent downtown is too expensive.

I'm sure my father wouldn't complain, but I'd rather live some place more suitable.

So here I am, walking into my new one-bedroom converted apartment in Murray Hill.

It's an interesting concept, one I had never heard of, but apparently, it's a super popular area for young twentysomethings to live in. They rent luxury one-bedroom apartments and put a makeshift wall up and turn half the living room into a second bedroom. Since I'm moving in after Sadie, I'm in the converted room. But it's fine by me; I get the balcony that overlooks the courtyard which is a huge plus. I have grown up traveling and being free, so the idea of being cooped up sometimes weighs on me. It's one of the reasons I hated the dorms so much. So this is the best of both worlds. I live in the city, close to school, but I also have the freedom to sit outside when I need air.

I'm sitting in my room on my first night in my new apartment bored and not sure what I should do for the evening.

As if conjured by my thoughts, Sadie pops her head into my room. "Let's go out," she says.

"I have work tomorrow."

"Come on, you're no fun. I need you," she whines. "Who else will be my wingman?"

To that, I laugh. "I'd make a horrible wingman."

"Oh, come on."

I let out a huff. Moving in with her is supposed to help me get out of my shell, so I nod. "Fine. But I don't want to wait in line somewhere." As the words fall out of my mouth, a plan forms to kill two birds with one stone.

I pick up the phone and call him.

"River Reed. I was wondering when you would call."

"Jaxson Price. I've been busy moving into my new apartment," I respond.

"How are the new digs?" he asks, and I smile as I look around my apartment.

"It's great. I love it."

"So not that I don't love the fact that you called, but to what do I owe the honor?"

"Me and my roommate want to go out," I state matter-of-factly as I move over to my bed and grab a shirt from my suitcase and start to unpack.

"And you thought this was a good time to start the plan."

I roll my eyes at his words. "Yes, although I can't see how it will work. Especially seeing as your brother doesn't want me. Hell, the man is avoiding me like the plague. He came to the office the other day and didn't say one word to me."

"My brother doesn't know what he wants."

"Your brother, without a doubt, knows exactly what he wants. And I will tell you it's not me."

"Well, Grayson is a complicated man, but one thing that's not complicated is he's jealous. Every time I mention you at the office, he looks like he's going to have a brain aneurysm."

"Um, yeah, because he hates me."

"No. Because he doesn't."

"Sure."

"Care to make a wager?"

"No."

"Chicken."

"My God, Jax, I'm young, but what are you, like ten? I'm not chicken because I don't want to make a silly bet about your brother."

"If you say so," he chides.

"Fine."

"Great. I bet he's throwing you up against a wall by the end of the summer. Hell, by the end of next month."

I roll my eyes at the stupidity of this conversation, but at least it feels good to laugh.

"Fine, what's at stake?"

"Hmm . . . you owe me a favor, and if I win, the same. We have a year to cash in."

"Ominous bet."

"That's why it's so fun."

"Or dangerous."

"It will be nothing illegal, don't you worry."

I let out a sigh. "Fine, whatever you say."

"Okay, great, so as for tonight . . . I'll pick you and your roommate up for drinks around ten. This is going to be fun." He chuckles into the phone before hanging up.

Do I even want to know?

CHAPTER TWENTY-ONE

Grayson

I COULD KILL HIM.

Actually murder my brother.

There he is, splashed on Page Six without a care in the world. But Jax being a headline for a gossip rag isn't new news. Nope. That's not the problem at all.

No. The problem is the girl he has draped on his arm.

My girl.

I shake my head. Not your girl.

She's nothing to you.

I look down at the image on my phone.

Right there in front of me are River and Jax.

Apparently, or so the article says, Jaxson Price has been spotted with a mystery girl. They were laughing, drinking, and having a great time.

My fists clench at my desk.

I'm pissed, and worse, I'm jealous.

She looks gorgeous, but in that dress, she's sinful as well. Her head is thrown back in a laugh, and they look so damn good together I could rip my brother's head off.

The worst part is that they make sense.

Whereas my feelings for her don't.

She's too young. She has her life ahead of her.

I'm old.

And who knows how long I have before I meet my maker. Could be decades, could be days . . .

It's not worth the risk.

As beautiful as she is, I can't chance it.

So, instead, I avoid her, because even without the age issue, she's still Tyler's daughter. The things that keep us apart are too much.

That doesn't mean I'm not pissed that my brother poached.

With my phone in hand, I stand from my desk and head out into the hall. My footsteps echo through the corridor as I make my way to his office.

I don't knock, just push the door open, nor do I bother with pleasantries.

"What's this all about?" I thrust my phone, already loaded to Page Six's website, in his face. He leans forward over his desk to have a better look and then lifts his gaze.

"She's hot." He shrugs.

"Stay away from her, Jax."

"And now why should I do that?" he asks, his brow lifting. "It's not like she has a boyfriend. Hell, she's not even dating anyone."

"Because you can't have her," I shout.

And instead of this scaring him, it seems to make his smile grow even bigger.

Fuck.

I just played my hand of cards without even realizing it and this smug bastard is loving it.

"Stop fucking smiling at me."

He leans back and crosses his arms in front of his chest. "I don't think I will actually, big bro. I think I will continue to smile because I have something you want, and you're too much of a chickenshit to go after it yourself. So yes, I'll be smiling."

"I can't."

"And why not?" he asks.

But I don't even know what to say. Or how to explain the rationale behind the real reason I can't.

So I say the one thing I can think of. "Her father—"

"Oh, cut the shit. You haven't spoken to him in years. So what that he was your friend? He's been out of your life for like eight years," he fires back. "If he was such a good friend to you, where the fuck was he when Dad died?"

"He didn't know."

"For fuck's sake, the whole world knew. All he had to do was open a magazine. I get it. You want to reestablish the friendship, and that's great. But at what cost? Because I don't see why you don't try."

The truth is, he's right. Tyler was my friend . . . once. What loyalty did I owe to him now, though?

But that's not the only reason.

So I still can't.

"It's not just that."

"Then what?"

I shake my head.

And he lets out a sigh. "Fine, be an idiot, but I'll have you know, your loss is my gain. The girl is pretty fucking fantastic. Not just because of her looks. She's funny, too. She's not like the other girls we know."

"Don't you think I know that?" I grit.

"Then what the fuck are you doing?"

"You just don't get it. You're young and don't give a shit about anything but yourself . . ."

"First. Not true. Second. Fine."

I cross my arms over my chest. "What do you mean fine?"

He doesn't answer and turns to work on his computer. "Jax," I demand.

"If you don't mind, I have work to do," he responds without looking up.

"Tell me," I say.

"If you aren't going to make a go at it, I am. Now if you would please leave my office."

Then he looks back down. I'm about to say more when Addison walks into the room. "What the hell is going on?" she asks, closing the door behind her. "I could hear you arguing all the way out in the hall."

"Nothing," I respond.

"Ask Gray," Jax says, and I want to hit him upside the head for his answer. It's bad enough that Jax is on my case. Now I'll have Addison there as well.

"What's going on?" Addison probes. Her voice is soft so no one outside the office can hear.

"Nothing." I turn on my heels and leave, slamming the door behind me.

I'm not sure why I'm so pissed because he's right. River is special. I should be happy for my brother. I should want him to have a girl like her.

But I'm not happy.

I'm anything but.

Before I can think twice, I'm in my office and back at my desk, but this time, I'm firing a text.

I can't help it.

I have to.

Me: Just wanted to make sure you're okay.

I lean back and stare at my phone. Once again, I'm doing something so out of character that I don't know what's wrong with me.

But the desire to reach out after talking to Jaxson is all I can think about now.

River: Who is this?

Me: Grayson.

I can almost imagine the shock when she reads that. I can see her type and erase and then type again.

River: How did you get my number?

Me: I have my ways . . .

I do, and his name is Jaxson Price. The idiot uploaded it to the company directory of important numbers a few days ago. It's been taunting me ever since.

River: I'm good. Thanks for asking.

I want to type more. I want to ask her if she wants Jax. I want to ask her so many things. But, in the end, I can't.

Not just because of Tyler, but because I can't be with her.

No matter what I want.

The rest of the week proceeds in the same manner. I spend half the time in my office looking at the gossip sites to see if Jaxson was still parading around with River.

I refuse to ask him what's going on there. Instead, I pretend to work as I search.

From across my desk, my cell phone starts to ring. Across the screen, I see that it's Tyler. I grab it and then swipe to answer.

"Tyler. What's going on?" I ask as I pull away from my desk and recline back in my chair.

"Not much, man, I was just calling to see what you're up to this weekend?"

"Absolutely nothing." I laugh at my old friend.

"Want to come out east and chill?"

No, absolutely not.

There is no way I can go out there. Not if River will be there. My desire to touch her is too intense, and I'm not sure it would be smart.

When I don't answer right away, Tyler starts speaking again. "Come on, man, it will be like old times. No women, we can barbecue, drink beer. Chill."

"No women? Where's Kim?" I don't say where's River, but that's really what I want to say.

"Out of town, and River's staying at some Hamptons share house," he says and my muscles tense. The idea of River partying at a house with Lord knows how many guys, has me irrationally jealous. But she's not mine, and she never will be, so I push it down.

"So basically you're bored, and have nothing better to do, so you want me to entertain you?" I joke.

"Yeah, basically. But don't pretend you have any other plans."

I laugh at that. Because I don't. And the truth is, as much as I have seen Tyler these past few weeks, there has always been work or some sort of drama. It would be nice to catch up with him.

I've missed him.

"You know what, okay."

"Great."

"I'll bring the cigars," I add for good measure, "If you provide the scotch."

Just like old times, before everything went to shit. It feels good to have Tyler back in my life. I understand that he felt betrayed and ended our friendship, but it still hurt.

The thing is, after my father died, and I realized how fleeting life could be, and that my own demise could be around the corner, I try not to let myself dwell on the past.

When I arrive at the house sometime later, it's eerie how quiet it is. Tyler is off grabbing the scotch and I'm sitting outside by the pool.

It's around eight p.m., and the sun has begun its descent, leaving the sky in brilliant shades of pink in the distance. I haven't spent much time appreciating a sunset, but now with no one here to distract me, I take it in.

As much as I have said I hate the Hamptons, that's not true.

I only hate my family's house. I hate the memories it holds for me. But staying here, although only a mile up the beach, feels different.

"Glenlivet, neat," I hear from beside me, and I pull my gaze away from the sky to see my old friend.

"You know me well, friend."

A small line forms between his eyes as if something is bothering him and then he takes a seat.

"What's going on?" I ask.

He lifts his glass and then takes a swig. Then he places it back down before burying his head in his hand.

"I would have been fucked."

"What are you talking about?" I ask. Leaning forward in my chair.

"Business was slow, and I'm bleeding money somewhere . . . Kim doesn't know. River either. And I was such a dick to you, and in the end, even though I was a dick, you came through for me."

"Addison set up—"

"Stop. Just stop. It's not just that. Maybe your sister did set up the meeting, but I'm not stupid. You helped me land Lancaster. You didn't have to work with me after what I did. But there you were, helping at every step to ensure I got the project."

"Listen, man, I might have helped with suggestions, but you got that gig on your own. With your talent," I say because it's true. I might have spoken to Spencer briefly about Tyler, but he worked hard.

"You still didn't need to fucking help me, not after what I did to you."

"You didn't do anything; you were upset."

"I wasn't even at your dad's funeral, man. I let my petty pride ruin our friendship, and for what? So that you could be the bigger man and help me anyway."

"It's not a big deal."

"No, Gray, it's a huge deal. And then after all that, before we knew Kim was pregnant, you came in and helped, again. Why? Why do you keep helping me?" He sighs. "I certainly don't deserve it. I haven't earned it."

"Because we are friends. And that's what friends do," I state. "Life is too goddamn short to hold grudges, man."

He lifts his glass and takes another swig. "Thank you."

"Don't mention it."

The two of us sit in silence for a minute before I turn back to him. "How are things? With Kim?"

"Good."

"And what about the money thing?"

"Shit is still tight. I mean Kim is planning this insane party for River, and I feel like I'm suffocating with the expense, but what can I do?"

"Tell her."

"I can't. With the baby, she's already too stressed? She's concerned that River isn't handling it well."

"And is she?" I ask. Because I saw how she handled the news the first time she heard, and it was obvious no matter how much she smiled, she was having a hard time with it, but since I haven't seen her around her parents since, I wonder if she's doing better with the news.

"She's okay. I mean River . . ." he starts and stops, and I feel like I'm a girl waiting on bated breath to hear what he's going to say. "Well, to say River has abandonment issues would be an understatement."

"So the news of the baby . . ." I led.

"She's had a hard life. Before she came to me, she moved around. Her mother homeschooled her. Kim and I have tried to take care of her, to show her she will always have a home with us, but some issues are harder to go away," he says.

His words resonate with me.

I know all too well what he's talking about. No matter how irrational my beliefs are sometimes for my future, they are still how I feel and no one will tell me otherwise.

I'm sure I will die young.

I'm sure like my grandfather and my father, I won't see my sixties. But unlike them, I won't leave behind a wife and children to mourn me.

After I watched my grandfather die, my resolve wasn't absolute. But when I was on the phone with my father that faithful day that he suffered a heart attack driving out east for the summer, I knew. Deep in my bones, I knew.

I watched my mom go from a vibrant woman; I watched as my father's death tore her apart and I knew right then and there I would never do that to someone.

I would never abandon someone.

Look at River . . .

She's the perfect example of why I can't form serious relationships. Because one day, like my father and his father, I'll be gone, and I don't want anyone left behind to pick up the pieces.

CHAPTER TWENTY-TWO

River

COMING HERE WAS A STUPID IDEA. WORLD-CLASS STUPID.
I'm not sure why I thought staying in a house with at least twenty single twentysomethings was a good idea, but Sadie and Alana insisted I should come. The thing is, I might drink, but I don't get shit-faced drunk. Not only because I'm not twenty-one, but also because that's not who I am.

Except for that one time. But the night I got drunk in front of Grayson doesn't count; I was hurting, and I didn't know how to cope. I got way too drunk that night and was way too hungover the next day. Not a mistake I care to make again.

Now, I'm standing with a plastic Solo cup in my hand as a full party happens around me. It's not that I don't like parties, but I was already in a bad mood before this shindig happened.

Sadie had told me there was a bed for me. But when I got here, the house was overbooked. So my choice is sleep on the floor or shack up with some guy. Shaking up is not an option, even if I have had five propositions already tonight for whose bed I should occupy.

I take a sip of the stale beer in my cup and shake my head.

Nope.

I'm out of here.

Moving through the thongs of people, I find Sadie.

"Hey, chica!" she shouts above the music.

"I'm going to get out of here."

"What, no!"

I nod, and for a second, I think she might object, but then a drunken guy flings his arm around her, and she starts to giggle. "It's fine. Go have fun, I'm heading to my dad's," I say before walking away.

It only takes me a few seconds before I'm swinging the door open and the summer heat smacks me in the face. It's fairly dark outside, the sun is almost completely set and the house we were partying at isn't on the beach, rather off a dirt road in the woods somewhere.

Pulling my phone out from my bag, I fire up my Uber app and order a car. It will take about five minutes for someone to get here. Which is much faster than I expected, but I'm sure they probably had a drop off at another party up the road. This area is packed with share homes.

I decide I'm better off walking toward the main road to pick them up. The driveways out here are long and winding and confusing as hell.

So in my heels, and the dress I'm in, I start my trek.

There is only one problem; these shoes are not meant to be worn out of the house. Actually, they aren't meant to be worn on a gravel driveway.

Each step feels traitorous right now, my ankle wobbling. But finally, I think I'm in the clear. The car should be here any second, and I only have a few steps left before I intercept the road where they are picking me up.

Of course, that's the moment my shoe decides to hate me, and down I go. On to the gravel driveway, my hands move to cover my face, but not before I slip and scrape my knee and my hand.

Shit.

Shit.

Shit.

I can feel pieces of stone in my knee and not only do I curse the driveway but I curse the damn shoes Sadie made me wear.

Pushing off the ground, my hand and knee burns but I stand nonetheless. I'm pretty sure I'm bleeding, and I turn back to look down the long driveway. Should head back and get my knee cleaned up, or just wait like the idiot I am?

Why did I decide to walk away from the party?

I let out a long-drawn-out sigh and look down at my phone. Well, walking back is a moot point, as the app tells me my driver is approaching.

It takes a few seconds, but after I double-check it's my car, I get in and sit in silence as we make the fifteen-minute drive out of the woods and back to the beach.

Luckily, at this time of day, there's no traffic, and before long we're pulling up to my dad's place.

When we park, I notice the lights are on in the house which is weird, because when I saw Dad at work, he said Kim was away and he would be hanging in the city.

But, obviously, that's not the case.

I step out of the car and pull out my keys.

"Hello," I say as I step into the foyer.

"Outside," I hear.

I lean down and pull off my heels and place hold them in my opposite hand as I start to limp in the direction.

As soon as I step out to the patio, I realize my father has company. Grayson Price is sitting at the table with him.

My mouth opens and it feels like I'm drowning.

"I—I didn't think you were here," I say lamely to my father.

"What happened to your leg?" he responds, and then I finally look down. My knee is gray from the gravel but little patches of blood are present as well.

"I tripped."

"What happened?" my dad asks as he stands and heads over placing a kiss on my head.

"I didn't want to stay."

"Did something happen?" It's Grayson who speaks this time, and so I turn my head in his direction. His eyes look dark. The green of his irises almost completely gone, and his jaw is set into a firm line.

"No." I shake my head, and I swear his shoulders seem to lower in relief.

"I'm going to get some Band-Aids or something. Go inside and clean it off . . ."

My dad heads inside the house and up the stairs, I'm assuming to find the first aid kit and I move toward the guest bathroom. I'm standing with the water running when I feel his presence behind me. He feels too big for the space. His body radiating a heat that makes my body feels warm.

"Give me that," he huffs.

I turn around and look up at him. "I can do it," I respond. Not really in the mood for his attitude today. My knee hurts way too much.

"I said give it to me." His voice holds no room for disagreement, so reluctantly I hand him the wet washcloth. "Sit," he orders and I do.

I sit on the closed toilet, and then Grayson does something I don't expect, he drops to his knee in front of me.

I swear the sight makes me feel weak and dizzy and I'm happy I'm sitting.

Wicked thoughts of him on his knees start to play out in my mind, making my cheeks feel even warmer.

Before I can stand back up and demand I clean my own knee, his hand reaches out. His large palm wrapping around my thigh to steady my leg.

If I thought I was warm before, I was wrong. My whole body feels like it will ignite as his hands touch my skin. Not even the cold compress pressed against my skin can calm the heat sweltering inside me.

I'm going to combust.

My head tips down to watch him, to watch as he cleans the wound. He doesn't look up as he works and a part of me is thankful but a bigger part begs him to look at me, to stare at me with those penetrating eyes and tell me I'm not alone in feeling this way. That I'm not the only one unhinged by what's happening here, He doesn't look though, just reaches the wash clothes back over to the sink to submerge it in clean water again. Never once looking.

I think my heart might beat out of my chest as I wait.

Thud. Thud.

Thud. Thud.

"All done," he groans, his head finally tilting up. Our gazes lock. A million unspoken wants and desires passing between us. The towel falls to the ground, and I expect him to let go of my thigh, but he doesn't. No, his hand still touches me, the pad of his fingers now dancing on my skin.

"I found the Band-Aids," my dad hollers.

Grayson pulls his hands away and stands and steps away so fast, I think I might have imagined the whole thing.

Like a dream.

"So what happened?" my dad asks from across the living room. I'm now sitting on the couch, Band-Aids on my now clean knee.

"I just didn't want to stay," I say but when he is still staring at me I know I have to give him more. "Okay, okay. There wasn't a bed for me."

"What?" My dad sounds horrified, while Grayson, on the other hand, looks like he's in his own personal hell.

"Yeah, so Sadie thought it would be like most weekends where there is always an extra bed in one of the rooms. Each room in the house usually has three to four twin beds." My father's eyes go wide at that. "So they have four twin mattresses on the floor, and you bring sheets and make a bed . . . I honestly don't know. I can see it being fun, I guess. But tonight it was insane, apparently, they were having this big party and so they opened the house to guests. Unfortunately, by the time Sadie and made it out there, all the beds were taken."

"So, if you didn't have the keys to this place, where would you have slept?" he clips out.

"Well . . . I had offers," I mumble and it's Grayson's turn to make a sound, or a cough, or some strange tortured noise bellows out of his mouth.

"Who offered you what?" He grunts from where he's sitting on the opposite couch.

"A bed," I clarify. "Guys offered me their bed, to—"

"Yeah, yeah. Dad here. No need to clarify," my dad chokes out and I laugh.

"Well, it's a good thing your dad has a place," Grayson huffs.

"But now I feel bad. I don't want to interrupt your—what is this? A boys' weekend?"

"Pretty much, but don't worry about it. We're happy to have you. Right, Grayson?" he says, and I turn to see Grayson who looks anything but happy to have me here.

"Sure."

I almost want to laugh at his gruff attitude, but instead, I move to stand and decide to call it a night. No need to put a damper on their drink fest, plus I saw the un-smoked cigars too.

"I'm going to bed, don't mind me." I start to head out the door.

"'Night," my dad says, and I notice that Grayson says nothing.

I head upstairs to my room and wash my face, change and go to bed. I'm so tired, sleep comes easily.

The next day I wake to find the house empty.

There was a note on the table that my dad and Gray went out for the day.

I'm actually happy to avoid him right now.

This morning when I woke up, I had remembered the way he touched me in the bathroom and a part of me was nervous to see him.

I'm like a blundering idiot in front of him. He's seen me at my worst and now he's seen me bloody and bruised too.

No. This is a good thing.

Maybe they will be out all day and night, and I won't have to worry about what dumb thing I will do next.

I spend the day swimming.

It feels amazing to be in the water. Each stroke of my arms helps me relax. By the time I get out, I see I missed a call from Sadie.

"Hey," I say, calling her back.

"Hi." I want to laugh at awful she sounds.

"Um, hungover much?"

"You have no idea," she groans over the line. "You missed a killer party."

"Sounds fun."

"Come back, we are partying all day and tonight."

"As tempting as that is—" I lie. It doesn't sound tempting at all. "I'm going to chill here. I'm alone in the house right now. It's kind of amazing actually."

"That does sound nice. Have fun," she says.

"You too," I respond and then I hang up.

The day ends up being rather relaxing. I swim. I eat. I take a nap and I even read a book. I haven't had much time to myself this summer. The last time I read was in Portugal when I waited for my mom.

Speaking of which . . .

I pick up my phone and try calling her again.

"You've reached Lily Pad. I'm stuck in a yoga pose and can't answer the phone right now. Please leave a message and I'll call you back. Namaste."

"Hey, Mom. It's me. This is the . . . I'm not actually sure how many messages I've left you now. I'm starting to get nervous. Call me back. Love you."

Standing from the lounge chair I head upstairs, it's late and my mind is going a million miles a minute to figure out what's up with my mom. Sure she's always been flighty, but this is so much worse. She's never disappeared for this long without speaking to me.

Lying down on my bed, I started to come up with an endless loop of possibilities.

I must fall asleep because eventually my stomach growls and my eyes jut open. Lifting my head, I peer around my room and realize the room is pitch-black except the moonlight that streaks across my room from the balcony window. Again my stomach grumbles, reminding me now only did I pass out, but I also forgot to eat dinner.

No wonder the sounds emanating off me sound starved. It's because they are. Or rather I am.

I'll have to grab a midnight snack, what time is it anyway?

Eleven p.m. Standing from my bed, I lift my arms up above my head, to get the kinks out of them from sleeping in an odd position and then walk to the door. Before stepping outside, I listen to see if anyone is up, but when I hear nothing, I'm pretty sure they are already sleeping so I decide I'm safe not to change out of my boy shorts and tank I fell asleep in.

Once in the kitchen, I keep the lights off and throw open the pantry to look for something.

I'm on my tiptoes trying to reach the cereal on the top shelf when I feel him step up behind me. The heat of his skin radiating on the exposed skin on my back. "Let me grab that for you," he says, his voice huskier than normal. I don't respond. I should say I can grab it myself, but no words leave my lips. My mouth is glued shut or frozen or I don't know because as he steps in to grab it, I can feel him . . .

I can feel all of him.

The air in my lungs seizes and the familiar feelings he stirs in me float to the surface. I'm a quivering mess inside, but I keep perfectly still as my backside, touches his front. His front that feels hard against me.

It can't be?

Or can it?

For a while now, I have felt that Grayson has wanted me, but this is evidence of the fact.

I want to move against him, feel him harden further

because of my ministrations, but I'm too scared to move—too scared that if I do, he'll leave.

"Here," he says, but he doesn't step back. Instead, he lowers his hand so the box is in my view. I turn around, and now I'm staring up at him.

We are so close, I'm sure he can feel me shake. I tilt my head up and meet his eyes.

Again they are dark, the green completely gone.

"Hello, is there someone down here?" my dad says from somewhere in the hallway outside the kitchen.

Grayson lifts his finger to his mouth to silence me, and with one hand he shuts the door completely.

"He can't find us," he says with no sound and I nod, but as the door shuts, so does the last bit of light.

In the darkness, my other senses are in overdrive.

I can hear and feel everything.

I can hear the movement of Grayson putting the cereal back on the shelf.

I can feel the pressure of his body pressed against to mine. *My chest touching his.*

I can smell his cologne wafting through the air and feel each inhale of oxygen he takes.

It's like I'm frozen in time.

Waiting.

Waiting.

Waiting.

It's delicious.

I pray for him to touch me again. To feel me again.

But engulfed in the darkness, he doesn't do anything more than hold me. His fingers on my skin, trying to keep me from moving.

It's torture. One I hope will never end.

But it does.

I'm not sure how long we stand there with his hand on my hip and breathing in the same air, but eventually, Grayson steps away, and I hear the hinge of the door.

Without a word he leaves. I'm disoriented and dizzy from it.

———◆———

A few days have passed, and I'm sitting out on my balcony, enjoying the calm of the courtyard.

When I sit out here, I'm not in the city. No, I'm transported back to France.

The view of the courtyard reminds me of the small village where Mom and I stayed last summer. The little balconies with small bistro tables. Red flowers draping off in vines down the side of the wrought iron.

I still haven't heard anything, and it's starting to weigh on me.

The phone rings, and I look over and see it's Kim. We haven't talked much since I've moved out.

I'm no longer mad at her or dad, but between moving out and work, I've been busy, plus I'd be lying if I also didn't know I was pushing them both away. On purpose.

"Hello," I answer.

"Hey, Riv. How are you, sweetheart?" she asks.

"I'm good," I respond.

"It's almost time for the Fourth of July party . . . aka the big day." Her voice rings with thrill. "Are you excited for your birthday?"

"To be legal? Hell, yes," I say. To have a party in my honor? Not so much.

"Is there anyone special you want me to invite, other than the usual?"

Her question has me going quiet. Is there? Other than my roommate and my new friends from work . . .

There's Jaxson.

"Jaxson Price," I respond.

"As in Grayson's brother?"

"Yes."

She doesn't speak for a minute. "I see . . . is there something going on with you two?" she asks.

"We're friends," I respond because that's the truth. We might be spending time together, but there is nothing there. I view him more like a brother than a lover. Unlike . . .

I wonder if Grayson will be there? I know she mentioned it to him, and he said he would, but that was a lifetime ago. Maybe he forgot.

A part of me wants to ask her if she did actually send him an invitation, but something stops me.

Maybe it's because I don't want to know if he was and then doesn't show. My heart can't handle that rejection.

"Okay, I'll invite him. Will you be driving up with your dad or taking the train with your friends?" she asks.

"Probably taking a train with my roommate on Friday."

"Sounds good. I can't wait to see you, birthday girl," she says.

"Thanks. Me too. See you soon," I say before hanging up.

Another birthday.

I pick up the phone and call my mom again. The same voice-mail picks up. When she gets to the part that says Namaste, I want to scream and beg that she shows up.

But, yet again, Mom won't be there, and it reminds me of Grayson.

Of the first birthday with my dad.

I wonder if he realizes how much that meant to me.

No. Probably not.

He probably doesn't even remember.

I sit outside for a few minutes longer before the heat of the day starts to get to me. These are the moments I miss going out east, and I'm happy to get back into the pool this weekend.

I miss swimming.

I miss the freedom it gives me. The clarity.

But since I don't have that option here, there is one thing that does help. Maybe it's time I start designing again. I stand, open the balcony door, and head back into my room. Rummaging around through my things, I look for the pieces of fabric I bought during my time in Spain.

I see a piece of leather that has been dyed blue. Blue like the ocean. I might not be able to swim today, but I can lose myself in the ocean. With the leather in hand, I open the next drawer and pull out a piece of quartz and then my tools.

A cuff.

I sit at my desk and start working.

When it's finally done, I look at the piece I created. It's beautiful. Soft leather. Striking color and then the simplicity of the earthy stone. It's going to look great on.

Maybe you should sell it?

I shake my head at the thought. It might be good, but it's not good enough. No one would want it. Standing I place it on my bed and go to grab a drink.

I find Sadie sitting in the living room.

"Hey. Were you sleeping?" she asks me.

"No. Just sitting outside. And then just fucking around in my room."

"Oh, how is it out? I have to run errands today. Are you working tomorrow?"

"I am."

"Sucks. Why can't you take the summer off?"

Because I want to prove I'm not my mom, I think . . . but of course, I don't say that.

"To pay the bills." I smile.

"I thought you were an intern."

"I am."

"For your dad."

"That, too."

She quirks an eyebrow. "And he pays you?"

"He does. Not a lot but enough that I can pay for my own social life." I laugh.

"Not this apartment." She looks around, whistling low.

"Lord no." I walk toward the bathroom. "I'm going to shower. Are you still coming with me on Friday?" I ask.

She pretends to think. "Hmm, let's see . . . big bash in the Hamptons? Free booze, umm, yeah."

I shake my head and head to the shower, smiling.

※

The rest of the week passes quickly, and before long, Sadie and I are on the sweltering platform of the Long Island Railroad.

Once the train comes to a stop, we board and take two seats by the front.

The train ride is about two hours, but at least it's better than hitting traffic. I should have asked Jax for a ride.

A helicopter doesn't hit traffic.

No. But it has Grayson Price probably.

This is my birthday weekend, and I refuse to let that man's mood swings ruin it.

It's the first time I'll see Kim in weeks, and although things are still a bit strained, they're getting better, and I don't want anything to send me into a bad mood.

Like being rejected again.

"So I never asked. Any hot guys coming to this shindig?"

"Just the guys from work, oh, and Jaxson Price."

Her eyes widen at that news. "What's going on with that anyway? You guys seemed pretty chummy at drinks a few weeks ago, but I haven't seen you with him since."

"We're just friends. Well, kind of, it's kind of new."

"Oh, is it . . . ?" she says playfully, waggling her brows.

"Not like that."

"It's always like that." She laughs. But it's not, and if she knew the truth of why we're friends, she would know it's not.

But I don't need anyone other than Jax knowing of my unhealthy obsession with a man old enough to be my dad.

Not true.

He would have had to be fifteen years old to be your dad, which means he'd had sex at fourteen.

So really, he isn't too old for me.

Too bad he doesn't see it that way.

With too many thoughts racing through my mind, I close my eyes.

When I feel someone touching me, I blink my eyes open.

"We're here," Sadie says.

"Sorry, I was lost in thought."

"No worries," she says, lifting her Kindle in the air. "I was plenty entertained."

"Reading anything good?" I ask as I stand and grab my bag from above.

"Just a forbidden romance." That makes my moves stop, and I turn to her.

"Really?"

"Yeah . . ."

"What kind?"

"You know, the usual kind. He's her stepbrother."

I shake my head with a laugh.

"What? He's hot. Something is so sexy about the forbidden . . ." She laughs, and I grimace.

Don't I know it?

Together, we step out of the train and start walking. In the distance, I can see my stepmom and dad holding a big bunch of balloons. She's running toward me like a little girl.

"Happy Birthday." She throws her arms around me, and I melt a little. Just a bit of the ice that had formed melts as Kim, the one person who always has my back, holds me. It feels like everything might actually be okay.

When she lets go, she looks over at Sadie and grabs her into a hug, too. Sadie looks taken aback but plays it off well. I don't think she's used to someone like Kim. There aren't many people like her.

The thought makes me realize that maybe I'm being too hard on her. She is here, after all, with balloons in hand to throw me a party.

Things don't have to change.

"It's so good to meet you, Sadie."

"Same," Sadie responds.

"Come on, girls. Let's go get ready for the party."

We walk over to where my father is, and I give him the first hug in two weeks. He holds me tight as if to tell me he loves me. I didn't realize how badly I needed that hug. But I do.

"Hey, Dad," I whisper.

He strokes my hair. "It's good to have you back." His words are clear. He's not talking about in the Hamptons.

"Dad, this is Sadie, my new roommate."

He reaches out his hand to shake hers. "Pleasure to meet you, Sadie."

"Same, sir."

"Oh no, don't call me sir. That makes me feel ancient." He laughs. "Tyler," he clarifies.

"Nice to meet you, Tyler." She looks back at Kim and smiles. "Kim."

"Okay, do you have any more bags?"

We both shake our heads.

"Then let's go home," my dad says as he grabs both our bags and starts heading to where the car is parked.

We all follow, and within a minute, we're traveling to our house.

When we get home, the house is in full swing. Workmen are setting up the tables outside as well as couches and tea lights. The house is being decorated, too. It's a massive party, apparently.

Not just to celebrate my birthday, but my dad has also invited his whole office to officially celebrate signing the papers on the Lancaster deal.

I wonder if Grayson will come.

I know Jax will be here.

He's been invited as my guest. But seeing as Dad's whole office is coming, I can only assume the Prices were invited, too.

I should have asked Jax.

But he's already on my case about his brother. I didn't want to stoke that fire.

Seeing as the house is full of commotion, I grab Sadie's hand and pull her toward the stairs.

"Come on, I'll show you to where your sleeping."

She follows, and before long, we are walking into the room.

"This is fantastic," she says as she looks at the modern room with sweeping views of the beach. "Your dad's house is amazing."

"Well, he is an architect," I say.

"A damn good one from what I can see." She plops down on the bed and looks up at me. "So, now what should we do?" she asks.

I don't want to admit I don't know, but I do anyway. "I don't usually go out much when I'm here."

"So then what do you do?" she probes.

"Hang by the pool."

She stands and looks at the pool below. There has to be at least ten workmen setting up around it. "Well, that's not going to happen."

I let out a laugh. "Yep. Not unless they want a distraction, and even if they did, that wouldn't be a good idea . . ."

"Yeah, no. By the looks of things or, better yet, by the looks of the party planner, she'd kill us."

We both start to laugh.

"We can go into town and have dinner."

"Your official birthday is tonight at midnight. We should be out for it."

"Or we can go have dinner and get to bed early, so we are refreshed for tomorrow," I say, lifting an eyebrow.

"You are such a lightweight. Hell, no. We are going out and celebrating. No ifs, ands, or buts."

It doesn't take long, but in the time it took me to shower,

Sadie has invited some of my coworkers over, Alana and Todd to be exact. They are sitting with their feet in the pool and each has a beer in their hand. I walk over, dressed to go out.

"Are we staying here?" I ask.

Todd is the first to speak. "No offense, but being around the boss man two nights in a row is a little bit much for me."

"So then why are you here"—I laugh—"drinking at 'boss man's' pool?"

"Well, I never said I wouldn't pregame . . ."

I shake my head at him while laughing. Kim takes that moment to walk over. "I know you are going out, but do you want me to whip up some apps before you go?"

"That would be amazing," I respond.

I grab my own beer. "Let the pregame begin," I salute her with my beer. I'm not used to having friends like this. Traveling and moving so frequently limited my friendships, but I love this group. We throw back shots, drink a ton of beer, and before I know it, we're ready to continue the party out by the beach.

———◆———

I am one hundred percent hungover today.

But I'm also officially twenty-one, which I guess makes it legal, at the very least. Lifting my hands above my head, I give my body a stretch. Then I open my eyes. From beside my bed, I see two pills and a note.

Take me, and then come downstairs for breakfast,
Birthday girl!
Kim

I would recognize her handwriting anywhere. My stomach turns at the thought of how awful I was to her. The sad part is, she knows me well enough to know I didn't mean it.

Another bad trait.

But maybe I can work it out.

Now that I have some space from my parents, I realize how much I overreacted. That's not to say I was wrong to move out. No, it was time.

At twenty-one years old, it's time I start thinking about what I want, so living by myself is necessary.

From across the nightstand, I hear my phone vibrate. A birthday text, I'm sure.

My mother maybe . . .

I pull it over and look at the screen. My heartbeat starts to flutter rapidly.

It's not my mom, and normally while that would upset me, the name across the screen has my mouth splitting into a smile.

Grayson: Happy Birthday.

He remembered.

River: Thank you for remembering.

He starts to type and then it stops.

I wonder what he was going to say? Shaking my head, I decide to go downstairs to take my mind off overthinking his lack of text.

When I descend the stairs, I make my way to the kitchen. The first thing I notice is the lights are off. The second is that it's eerily quiet.

It doesn't take a rocket scientist to know that once I turn the corner, I'll be met with a birthday surprise of some sort . . .

I walk extra hard, letting my slippers echo through the space to announce my impending entry.

"Happy Birthday!" my dad, Kim, and Sadie shout as I enter the kitchen. There are balloons everywhere. If I had to hazard a guess, I would say about twenty-one of them are floating about the room. In the center of the island are rainbow pancakes.

Whipped cream.

My favorite.

It's truly the best way to start off today.

Some birthdays have been good, and some not so much . . . but I have a good feeling about today.

"Happy Birthday," my dad says again as he gives me a kiss, and then Kim steps up. When I look at her, I notice for the first time that she has a small bump. I'm shocked to see it, but instead of staring, I give myself a little shake and smile down at her.

She has tears in her eyes as she pulls me into a hug. "No matter what happens," she says, her voice tinged with emotion, "you will always be my daughter."

Now tears fill my eyes.

I hug her tighter.

"Kim," I start, but she lifts her hand.

"Today is your birthday. Today, we celebrate."

There is plenty we need to say to each other, but that conversation will have to wait because I have a big stack of pancakes with my name on it.

After we finish, Sadie and I head upstairs to hang out and rest. Tonight is a big night.

Around five p.m., the door to my room opens, and hair and makeup is here. Kim pulled out all the stops for tonight's celebration, even sending in a stylist to dress me for the night.

By the time eight p.m. rolls around, I feel like a princess.

Tonight, my blond locks are blown out in sexy beach waves, and my eyes are smoky with a red lip. I'm wearing a skintight red bandage dress that accentuates every single curve.

The dress is so tight; there is no room for anything under, so I walk down the stairs to my party very carefully.

Commando style was not made for stairs.

The party is just beginning. Not many people are here yet, and the few who are, are outside already.

Sadie steps out from behind me and takes my hand in hers. "You ready?"

"I am."

The doors to the patio are open, and when I step outside, my breath leaves my body.

Kim has created a luxurious space, filled with tea lights and chandeliers hanging from the trees. Even the pool has little lanterns floating inside it, illuminating the waters.

It looks straight out of *A Midsummer Night's Dream*. As though anything is possible in this fantasy.

The first person to approach is my father. I step into his arms, and he gives me a kiss on the forehead. "You look beautiful," he says. "Happy Birthday, sweetheart."

"Thanks, Dad," I respond. "And congratulations on the account."

"This party is not for me." He laughs. "We just used it as an excuse to have a massive party for you."

I shake my head while laughing, tears filling my eyes again. The sense of family, of familiarity, is overwhelming and strange but not unwelcome.

I haven't even been here five minutes, and my emotions are already all over the place.

Guest after guest greets me, wishing me a happy birthday. All my coworkers come over. I look around the room. I wonder if she was invited. If she will show.

"Who are you looking for?" Kim asks as she walks up beside me.

"My mom," I admit, and I can see her cheeks pinch in.

"I'm sorry, River. She's not here."

Another tear falls down my cheek, and she wipes it away.

"Not at your party, miss. There is no crying at your party. Only celebrating. And since I can't drink a toast to you, I expect you to drink double for me."

I know she's joking since she rarely drinks to begin with. But she is trying to lighten the mood, and I appreciate the attempt.

Kim lifts her arm and summons a waitress with champagne flutes. "If you see her glass empty, make sure to refill."

I stare at her.

"What?" she asks.

"Thank you . . ." I start again, getting choked up with emotion. She takes my free hand in hers.

"It's not the time, but I understand. But I want you to know I will never leave you."

"I know."

And I did.

I acted like a scared little child, but being here now and seeing her love, I know she wouldn't.

She's not my mom.

No, she's the woman who chose to love me unconditionally no matter what.

"I'm sorry for what I did. Leaving without talking to you. I knew you knew I was having a hard time . . . but I left anyway." I look down, ashamed of how I ran from them.

"Your father and I love you very much."

I nod but continue to look down.

"River."

I look up.

"Go have fun. Enjoy yourself. Dance. Be young and stupid and have fun."

"I'm not sure you're supposed to say that."

She winks. "Well, I just did."

Sadie chooses that moment to come over and pull me away. The DJ is playing already, and most of the guests have arrived.

As Sadie pulls me to the dance floor, I notice that Jaxson is there. He walks over, swagger and all. Then he grabs me and pulls me into his arms. Giving me a hug and lifting me at the same time.

I start to laugh, my head falling back as he carries me to the dance floor.

"You look gorgeous."

"Thank you."

"It's perfect."

He sets me back onto the floor, but I'm still firmly encased in his arms. "What's perfect?" I ask as I incline my head at him.

"You'll see," he says as he looks off into the other direction, and I follow his gaze. It doesn't take me long to see who he's looking at.

From across the patio, I see him standing, more like scowling, and then he's stalking across the distance with one purpose, to get to us.

I'm still in Jax's arms when he makes it over, and Jax is laying it on real thick.

By the bulging vein in Grayson's neck, I know he's not happy.

"River, Jaxson," he grits through clenched teeth.

"Hey, big bro, happy to see you could make it. I was under the assumption you weren't coming." He smirks, and Grayson's jaw tightens further.

"I changed my mind," he murmurs, and then he looks over at me as if he just remembered I was standing there.

His gaze sweeps back to me, and then he looks at Jaxson's arms. I wonder if he'll let me go, but Jax just holds on tighter, and I can feel his fingers running circles over my exposed skin.

"Aren't you going to wish the birthday girl a happy birthday?" he says. "She's twenty-one now."

"Happy Birthday," he hisses as if he's mad at me. For what, I don't know, but I assume he's not happy to be here.

Maybe Jax was wrong.

But he texted you this morning, so why is he mad now?

My stomach tightens. It feels like it's churning with emotions, and I don't know what to do with it.

The party has just started. I have already cried once and feel like I might cry again.

I push off Jax's arms and reach my hand out to him. "Come on, Jax," I say. I don't pay one more ounce of attention to Grayson Price.

I'm sick of his confusing behavior. One minute, he looks at me as though he's a starved man and I'm the last meal on earth, and then next, it's like he doesn't give a shit about me at all. If today he's going to act like the latter, then I don't need to stand around and let him reject me.

After living with rejection every day, I refuse to let it ruin my night.

We start to walk away, leaving Grayson standing alone. I keep moving faster until we are at the opposite side of the room.

From where we are now standing, I see my father's cousin. He inclines his head and gives me a nod.

Not a smile.

Typical.

My father's cousin Cyrus reminds me a lot of Grayson.

Both rich, both handsome, and both condescending jerks.

No . . .

That's not true. Grayson has a good side. I've seen it.

Cyrus is just plain ruthless.

I nod my head back, and Jaxson looks from him and then back at me.

I shrug. "Come on, let's go get a drink." We head toward the bar, and I see Sadie and Alana.

"Shots for the birthday girl!" Sadie shouts as I make my approach, and by the time I get there, tequila shots are lined up.

"To the best birthday and the best birthday girl ever." She lifts her glass, and she's obviously already drunk. I need to catch up. Lifting my glass off the bar, I take the whole thing in one swig. It warms my body no matter how chilled I am, making me instantly feel looser.

That is, until I look toward where I left Grayson. He's standing in the same spot, his gaze trained on me, but now a beautiful brunette stands beside him, talking to him. Her hand resting on his arm as she throws her head back at the words that come out of his mouth. He's too far away for me to make out what he's saying, but he's still staring at me while he says it.

Whoever she is, she eats it up, and when she strokes her hand up his arm, pulling his attention back to her, he looks away from me, breaking the connection. It makes me so jealous I can't think straight. Turning my head away, I lift my hand and signal for another shot.

Sadie squeals, Jaxson shakes his head but shrugs, and the next thing I know, we are taking another round and then a third. With each shot we take, I turn to glance back and see he's still talking to her.

By the end of my fourth shot, my hands are shaking from the adrenaline. I turn on my heels and run through the door and into the hallway of the house.

I need to get away. Get out of here. I start toward the side entrance. If I go out that entrance, I won't have to see anyone. No one will know . . .

I'm walking toward the door to make my escape when I hear footsteps behind me. I don't know who it is, but I refuse to turn around. I do hear my name, but I don't want anyone to see me like this. I can't believe that not only is he a dick to me at my own party, but to watch him flirt . . .

It's too much. That's when I feel hands reach out and push me toward the adjacent open door.

"What the—"

"Shh," he says, and I'd know that voice anywhere.

"What are you doing?"

He doesn't answer me.

"What is your problem?"

"You think I hate you?" he growls, taking a step toward me.

"Yes," I whisper.

He advances, and I step back. "You really think that's the problem?"

"It's pretty obvious, to be honest. You haven't been shy with your repulsion toward me."

He moves in until my body is firmly pressed against his, his erection pressing against my stomach.

I let out a gasp.

"Repulsion, River, huh?" He grinds up against me. "That what it feels like? Or maybe it's something else? Do you think my anger is something else?"

"What else can it be?"

"Self-preservation." He's so close I can feel him breathe. I shouldn't want him to kiss me or move any closer. To place his mouth on mine. He's a dick, but I can't help myself. I need to taste him.

Just once.

The sexual tension has been crackling around us for hours, for days, for weeks.

Without a second thought, he crushes his lips to mine.

It feels like a series of fireworks explode inside me at the feel of his mouth. We are all teeth and tongue.

The kiss is desperate, and then he pushes off my lips. "Why do you do this to me?" he rasps. "Why do you torture me?"

I wonder if he will stop it now, if he will go back to pushing me away, but instead, I feel his fingers on my thighs, and his mouth touches mine again.

Each new swipe of his tongue makes me moan into his mouth and then when I feel his fingers teasing the hem of my dress, I swear might die.

"Fuck," he grits out when he finds me bare underneath. "All this time . . . you were naked underneath this scrap of a dress."

"I was," I purr. "Is that a problem?" My voice is coy. I know I shouldn't taunt the beast, but I can't help it. "I really can't keep up with you. One minute, you're hot, and then the next minute, cold. Then you grope me. What's next?"

"Grope you? You make it sound like you don't want it."

"I don't." I narrow my eyes at him as I cross my arms.

I step back until my body becomes flush with the washer, but he steps toward me, his arms reaching out to close me in. Glancing up at him, I can see his calculating grin. He has me, and he knows it. This game of cat and mouse is about to come to a head.

"So you don't want me?" His voice is deep and husky as he moves his head, placing his mouth dangerously close to mine. My breath hitches in my chest, my heart thrumming erratically. He descends . . .

Firm lips probe mine. His tongue sweeps inside my mouth, and I melt as all resistance has completely faded away. The kiss intensifies, his lips growing hungrier. Grayson's fingers glide down the exposed skin of my neck, down my collar, his hands lift the hem of my dress until it bunches at my waist, and my body trembles with anticipation.

His hands then grip me under my arms, and he lifts me into his. The movement places me on the cool surface of the washer. Wrapping my arms around his neck, I deepen the kiss. Our mouths collide in a frenzy of passion. Just as I start to lose myself in him, he suddenly pulls back and removes his hands from around me. The sound of the zipper being pulled down reverberates through the room, and a harsh moan leaves my mouth as his large hands touch me.

Then I feel him, pressing himself against my heat, probing my entrance. "I need to fuck you now," he says through gritted teeth. He readjusts his hands to cup my ass as he begins to stroke me. "Tell me to fuck you, River. Tell me you want me inside you. I need to hear you say it." The soft nudge is enough to make my inner walls quiver. "Dammit, River, say it. Tell me to fuck you." He pushes forward, just the tip, torturing me.

I can't resist. I want this. I've wanted him for so long that, like him, I can't wait another minute. I want him to fuck me and make me forget everything else.

"Fuck me. Now!"

With one sudden thrust, he's fully seated. I moan at the sudden invasion.

It feels so good.

He slams into me hard and fast.

I gasp and moan with each thrust. I claw at his back, needing him closer, needing to close the space between us. I beg and pant until he's fucking me so hard, I don't know where he ends and I begin.

It feels amazing with each move, with each thrust.

He pulls out.

He slams back in.

Out.

In.

If anyone walked by, they could hear the sounds of our moans, the sound of the washer hitting the wall as if the spin cycle is on.

CHAPTER TWENTY-THREE

Grayson

Fuck.
   Fuck.
Fuuuck.

I pull out, looking down at my dick, now half-mast. The evidence of our tryst glaring back at me. What the hell did I just do?

I wasn't thinking. That's what. I saw her with Jax and I saw red. So when that woman approached me . . .

Goddammit.

I wanted to pretend I didn't care. But when I saw her face. Saw the expression. The hurt. And then she stormed off.

I have seen River upset too many times to know I had hurt her, and by the looks of things, I'd hurt her a lot.

Chasing after her was a bad idea.

Kissing her . . . another bad idea.

Then fucking her.

Shit.

Feeling her heat around me, I was lost.

And now with my dick in my hand, I realize the worst part.

I fucked her raw.

No condom.

And I came inside her.

"River," I say, looking down at myself and then at her. My jaw tightens. "I didn't . . ."

"You're fine. I mean, as long as you're clean . . . I'm on the pill."

She lowers her legs to the ground and jumps off the dryer.

I watch as she rights her dress.

"I'm clean." My voice is tight. My chest tighter.

I came to a party to celebrate my friend and slept with his twenty-one-year-old daughter.

I'm officially the biggest asshole in the world.

This is low.

Even for me.

I never said I was perfect. Far from it. I'm an asshole. I'm cold and don't let people in, but this is the opposite of all my "winning traits" and worse.

She stands in front of me, staring.

I don't even know what to say now, which is odd because I always do.

"You should sneak out first," I finally decide to say.

"Are you serious right now?"

"Yes."

She shakes her head back and forth.

"You really are a dick."

"River." I reach out my hand.

"No. Don't River me." She steps around me.

I grab her arm, pulling her toward me and placing my lips at the crook of her neck. "I didn't mean it like that. We can talk about this." I kiss her neck. "Whatever this is later. But right now, we can't have anyone seeing us. So you sneak out, and I'll follow." I feel the tension leave her body.

"Okay," she says as she pushes off me and turns and looks me in the eyes. I can see the uncertainty, but she just gives herself a little shake before moving out the door.

I let a few minutes pass before I attempt to leave. I pop open the door and look left and right. No one is there, so I step out into the hall. I make a quick right and head back to the party. I don't make it more than five steps before I see Jaxson propped back against the wall.

He looks like a smug shit.

Crooked smirk and all.

You'd never know now that he is one of the Price heirs.

He's wearing a hat, for crying out loud.

His arrogance tells everyone that he's someone—that he's important—but all it tells me is that he knows.

"Taking a break from the party?" he asks, and I just shrug. "That's not an answer."

I start to move past him. "If you're so smart, why do you ask stupid questions?"

"Just need the confirmation of what went down in that room." He points at the laundry room where I had just left. "Seeing as she looked thoroughly fucked, and you look pissed to all hell, I'm going to assume you banged her in there and are now spiraling into the typical Grayson self-loathing portion of the evening."

"You're an ass."

"Yes, I might just be, but at least I'm not afraid to let people in."

His words stop me, and I double back. "You don't know anything about my fears," I hiss.

"And whose fault is that? Huh, Grayson? I'm your brother, and you don't talk to me. You don't talk to Addison either. Who the fuck do you talk to?"

Dad.

I talked to Dad.

And before that . . .

I shake my head.

"No one," I holler back, my anger palpable at his line of questioning. But Jaxson will never understand, or maybe he will. The things that haunt me don't bother him. Never have, never will.

Although we're cut from the same cloth, and genetically, we share the same genes with whatever that entails for the future; he isn't hounded by fears like I am.

No.

Not Jax.

Jax doesn't have a care in the world. He doesn't worry about the future or what will happen if he's gone too early.

He lives a life for the here and now.

While I'm plagued by the doubts. I'm plagued by the what-ifs.

Before he can speak, I turn back around and head out the door. I head straight toward the bar.

I need to find the goddamn bar.

My brain is screaming about what Jax had said, and the thoughts and feelings it brings up, and on top of that, I feel sick about what just happened with River.

I need a goddamn drink.

I also need to get the fuck back to the city.

But I can't leave yet. Not until after the fireworks apparently, so instead, I have to pretend. I have to act as though nothing happened between River and me.

It shouldn't be so hard. I'm always an asshole, so no one should suspect anything. No one other than Jax. Tyler barely knows me now, so he shouldn't be able to tell. That and I can avoid him too. Yep, that's my plan.

I keep walking, sidestepping drunken people dancing in the middle of the space. Spotting the bar, I head toward it. A few people are standing around, mingling and talking.

Tyler.

I have no desire for fake pretense now, and that's exactly what will happen. If I go over there, I will have to make small talk and pretend I didn't just fuck his daughter.

I can still smell her on me.

This isn't good. But I want a drink, and I don't want to wait for him to leave.

There has to be another bar set up somewhere. I let my eyes scan the room, and instead of finding a bar, I see her.

My brother is right. She looks as though she just got fucked.

Her head is thrown back, and she's laughing. It's obvious what just happened isn't weighing on her like it does me.

Must be nice.

Must be nice not to have the weight of the world on your shoulders.

Sitting so heavy you feel like you can't breathe.

Fuck it, I'm getting a drink. Even if that means I have to look Tyler right in the eye as I do.

I have mastered my facade. I can handle him.

As my feet take me over to my destination, my head pounds like a freight train.

Don't think about River, I tell myself.

Not the way she tasted, or the way she felt, or the way she came around you . . .

I reach my hand to the collar of my shirt and pull it away from my skin.

It feels like I'm choking.

"Hot?" Tyler says as I stand beside him at the bar.

"Yeah."

"You look a bit stressed. Everything okay?" he asks, concern etching his face.

"Just peachy," I say, looking away from him and around the patio. I catch her again, and this time my jaw tightens.

"They're young but harmless. You remember what it was like to have fun, right?" He laughs.

He mistakes my uncomfortable demeanor for annoyance at the drunk kids dancing around the pool.

I'm okay with that.

At least if he thinks that, he won't know the truth.

"We all have to grow up sometime," I mumble under my breath.

"Don't I know it." He sighs. "I can't believe I have a twenty-one-year-old daughter and another on the way."

I turn my head back toward him. "It's kind of crazy," I say.

Just as Tyler is about to say more, the bartender cuts in. "What can I get for you, sir?" he asks us.

Tyler lifts his hand. "You first."

"I'll have a scotch neat," I respond.

"How about we do a shot instead?" he says, and I give him a nod.

"Tequila?" I ask.

"Sure." He turns back to the bartender. "Extra chilled." The bartender starts to grab ice and a shaker, and before I know it, two large shots of Don Julio are placed in front of us.

"To what?" I ask.

"To my baby girl growing up," he answers, and it feels like he's punched me in the gut.

I don't reply. Instead, I just lift the glass and take it down. The liquid streams down my throat. Smooth and cold.

Refreshing among the heat of the night. But it's not enough against my throat. I need one more, or maybe two.

"Another," I say as I drop the glass back onto the bar.

"Another," Tyler responds with a smile and then pats my shoulder. "Good to have you here," he says.

But it doesn't feel good to be here.

No. Not at all.

Because being here means I have to see River and seeing River means I have to feel.

Something I try my hardest not to do.

Multiple shots later, I'm drunk. Very drunk. Stumbling drunk. Needing a moment to myself, I grab one of the large blankets from the pile Kim has set up to bring out to the beach. I then head down to sit by the water.

A little way up the beach, I can see the fire from the bonfire crackling. A group congregates around it, drinking and laughing.

Having no desire to socialize at this point of my night, I lay the blanket down and then plop down on top of it.

"Why are you by yourself?" a familiar voice says.

Turning over my shoulder, I peer up at her. "River, what are you doing here?"

"I saw you walking from up over there." She points at the bonfire. "And wanted to make sure you were okay. I felt it was only fitting, seeing as where you are sitting," she mumbles, but in my drunken state, I have no idea what she's talking about.

"Do you mind if I sit with you?" she asks, and I shrug as she lowers her body to the empty part of the blanket.

When time stretches between us without a word, she sighs. "It's not a big deal, Grayson."

She's lying. It's a huge deal. She knows it, and I know it.

"I'm an adult," she continues. "I can sleep with whoever I want to."

"I hardly call what we did sleeping," I mutter back.

"No. I wouldn't either. But you don't need to get solemn about it. Or be an asshole. We were both there. We both made a decision. Stop beating yourself up."

"I'm not beating myself up."

"Then why are you all alone in the spot where people beat themselves up and feel sorry for themselves?" She shrugs.

"What are you talking about?" I ask.

"Figures."

"What figures?"

"Nothing," she mutters as she shakes her head. "It's not important." Her voice is low and sounds sad, but I'm too much of a selfish bastard to ask her what she's talking about.

"Are you always like this?"

"Always like what?"

"Miserable. I've seen you smile once, maybe twice. It must be exhausting."

"Says the girl who had a mental breakdown when she found out her dad is having a baby. Pot meet kettle."

"Wow, on that note . . . I'll be going."

I reach my hand out before I know what I'm doing. Her skin is sticky from the salt in the air and hot to the touch. I shouldn't be touching her. It makes me feel too much, but now that my hand is on her arm, I can't find it in myself to let go.

"Don't."

She stares at me. Probably trying to see something behind my words. Some piece of the puzzle as to why I'm so fucked up. But she won't find anything; I keep my thoughts tied up tight.

"Why should I stay?" she whispers.

"Because I asked you to," I respond.

"That's not enough."

"Because I need you to. Because I'm fucked up, and I know it, and I hate it, but when you're around, it makes me forget why . . . and right now, I want to forget why."

She sits back down after my word vomit.

"Okay, I'll stay, but you have to stop this. You have to stop treating me this way. You either want me around or don't."

"Of course, I want you around." I run my fingers through my hair. The strands are knotted, and I pull on my scalp. But it makes me feel better, the pain.

"Then why?"

"Because I'm too old for you," I say. It's a bullshit reason. I know it, and she knows it.

"Age is only a number."

"Sweetheart, you know it's a cliché. Our social circle will take one look at us, and I'll be the cradle snatcher, you the arm-candy I saved from herself and from financial demise. We'll be a caricature, the talk of Manhattan, and not in a good way. Besides, your father . . ."

"Who cares about my father? I'm an adult."

"*I* care about your father," I press, but even that is not the real reason for my hesitation. I'll never get over the look on River's face when she broke down about being left behind. How can I knowingly enter into a relationship with her, when I could end up leaving her too?

"He doesn't have to know . . . We can do this, and he doesn't have to know. I want you. I'm not ready to let you go, and I know you want me. Why can't we? Not forever, but just for now?" she asks.

And maybe it's the booze, or maybe it's the way her hand feels against my skin, or maybe it's just that I'm just so fucking tired of pushing her away, but as I open my mouth to say no, I shut it.

Why can't I?

Why can't I indulge in this for a little while longer? Once wasn't enough. I don't know how long it will take to fuck River Reed out of my system, but I will. I could. And then I can go about my life.

Sounds like a solid plan.

My hand still touching her skin, I look up at the sky.

Knowing full well this won't play out well but not caring.

We stayed on the beach for a while, doing nothing more than holding hands. If anyone passed, they couldn't tell. But the heat and desire that coursed through us was enough to light the night on fire.

Eventually, this would sizzle and no longer be, but for now, in my drunken state, I enjoyed the illusion that it could work. I enjoy the bubble.

When the last of the bonfire flickers and the stars provide the only light in the darkness, I know no one can see us now.

I'm not sure what will happen tomorrow, so if this is it, I seize the moment. I turn to her, but with only the moonlight and stars for light, she looks like a goddess sent down from the heavens.

Unreal.

Not mortal.

One I shouldn't touch but can't help to.

Cloaked in the darkness, I bridge the space that separates us on the blanket.

Our faces are now only inches apart, and with every exhale she takes, I can feel her breath.

Her eyes are filled with desire.

Dropping my gaze, I take in her full lips.

A ragged breath escapes her trembling lips as I move my thumb to trace them. She shakes against my ministrations, breathing heavily. Moving my hand, I cup her face and move in to kiss her. The kiss starts off soft at first, but when I know she won't push me away, I deepen it.

Pressing my lips firmer to hers, I kiss her faster. Rougher. It tells her how much I want her. How desperate I am to once again be inside her. The moment might not last; this may never happen again, and the thought makes my moves primal.

It makes me desperate.

"Naked," I growl. "I want you naked this time." If I thought fucking her in the laundry room was a stupid idea, this is even worse, but under the stars, beneath the moonlight, I can't think of anything else than feeling her naked body underneath me as we join.

"Okay," she whispers, slowly unzipping her dress. I move my hands behind her back and help her.

Against the sound of the waves crashing, I can't hear it, but in my mind, the sound of the zipper lowering echoes.

I'm doing this.

I shake away any doubts.

My need to be inside her outweighs all logic, all objections.

It outweighs everything.

I bury my nose in the crook of her neck and then drop delicate kisses in a path down to her collarbone. With the dress now off, I can see all her skin, and I continue to kiss her. Touching her.

Down.

Down.

Down.

I trail my lips down until they reach the hollow of her chest. Then I let my mouth take possession of each peak, licking and sucking until her body quivers with need.

I lift off her breast and start to trail farther down.

My eyes roam over her body as I make the descent and then part her legs. I angle my body between them and kiss all the way up from her ankles until I meet the inside of her thighs.

I lick her.

Suck her.

Desperate moans escape her mouth. She purrs beneath me, begging me with her movement to pick up my pace, and so I do. I answer her cries and start to flick and then suck in a maddening pace that has her gripping my hair and falling over the edge.

I move away and remove my pants, climbing up her body until I'm aligned with her.

When our bodies are positioned, I push inside her slick heat. The feel of sinking inside her has me releasing a groan of satisfaction and a moan of pleasure escapes River's mouth.

I pull out and then thrust back in.

Her thighs clamp around my waist, and I feel her tighten around me, coming undone. A tingling feeling spreads across my body as well, and I know I'm almost there too.

I push forward a few more times until my body jerks within her, following her over the edge.

As we allow our racing hearts to calm, reality comes crashing down on me.

What have I done?

It was dumb to have sex in the laundry room, but having sex on the beach is just suicidal.

Anyone could have caught us or, better yet, caught me.

River has done nothing wrong, but me?

I'm in a world of shit if Tyler finds out.

Pulling out of her, I sit up.

"Are you leaving?" she asks.

"I think it would be best."

She inhales, her eyes closing and then reopening. "And us?"

"I'm not sure," I admit on a sigh. I need space. To breathe. To get back to the city and think about what I'm doing. *Who* I'm doing. "How about when you're back in the city . . ." I lift my hand and rake it through my hair. "How about you call me when you're back, and we take it from there?"

She nods, but she doesn't answer, so I lean down and place my lips on hers.

"Call me," I say again, and then I get dressed and head up the beach and back to the path to the party. By the time I'm back on the patio, the party is winding down here too.

Only a few people are milling around. I don't see Tyler or Kim, so I let out the breath I'm holding.

Who I do see is Jax.

He smirks like usual and then walks over to me.

"Where've you been?" he asks like he already knows the answer to that question.

"On the beach."

"Alone?"

"Yes."

He nods at me, but luckily for me, he doesn't press. I know he knows, but I appreciate him not saying anything.

"Come on, let's go." I start to walk to where the driver is parked. It was smart not to drive. I'm not sure about Jax, but I'm certainly not sober enough.

We head to the car, and our driver opens the back door for us. At times like this, I would have liked for Jax to be in his car because I really don't want to speak, but lucky for me, he remains quiet. Before long, we are rolling up to our own house.

A place I hate to go.

But no matter, I head straight past the door to the house.

"Where are you going?" Jax asks.

"To the guesthouse."

"You still won't sleep in the main house?" He stares at me.

"No," I say and walk away.

Normally, I'd go back to the city, but it's late, and I'd rather have a fresh start tomorrow and leave then.

As I close my eyes and fall asleep, I let my mind drift to the events of tonight.

CHAPTER TWENTY-FOUR

River

I'M BACK IN THE CITY. CLUTCHING MY PHONE IN MY HAND, I'm not sure if I should call.

He said I should, but on the list of good ideas I have, I'm not certain it would make it to the first three hundred items.

When I woke up the next day, sand still in places I don't care to think about, I didn't regret what happened. How could I?

And now that I'm back in the city, while I still don't regret it, I'm not sure what to do.

My feelings for Grayson Price are complicated enough.

A part of me always saw him as a savior, but seeing him now after all these years, I've met another side of him. A darker side.

He's not the same man from all those years ago. Nor is he the same man that my childhood brain attached itself to. I'm not sure what to think of this version. Obviously, the attraction is there but . . .

A groan escapes.

The whole weekend event has me not able to think.

After sitting and staring at the phone for an hour, I send the first text.

Me: Hi

Grayson: I didn't expect you to text.

Me: Did you not what me to?

Grayson: I told you to call not text.

I stare at my phone, thinking of how to respond. I decide to put all my cards on the table. If I'm going to be rejected, I'd rather it be now when I'm home in my apartment and don't have to see his face as he does it.

Me: I was thinking about you.

He doesn't type anything, so I continue.

Me: Have you thought of me?

My hands start to shake, the phone rattling in my hand. I can't believe I said that and now I have to wait for him to answer, and it feels like an eternity.

I swear I can hear the hand of the clock ticking slowly.

Tick.

Tock.

Is he ever going to answer, or have I officially pushed him too far?

Grayson: I have.

Me: I want to see you again.

Grayson: When?

My heart starts to hammer in my chest. I'm going to see him, and we're going to do this. I'm going to have a—have a what? A relationship? No. An affair. Yeah, that's what this will be . . . it will be a torrid love affair.

The type that's written in romance novels.

The type that doesn't end well, and when the time comes, we will go our separate ways. Because I know he's not offering me anything.

This is the moment when I should run. The moment I should text back that I have changed my mind.

Because I'm not sure I can handle him leaving me.

But at the same time, I don't think I can handle never having him touch me again.

I can do this.

I can enjoy him for a limited time and then let him go.

I have survived others leaving me. I can survive Grayson Price too.

Me: Tonight.

I respond. It's brazen, but I can't turn back now.

Grayson: Come to my place at 8pm, and I don't need to tell you not to tell anyone.

He fires off his address, and then I place my phone down on a large exhale.

I know I'm playing with fire, but sometimes, you need to be burned to feel.

And he makes me feel.

Hours later, I'm dressed and ready to head over to his apartment. I opted for a pair of skinny jeans, a black T-shirt, and ballet flats.

I'm not sure what we are doing, if anything, so I figure I'll keep it casual with the attire. As I step out of my apartment and head uptown, I can feel the energy rolling off me.

I'm nervous.

And I'm not sure why.

Grayson and I have already had sex, so I shouldn't feel this way. Plus, we have spent plenty of time together as well.

But this is different.

I shake my head, trying to not psych myself up.

It's not really different. Sure, we are alone, and sure, unlike in the past, we are spending time together with the assumption we will have sex.

I wonder what it will be like.

Will he just rip my clothes off when I walk in?

Or will he at least feed me first?

My stomach tightens at thinking these thoughts. I'd be lying to say I wouldn't be hurt if he just sleeps with me and then asks me to leave . . .

But isn't that what I signed up for when we decided to be "sex buddies"?

We fuck.

I leave.

It's fine. I can handle this because I control it. It's on my terms. I'll be the one leaving.

For once in my life, it will be me.

Walking over to the side of the street, I lift my hand in the air and wait for a yellow cab to pull over.

I fire off the address and we're on our way.

As we weave through the traffic, I watch the lights and the colors. I watch as buildings pass and numbers on the streets increase. With each block put behind me, more butterflies flutter inside me. By the time we arrive, I'm basically shaking.

Not just from excitement but also from nerves.

I'm doing something completely out of character. I'm not one to carry on relationships like this.

Yes, I wasn't a virgin before Grayson. But with the need to be different than my mother, I only ever had sex with one person. It was the summer I lived in France. Mom and I rented an apartment overlooking the Louvre. He was French and experienced, an artist . . .

It was beautiful for what it was, but even then, I held the cards. I left.

The soles of my shoes click on the pavement as I approach the building. The door is opened by the doorman on duty. I step up to security behind the long Lucite desk in the entry.

"Ms. Reed for Mr. Price," I say.

"The elevator for Mr. Price's apartment is around the corner and to the right."

I wonder if this is like his office, a private elevator just for him.

I walk over to the elevator, and lo and behold, it is. I press the button, and it opens, but once inside, there are no other buttons to press.

The elevator closes and starts to move.

Up.

Up.

Up.

All the way up to the penthouse. I expect the door to open into a hallway, but instead, it opens up to the most beautiful apartment I have ever seen. It's large and open, modern and airy. Floor-to-ceiling windows overlook the park, making the wall almost all glass. The only place with no window is the wall with the elevator, it seems, and one section that leads to what must be the bedrooms.

My mouth hangs open. I've never seen a place like this before. Ever. It's incredible.

In the distance, I can hear the sound of footsteps. That's when I see him, emerging from the hall.

"River," he says in greeting.

"Hey, Grayson," I respond.

He walks over to me, and as he does, I take him in.

Tall and handsome.

Gruff and reserved.

He looks amazing, though, even wearing the normal scowl on his face.

I'm actually not shocked to see that look. I had hoped he would be smiling, but alas, I guess not.

When he stalks over to me, I can smell the faint scent of soap and cologne . . . It's delicious, like him.

I expect him to yell, but instead, he leans forward, grabs me, and pulls me until I'm flush with his body.

I'm shocked, and before I know it, I'm swimming in the hottest kiss of my life.

His lips find mine. Plundering. Devouring.

He kisses me as if he's starving. As though I'm his last meal on earth.

My body sinks against his, and I let him lead the kiss, my brain too fuzzy to understand anything more than his mouth on mine. When he finally pulls away, I'm breathless and dizzy.

"Let me get us a drink," he says, and I shake my head, confused by what just happened.

I did not expect him to kiss me like that in the foyer . . .

But the way he pulls back and stalks off has me wondering what tonight is?

Then a thought pops into my head . . .

Maybe I had tonight wrong. Maybe this isn't a chance affair; maybe this is the big brush-off. Maybe I'm here so he can let me down easily.

The muscles in my back tighten, and I start to feel lightheaded.

Maybe that was our last kiss.

"River, are you okay?" His brow is furrowed. He's a few feet ahead, but I don't move with him.

Instead, I incline my head. "Before I walk any farther . . . tell me what this is."

"What do you mean?" He scrunches his nose.

"Are you here to let me down easily . . . ?" I trail off, my voice betraying my nerves.

That's when the scowl leaves his face and changes to what looks like rage . . .

He's quick to get to me, his hands bracketing around me.

"You think you're here so I can let you down easy?" he hisses, his fingers pinching my skin. "You think I would risk so much to let you down easy? No, River. You're not here for that."

"Then what?"

"You're here because no matter how hard I try, I can't stop thinking of the way you taste on my tongue," he lashes out.

"And so . . ."

"And so . . ." he presses, "that's why you're here, because since Malaga, I can't stop thinking about you. I wanted you that night and every single day since then. I have fought every single day not to grab you and make you mine." His voice is so angry; it's like he hates himself for feeling this way, and that thought sparks a flame of anger inside me as well.

"So why don't we skip the pleasantries and just get to it?" I snap back.

"God, you're infuriating," he chides before turning around. "We are drinking because we will both need it as we talk about this," he says over his shoulder, and he's right.

We will both need a drink.

I don't have to walk far to be in the kitchen. Technically, due to the open floor plan, I'm in the kitchen now. There are no upper cabinets in the kitchen, which is odd. Where there should be a backsplash is windows.

Although beautiful, it's extremely odd and also feels completely out of character for Grayson.

"What?" he asks as he walks up to the island and places a bottle of wine down.

"Your apartment. Don't get me wrong, it's super cool, but it doesn't seem like you."

"Funny story there. Your father designed the remodel of it actually. When I first bought it, I was around your age . . . and your father was studying to be an architect," he says offhandedly, but I can tell by the way his brows pinch in, he doesn't like talking about my father.

"It just doesn't—"

"Fit?"

"Yeah," I admit.

"I was different back then." He shrugs. Then he lifts the bottle. "Hope you like cabernet."

"I do. I might have just turned twenty-one, but my mother always let me drink wine." At the mention of my mother, my stomach drops. She still hasn't called me.

How is that possible?

"What's wrong?" Grayson asks as he pours two glasses and hands one to me. I lift the wineglass to my mouth and take a sip. It's more robust than I'm used to, and I'm sure it's more expensive than I'm used to.

When I don't answer and just take another sip, Grayson reaches out and sets my drink down.

"Talk to me."

"It's nothing."

"It's obviously not nothing,"

"It's just my mother . . . I haven't heard from her. She didn't even call me on my birthday."

Grayson's brows furrow, and then he picks up my glass. "Come on, let's sit on the couch." He leads me to a gray couch. All the features in this place are monochromatic in black, gray, and white. I imagine he chose this one because of the color and our wine.

When I sit down, he places the glass back in my hand, and then once I'm done, I place it on the Lucite coffee table in front of us.

"As I'm sure you know, my mom has always been a free spirit. She teaches yoga. But she doesn't teach yoga in New York. No, not my mom. Not Lily Pad. She teaches yoga in, like, Nepal. So growing up, we traveled. We lived out of suitcases. I was home-schooled. I didn't even know about my dad until I was twelve. Which you know already since you were there the day she dropped me off at my dad's house." He worries his lower lip. "I'm used to her going away now. She always leaves."

"So what happened this time?" he asks, his voice heavy with concern.

"We were supposed to meet up in Portugal, but she never showed up, and well, she didn't call me."

"Wait. She didn't call to tell you?"

"No. Not even on my . . ." I trail off, my emotions rising up and making my jaw tremble.

"She didn't even call on your birthday?" he grits through clenched teeth. He's angry. Seething angry.

I shake my head and then look down at my hands in my lap. I can feel the tears welling in my eyes, but I don't want them to fall. It seems every time I'm with this man, I'm crying or upset or something. Grayson moves closer to me, his hands reaching out and tilting my jaw up. A lone tear escapes my eyes. "I don't normally cry this much," I hiccup as another tear falls, and he swipes it away.

"You don't have to explain." He moves me into his arms and holds me to him.

Finally, when I'm sure I'm okay, I move away, but he keeps me close to him. "It's fine. I'm okay. Let's talk about what you wanted to talk about."

"No," he says, standing abruptly.

"No?" I ask as he takes my hand in his and he moves me to stand as well.

"No. We aren't talking about any of that shit right now."

My chest starts to tighten.

"Then what are we going to do?"

"The first thing I'm going to do is this." He leans down and sweeps me into his arms, cradled to his chest. I tilt my head up, and he's looking at me with deep hungry eyes.

"And then?" I croak.

"And then I'm going to thoroughly spoil you. I'm going to ravish you. Feast on you. Until you are begging, writhing beneath me and only then will I stop."

My eyes go wide at his words, at his unspoken promise. And I shiver. "Okay."

He walks us into his room, my body growing hot. Once inside, he drops me on his bed.

"Lean back on your elbows . . ."

"Why?"

He looks at me in a way he has never done before. Like I'm dessert, and he's ready to dine.

"Because I'm hungry," he says as he pulls the button of my jean, unzips the zipper, and pulls off my pants. When he sees I'm left in black lace panties, he shakes his head.

"Although you look beautiful, I think I liked your birthday outfit better . . ."

"And why is that?" I ask as he grabs the lace and lets it snap back against my skin.

"Because these need to go." And go they do. He yanks them down, leaving me completely naked, and leans in.

His mouth hovering against my skin, I push my hips up,

trying to get him to touch me, but that only makes him take his time. He slowly kisses up my thigh, but still, he doesn't touch me where I need him most.

"Beg," he says, and I know he wants me to. He said it before.

"Please," I do as he commands and beg.

"Please what?" he taunts back.

"God, Grayson, just do it already." With that, he laughs. A sound I will never grow tired of, and it only makes me hotter.

"Please what?" he says again.

"Please fuck me."

"With my mouth? Or with my cock?"

"Both."

And he does. He answers all my pleas, and he fucks me with both.

Over and over again.

All night.

CHAPTER TWENTY-FIVE

Grayson

TONIGHT DID NOT GO AS PLANNED.

I planned on telling her that this couldn't be a serious relationship. That we could enjoy each other's company, but that it couldn't go any further.

She was an itch I needed to scratch, an addiction I needed to kick, but I needed a few more fixes before I gave her up. Then she started talking about her mom, and I knew it wasn't the time for that conversation.

So instead, I worshiped her.

All night.

Looking over at the clock, I see that it's three a.m. Not good. I have work tomorrow, and now I'll most certainly be useless.

Not only that, but it's not good because she is sleeping over.

Sleeping over is rule number one in the just sex talk.

Day one of this thing and I've already fucked up my rules.

I'm a mess.

I look over at her. She's curled up on her side, her blond locks fanning across my bed. She looks so small among the sheets.

She looks insanely gorgeous, and if I didn't have work tomorrow, I'd consider waking her for round two, but I don't. Instead, I stand and walk into my bathroom. The lights are bright against the dark of the night. I splash some water on my face.

I need to get my shit together.

I need to talk to her.

Especially after what she told me about her mom.

This girl has been left too many times, and I need to tell her now I don't plan on staying.

Not just because of her dad, but also because of me.

I'm so much older than she is.

Too many years separate us. She has her whole life ahead of her, and who knows how long I have. My father died young. My father's father, too.

All the men in the Price family do.

It wouldn't be fair to her. I walk back into my bedroom and get back under the sheets with her. It's like her body knows I'm here because even in her sleep, she seeks me out, curling around my body for warmth.

It feels good to have her here, but it's not something I should get used to.

With an inhale of my breath, I will myself to fall asleep. My brain still races, but my thoughts are no longer about ending it, though. No, instead, now I'm thinking of the story she told.

About her mother.

What kind of mother doesn't show up for a trip with her daughter?

I don't know much about her, and I do know she's flaky, but this seems more than flaky. I want to ask Tyler about it, but then he'd know or at least question my interest in River. Since River and I have no future, there is no reason to tell him or bring up suspicions.

No.

I can't ask him.

But still, the story doesn't sit well with me. Something is going on, and River deserves to know what.

Looking over at her, I watch her sleep. She looks peaceful, but when she's awake, it's obvious this bit of knowledge she doesn't know haunts her.

A need to find out everything about her grows inside me.

It would be easy to find out information. Only one phone call would have to be made, and I'd be able to supply River with all the answers she needs. But the question is, should I? Should I meddle in something that is not only not my place but also something I probably won't be here to see how it's resolved?

But at least she would have answers.

I resign myself to help. Even though I'm not asked, I'm going to speak to my brother tomorrow, and Jaxson will be able to find out where her mom is. We don't like to talk about Jaxson's extracurricular activities, but it still doesn't change the fact he is one of the best hackers in the world.

If there is something to find out, he will.

Normally, I wouldn't get my brother involved with this since it's River, but he already knows I screwed her. I might not have confirmed it, but he knows. At this point, Jaxson is the only one I can talk to about this anyway.

I'll probably regret bringing him into this, but what other option do I have?

I nod to myself.

Yes, that's exactly what I'll do.

Tomorrow, I'll clarify with River that this is just fun. I'll make sure there are no false illusions, and then I'll get Jax to find out the information.

Now that I've settled on my plan, I find that sleep comes easy.

Before I know it, my alarm goes off. With a stretch of my

arms, I expect to collide with River, who slept beside me all night, but when I find nothing, I pop my lids open.

My bed is empty.

Huh.

It's five a.m.

I step away from my bed and head into the kitchen. Maybe she couldn't sleep and made coffee. That will actually work well. We can talk over breakfast.

All the lights in the apartment are off.

It's dark.

Pitch-black. The city lights shimmer and shine through the windows, and that's when I see the note.

Grayson,

Thanks for last night.

~River

I take the letter in my hand. What the hell? She left. In the middle of the night, she snuck out as if I'm her dirty mistake.

I should be happy. If she's leaving in the middle of the night, that means I won't have to have that awkward talk about just sex.

It's obvious from this note that is all she wants too.

Good.

Great.

This is perfect.

I look down at her tiny handwriting.

This is good . . .

Then why does a part of me feel empty?

My morning is odd, to say the least. Having River treat me like a bad one-night stand doesn't sit well with me.

To be honest, I fucking hate it.

I'm at my desk now, drinking my morning coffee and checking my phone for the millionth time.

It's like I'm a damn high schooler. That's the way I'm acting at least.

I debate texting, but I don't.

Lie.

I have started and erased twenty variations of a text.

I want to laugh at the cosmic irony, but I don't.

So instead of dwelling on it, I stand from my desk, shove my cell phone in my pocket, and head out the door to Jax's office.

I don't bother knocking. He never does, so why should I?

I find him behind his desk. His hair is the usual completely not professional bedhead he has. He's wearing a hat, backward this time, a T-shirt, and although I can't see under his desk, I'm sure the rest of his outfit is complete with jeans and sneakers.

He is my polar opposite.

"Grayson, what brings you to my humble abode?" he asks, his signature smart-ass smile gracing his face.

"A hat? Really, Jax?"

He shrugs. "Don't like it?"

"No."

"Too bad. This is my office and seeing as you're standing in it at"—he looks over at the clock on the wall—"nine a.m., it's obvious you need or want something, so spit it out and tell me so I can get back to my game of Solitaire."

"Are you really playing Solitaire?"

"Yes."

"Can I sit?" I ask.

"Wow, this really must be important."

I nod at his comment.

"Fine, I'll stop playing." Once he closes down his game, he looks back over at me. "Now what can I help you with?"

"I have a favor to ask."

The smile on his face spreads into a full-fledged smug grin. He loves when someone calls in a favor because it means he gets a favor back, eventually.

"It's not for me . . ."

"Interesting."

"It's for River."

"Even more interesting."

"Can you just be serious for a minute?" I snap.

"Is she okay?"

I lean back in my chair. "She is. She actually doesn't know I'm asking this for her."

Jaxson cocks his head and waits for me to continue. He's tapping his fingers on his desk as he waits.

Jeez, he's annoying.

"Do you mind?" I ask, signaling to his fingers.

"Well, then get on with it."

I let out a long sigh. "I need you to find her mother."

"Okay . . . why do we need to find her?"

"Well, she never showed up to their mother/daughter trip."

Jaxson's eyes go wide.

"And she didn't call either."

"Oh, shit."

"I know, but that's not the worst."

He stays quiet, but I can see the tension in him growing. He might mess with me about her, but I can also tell he genuinely likes her.

"The worst part is, she never even called on her birthday, so basically there has been nothing from her for over a month. Apparently, she does occasionally do flaky shit, but . . ."

"But this is a whole other version of shady."

"It is."

"Okay. I'll look into it. Might take me a few days, depending on what's going on. And after I find something . . . ?" He doesn't say if. That's how good Jax is at this. It's not an if, it's a when. "What do you want me to do with the information?"

"I want you to come to me. We don't know what you are going to find out. Depending on what we find out, well, I might not want to tell her."

"Gray—"

"Just find out what's going on, and we can worry about it later. Okay?"

"Fine. But you'll owe me."

I roll my eyes. "I know."

With that, I stand from the chair and head back to my office. My coffee has cooled, but I still lift it to my mouth to drink, tasting nothing. Now with that settled, I sit forward in my chair and turn on my computer.

I check my emails and then look at stocks. But everything is falling flat, and I can't concentrate. Suddenly, my phone is boring a hole in my pocket.

I whip it out and look at it again.

I can't believe I have been reduced to this.

But it doesn't matter how much I want to stop; I still find myself scrolling through my phone and pulling up her contact number.

No. I can't call her, but texting . . .

Before I can't think twice, I'm firing up a text.

Me: Dinner tonight at 8pm.

A few minutes pass and she doesn't respond.

So this is what it feels like . . . all the times I have been an as-shole to a woman by not answering her text comes back to slap me in the face. I'm about to storm out of here and do something dumb, like yell at Jax to track her or some stupid shit, but then my phone vibrates on my desk.

River: No hello?

Me: No.

River: Any reason?

Me: What's the point of a hello when you never said goodbye. Since we didn't have breakfast, you owe me a meal. I'll see you at 8. Park Bistro.

Then I throw my phone down, annoyed that I'm letting this girl get to me.

I tell myself it's fine. Tonight, I'll get the upper hand back.

But something tells me I'm wrong.

CHAPTER TWENTY-SIX

River

I STARE AT MY PHONE.

Did that really happen?

Yep.

The texts are still there.

I'm seeing Grayson again . . . tonight.

Still staring at his last message, I realize he's not happy about me sneaking off last night.

It was a smart move on my part. The truth is, I should never have allowed myself to fall asleep, and I was barely sleeping at that.

More like thoroughly fucked and in a coma.

But I knew I had to wait for him to fall asleep before I could sneak out. Grayson wouldn't have let me go, and I needed to leave, so I waited until his breathing leveled out, and then I snuck out.

Lo and behold, I'm shocked that he texted me today and demanded dinner.

I should say no.

But I'm not that strong. I know I'm standing on precarious ground with Grayson Price. Playing with fire, really.

I'm not ready to walk away.

But I can't let him leave first.

The day crawls by painfully slow. I'm nervous about dinner.

I have a feeling he's going to want to talk about what this is. There's no point, so when I see him, I plan to beat him to it.

Work is slow today. It's Friday, which means no one is here. I chose to stay in the city this weekend. My father is already in the Hamptons, and most of the employees leave early. Most companies in the city have "Summer Fridays." Technically, we are open until five p.m., but no one is here after four p.m.

Most people leave after lunch.

Some don't even bother to show. So that means at four fifty p.m., I'm the only person in the office. And I don't mean that in a figure of speech sort of way. I am literally the only person here. Even the receptionist has left to beat the traffic home.

I finish my filing, and then I too leave for the day.

Having dinner with Grayson has me frazzled, so a fresh blow dry and professional makeup might help calm my nerves.

Two hours later, it's seven p.m.

I'm already dressed. I showered earlier, and I have my hair and makeup done.

Sadie walks in the front door and takes one look at me and stops in her tracks.

"Umm, wow. Hello, hot stuff. Where are you off to tonight?" she asks.

"Just to dinner," I say.

She lifts an eyebrow. "With who?"

"No one."

She marches over to where I'm sitting, hand on her hip, and cocks her head. "No way you don't have a big date tonight. Have you looked at yourself in the mirror? You're hot. Which means you're trying to torture some poor idiot. So who is it? Is it Jaxson?" she leads.

I shouldn't tell her.

I know I shouldn't.

But I can't help the words that slip from my mouth. Someone has to know. The secret has been tearing me apart.

"Grayson Price," I spit out before I can stop myself.

"Holy shit!" she exclaims, her hand clamping over her mouth in shock. "You're banging Grayson Price?"

I plead the fifth with my eyes. That doesn't help much, though.

"Umm, no. You need to tell me rather than some dumb head nod. How did it start? Oh my God. Is it good? I mean, of course, it's good. He's damn delicious, but like he never smiles at all. Does he smile in bed?" She just keeps rambling an endless string of ridiculous questions until I finally lift my hand to silence her.

"Okay, okay. One question at a time."

"How did this happen?"

"As you know, he was at the party . . ."

"Oh, cut the shit, it wasn't some random hookup at the party, and you know it. Tell me the truth."

"You can't tell anyone."

"Okay."

"No, I mean it, not one person. You might not realize it, but for as big as the city is, everyone knows everyone, and everyone knows Grayson Price."

"This is true," she agrees.

"Okay, so Grayson is childhood friends with my dad."

Her mouth drops open.

"Oh my God. That's scandalous."

"I know. But it . . ." I try to think of a way to get her to understand. "He and my dad haven't spoken in years. They only reconnected because of this deal Grayson brought to my father."

"Okay, so it's not like you have been doing Sunday night dinner with him and your dad," she says as if this makes everything better, but technically, I have.

I grimace.

"Oh, you have . . ." She cringes.

"Well, not really."

"How is it not really? You either have or you haven't."

"Fine." I roll my eyes. "I have. But not only Sunday nights," I joke, trying to take the edge off the conversation.

"So you're banging your dad's insanely hot friend, which makes it forbidden, which makes it hot as well."

"Basically," I admit on a sigh.

"Damn." She pretends to fan herself. "So how is he in bed?"

"Amazing."

"Does he smile?"

"Nope."

"Hot." She laughs, and that makes me laugh more. "So now you have what, a booty call?"

"Well, actually, we have dinner." That makes her eyes widen.

"As in a date?"

"No. As in dinner." She shakes her head at my words.

"Dinner is a date, dear. Just be careful, okay? Fucking is one thing, but dinner . . ."

"I know. I know. Trust me, I know," I drawl out. "Plus, I plan to tell him this is just sex. Maybe friends with benefit, but nothing more."

"If you say so."

"I do. Now, if that's all the questions, I have to head out. It's already seven thirty, and I have to catch a cab and head to the restaurant."

"Have fun." She smirks.

"Thanks," I say before heading out the door.

Tonight is not a date. No, tonight is more like a meeting to set up parameters.

Or at least that's what I tell myself.

Maybe if I say it over and over again in my mind, I'll actually believe it.

I opt for a cab. Usually, I'd prefer to walk in the city, but right now, with the outfit I'm wearing and especially the shoes, walking isn't an option.

It's not that I'm overly dressy.

I'm in a black romper, but my wedges are high enough that I'd for sure trip and fall if I tried to walk the ten blocks to the restaurant Grayson has picked. So instead, I hop in a cab and have them drive me to my destination.

The restaurant is quaint for New York City. It resembles a barn, which is odd for the location, but it works. With wood-paneled walls, candles, and tea lights, it's the type of restaurant you'd find in the country. But I like it.

It's not pretentious.

That's the one thing I have noticed about Grayson and really like. For as much money as he has—planes, helicopters, car and driver, and hell, even his apartment—the man is not pretentious.

Arrogant? Yes.

Pretentious? No.

My eyes scan the room for him, but I don't see him anywhere, so I walk up to the hostess stand.

"Hello," I say, and she smiles. "I'm looking for Mr. Price."

"Oh yes, Ms. Reed. Your table is right this way."

I follow the woman as she weaves her way through the restaurant until she turns into a smaller dining room.

There is a view of the kitchen from the table. And you can see the chef making dinner.

"The chef's table," she says as she pulls out my chair to sit. Grayson isn't here yet, but I take the seat anyway.

Now alone, I watch the hustle and bustle of the kitchen, so completely enthralled that I don't notice him approach.

But when I feel a hand on my shoulder, I startle and turn to look and find him standing behind me.

"Sorry I'm late," he says before walking away and pulling out the seat beside me.

"It's okay. I was enjoying the show," I respond, pointing at the display in front of me.

"That's why I like it here. Not only is it farm to table, but you can reserve this table and watch the magic happen."

I take in what he says and store it in my Grayson file. I wouldn't have expected him to say that. Just like I didn't expect him to fly me to Maine for lunch. Or text me . . .

This man is full of surprises.

Now sitting beside me, we don't speak. With the quiet all around us, I start to nervously fiddle with the glass in front of me. Gliding my fingertips along the surface of the cold glass.

Grayson reaches his hand out to stop my movements, his warm and rough pads of his fingers caressing my skin. Instead, he draws out circles on my flesh, making goose bumps break against my skin.

"There's no reason to be nervous, River," he says. But his voice is rough and gravelly and does something to my insides. It's as if he's seducing me by just speaking.

I give my head a little shake to right my thoughts. "I'm not nervous. I'm just waiting."

"Waiting for what?"

"For whatever you want to say."

"Maybe I just want your company."

I lift a brow at him. "You have something to say. But it's okay. I'll say it first. I am under no illusion that this will be anything more, so you don't actually have to have the talk with me," I say.

His jaw tightens a fraction, or maybe I'm just imagining it, but it looks like my words have upset him.

"Is that what you think we are doing here?"

"A public place . . . to tell me that this is all it will be. Don't worry, you don't have to let me down easy. We're cool." I shrug.

"One, we are not cool. Two, I'm not letting anyone down easily," he responds or actually snaps back.

"Fine. Not now. So I guess this is the talk about no future. But what I'm trying to say is I know that, so it's cool. I enjoy being with you," I nonchalantly say, "and you enjoy being with me. Let's just have fun."

There, I said it, but even though the words leave my mouth, and even though my back is straight, I still feel tied up inside. I'm trying to be the one to set the terms. That way, I can't be hurt, but even saying them hurts. I won't let him know that. But it does.

"Well, thank you for that. It was enlightening. Now, do you mind if I speak?"

I motion my hand to tell him to go on.

"Yes, you are right. I'm not looking for a relationship."

"See, great, this is perfect. We are on the same page." I smile, and he inhales sharply.

"Let me speak, River," he snaps. "I enjoy your company, and you are right, this can't go anywhere. Hell, your father can never know. But seeing as you have said this, I guess I don't have to say anything else on the matter."

"We can be friends who fuck."

"River."

"Or is friends out?"

He looks like he wants to strangle me, but instead, he takes a deep breath. Inhaling and then exhaling. "We can be friends who fuck." He sighs.

"See, great. Now that we are on the same page, let's eat."

He shakes his head at me, and he laughs. The sound is intoxicating; I want to hear it over and over again. I want to be the one to make him laugh because the feeling is powerful and all-consuming.

And right here at the table, despite my big speech . . .

I know I'm fucked.

"So what's new at your office?" I ask, not wanting an awkward silence to descend.

"The office, really?" The corner of his mouth twitches. "Can't come up with something better than that? Especially, after the whole friends bit."

"Fine," I huff. "What do you want to talk about?" I ask.

He leans forward, his elbows now on the table. A shadow is cast from the illumining light of the candle, making my breath hitch from the look in his eyes as he gazes at me, and then down to my hand resting on the linen beneath me.

"I want to talk about that," he answers, tilting his jaw to signify the bracelet that sits heavy on my wrist.

"Nope. Next question." I laugh, trying to play it off as a joke. But I don't want to talk about the first bracelet I ever made, the one that sits on my wrist every day, the one that I have had since I was a little girl and my mother took me to Mexico. Where in a small town called Pátzcuaro, I learned to work with silver.

"Then what?"

"How about you tell me what your favorite color is or your favorites movie."

"As you wish." He sounds amused, and then in the middle of the quaint restaurant, Grayson and I trade favorites until I know every useless piece of information about him, from his favorite candy—*he only likes dark chocolate*—to the fact that he runs every day, rain or shine.

But when dinner is over, and as pleasant as it ended up being, there is still a strange tension in the air that hasn't subsided.

We both know what this is now.

I'm not sure if tonight starts our affair, but by the time we walk outside, I'm curious to find out.

"I'm that way. Thanks for dinner," I say as I turn to look at him.

"I'll walk you home."

I shake my head. "You don't need to."

"I know I don't, but I want to . . ." He lifts his hand to touch me, his fingers tracing my bottom lip. I shiver under the touch, my body growing needy for more. "We haven't had dessert yet." He smirks.

"My roommate is gone for the night," I respond, and his lips split into a large smile.

"Lead the way."

——————◆◇◆——————

This morning, we met for brunch. We have started to meet for breakfast or brunch on most days.

Today, we are walking down the street together, bellies full, and our bodies almost touching, but we don't touch.

Even though a few weeks have passed since we have

discussed keeping us a secret and I haven't mentioned it since, it still bothers me.

I don't actually want to tell my dad, and I have no real desire to go public per se, but the fact that he won't, or doesn't want to, is what keeps me up at night.

The fact that he won't fight for me.

With each step, I can feel his fingers hovering close, but they don't connect, and with each step, I grow more and more annoyed.

I know we are not telling people about us, but right now, we are all the way in the West Village, and nowhere near anyone we know. Who would see us if we did touch?

I stop my movements. Grayson takes an extra step before he realizes I stopped walking.

He halts and then turns around to face me.

His eyebrow lifts. "Is everything okay?"

When I don't move, he takes the few steps until he's standing in front of me. His gaze is unwavering as he waits for me to speak. I study him for a minute, memorizing the line that forms on the side of his lips as he waits. The sign of his impatience. The small divot on his cheek.

These small imperfections that I have grown so fond of. Although they make him tough and cold to some, I love every imperfection that mars his skin because they make up Grayson Price, a man I have always cared for, but now all I want to do is make him smile. Make him laugh. I want to see the lines form in a different way. But first, before I invest any more time, I have to know . . .

"Am I your dirty secret?" I ask, keeping my voice low so no one around can hear.

The familiar line between his eyebrows when he is

confused appears, and he reaches out and ushers me away from the middle of the sidewalk and toward the building.

"Well, am I?" I break my arm away from his and take a step toward the brownstone beside us. The street is relatively quiet, almost like it's off the beaten path of typical New York traffic.

A part of me wonders if that's why he brought me here. I turn my head back to the restaurant where we just ate dinner and then lift my brow in speculation.

"Hardly."

"Then why take me here or, to be honest, any of the places you have taken me to? They're always quiet and empty. Not popular."

"I take you to the places I like to eat, River."

I tilt my head at his answer.

"You know I'm private, and these are the places I go. These are my favorites. I don't take you to the trendy spots, not because I'm embarrassed by you, but because I hate them. I hate the scene; I hate being recognized." He looks away from me above my head. "I thought you knew that about me."

"B-But . . ." I start to say and stutter. "You don't touch me in public. You don't kiss me."

"River, it's hard."

"I know but—"

"But what?"

"It's not that I don't want you. Never think that. I just can't risk someone seeing us."

"Then why bother taking me out in general?"

"Because I want to be with you. I just . . . We need to be careful."

I know I'm being silly, but those ugly insecurities have

a way of surfacing at the worst times no matter how I try to push them down. "Why? My dad isn't even here. He's in the Hamptons."

"River, you know that's not it. You see how they hound Jax. Hell, even you got photographed with him."

"You knew about that?" I whisper.

"Of course I did. Wasn't that the goal?" He's trying hard not to sneer.

I look down and then back up. "I didn't think you cared at the time."

He steps into me, and my back hits the distressed and aged brick of the building. He lifts his arm to box me in.

"You think I didn't care?"

"Yeah."

"I cared," he grits out.

"Why?"

"Why? Because you're mine, not his. Since I first saw you in Malaga, I wanted you, and seeing that my younger brother, someone probably better suited for you, could be with you, drove me insane."

His leans in and is now so close that his lips hover above mine. "Don't think I don't kiss you in public because I don't want to. I do. I want to grab you . . ." His hand leaves the wall and grips my hips. "I want to kiss you. I want to tell the whole world that you're mine."

"Then do it," I breathe. He lets out a sigh, and the air that escapes his mouth tickles my skin.

"I can't." When he pushes off me, I groan at the loss of his presence before he forcefully grabs my hand in his and pulls me with him.

"Where are you taking me?" I ask as I try to keep up.

"Back to my place, so I can show you just how much I want you, regardless of what I do out here."

"Okay," I squeak.

I might not have won that battle, but I'm not giving up on winning the war.

CHAPTER TWENTY-SEVEN

Grayson

A WEEK HAS PASSED SINCE RIVER CALLED ME OUT ON THE restaurants I take her to. Things are the same. We see each other often, and I enjoy my time with her. Every day that passes, it becomes harder to remember why we are hiding, but then I remember that we can't get serious, not because of just her father but because the idea of us being serious, and then something happening to me—something to take me away from her—is something I can't bear.

So even though a part of me wants to throw caution to the wind and fight to be with her, I also know that when my times comes . . . I can't do that to her, so instead, I keep the status quo.

But since I'm a glutton for punishment, I can't say no to her when she calls, which is why she is standing in my office today. Even though, I know it's risky, I just don't care.

"To what do I owe this visit?" I smile up at her from my desk.

"I had documents." Her lips turn up into a smirk, and I know she's lying.

"You do?"

"Nope."

"Ms. Reed." I shake my head. "What am I going to do with you?"

"I can think of a few things," she responds, raising an eyebrow.

"Come here," I command, and she does, walking over with a coffee in hand.

She lifts it up. "When you said you were too busy to have coffee this morning, I thought I'd bring coffee to you instead."

"That was very considerate of you."

"What can I say? I'm a considerate girl."

I take the coffee out of her hand and take a sip. The fresh brew is still warm. Placing it down, I pull her to sit on my lap and place my lips on hers.

"You shouldn't have come." I kiss her lips. "But I'm happy you did."

"I just couldn't stand the idea of you not having coffee since you are such a busy man. And I do love me a good cup of Joe."

"Thank you." I lower my lips again to hers, and her mouth opens for me, so I deepen the kiss.

My hand reaches out and starts to unsnap the buttons on her blouse. Then I lean forward and start to trail my tongue across her skin, down her neck, to the swell of her breast.

"What are you doing?" she whispers.

"Having breakfast," I respond. When she first walked in, I had anticipated this, but now that she's here, sitting on my lap, I can't think of anything but sinking inside her.

My tongue continues its path, and as I'm about to start my trek lower, the intercom on my desk rings.

Still kissing her skin, I lift my hand and press the button.

"Yes," I say between swipes of my tongue.

"Mr. Price, Tyler Reed is here to see you," my assistant says through the line.

I stop my ministrations and hit the mute button.

"Oh my God," River whisper-shouts. "I have to get out of here."

"Does Nicole know you're here?" I mouth to her.

"No. She didn't see me walk in."

"Fuck."

"That probably means he's outside the door already."

"Doesn't he need to get buzzed up?" she asks.

"I put him on the list."

"Shit."

"Mr. Price?" Nicole's voice says.

I place my hand over my mouth to silence River before taking the phone off mute.

"Sorry about that, send him in."

I'm about to tell River to get in the seat across from me and I'll come up with a plausible story when the next thing I know, she's sliding beneath my desk.

What the fuck is she doing?

"You need—" I start to say but just as I'm to tell her to get out from under there, the door swings open.

"Gray."

"Tyler," I respond. "Take a seat." I signal my hand out across my desk.

He does.

Now with him sitting, I try to act calm and collected, but I'm finding it rather hard to drop the facade, knowing where his daughter is.

"What's going on Tyler?" I ask, and just as I say his name, her hands rest on my thigh. I swear I start to choke as her fingers move. I can tell she's trying discreetly to get comfortable down there, but does she have to touch me? Do her fingers have to move up my thigh?

This must be what hell is like. My dick getting hard with the girl's dad in the room.

I swear I'm in high school.

Tyler is speaking, but I legitimately have no idea what he's talking about.

Again.

Why does this keep happening to me?

I have to shake my head to right myself.

"Wait, what? Sorry."

"You okay?"

"Yeah. Sorry. Go on. Actually, repeat what you just said." I try to concentrate on him, not thinking about the fact that I have a partial naked River under my desk with her hand dangerously close to my crotch.

I can do this.

I can pay attention.

"I was just here to ask you, typically"—he looks uncomfortable—"when can I expect payment from Lancaster?"

"Is everything okay?"

"Yes. Well, no." He lifts his hand and runs it through his hair. "The party ate away at the money you paid me to do the initial sketches," he admits on a sigh.

"Already?"

He looks down. Things must have been a lot worse than he implied.

"I can speak to Lancaster, but if you sent him an invoice, they'll pay before it's due." His shoulders visibly loosen at my words.

"Okay."

"Do you need help?" I ask, leaning forward in my desk.

"No, of course not. We're okay. But with the baby . . . and

River's rent . . ." He swallows. "Things just got away from me, I guess." He looks down and up. "I swear I need to find time to look at the books and cut back somewhere, but I'm so busy."

"Do you want me to look?"

"I couldn't ask you to do that; you've already done too much," Tyler says before he stands. "Thanks for listening to me ramble."

"Anytime."

"You're a good friend."

Hardly. Actually, I'm the worst. I give him a tight smile.

"Okay, I'll get out of your hair."

I laugh 'cause I'm still at a loss, and then he leaves and walks out the door. A sinking, horrible feeling builds in my stomach.

"Is he gone?" River whispers, and I look down, seeing Tyler's daughter, the evidence of what an asshole I am, under my desk.

I push back my chair, and she steps up.

"Why did you do that?" I say, my voice rough with a mixture of confused feeling.

"Well, where else was I supposed to go?" she asks.

"You could have said you were dropping something off."

She lifts a brow. "Yeah 'cause he'd believe that."

"Fine."

"Don't be grumpy."

"How am I not supposed to be? I had to talk to your dad with a straight face all while your face was painfully close to me."

"Sorry," she responds in a coo.

"No, you're not."

"No, I'm not. I couldn't hear much under there. What was my dad going on about?"

"Nothing. Everything is fine," I lie.

"What aren't you saying?" She lifts a brow and crosses her arms in front of her chest. Something tells me if I don't tell her the truth, she won't be leaving my office anytime soon.

"The truth is, he's overextended himself, and money is tight. But honestly, he's about to get a huge check, so don't worry about anything."

She inclines her head and looks at me, reading me to see if I'm lying, again. When she's satisfied, she smiles.

"I should get out of here," she says, before fixing her blouse and striding out the door.

Leaving me to work in the state I'm in.

Shit.

CHAPTER TWENTY-EIGHT

River

DAYS HAVE PASSED SINCE MY NEAR RUN-IN WITH MY FATHER under Grayson's desk. I'm working late at the office on a Friday. Everyone here has already left, and I'm the only one left. I'm actually planning to head out to the Hamptons this weekend but not until tomorrow. I'll hop on a train first thing in the morning. I could have gone today, but I wanted to help out here.

Grayson's words from the other day about my dad and money linger in my head. I had a small idea that Dad was having financial problems, but now that Grayson mentioned it, I realize it's much worse than I thought. I feel bad milking money off him, which is why I'm here working late. I figure the more I do around this place, the better it will be for his business.

Maybe I should get another job, one where my father isn't the one paying me. Then I won't need his help to subsidize my rent.

Or maybe . . . An idea popped into my head. Maybe I can help him even more. I'm not a genius, but I do you have a 4.0 average in business. Maybe . . . I could look over his books.

I mean he wants me to work with Larry, but Larry seems frazzled all the time. Maybe Larry is missing something, and I can help.

The thing is, Larry won't ask for my help if there is an issue. And there is no way if I tell him what I'm doing he'll let me.

But what he doesn't know what hurt.

If anything, it can help, and if I find something, I can always tell him, and he can take the credit for all I care.

With my mind resolved, I take another peek around the office, and once I confirm I'm alone, I head into Larry's office with a zip drive in hand. His computer has a passcode, but I've seen him enter it.

It's not like I'm breaking into his stuff, I tell myself. This is my dad's company.

So technically, it's okay. Plus, I won't look at anything but my dad's books. No emails or whatnot.

Imagine if he has dirty pictures on there.

Barf.

Thumbing through the files, I'm quick to download them, and I'm out of his office before I can even think twice.

I'm not sure when I'll get around to looking at the files, but hopefully, I can find somewhere we can cut costs to make this company more profitable.

I'm surprised to see that Grayson sitting outside by my parents' pool when I finally make it to their house today.

From where he's perched on the chair at the table, I see his lip lift slightly. I know if we were alone, a smirk would line his face, but he's trying very hard to keep his face completely neutral.

"Look who decided to drop by for lunch," Kim says.

Still looking at him, I lift my hand and give him a little wave. He nods his hello. He looks so good in the early afternoon light. I can't see his eyes behind his aviators, but I can imagine behind the lenses they are staring at me.

"When are we eating?" I ask because it's the only thing I can do to make myself not approach him and kiss his full lips.

"Your dad is on the way back with lobster rolls."

"Lobster rolls?"

"Yeah, Grayson said he was in the mood, and I know how much you love them, baby."

The memory of him whisking me away plays out in my head. Although things were different then and tense, I warm that he remembers that I had said it was my favorite and he wanted to make me happy.

"Yeah, I do love them," I respond.

Walking over, I take the seat directly beside him. This close, I can see his smile tip up further. To anyone who doesn't know him well, he's not smiling. But since I have been studying that look for weeks, I know he's thoroughly amused.

He's here to torture me.

As if he's reading my mind, I feel his hand brush against the exposed flesh of my thigh. I'm thankful the table is set today with linens, or Kim might see it when he places his palm on me, his fingers wrapping around and squeezing lightly.

I cough, more like choke, not expecting him to do that, but for some reason, he starts to trail his fingers on my skin, and I feel like he's getting me back for the incident in his office.

Karma is a bitch.

I know that's what this is. This is his way of getting me back.

Grayson sits back, all while he continues to stroke me. A shiver runs down my spine at his touch. Slowly his fingers start the climb, and I swear it feels like my heart will explode. With each inch he moves, the tension inside me crackles, and the air around us intensifies. By the time he's right at my bikini bottoms, I swear my body lights on fire.

The oxygen I inhale burns my lungs as I wait for him to touch me there.

"I need a drink." He stands abruptly, removing his hand. "Kim, what do you want?"

"You don't have to—"

"Sit. Rest"—he looks over at me—"River will help me." I don't need to see his eyes to know what he's thinking, but when he lifts his glasses off his face and places them on the table, I can see it clearly written in his enlarged dark pupils.

"Umm, okay," I say and look over at Kim, who looks completely oblivious.

Grayson starts to walk, and I follow him.

Once in the kitchen alone, Grayson wastes no time pushing me against the wall. His mouth descends before I can even process what he's doing, and his tongue slips into my mouth, sweeping against mine.

The beat of my heart intensifies with the thrill of what's happening—he's kissing me, here, in my father's house, with Kim right outside.

She could catch us.

My father could come home and see us like that.

I'm not sure what it is, but we are kissing each other with a frenzied clip because our time is limited to a stolen moment or two in the kitchen.

Grayson pulls my body to tighter to his, deepening our kiss. I allow myself to melt into him. A moan escapes as he brings his hands up my sides to just below my breasts.

I need him to touch me, and he does.

His hands touch my breasts, making my nipples pebble and my core tighten.

He grabs harder, pushing his body deeper against mine,

and I can feel his erection up against my stomach. I wonder if we have time . . .

"Got the rolls, where we eating?" I hear my father shout as he walks in through the door that leads to the garage.

"Shit," Grayson mumbles under his breath and pushes off me.

"Hey, guys. What are you doing?" My dad walks into the kitchen.

"We were just getting drinks," I say lamely. "Grayson was helping me."

"What do you want?" Grayson says, turning to my father. Grayson looks perfectly collected as he speaks, as if we weren't just making out.

"What are you having?"

"Beer," Grayson answers.

"I'll have the same," my dad says before he turns to walk outside.

Once he's gone, I turn to look at Grayson and let out the breath I was holding. "That was too close," I whisper.

"You're right."

"So then why did you come? And why did you do that?"

"I missed you . . ."

"It wasn't smart." I lift my brow.

He nods. "Next time, I'll find us a place to be alone." He doesn't elaborate; instead, he turns and walks away from me, two beers in hand.

CHAPTER TWENTY-NINE

Grayson

I WANT TO SPEND MORE AND MORE TIME WITH RIVER. SHE has become my drug of choice, a dangerous habit I can't kick.

Today, we spend the day walking around the Upper East Side.

"It's going to rain," she says, her face tipped up.

I look up at the sky. "No, it's not."

"It is. One hundred percent. We should wait here?"

"Don't be ridiculous, River. I'm not standing in this store to see if it's going to rain."

She shrugs. "Fine, but I'm telling you, the sky is about to open and swallow us whole."

"And you know this because . . . ?" I trail off.

"In my spare time, I'm the weather girl." She rolls her eyes. "Because as you can see right there"—she points up at the sky— "that is a big-ass black cloud that screams torrential downpour."

"Big-ass cloud, huh? You sure you want to go into business? Because I feel like you could have a very promising career in weather."

She bursts out laughing. "Did you just make a joke, Mr. Grumpy Pants?"

"It appears I did. I must be losing my grumpy touch." I smirk back. "It seems you're a bad influence on me. But whatever you do, do not tell my brother."

"Mission complete, and no, I wouldn't dream of telling Jax. He would never let you live it down. Now I just need you to belly laugh, and my work here is done."

"Well, that is not going to happen."

"Challenge accepted." She laughs, and I shake my head.

"This isn't a TV sitcom; you won't get me to belly laugh."

"I bet I do. And when I do, you owe me a prize."

"What do you want?"

"A trip."

"I'd take you on one anyway. Where do you want to go?"

"Anywhere where it's just you and me."

"Done. Regardless," he says.

"Come on, let's try on hats," I say, taking his hand in mine.

"Hats?"

"Well, we have to kill time before the storm hits, so we might as well kill time in a store." I look at the store she's pulling me in. It's all oversized hats like the ones they wear in England or to the Kentucky Derby.

With a shake of the head, I follow her inside, and she starts to place one, then removes it and replaces it with a fresh hat. One after the next, and as much as I smile, no belly laughs form.

Not even when she starts to impersonate famous actors and different accents to match the hats.

Belly laugh or not, this is the most fun I've had in years. The most fun I've had since my father died, that's for sure.

Being with River is easy.

Notwithstanding the obstacles we face and the lack of a future, actually spending time with her is easy.

She makes me feel young and carefree.

I like it.

With an overly dramatic sigh, River puts the last hat back and turns to me.

"Fine, Mr. Grumpy, let's go. There is no helping you." She takes my hand in hers and pulls me out of the store and down the block.

It's crazy that we are walking hand in hand down Park Avenue, but I'm having too much fun to care if anyone sees me right now.

"Where to next?"

"Let's see if dessert loosens you up."

"Are you for dessert? Because that most certainly could help."

"Sex joke." She rolls her eyes. "Typical. Men."

Hand in hand, we continue to walk until she pulls me into a popular cupcake store. I meander around the room as she places her order, and when I see her at the register, I walk over and take out my wallet.

"My treat," she says, waving off my money. "Let's go."

"Any other places?"

"Nope, just back to your apartment," she responds with a smirk.

The endless possibilities of all the things I can do with the icing play through my head as we start to walk home.

I'm so wrapped up that I miss the telltale sign that the storm is going to hit.

But when I hear the crack of thunder, I notice the sky is black, despite the time of day, and the wind has picked up. Then out of nowhere, the sky opens up and basically swallows us whole just as River predicted.

"Oh my God, should we take shelter or maybe grab a cab?" River says.

I can't even see three feet ahead of me, but I can see River stuff the cupcake boxes in her shirt for protection.

"Priorities." She shrugs.

No cabs.

No umbrella.

No shelter in sight, and she's worried about the cupcake.

The damn cupcake I intended to eat off her body.

And that's when it happens.

In the middle of Park Avenue, drenched to my core, every single inch of me saturated in water like a drowned rat, I laugh. And not just any laugh, the one she's been waiting for all day, and at that moment, I know that River is special because right there, in the rain, River starts to dance in the street.

"I did it. I did it."

Water belts from all angles, and it makes me laugh harder.

"It's coming from everywhere." She giggles back. "I swear it's coming from the ground too."

And she's right. The rain is coming from every direction. Up. Down. Left and right. And I just can't stop laughing.

I laugh so hard my belly hurts.

I laugh so hard I can't tell if tears are leaving my eyes, and I don't stop laughing until I reach for my little River, pull her toward me, and seal her mouth with mine.

Right there on one of the busiest streets in New York.

In the pouring rain, I kiss her and kiss her and continue to kiss her.

Water pools between our faces, dripping off my nose onto hers, and it's almost cathartic.

Like a *river* has run over me and cleansed me of my past.

Maybe only for a brief minute, but I feel cleansed and free.

I pull away after a minute. "Come on, let's get home. It's only a few more blocks. Think you can make it?"

"There is nothing more that can get wet," she says. When I raise an eyebrow, she swats me.

"Head out of the gutter."

I take the hand she swatted me with and lead us home to my apartment.

When we finally arrive, we leave a pool of water in our wake.

The elevator opens to the foyer, and when we step inside, we are so wet, I can't help but laugh again.

"That's what it took? A little rain?" River states as she stares at me laughing in my apartment.

"A little rain? That was a monsoon."

"Told you it would be killer, and I got you to laugh." She giggles. "A full belly laugh. And that took less time than I thought. Here, I thought I would have to smash this cupcake on your face."

"Don't you even think about doing that. You already won."

Still holding the cupcake, she steps toward me with a wicked gleam in her eye. "River," I mockingly scold. She wouldn't dare.

Still drenched from the rain, she steps closer to me, her dripping wet legs touching mine.

"You wouldn't dare," I say as she lifts the cupcake toward my face.

Her smile deepens, and then before I can stop her, she's smashing the cupcake on my face.

The sound of her laughter echoes through the room, breaking down the little resistance I have left for this woman.

Reaching out, I grab her and pull her to sit on my lap, and then with the cupcake still on my face, I kiss her.

<hr />

It's been weeks since I started to see River in secret. I got to have exactly the relationship I wanted from her without even having to ask for it.

She offered herself on a platter before me, the perfect dish, and who was I to say no?

Obviously, I couldn't. Not when I was still unsatisfied.

With River, it was like my thirst for her could never be quenched.

It needs to be, though. The only problem is, the more I keep spending time with her, getting to know her, the more and more I want.

I keep thinking this will be the last time, and I will end this soon. But like the addict seeking his next hit, I'm addicted to River Reed.

As much as I want to say I keep going back for the incredible sex, it's not just that.

It's more.

Despite what I wanted, it's more.

I like her. Enjoy her company.

She makes me laugh.

Not many can break through the walls I have built, and she has. She didn't just break through them, though. No, River took a sledgehammer, and now I'm the idiot with a smirk on my face in my office looking at her texts.

Like now.

I'm sitting at my desk leaned back in my chair. Not my typical position. Usually, my shoulders are tight, and I'm sitting upright. But not now.

Nope.

Now, I'm sitting back reading my texts.

River: What are you doing?

Me: Working. As most mortals do on a Monday.

River: I work.

Me: Hardly.

River: I'm bored.

Me: Go be a mortal, then.

River: Nah, kicking it upstairs with the gods sound better. Come entertain us.

My smile spreads further on my face. How I'd love to do that right now.

Playing hooky with River sounds like the perfect solution to the Monday blues.

Me: Send me directions to your cloud.

River: Got your private jet ready?

Me: All fueled up.

River: Oh . . .

Me: Oh???

River: I'm at Bloomingdale's. Surrounded by mortals. A rescue mission would be appreciated.

Me: At Bloomingdale's? No thanks. It was nice knowing you.

River: Don't you want to see me trying on dresses?

Although the visual of River trying on dresses has my pants growing tighter, the answer is still no.

Me: You really don't have a deeper understanding of what guys like to do in their spare time, huh?

River: Even if I'm naked?

Fuck. Now *that's* a visual I don't need to have at my office. How the hell am I going to concentrate on my meetings today with her telling me she's naked?

My phone rings, and I press the speaker button.

"The conference room is ready for you, Mr. Price."

"Thank you, Nicole," I say as I stand and adjust my pants. Luckily, this distraction is exactly what I need.

Grabbing the papers on my desk and the phone, I head down the hall and into the conference room.

Tyler is sitting there.

A wave of guilt spreads through me. I stare at him for a minute when I sit, and he quirks a brow.

"Everything okay? You look . . . extra serious."

"My brother is just his normal self. You don't see him in the office often. This is his pleasant look." Jax steps in, saving the day.

He must know what's wrong with me. Normally, I wouldn't appreciate the poke, but this time, I do.

"What Jax said. So what have you got?" I ask.

Now that it's out there that I'm always a dick at the office, I play it up.

"See," Jax says, and Tyler laughs.

Tyler then proceeds to show us what he plans to do with our land. The Lancasters are here, too. They opted not to buy the land outright, so we have to sit in on the meeting to approve the construction.

The plans are different from what Lancaster usually goes for, but in true Tyler fashion, he nails it. He's incorporated the Moroccan designs into the mountain, so the building looks like it's part of the land rather than a hotel.

It's fantastic.

As he begins to show us the interior, my phone pings on the table.

Everyone stops talking, and I silently curse myself for not putting it on vibrate when I see who it is. It's a text from River.

There, staring back at me is a picture of a very naked River. The very naked daughter of the man sitting right in front of me. My throat closes up, and I let out a choked cough.

"Are you okay?" Tyler asks.

I reach for the glass of water in front of me.

"Yeah, I'm fine . . ."

"Must have been some text," Jax taunts from beside me. I want to strangle him.

Tyler lifts a brow and then catches on, and it rises even farther as this time, a smirk forms.

"Ahh."

"No. It's nothing," I say.

"That's not a nothing text. How about you show us?" my idiot brother presses, and now it's official. I'll kill him.

"Nothing for your eyes." I hiss, and Tyler bursts out laughing.

"Must be some text, all right."

"Jeez, guys. Drop it."

I swipe my phone and fire back.

Me: Stop texting. Your dad is here.

River: Oops. Still?

Me: YES.

I place my phone back down, and Jax smiles, enjoying this way too much. "Can we continue now?"

I wave my hand, and Tyler continues the presentation.

He talks for about another thirty minutes, but I don't hear one word. Instead, I stare at my cell on the desk.

Luckily for me, it doesn't ring.

Not until I'm back at my desk and sorting through my emails again.

River: Still there?

Me: No.

About an hour later, my door flings open, and I'm met with River's face holding two shopping bags.

"Are you kidding me? Why are you here?"

"What do you think?"

"What are you doing?"

"Stop being so cranky. Maybe you need to get laid? I can help with that . . ." When I don't speak, she shrugs. "Fine. Since you stopped responding, I figured I would come here and just show you what I bought." She walks farther into my office, bags still in hand, hip cocked.

Daring me to tell her to leave.

I won't.

"Close the door."

"Yes, Mr. Price," she coos, and I know she's up to no good.

The sound of the door closing echoes in my office. "Lock it," I rasp through clenched teeth. This girl has been teasing me all day, and now that I have her here, I'm going to have my way with her.

She gives me a coy look as she drops her bags and locks the door.

"Well, you made a big deal about what you bought, so are you going to show me?" I ask. And her smile spreads farther on her face.

"I can do that."

I stand from my desk and make my way to the other side. Crossing my arms in front of my chest, I wait.

She's wearing a cotton dress. Slowly, she drops the strap off her shoulder, and once they are both dropped, the dress pools on the floor beneath her. Now she stands in front of me in her ballet flats, a bra, and lace underwear.

"What did you buy?" I hiss.

My heart beats rapidly in my chest.

She turns around and then bends down, and I get a perfect view of her ass. Almost bare except for her thong.

She lifts something. It looks like a scrap of material, and that's when I look at the label on the bag.

Agent Provocateur.

Fuck.

"I bought this for later," she says in a seductive voice.

"Is that so?" I push off the desk behind me, and she steps back until her back hits the door behind her.

Lifting my hands, I run the pads of my fingers across her jaw, down her throat, and to the swell of her breast.

"Take it off. Take it all off." I step back and wait for her to undress. She does it fast, and I appreciate the speed.

I don't have all day with her because I do have to get back to work eventually. I step aside and stare at her.

"On the desk," I order.

"What?" Her eyes are wide at my command.

"Get on the desk," I grit.

She follows orders well, moving quickly to sit on the edge of the desk.

"Lean back."

She does.

"Show me."

Slowly, but as ordered, she spreads her legs.

My lips tip up, and I make my way, more like stalk, over to her.

"I don't have time to taste you," I say as I unzip my pants. I don't bother taking them off or removing my jacket. Instead, I just pull my cock out. "I'm going to fuck you. And you aren't going to make a peep. Do you understand?"

She nods.

"Good girl."

I align myself with her core, taking her legs and bracketing them around my hips.

And then I thrust in all the way to the hilt. She feels amazing.

The perfect fit.

This must be what heaven is like.

I start out slow, leisurely drawing it out, but soon, the need to increase my speed and force is almost maddening, torturous. I cup her backside and angle her body upward, slamming into her again and entering her fully, reaching deeper than I thought possible. Pulling all the way out before pounding back in.

My strokes grow harder with each new thrust of my hips. I quicken my pace until I'm fucking her at a punishable speed. Her body starts to shake, her inner walls grasping me.

I watch as her mouth clenches, trying her best not to make a sound, then she's biting her own hand to stifle the scream threatening to expel. I can feel her come apart all around me.

It doesn't take me long, but soon I'm falling over the edge. I'm gritting my teeth and pouring myself inside her.

I allow my chest to fall forward, placing my head in the crook of her neck. I'm still cradled inside her body.

The phone on my desk starts to ring.

"Fuck," I say as I pull out.

I miss her warmth instantly. As I said . . . I'm a junkie, and she's my drug of choice.

"I have to get that." I sound like a dick. I just fucked her, and now I'm kicking her out, but if she's upset, she doesn't appear to be.

Instead, she nods with a genuine satisfied smile and walks to retrieve her clothes.

"Price," I answer.

"Gray, Jace here."

"Talk to me about my money," I say to Jace Montgomery. He runs the hedge fund where I keep a portion of our money.

He starts to ramble about something, but I really have no

idea. I'm too busy watching River shimmy back into her clothes and right herself. She picks up her bags and is unlocking the door.

"Jace, hold on a minute." I press the hold button, and River turns around as I put the phone down on the desk. Walking over to her, I tilt her head up.

"Were you going to say goodbye? Or just sneak out again?"

"You're on the phone," she answers.

"Not a good answer."

I lean down and place my lips on hers, licking the seam as she sighs against me.

"Goodbye," she whispers.

"Goodbye." I chuckle back.

I turn to walk back to my phone call.

"River," I say over my shoulder, and I hear the door open.

"Yes?" she says.

"Be at my apartment at seven p.m."

She doesn't respond. She knows better. I hear the squeak of the door opening and then closing.

"Sorry about that, man. Now, what were you saying?"

I sit back down at my desk and move to open my computer. Back to work for me.

A smile spreads across my face. Suddenly, work doesn't seem so bad.

CHAPTER THIRTY

River

G RAYSON AND I SPENT A LOT OF TIME TOGETHER, BUT WE are still not more, nor will we ever be. The thing is, getting to know him and making him smile is enough for me. With every day that goes by, I learn so much about him, and despite the front he puts on, he's pretty amazing.

Things are tricky this weekend, though. This weekend we are in the Hamptons again. More like I'm in the Hamptons, and I'm waiting on bated breath to see if he's coming out here to see me.

He said he's not.

But I don't believe him.

That's what he said last weekend, and he showed up.

One thing I do know is that Grayson is insatiable. He can't go a day without fucking me, so I wonder just when he will call, tell me he's here, and whisk me away for an impromptu romp in the sand again.

"Everything okay, River?" Kim asks as she walks across the patio.

"Umm, yeah. Why wouldn't it be?" I respond, lifting my gaze from my cell.

Still nothing.

No texts.

No calls.

Nothing.

"Because you are staring at your phone like your life depends on it," she answers matter-of-factly.

Shit.

I'm being obvious, and now she'll ask questions. Something I can't have.

"Just waiting for Sadie to call," I lie.

"Oh, she's in the Hamptons? Why didn't you have her stay with us?"

Fuck. Yeah, why, River?

Note to self: Next time you are going to lie, have a good excuse ready.

"Umm . . ." She rolls her hands for me to continue, so I do. "Because she is at the summer share house?"

"Are you asking? Or telling." She's too smart for her own good. And knows me far too well for this not to blow up in my face. I have to get out of here.

"Telling and as soon as she texts me—" And as if on cue, my phone vibrates, but it's obviously not really her. "Speak of the devil," I say, continuing the farce. "Got to run." I stand and head into the kitchen to grab the keys to the spare car I use when I'm here.

I'm not even sure where we are meeting.

Me: Where should I go?

Then Grayson fires off an address only a mile up the beach.

Odd.

Less than five minutes later, I'm pulling up to a large mansion. The type of home a celebrity would own.

The type of home a Price would own.

I park the car, and I see him standing on the edge of the

circular driveway, but not by the front door. No, instead, he's standing by the gate to the backyard.

Maybe he wants to swim?

I step out of the car and greet him. "Hi."

He leans down and places a chaste kiss on my lips, before taking me around back.

"Are we swimming? I didn't bring a bathing suit."

"We aren't going swimming." He smirks.

"Then where?"

He pulls me past the pool to a small house on the property.

"What is this place?"

"Guesthouse," he says. Swinging the door open, he pushes me up against the wall and kisses my neck.

"Wait. Stop." His lips halt their movement. "Whose house?"

"Mine."

Now I actually push him off me completely, the blood in my veins boiling. "You can't even fuck me in your own house? You need to fuck me in the guesthouse?" I hiss.

"It's not like that."

I place my hand on my hip, tapping my foot against the tile floor.

"It was my grandparents."

"And . . . why don't you stay in the main house?"

"I don't like to go inside," he mutters under his breath before storming out the door and onto the patio. I follow him, not sure what just happened.

I find him sitting on a lounge chair overlooking the pool. He won't look at me, so I sit beside him on the same chair.

"Talk to me. Why don't you go inside? Why don't you stay here?"

"My grandfather died in this house, and I was here."

My heart thuds rapidly at what he just said. I had no idea, and now looking at him, I want to ask more. Find out more. But without another word, I watch as Grayson strips off all his clothes and stalks toward the pool.

This conversation is obviously over. After dropping that bombshell, I'm not sure what to do, and when he gets closer to the pool, I'm not sure what he is doing either.

Then he dives in. The water slushes against the pavement beside the pool and waves surround where he is now submerged.

His head pops out of the water, the droplets of water in his hair glistening against the sunlight streaming down from above.

"Get in," he shouts to me.

"I still don't have a bathing suit," I say, raising an eyebrow, and his lip tips up into a smirk.

"And you still don't need one. Jax isn't here. No one is."

I look back at the house. The house Grayson refuses to stay in. It doesn't appear anyone is here, so I shimmy out of my clothes and walk to the shallow end.

Unlike Grayson, I don't dive in because I don't want to get my hair wet. Instead, I slowly walk in until the water covers my breasts. Grayson dives back under, and underneath the water, I can see him swimming toward me. He pops up at the exact moment, pulling me under with him into the deep end, and then he releases me.

Kicking my legs, I tread water, and then he reemerges. "Hey!" I shout. "I didn't want to get my hair wet."

He moves closer, and this time, he pulls me toward him, both of us treading water together now.

"I have never had sex in a pool before," I breathe out. He pulls me closer, his lips connected with mine.

"Then we are going to have to remedy that," he says between each swipe of his tongue.

And he does.

All day long.

———◦———

Now I'm back in the city, waiting and wondering when he's going to call to tell me the plans for the night.

When I get home, my phone rings, and I anxiously look at the phone to see what he says. He's pretty demanding when it comes to our dates.

Grayson: Bryant Park. 6pm.

Me: What?

Grayson: I'm stealing Kim's idea.

I scrunch my nose because I have no idea what he's talking about. So I do what anyone would do in this situation, I google it.

Bryant Park summer events.

Tons of articles pop up, but the one that stands out and reminds of something Kim would do is Movie Night. That has to be it, so I click on the link. Sure enough, I'm right. Apparently, every week during the summer, Bryant Park plays a Monday Night Movie. It seems, according to the articles I skim through, that in the center of the lawn, a large screen is erected, and a classical movie is played.

Me: Where should I meet you?

Grayson: Outside the Bryant Park Hotel.

Two hours later, I find him leaning against the wall of the Bryant Park Hotel. As soon as he sees me, he comes over and places a kiss on my lips. We walk across the street to the park. I can't help but smile to myself. This date is pretty perfect, and it hasn't even started yet.

If this is a date?

It has to be. Even though we said this was casual, movies are dates.

I'm so lost in my own thoughts that I don't notice that Grayson has stopped walking. I look up and realize he has found a clear spot in the grass. I also notice he has a basket with him.

How did I not see that?

Because you were too busy lusting over him. Grayson lays out a blanket, and then he pulls out a bottle of wine with two plastic cups. Cheese and grapes are next. For a man who doesn't date, he sure did put together quite the spread. "So how's work going? Do you like working with your dad?"

"Honestly?"

"Yes, of course. Honestly. I won't tell him."

"I hate it." I sigh.

"How come?"

"I always wanted to be boring and predictable . . ." I admit. "But working behind a desk is a whole other level when you work for your dad. So yeah, well, I kind of hate it."

He bursts out laughing, and I follow suit.

"So what do you like to do?"

"I don't know."

He lifts his hand and touches the bracelet on my wrist. "You made this, right?"

I nod.

"And this, too?" he asks as he touches the charm bracelet next.

"Yeah."

"And how did you feel when making it?"

"Well, I kind of love it."

He lifts his brow at me as if he's trying to tell me something.

I touch the necklace on my neck that I made, too. "You mean make jewelry? You think I should make jewelry? And what? Sell it?"

He shrugs. "Why not?"

"I-I . . ."

I don't know what to say. All I know is I can't do that. That's the kind of job Lily would tell me to do. "I can't." I take a gulp of my wine and turn my head toward the large projector screen.

The movie begins to play, and Grayson moves closer to me. Laying his hand gently on my thigh, he traces circles on my skin.

"I'll drop it for now."

I smile up at him, silently thanking him, and he leans forward to place a gentle kiss on my lips.

"For now. But I'm bringing it up again."

I nod, and then my eyes flutter closed, and I bask in his warmth. Our bodies are so close that I can feel his heat radiating off him and through me.

Opening my eyes, I peer up at him, and he drops a kiss to my lips.

Making tonight perfect.

———◆———

For the past few days, during my free time, I have studied the files I lifted off Larry's computer. Last night, around three in the morning, bleary-eyed and all, I finally found something.

So now back at work, eyes red from lack of sleep, I make my way into Larry's office. Closing the door behind me, Larry looks up.

"Do you think you can just barge into my room because your daddy owns the place?"

"No, but I found some discrepancies in the accounts and I figured I'd give you the opportunity to explain what happened before I burden my father with trying to figure it out."

My father has way too much going on for me to go to him with a few missing dollars, and I don't want to start trouble if there isn't any.

"You don't want to start trouble for me regardless of what you think you saw or heard."

Heard or saw?

What is he talking about?

But then something pops into my head . . .

The first day comes into my mind. Thoughts start to whirl around. What if it wasn't a mistake that Larry didn't catch? What if Larry was causing the mistake?

I need to bide my time and look into it but . . .

"Because I know about you," he says, and I whip my head up.

"Excuse me?"

"That's right, little girl. Your father might be blind, but I know about you and Daddy's friend. I wonder what your father would say if he knew you were having a secret affair with not only his business colleague but also someone he thinks of as family? Yes, that's how he explained him to me. The brother I never had. The brother he thought he lost. It's funny what a man will tell you when they're drunk at a party. Say, one at his beach house . . . at his daughter's birthday party." His lip tips up into a nasty smirk. "One with a laundry room right by the bathroom."

His words hover over me. I feel ill.

"You can't—"

"Tell him?" He smiles wider. "Don't worry, I won't. Just like you won't tell him this conversation happened."

I nod.

Not because I can't find my words, but because if I open my mouth, I will rip into him, and he'll know I'm not dropping this.

I school my features and leave.

When Grayson texts to make plans, I think about telling him what Larry said to me earlier, but when I read the text, I decide to not tell him yet.

Grayson: I'll pick you up at 4pm.

Me: For what?

Grayson: That trip I owe you.

There is no way I can tell him now. It will ruin the whole trip, and I'm too excited to do that. Hell, my hands even shake with my excitement. I know he said he would take me away, and I did win, after all, but I didn't actually expect him to.

I basically bounce around the office all day in my anticipation, but I have to be careful, or I run the risk that my dad will ask me what I'm doing this weekend. That is a question I can't answer. Another thing is . . .

I don't usually sleep over with Grayson. Normally, I duck out before he wakes. Going on a trip is pretty serious, and I can't afford to think this will be more.

Stop.

I can't micromanage this like I do everything in my life.

Just have fun.

Having fun doesn't mean you are like her.

Once the day is over, I hurry back to my apartment. I don't have a lot of time, and I still have to pack.

He hasn't told me where we are going, but since it's August, I can't imagine I will need any warm clothes, and since it's Grayson, I cannot imagine I'll need any clothes at all.

With not much time to spare, I pull out a few sundresses, a cardigan, and my jean jacket just in case there is a breeze at night.

Then I open the lingerie drawer. My lips spread into a smile as I pull out a few pieces I bought to show him but haven't had the right moment to.

This trip will be the perfect time.

"Where are you off to?" Sadie asks from her perch in my doorway. "Hamptons?"

"Actually . . ." I bite my lip. "I'm going away with Grayson."

"You are? Does this mean it's getting 'serious'?" She air quotes.

I shake my head.

"Then why are you going? Don't you think it will just make it harder when it eventually ends?"

"I'll be fine," I say, not sure if I'm lying to myself or her at the moment. In all reality, I usually have my heart tucked away like Fort Knox, but Grayson is different. He's always been different.

She lifts an eyebrow, basically calling me out on my shit.

"Seriously, I have it under control. I can handle it," I respond, and she lifts her arms in surrender.

"If you say so." She takes that moment to step closer and peer into my open suitcase. "Where are you going?"

"No clue actually."

"That should be fun." She eyes the piece of lingerie sitting on top and smirks. I laugh, and she giggles, too.

I'm bouncing off the walls by the time I receive the text telling me he's here. With a final wave to Sadie, I grab my bag and head out the door.

When I step outside, I see his car parked. I don't wait for him to get out before I'm heading over to the car and tapping on the window. He's just hanging up the phone as he rolls it down.

"Wait there, I'll grab your stuff."

"Just pop the trunk." He shakes his head, and I roll my eyes. "I'm a big girl. I can get my suitcase in the trunk." Again, he shakes his head, and then he throws open his door and heads over to where I'm standing.

Before I can object, he pulls me toward him and places his mouth on mine. I'm so shocked by the sudden movement and the public display of affection that my mouth opens. We kiss on the sidewalk for a moment before he pulls away with a smirk.

"What was that for?" I ask, my cheeks warming.

"I couldn't wait until we were alone, so I said fuck it."

I start to laugh, and he grabs my bag with one hand, as the other opens my door. I slip into the passenger side as he places my bag in the trunk.

"Where are you taking me?"

"Wouldn't you like to know?" He laughs, and I swear I will never get used to this magnificent sound. Screw waves breaking on the shore. This is the sound that lulls me into tranquility.

It makes my body grow hot, and butterflies erupt in my stomach.

"I would, but since you suck, I'll just sit here and try to guess."

"Suit yourself," he responds, and I fasten my seat belt as he pulls away from the curb.

"Is it drivable?"

A grin tugs at his lips. "No."

"Are we taking a plane?"

"No."

"Are we staying in the city?"

"Jeez, River, can you let there be any surprises?"

"Umm, hello. Maine. Lobster. That was a surprise."

"True." He smirks but doesn't say more.

I shake my head at him. "So that's it. Nothing else? No more details?"

"Nope."

When I go to say more, he reaches his hand across the console to stop me from asking more questions. I turn my face toward him, and even though he's facing forward, I can see a small smile lining his cheeks.

I let out an overdramatic sigh. "Fine." My comment is rewarded with a squeeze of the hand, and I can't help when my lips split into a smile as well.

We continue to drive, and then we are pulling off toward the pier.

The pier where they keep boats.

"Are we sailing?"

Nothing.

Crickets.

We weave our way closer and closer, and before I know it, we are pulling up to where the yachts are docked.

"A yacht. We are going on a yacht?"

"We are. And wasn't it so much more fun not knowing?" He smirks. "Come on."

Grayson steps out of the car, and I follow suit, and before I know it, he's leading me to a sleek white yacht. It's huge and gorgeous, and I can't wait to go on board.

Together, we make our way down the dock to where the boat is tethered.

"Hello, Mr. Price. Lovely to see you again. Hello, Ms. Reed," says the man standing in front of me. "I'm Nigel, the head steward. You can leave the bags right here, and we will have them unpacked and placed in your cabin."

"Thank you, Nigel," Grayson says as he takes my hand and leads me aboard.

My breath leaves my body "Is this yours?" I say in awe.

"It's owned by Price Enterprise."

"So, yours," I quip.

"Ding, ding, ding. Come on, let me show you around."

For the next ten minutes, he gives me a tour, and by the time we're on the aft deck with glasses of champagne in hand, my head is spinning with excitement.

"Cheers," he says.

"To what?"

"To enjoying the present." The toast is ominous, and normally, I would try to nitpick its meaning, but here on this boat, with the perfect sunset on the horizon, I just enjoy the moment.

Together, drinking champagne, we look at the dark blue water and the pink skies and sit in silence as the boat makes its way out to sea.

Once we've finished our drinks, he stands, taking my hand in his, and leads me back into the boat. We walk down a hall, and then he pushes open a door. We aren't even inside before his mouth is on mine.

Lifting me into his arms, he walks me toward the bed. He

places me down in front of it, and then he makes quick work of removing our clothes.

Once naked, he's pushing me down and hovers above me.

A shudder runs through my body as I feel him separate my legs and fit himself between them.

The look in his eyes is wild, and I want to grip his waist and pull him into me, but I don't. I allow him to watch me with those hungry eyes. Like a predator stalking his prey.

And I wait desperately for him to pounce.

It feels like time stands still as I wait. But then he aligns himself with my core.

Every part of my body quivers with anticipation. Finally, I feel him brush against my entrance, and I lift my pelvis.

Our eyes lock. And then and only then does he slowly push inside me. It feels too good; as though I'm complete once he's fully engulfed in my heat.

His hands reach to cups my face, and as he starts to thrust, he peers into my eyes.

He moves inside me, never breaking our stare.

Over and over again.

Deeper and deeper.

But he never pulls his gaze away.

Not once.

Not as I cling to him.

Not as I scream my release.

Not as he reaches his own climax.

He never looks away.

Once we are both spent, we lie panting, catching our own breaths. His heart beats erratically against my own.

This feels different, and the thought of what it might mean scares me. My brain is running a mile a minute, but he kisses my lips and then lifts off my body, breaking the connection and ending my wayward thoughts.

He stands from the bed and enters what must be the bathroom. He comes back a moment later with a towel.

"You hungry?" He smiles.

"Always," I respond.

———◦———

The next morning arrives too fast. I don't think I have ever slept better in my life. I'm not sure if it was the rocking of the yacht, or being in Grayson's arms, but I could get used to this.

We spend the early part of the day walking around Cape Cod. Hand in hand, we maneuver our way through the streets, going from boutique to boutique. After we shop for a bit, Grayson pulls me through an alleyway that opens into a bustling market.

"What is this?" I ask.

"Farmer's market?" he responds. "Want to go in?"

I nod with excitement. Together, we look at each table set up along the street. Some have food, some knickknacks, but the one that gets me excited is the one that is set up with fabric.

"Do you like it?" Spencer asks, stepping up behind me. My eyes are wide, and my smile wider.

"I love it."

I start to touch each piece of fabric, imagining what I can make. When I get to the leathers, I'm practically jumping up and down. There are so many colors and lengths, I imagine a choker I can make with one that's silver. I would just need to find the right stone to wrap in metal.

"I like to see you happy," he says against the shell of my

ear. The warmth from his lips teases me as he speaks, causing my heart to pound erratically at the sensation.

"Thank you for taking me here," I say, turning my head over my shoulder so I can see his eyes.

His arm snakes around my waist, and then he presses his mouth to mine. "Anything for you," he says between kisses, and I know he means it.

After a few more pecks on my mouth, he pulls away and reaches his hand out. "What are we buying?" he asks, taking a few pieces of leather in his hand.

"Me, not we," I answer.

He shakes his head and proceeds to lift a brow. "You aren't paying."

"Gray—"

"Don't Gray me," he says, reaching out and taking my hand in his. He lifts and kisses my knuckles. "I want to do this for you. Seeing you smile and watching the wheels turn in your brain makes me happy, and I want to be a part of this. Please."

His words do funny things to my heart, and I find it hard to respond.

"Thank you." He drops my hand and grabs even more material, enough for me to make a ton of new cuffs and necklaces. Once he has all that he's going to buy, he walks to the register and pays.

A warm feeling spreads through my chest. I can't remember the last time I was this happy, and that scares me.

Because from what I have learned in the past . . .

Nothing good stays.

CHAPTER THIRTY-ONE

River

WHOEVER SAID TIME FLIES WHEN YOU'RE HAVING FUN knew what they were talking about. The summer is almost over, and I can't believe how fast it passed. I've been with Grayson every waking moment since we came back from the trip.

"Come on, we're going to be late," he says against my skin.

"Where can we possibly have to go at . . . ?" I open my eyes and look over at the clock next to his bed. "What time is it? That can't be right." I rub at my eyes. "No way is it seven a.m."

"It is."

"Who wakes someone up at seven a.m. on a weekend?" I cover my face with the sheet. "I'm going back to sleep."

"Like hell you are. We have an appointment."

When I don't answer him, I feel a tug, and then the bedding covering my naked body is ripped away from me.

Now naked in his bed, I open my eyes slightly and see Grayson staring at me with a robe in his hands.

"Do you mind?" I say as I stand, taking the robe and making my way into the bathroom.

"And you call me grumpy," he says, and I turn over my shoulder and give him my best death stare.

"You're grumpy all the time. I'm only grumpy when I wake up."

"Is that why you never sleep over?" he asks.

My stomach twists at his words even though that's not the reason. The reason is so much worse than a bad mood. Old feelings and deep-seated insecurities of people leaving me start to gnaw at me.

I'm not sure how to answer, so instead, with my tongue weighed down with my reasons, I nod my head and turn back to the bathroom.

"I'll make breakfast as you shower. Don't take too long."

With a salute, I close the door behind me to do my morning rituals.

It can't be more than fifteen minutes later that I'm in the robe Grayson provided and padding my way into the kitchen.

In front of me are the fluffiest pancakes I have ever seen.

"You cooked?"

"What did you think I meant when I said I'd make breakfast?"

"I guess I assumed you would toast a bagel."

"Shit, I could have just done that and still impressed you?" He laughs, and I love the sound. I didn't realize how much I wanted to hear it until I heard him laugh with my dad. Now months later, to know that I have brought this man happiness . . . Well, it does silly things to my heart.

I had set out to go against my better nature and let him in—to give him parts of myself I don't normally give—and seeing him smile and laugh proves I can be that carefree River I was with my mom with him too.

"I'd be impressed no matter what you do."

He smiles at my comment and then motions down at my plate. "No more talking, eat." He winks as if he's joking, but I know it's just as hard for him to let me in as it is for me to let him in.

Lifting my fork, I take a large bite. It's so good, and since I'm famished, I eat it in record-breaking time.

"You ate that fast," he notices.

"I was hungry."

"I'll say. Well, now that we're done, I'll grab a T-shirt you can wear with your jeans from yesterday, and we can head out."

"That's okay to wear to the appointment?"

"You'll see."

Thirty minutes later, Grayson is weaving in and out through city traffic. We're in the Village again, not too far from where we had brunch when he pulls over to what looks like a small abandoned storefront among a bunch of small boutiques.

He parks the car and then turns to look at me. "I'll show you." Then he's out, and I'm getting out too.

We walk over to the abandoned building, and Grayson opens the door.

Inside, it's empty except for a few pieces of furniture. A glass display case is what I notice; it's made of stainless steel with what seems to be a barbed wire design on the legs.

"What is this place?"

"I own it." I tilt my head and shake it, not understanding. "Well, my company owns it. It was recently used as a jewelry store." He points at the case. "You wouldn't have to keep that if you didn't want to."

"What are you saying?" I ask, still staring at him. I'm starting to have an inkling of what he's implying, but he needs to spell it out for me.

"If you want it, it's yours."

"For what?"

"To sell your jewelry."

My mouth must drop open because he couldn't possibly have said that. "You want me to open a jewelry store?"

He walks over to me and takes my hand in his, his fingertips tracing the charm bracelet on my wrist.

"I do. Tell me about this bracelet?"

"Why?" I whisper back.

"Because it's important to you, so it's important to me."

I close my eyes. When I open them, Grayson is staring at me, imploring with his green eyes for me to trust him with this story.

So right here, in the store he hopes I'll take, I do.

"I know I told you about my time when I lived with my mom . . . This piece, I made with her. It was right before I came to live with my dad. She helped me create it, and then said, we would make a charm for every city, every country we travel to." I lift my wrist and shake it, the metal rattling with the movement.

"Are they all the cities you traveled to with her?" he asks.

"All the important ones."

I can feel his fingers touch the charm from last year but he never takes his gaze off mine.

"I think you should sell your pieces, they are beautiful and they are part of you. Let me help you."

"I don't . . . I couldn't."

"You don't have to say yes now. I just want you to think about it and know it's here." My heart starts to beat rapidly in my chest. "River, you have talent. It would be a waste for you not to use it."

"You can't give me a store," I say.

He lifts his finger and touches my lip.

The intimate move makes me feel exposed. His gesture is life-changing and more than I could ever hope for. He sees me.

The real me.

He sees my passion and love and wants me to cherish it.

I should say yes; I should throw my arms around him and say yes.

His gesture means more than anything he could ever know. But a part of me doesn't know if I can. I started this because of my mom, but I'm not sure if I can continue it. Wouldn't that make me like her?

A hopeless romantic.

Taking something that's not mine to take.

She took a baby from my dad, a man she would never be with.

And I'll what? I'll take a store.

No.

Eventually, I'll say no.

I have to. No matter how much these mean to me, I can't be like her.

Not now.

Not ever.

CHAPTER THIRTY-TWO

Grayson

DAYS HAVE BECOME WEEKS, AND SUMMER IS NOW OVER. I'm happy about the possibility of no longer having to go out east.

But since the weather is still nice, you might have to.

I turn to River, who's walking beside me. Once again, like every day this week, we both grab coffees and walk in the park together.

We have become more brazen about being seen in public, but that's only because we know Tyler and Kim are in the Hamptons.

Another reason I hate going out there.

Not only are there enough memories to suffocate me, but we also have to hide. I hate hiding.

"Are you going out east this weekend?" I ask.

"I assume," she responds. "Why? Do you have other plans?"

"Yes."

She stops walking, so I stop as well. "And what, pray tell, are your other plans?" Her eyebrow lifts.

"Keeping you locked up in my apartment all weekend." I chuckle.

"We cannot stay indoors all weekend."

I let out a long groan. "I really don't want to go back to my grandparents' old house."

"Then tell my dad you are staying with us."

Now I'm the one to lift an eyebrow. "Because that's not obvious . . ." I trail off for emphasis. "The only thing more obvious would be if I kissed you in front of him."

"So then why don't you?" she says nonchalantly as if that's even a possibility.

Or is it?

I care for River.

But to come out to her parents?

Could we talk to them, and better yet, do I want to?

It would certainly make my life easier, but at what cost?

It's not like we can be together. I mean, River knows no matter what I feel I don't want a relationship with her. I won't fall in love. There is no happily ever after for me.

But at the same time, I like spending time with her.

Maybe we could say we are friends.

I'll have to think about it, but not now. Today is too nice a day to deal with daunting tasks like thinking about the future.

I'm always plagued by the notion of my impending doom. I just want one day when nothing plagues me, and I can just enjoy being with her, even if it's a false reality.

Even if it's fleeting.

We continue to walk through Central Park, passing people playing Frisbee.

At some point, we take a seat on the grass and just be.

It's amazing.

"What are you thinking about over there?" she asks from where she's resting on my shoulder.

"How perfect this is," I say.

"It really is." Her voice is whimsical as she speaks. A soft and content smile lining her face.

"What about you? What are you thinking about?"

"I was thinking just how much I love to people watch." She tilts her head to a couple a few feet away, and then whispers, "What do you think their story is?"

"I really don't know."

"Come on, that's not fun. Tell me what you see?" she asks, and I shake my head because I can't come with up anything. "Fine." She sighs. "You're no fun. Here's what I see. He's a foreign diplomat, traveling abroad to do business for his country, and she is the maid at the consulate. They are having a torrid love affair," she says with all seriousness.

"That's ridiculous."

"Then you tell me what's going on over there?" she says, tilting her head back to look into my eyes.

Her eyes sparkle with delight, and I realize I love this look in her eyes. "Fine, I'll play along." I look toward the couple. They are talking fiercely but not in argument. Passionately. "They are having an affair," I say. "That's why they are arguing. They are in love, but she won't leave her husband."

"You think that's it?"

I ponder this theory.

"Maybe you're wrong. Maybe he won't leave his wife, and she's scared. Scared to make the big sacrifice and then end up alone."

Suddenly, I realize we are no longer talking about that couple. We might be outside, but it feels like the imaginary walls of the park are closing in on me.

"There," I say, pointing at a group of men playing Frisbee. "They're talking about the girl they triple-teamed last night," I say in jest, but it does the trick when she laughs. A sound I will never grow tired of.

"Do you think it was an RH?" she asks.

"What the hell is an RH?" I respond.

"Reverse harem. Basically, they all love and date and satisfy one girl's needs." She blushes as she says it.

"Reverse harem sounds awful," I respond.

"Why is that?"

"Because then you have to share, and I don't share." My words come out deeper than I intended, but if she notices, she pretends she doesn't. Instead, she points at another group and starts the game all over again.

But the day is perfect, almost too good to be real.

A series of screams and sirens in the distance changes things in an instant. When we turn the corner, leaving the park, I see it.

A middle-aged woman, probably in her late forties, screams for help.

On the ground is a man . . . and beside him, a younger man doing chest compressions.

"Help him," she screams, and someone holding her coos that the ambulance is coming. I hear it. It's quickly approaching.

My heart starts to race as I am mentally pushed back to a time when I was leaning over a body, and I was the one trying to save a life.

But life is fleeting, and I wasn't able to save him. I wasn't able to save my grandfather or my father.

They both died.

I look over at River, her eyes lined with tears. She would never be able to handle me leaving.

It wouldn't be fair.

It might be sunny, but a black cloud has fallen over us. I can feel it hovering. River doesn't know it yet, but our time has always been limited, and the grains of sand are running out.

CHAPTER THIRTY-THREE

River

GRAYSON AND I ARE AT A STANDSTILL NOW. NO MATTER how much I repeated it to myself that it was on my terms, that we were just sex buddies, that I was in control, I honestly thought after this summer we would be more.

But weeks have passed, and nothing has changed. Actually, he's been growing distant now that I think about it.

I know we have no future. It's only a matter of time.

I just thought we had more time.

The thing is, I know he's been busy the past few days. So maybe that's why he seems distant too.

I tend to be overdramatic and irrational, so I try my hardest to rein in my emotions and tell myself my brain is just being overdramatic.

I'll see him tonight, and then I'll know where we're at. As if by some cosmic tragedy, I open the Internet browser on my phone to the society pages of the New Yorker. There he is in his glory.

Standing with his sister at a fundraiser.

My stomach plummets as I realize he was there last night. This is the reason he didn't call. He was out being a "Price" in public. I look for Jax in the background, but then I remember he's out of town.

Probably another reason I had no idea about this event. Grayson probably thought I wouldn't even know about it.

That thought doesn't sit well with me.

It just reiterates to me that if I'm going to act, I need to act soon. I can't let myself grow any more attached to his company.

I scroll down to the next image, and I see him in a picture with a busty brunette. She is the polar opposite of me.

Fake.

She's dripping in diamonds, and she appears to be in her mid-thirties.

She's closer to his age, and a better fit for him for sure.

Maybe this is the real reason for his distance.

Maybe he wants to be with someone closer to his age and social standing in society.

I can't jump to conclusions, though, not without asking him. Without second-guessing myself, I send him a text.

Me: Are you busy?

Grayson: Yeah.

His one-word answer gives me pause. Is he with her right now? Did she sleep over . . . something I won't do?

Is he replacing me with her?

My brain formulates crazy stories about their love affair. Even though I know it's just one picture and probably meant nothing, I can't help the stories my imagination is weaving.

Me: Can I come over later?

Grayson: Yes

I can't shake the feeling he's hiding something, and I won-der if this is the moment. Tonight. The moment I leave. Because, for once, I won't let someone leave me. I will leave them before they can hurt me.

The thought is sobering, and I feel the pain all the way through my bones. The fear of what tonight will bring lingers throughout the day, a nervous energy coursing through me.

I try to stay distracted by creating new pieces of jewelry. Today, I twist metal. I hang it from a leather band Grayson had bought me and make it into the length of a choker.

While in the zone, I had created a broken heart without realizing it. This whole time, I have deluded myself into thinking I could separate my emotions from sex. Although I've loved a part of Grayson since I was twelve, I could hold back a part of myself and not fall in love.

But looking at this piece, I understand how stupid I was. It's too late. No matter what the outcome is tonight, I have already given my whole heart to Grayson Price.

Hours later, I show up at his apartment. I said I'd be here at 8:00 p.m., but I'm a few minutes early. The doorman knows me now, so I just nod and head to the private elevator.

When I walk in, he's not in the living room or the kitchen.

I continue my path to the bedroom. When I'm there, I can hear the shower running, and the steam filters in through the open cracks in the door. From the corner of my eye, I see his phone sitting on the bedside counter. Before I can think twice, I'm stalking toward it and pick it up.

I know what I'm about to do is wrong, but I can't find the strength to stop myself.

I'm surprised it's not locked when I touch the screen, but maybe he was just on it, and that's why.

Pressing the button to see his last call, it shows a bunch of numbers I don't know.

This isn't going to answer any of my questions. The man is super busy and must get a million phone calls a day.

Maybe his email will tell me more. I'm about to hit the icon when I hear his voice.

"What are you doing?"

I drop the phone. A crashing sound echoes around us for what I just did. I was snooping, and worse, I got caught.

"I-I," I stutter. What can I say? There's no excuse I can offer up. Not when I'm basically caught with my hands in the cookie jar or, in this case, on his phone. He steps closer, and that's when I realize what he's wearing. Nothing. Well, that's not true. He's wearing a towel. It's slung low on his hips, and little drops of water trickle down his chest, over his abs, and down to the V that dips low beneath the fabric.

Subconsciously, I lick my lips, expecting him to be angry. Maybe yell. Maybe throw me out. But what he does shocks me more. His lips tip up into a seductive smirk, and he comes closer. Each step he takes makes me shake, more and more.

I'm not afraid of him. Not really. That's not the reason I shake. I shake from the anticipation.

"What were you doing, River?" He takes another step.

"Looking at your phone," I whisper, barely audible.

Closer.

"And what were you expecting to find?"

Closer.

"Why?" I squeak.

He's here now. Standing directly in front of me.

"Why what?"

"Why you haven't called," I admit, hating myself for being so weak. Hating myself for letting my emotions get too far.

I have always cared about Grayson.

Ever since the first time we met all those years ago, but now I let my emotions get in the way of things. It's one thing to care; it's another thing to hope.

"And you think you'll find it there?"

I look down, ashamed.

"Did you think you'd find texts?"

Nothing from me.

"Did you think you'd find another woman?"

I can't take this. I don't move.

He steps in, his body pressed against me, my legs hitting the foot of the bed.

"You won't find anything," he says. "And do you know why?"

I shake my head.

"Because there is nothing to find. Want to take a guess at the reason?"

Again, I shake my head, this time dropping my head. He doesn't let me, though. Instead, he cups my jaw and makes me look at him.

"Because all I want is you. All I see is you. I'm obsessed with you." His words are rough, abrasive. He hates himself for it. I can tell by the way he grabs me roughly and throws me down on his bed. Then he's on me, pouncing and kissing me, telling me with his mouth, with his tongue, and with his teeth just how much he hates that he wants me. The towel falls away from his body. My dress is lifted and then somehow the lace that separates us is gone. Before I can think or breathe or anything, he's in me.

Pressing, thrusting, fucking.

It's angry.

It's desperate.

It's hate and something else all rolled into one.

It's obsession.

I kiss him back with the same intensity. Giving everything I have.

Telling him I hate myself, too, because I might have always

loved Grayson Price, but now this feeling I have is so much more.

We cling and claw. We fight for possession over each other.

"Come," he shouts, demanding it of me. He won't come until I do. I'm almost there; so close I can taste it.

"Need more," I plead. "Harder."

And he answers my pleas by fucking me so hard and in such a primal way that I'll have bruises. But I don't care. I welcome the pain.

I welcome the feeling.

He reaches his hand between us and rubs me faster as he fucks me harder. His tempo increases, the friction of his finger matching the beat, and then I feel it.

I feel the burning inside me.

I feel the rise and fall.

I feel everything.

I come undone.

I come undone with tears in my eyes, and then he comes. Deep inside with no barriers between us.

Just us.

Feeling.

CHAPTER THIRTY-FOUR

Grayson

I INHALE DEEPLY INTO HER NECK.

What the fuck was that?

Our bodies are still joined together. Our hearts still beating as one.

In my life, I have never experienced anything like that. The need to brand her as mine was all-consuming. The fact she thought there was someone else infuriated me.

I stopped thinking rational thoughts at that point. I needed to show her without a measure of a doubt that she was all that mattered, that she all I saw.

I needed to possess her. Now as I come down from my high, a high only River can give me, I realize how rough I was. But how could she ever think there was anyone else? That's why I stayed away. Not because of another woman, but because I realized there would never *be* another woman.

The thought scared me. I'm not scared of much, but this, falling for River, scares the fuck out of me.

I needed space because the truth is, I can't be with her. No matter how I feel, I can't.

She's so young.

Too young.

If something were to happen to me, like my father and my grandfather before him, she'd be devastated.

I love River too much for that.

Love.

I love River.

How the hell has this happened? I tried to be careful by keeping her at bay and not letting her in. But shit, it happened anyway. Each time I tried to push up my walls, she pushed them back down. Each time I tried to keep my feelings out, to keep myself leveled, she pushed her way in.

But how?

She made you smile.

Laugh.

Feel.

She made you feel so goddamn much, how could you not fall in love with her?

Shit. Shit. Shit.

Is the room hot? Warmth spreads across my skin as though my body is on fire and I'm being burned from the inside out.

I can't breathe.

My chest feels like it's caving in. Painfully. Like I'm suffocating.

I pull out of River and sit up fast.

She looks up at me. Her eyes look hazy from her orgasm, but then she sees my face, and her brows knit together.

"Are you okay?" she asks.

I stand.

"I need air," I say, pushing away from the bed and stalking out of my room.

I walk straight to the fridge and open the door. The cold air hits my face, but it doesn't cool me fast enough. It doesn't shut out the voice. The one telling me it has to end.

The one saying you fucked up.

You fell for the one person you shouldn't.

I made a promise a long time ago never to fall in love.

Never to marry.

I made a promise to stay single and alone.

And then River happened.

All I want to do is be with her—kiss her, feel her, and love her.

I'm not sure how much time passes, or how long I stand in my kitchen buck-ass naked in front of the fridge, but eventually, I hear the telltale signs I'm not going to be alone for long. In the distance, I hear the pitter-patter of her feet.

I don't turn toward her. Not as she approaches, the steps getting closer and closer and River's fragrance permeating the air. I don't move.

I don't move when she's directly behind me.

And I don't move when she touches my back.

My lungs expand and deflate.

Waiting.

For what?

Clarity?

Or maybe for her to speak.

And then she does.

She speaks, and I'm not ready for what she has to say.

"Grayson . . ." She pauses, and I imagine from behind me she worries her lips. "I don't think this is working," she says, and I want to turn around and ask her why. I want to see if I hurt her. If she hates me for the way I just treated her.

I don't, though.

I'm too much of a pussy to turn and look into her eyes. Because I'm afraid I'll tell her I'm sorry and beg her to stay.

If I see her, I'll drop to my knees and tell her I love her . . .

So I can't. Instead, I focus my eyes on the jars in front of me. I study the line of the bottle, the color of the label.

I might be a selfish prick, but I'm not selfish enough to condemn her to my mother's fate. To condemn her to a lifetime alone.

"I'm going to leave," she says.

Still no words leave my mouth.

I don't trust myself.

"Goodbye, Grayson."

Silence.

I can feel the loss of her presence immediately as she leaves the room. In the distance, I can hear the faint sound of her getting dressed.

Red.

That's the color of the label with silver lines . . .

Script writing.

French words.

The elevator opens.

Then closes.

And I grab the bottle.

I grab the bottle and throw it. It hits the elevator doors, shattering on the floor. Blood red liquid pools in the spot where she just was.

It feels like a part of me lies on the floor. Like my heart was ripped out and is bleeding all over my marble.

And I do believe it is.

CHAPTER THIRTY-FIVE

River

I HAD TO DO IT.

I had no choice. I instantly knew something was wrong. Without a measure of a doubt, I knew our expiration date had come.

I couldn't let him leave me, so I did the only thing to save myself.

I left first.

On my terms.

It hurt that he wouldn't look at me, but now in the safe confines of the cab on the way back to my apartment, I know it was for the best. If I had looked into his eyes, I never would've had the strength, and if he had objected, I'd be in his bed now, but what would tomorrow bring?

I always knew this wouldn't last; I'd just hoped I had more time.

Back at my apartment, I let myself cry. I let myself feel all the emotions I need to feel.

I bury my head into my pillow, fresh tears splashing on the silk. Even though I knew this day was coming, I let myself believe. Now, I can't help the onslaught of emotions pouring off me. They hemorrhage from my body in waves.

Like a dam bursting.

Like a free-flowing river.

I can't control them. Nor can I stop them.

Instead, I let them expel from my soul. My sobs the only noise in the otherwise quiet apartment.

Reaching my hand out, I swipe the tears across my face. The moisture collects on my fingertips before I wipe them on the bedding. That's when I hear the creak of my bedroom door, and Sadie steps into my room and sits on my bed. I haven't told her what happened, but it wouldn't take a rocket scientist to know.

"It's going to be okay," she says, and I feel her hand reach out to grab mine. It feels good to have her here and comforting me.

"Thank you," I whisper.

"For what?"

"For being my friend."

"Always."

We sit in silence for a few more minutes, and when my tears stop, I look up at her. "I don't know what to do now?"

"What do you mean?"

"With Gray . . . I don't want to see him, and he's still working with my dad."

"Tell your dad you need to get ready for school."

Yeah, that's what I'll do. But then I think about the fact that I never finished looking over the books. I still haven't found what I need to help him.

But that's something I can work on at home.

If I'm not at the office, I'll have more time to go through the files.

Yes, this is exactly what I'll do. Kill two birds with one stone. I won't have to see Grayson, and I can dedicate my time to figuring out what's going on with his finances.

CHAPTER THIRTY-SIX

Grayson

I DON'T WANT TO BE IN THE OFFICE TODAY.

It's been two weeks. Two weeks since I let River walk out of my life.

The empty feeling inside me won't dissipate, and any distractions haven't worked. Not for my lack of trying.

Running, which usually helps, doesn't anymore. The gym bores me to death. My normal activities to keep my mind preoccupied no longer work.

All I can think about is her.

Will I ever see her again?

I'm lost in my endless train of thought when the door to my office opens. I'm not surprised to see Jax standing in front of me. He always makes it a habit to pop in when his presence isn't welcome.

"Get out," I say as he enters and closes the door.

"If you are so miserable, then why don't you get back together with her?" he says.

As if I'm the one who dumped her. I mean, sure, I was planning to, but she beat me to it.

"You have no idea what you are talking about," I answer.

"So why don't you tell me?"

I lift my hands and cover my face. "Get out."

"Tell me. It's been two weeks. You have been a fucking

dick to everyone in the office. I don't normally give a shit about your behavior, but Addy would care. And seeing as she is not here to slap some sense into you, I feel I must step up to the job."

"Look at you, taking work seriously," I chastise.

"Spit it out, or I'll call our sister and tell her half our staff is planning to quit because you're being an even bigger prick than normal."

"Oh, shut up. I'm not that bad."

Or am I?

"You made Nicole cry yesterday."

Apparently, I am.

"Shit," I mutter under my breath.

He nods. "Yeah, shit. So talk, tell me what's going on. Because if you don't, I'm just going to hack into your shit and find out anyway. This would be so much easier."

"She dumped me," I admit on a sigh.

His eyes open wide, and his mouth actually hangs open. "Really?"

"Yes, dick."

"I-I don't even know what to say . . ." He shakes his head. "I mean, I was so sure." He stops talking and just looks confused.

"Sure of what?"

"Nothing," he answers. "Obviously, you did something. So what was it? Was it your winning personality? Went back to being an ogre?"

"Shut up, and nope. Nothing." Only fucked her and then left her . . .

"Do you think she'd take you back?" he asks.

"Never going to happen. The truth is, she did me a huge

favor. I was planning on ending it with her anyway, so at least I'm not the villain now."

"Oh." He stands there perplexed as if he has no idea what happened. Kind of like how I stood in front of the fridge all those days ago.

"What did you want?" I ask because obviously he came in here for a reason. That's when I notice he's holding a manila file. "What is that?" I ask, pointing at what he's holding.

He looks down at his hand as if he's just now remembering that he is holding something. "Forget it. It's moot now. I'll handle it," he says.

"What are you talking about?" I ask because there is no way I believe that folder doesn't concern me in some way or another. Why else would he be in here with it?

"It's about River."

That makes me jerk my eyes up.

"Give it to me," I say, my voice forceful.

Reluctantly, he hands over the file, and I all but rip it out of his hand. Flinging it on my desk, I start to read the information Jax has gathered.

This is about River's mother.

Phone records.

Credit card information. Which it seems she hasn't used in quite some time. Pages and pages of details.

Then I reach a page about medical records.

My eyes go wide.

This is dated almost nine years ago.

The summer River's mom dropped her off at her father's.

River's mom didn't just disappear to party. She didn't leave her kid because she wanted to have a good time. No. Not at all. Far from it. River's mom left because she was sick.

And from the looks of these records, very sick.

Then I turn the page and see the last piece of the puzzle clicking into place.

A small medical center on an island in the Caribbean.

Within a day of locating River's mom, I'm on a plane to the small medical center.

When we land, I expect to be brought to a major city, but instead, I'm brought to a small run-down building on the beach. The closer I get I notice it's more like a hut.

What the hell is this place?

I step inside and find myself in the main lobby. It's actually larger than it appears from the outside.

In my suit, I'm out of place. People look at me like I made the wrong stop, and maybe I have, but I won't know until I ask.

That's when I notice a young blonde sitting behind the desk.

I walk over.

"Hello," she says in a what seems to be a Boston accent. She looks to be River's age, maybe a little older.

"What is this place?"

"This is a free medical clinic for the village. We provide healthcare to locals who can't afford to go into the city."

"I'm looking for an American, late thirties."

"Oh yes, Rain."

I shake my head. "Her name is Lily Pad."

"We only have one American here. Follow me."

I do. We walk into a room, and there, lying on the cot, is a woman about my age with what would be sun-kissed locks, but instead, they appear matted and dirty.

I take a step closer.

Her eyes are closed, but then they start to flutter. Eyes I would know anywhere stare back at me. This is River's mom.

I stare at the woman in the bed, the woman so fragile and small if I didn't know what I was looking for, I wouldn't know it was her . . .

But the eyes.

Those eyes are the same ones that haunt my dreams.

She looks at me but has no recollection. Back when we were in high school, we only met once, so I don't expect her to know me. But she doesn't even move with me standing here. She just stares at me.

"Why is she here?" I ask. Even though I'm pretty sure I know the answer.

"The patient was found unresponsive and was brought in."

I nod and start to walk away. My hands are fisted at my sides.

She looks like she's knocking on death's door. I need to get her out of here. They are not equipped to treat her here.

Picking up my phone, I order my jet to be ready and fueled. "I'm going to need to take her to a hospital."

"You can't do that, sir. She's unwell."

"With all due respect, I know she's unwell. But I also know that this woman was in remission from cancer . . . by looking at her, I'd have reason to believe that she very well might be sick again."

Her mouth drops open, and she doesn't know what to say.

"Rain never mentioned—"

"Her name is not even Rain, so it doesn't surprise me she hasn't mentioned her previous illness," I hiss back.

The woman shuts her mouth.

"Now tell me, do you have an ambulance?"

She shakes her head, and I pick up the phone and call my assistant, telling her everything I need. Not only will I need my plane, but I'll also need a full medical team and equipment for transport.

And in my usual way, I give her a tight budget to accomplish these goals, but money talks, and I have enough to make this happen.

Hours pass, but in the end, I got everything I needed to transport her off the island and back to New York.

I'm fucking tired.

Beat.

But I don't think about that. Inside, I spend my time figuring out how I'm going to tell River.

I'll wait until I hear from the doctors before I do.

Only then will I know what to say.

She's responsive and awake.

She's also in a private room and at a world-renowned cancer treatment center in Manhattan. I might have pulled a few strings. It pays to be a donor, apparently. Luckily, she is awake enough to allow me to sit in when her doctors come to talk to her and tell her that not only has her cancer returned but also that it's worse this time.

Much worse. I know it's time I tell River. But my heart aches at the knowledge I'll have to bring.

There is no choice, though. I pick up my phone and dial her number. She doesn't answer, so I scroll to someone else who can help.

"How bad is it?" Jax asks.

"Bad." It's really bad. The thought of telling River has my heart tightening in my chest.

"Have you told her yet?"

"I'm about to . . ."

"But?"

"How did you know there was a but?"

"There is always a but, or you wouldn't call me."

"That's not true."

"It is, Grayson. You're a selfish prick, but it's okay, I love you anyway. So what do you need from me?"

"I need you to track her phone and tell me where she is," I admit.

"No problem, man."

"Thanks," I say, before hanging up and heading back over to sit with River's mother.

"I'm going to tell her."

Her mouth opens and then shuts.

"I know you wanted to protect her, but it's time she knows. I won't keep this secret from her," I say.

She nods, then closes her eyes.

She's asleep within seconds.

I must fall asleep too in the chair because I wake to my phone vibrating in my pocket.

It's a text from Jax.

Jax: Hamptons.

Me: Appreciate it.

And I meant it. I haven't always been the best brother. To be honest, I've pretty much been a piss-poor one. At least to Jax. I need to start being better about appreciating him.

One thing I have learned from looking at River's mom is that life is fleeting. It can slip away in a minute, but that doesn't mean you give up.

Looking at her mother in the bed, I realized that.

She had given up.

The moment she realized her cancer might be back, she had abandoned River.

I see that now.

She was ready to die alone on that island. Even if I do die young, I don't want to die alone. I want to live for the years that I have and cherish them. It might not be with River, but she deserves the choice.

And as for my brother, I'm done being a dick.

He has shown me over and over again that even though he is a smart-ass, he has my best interests at heart.

It's time I return the favor. I always knew Dad would want me to take care of my family. But I always assumed it meant money, jobs, and the business.

Now seeing River's mom and seeing what can happen, I realize there are more important things to my relationship with him. And the same goes for Addison and my mom as well. After this is over, I'm going to be better.

―――――――•◦•――――――――

It takes a little over two hours to drive to River's father's house. With the season being officially over and the weather getting cold out, there is no traffic. Normally, I fly, but I needed time to think, so I opted to take my car.

When I get there, I don't ring the bell. Nor do I park in the driveway. Instead, I park on the street and walk straight to the secluded alcove by the dunes on the beach. Then I pull out my phone.

Me: I'm here and need to speak to you.
River: Okay.
Me: Meet me by the dune.

I know I don't have to tell her or remind her where that

is. It's where we spent that evening together. It's where it all began.

I stare out at the ocean in front of me. The sun is starting to fade in the distance. The sky is a vibrant shade of pink. I don't hear her approach. The crashing waves muffle the softness of her footsteps, but I feel her.

She sits beside me, and her leg touches mine. I'm surprised she's this close.

"River . . ." I start and then stop myself. I'm not even sure what I'm going to say, but already my words feel lodged in my throat. "I have something I need to tell you. I found your mother."

I look away from the water and in her direction.

Blue eyes meet mine; they are full of so many questions, and so many feelings I can't even comprehend. Lifting my hand, I touch her trembling jaw. A move I shouldn't do, but I need to touch her right now. "Your mom is sick."

The muscle in her throat strains as if she is trying to find the words for the questions she has.

"Your mother . . . your mother has been sick for some time."

"What do you mean sick?" Her voice is barely a whisper, pain evident in each word.

"River—" I start to say, but she lifts her hand and starts to shake her head.

"No. Spit it out. What do you mean?" Her voice rises an octave.

"She has leukemia."

A range of emotions passes over her features, and then I see one I'm not expecting. Anger.

She starts to pull at her hair, a silent scream falling deafly from her lips, but I know her, I feel her, so I hear her.

I pull her toward me.

Into my lap.

And she falls apart. Once in my arms, she lets go of every-thing. She hits my shoulders. My back.

Screams pour from her mouth, and I just continue to hold her. I hold her through the screams, through the curses, and then when the tears come, I pull her closer and kiss her tears away.

"Why?"

"I don't know," I say against her cheek. Our faces are pushed together, her damp skin rubbing against mine.

"Was this why she never showed?" she whispers.

"Yes, sweetheart, it was." And I sure as hell hope it makes her feel at least a little better about Portugal.

"And why she didn't call."

I nod, and at the movement, fresh liquid coats my face as she cries harder.

"What do I do now?" she asks.

I pull away and take her hand in mine. "We go to see her."

"We?"

"Yes. We. I let you go. I know you left me, but I gave you no choice. I let you go, but I'm here now, no matter what, even if you don't want me. And we are going to see what we can do to help her."

She nods, and I move to stand, holding my hand out.

"I got you," I say and pull her up from the sand.

Together, we take the path to where my car is parked and I open the door for her.

"My dad?"

I shake my head. "I don't know if he knows or what he knows. I wanted to tell you. It wasn't my place to look—"

She lifts her hand.

"Thank you for doing it." She narrows her eyes. "But why?"

I know she's asking me why I tracked her mom down, why I came here, and why I'm taking her to the city.

Why am I doing this all for her?

I want to tell her I love her, but now isn't the time for that.

Right now, it's about River, not my own damn issues. So I'm no longer going to be selfish. I might want her in my arms again, and I might want to kiss her lips and make love to her, but right now, that isn't what she needs. She needs my strength and my friendship, and that's exactly what I plan to give her.

"River, despite what you think of me . . . and I'm sure your opinion of me isn't the best right now, all I ever wanted was you to be happy. It's not the time or the place to talk about this, but when you are ready, I do want to talk. Because all that matters to me is your happiness."

"Okay," she says, her voice low and uncertain.

It's not the right time, I tell myself. *But we will talk.*

And when we do, I will put all my cards on the table. I will tell her everything, and she can choose.

And whatever she decides, I'll support her. Even if it's not what I want, I will.

No matter what.

CHAPTER THIRTY-SEVEN

River

I NEVER EXPECTED TO SEE HIM AGAIN, AND I CERTAINLY NEVER expected to see him come to me and tell me my mother is sick.

We are halfway to the city, and my body is still shaking. I can't stop it. My knee bounces and my hands twitch. They are moving so badly that Grayson reaches between the space separating us and holds my hand steady.

"Everything is going to be okay," he says sternly, and although I don't necessarily believe him, I appreciate the effort.

"I hope so." I inhale and then exhale, but it feels like I'm not sucking in enough oxygen the closer we get to the hospital. By the time we pull up, I'm on the verge of a panic attack as to what I will find.

Strong arms wrap around me and hold me.

"It will be okay. I promise you, it will be okay. No matter what happens, you will get through this."

When I don't speak, he stops his ministrations on my back.

"Look at me."

I do. I look up and find deep green eyes, so sharp they pierce me.

"I promise you," he says, and for some reason, I believe him. I believe that Grayson Price would move heaven and earth to see me happy.

Even after everything he did, he would.

Once inside, we make our way down the hall, up the elevator, and into the private room.

When I turn the corner, I see her.

My mother.

But the woman looking back at me looks nothing like the woman who raised me.

This isn't the woman with shiny blond hair who would dance in the moonlight. The one who made tents on the beach and taught me the names of all the stars.

No, this woman is a stranger.

Her once vibrant eyes are hollow, and her skin is pale and paper-thin.

"Mom," I call out to her.

I can't bring myself to call her any of those ridiculous names she's asked me to in the past.

"River." The word is choppy, raspy, with a dry throat.

"Let me get you some water, Mom." I move away from the bed and grab the pitcher and then fill the glass.

I lift it to my mother, who takes a sip, and then I take the glass back. She gives a little cough and then looks at me.

"Thank you for coming,"

"Of course, I'd be here."

"I'm sorry . . ." She trails off, and I'm not sure what she's sorry for. Is she sorry for not calling? Or being an absent mother? Or is she sorry for not telling me?

I told myself I didn't want to fight, but at the same time, I can't go on like this. I need the truth, no half-truths and missing information.

I try to breathe through the anger I feel. A hand touches me from behind, and I see Grayson. He gives me a small smile, calming me once again without words.

"Why didn't you tell me?" I ask her. My voice is steady, hiding how I feel.

"It wasn't like before, and I was scared," she says, and her words hit me in the stomach. Before?

"Like before? What do you mean like before?" The walls around me feel tight. It feels like they are shrinking around me.

"River, when you were twelve, I was diagnosed with leukemia . . . I needed to undergo chemo and radiation. I couldn't handle . . ." She trails off, her voice weak.

"You dropped me off at my father's because you were getting chemo."

"Yeah."

"So when you left me on his doorstep . . . ?"

"I was sick."

"Why didn't you tell me? Why couldn't I stay with you? Help you?"

"I didn't want to hurt you. I didn't want to burden you."

"Burden me? Burden me?" My voice is too loud. I know I have to calm myself, but I'm having a hard time. "This whole time, I thought you left me. I thought you abandoned me."

"I'm so sorry," she croaks as tears slip down her cheek. "I thought . . . I thought . . ." Her tears pour down faster. "Thought I would die, and I didn't want you to feel the pain of having to watch me."

"I'd rather feel the pain and be with you. You can't protect me from hurting, Mom. I needed you, and you weren't there."

"I know."

Fresh tears form in my eyes.

"I needed you . . ." They fall down my cheek and pour out of my soul. "I needed you so much," I sob. "I had no one. I was in new surroundings. I was confused and angry, and I didn't want to—" I stop my words.

This isn't the time or the place for this argument. My mother is here now, and she needs my help.

I push down all the words I want to say and square my shoulders because I know she isn't strong enough to hear them today. One day, I'll have to think about what her actions did, and one day, I will forgive her, but right now, I can't think about either. I need to focus on her getting well.

I lift my hand and touch my necklace, touch the sea glass hidden beneath.

The jagged end, beaten beneath the ocean to form something beautiful, and then I turn to Grayson. "Do you mind finding her doctor for me?"

"Of course."

When he steps out of the room, my mom's soft voice rings through the air.

"That man truly loves you."

"No, he doesn't," I respond.

"I don't know a man who would do what he did without love."

"That's just Grayson." I shrug, and she shakes her head.

"No. That's love." And then her eyes flutter shut.

It doesn't take me long to find Grayson and the doctor. Neither is smiling as I make my approach. If anything, it's like her fate is already sealed.

He proceeds to tell me the diagnosis and our options.

By the time he's done speaking, my body shakes with tears.

Choices have to be made.

My mother needs a bone marrow transplant.

My body feels numb from what the doctor has told me. It feels like my head is a balloon, hovering above my body.

Options: best and worst pound in my brain.

Everything spirals around me.

Not just about her illness, but also about how my whole life was a lie. Well, not my whole life, just the past nine years.

The truth is, my mother got sick, and that illness, unbeknownst to me, changed my whole life.

And I don't know what to do about it.

How to act?

What to think?

But I do know one thing I must do. I need to talk to my father and Kim and find out how much they knew. And if they knew something, I want to know why they didn't talk to me about it.

Grayson has been amazing through this whole process, but I'm not sure what it means. I'm not sure if there is even a future between us. So many unanswered questions.

This could be, as my mother said, love.

Or it could be obligation to help since he is friends with my dad.

I have no idea, but the truth is, I'm not even ready to think about it yet.

So instead, he drives me back to the Hamptons, and we sit quietly. Although the season is technically over, my stepmom isn't ready to move back to the city.

I can understand that. Apartment living isn't ideal.

When we pull up to the house, Grayson stops the car, and I look at him. "Are you going to come in?" I ask.

"I don't think that's for the best."

"Yeah, I guess you're right. I wouldn't even know how to explain why we are together."

He nods, his lips tight.

"If you need me . . ." He trails off.

"I know. And thank you." I lean across the console and brush my lips to his cheek. I linger longer than I need to. I'm not sure what the future holds. For all I know, this will be the last time my mouth touches his skin.

I hear his intake of breath, but he doesn't kiss me back. He doesn't move other than the rise and fall of his chest.

After a few seconds, I move away and push open the door.

My stomach flip-flops as I pull out the key and walk inside.

"Hello?" I say as I walk through the foyer, looking for them.

It doesn't take me long. I find them together on the couch in the family room. Kim is resting her head on my father's chest.

I observe them for a minute. My dad's hand rests on her swollen belly. Slowly, he runs circles on it.

The picture in front of me is beautiful. They truly look at peace. They have no idea the hell I'm living, or what their decisions have done to me. I want to be angry. I want to yell and scream that while they were in their perfect bubble, I was finding out my life was a lie. So I do.

"How much did you know?" I say loudly from where I'm standing.

Kim jumps at the sound of my voice, and my dad tenses.

"What are you talking about?" Kim asks, and it dawns on me that she might never have known. But Dad, he must have known. No way was he taking in a young girl unless he knew.

"How. Much. Did. You. Know. About. My. Mother," I say, enunciating each word to get my point across.

His mouth drops open as realization hits.

"How do you—"

"How do I know?" I shout. "I know because my mother is sick again."

I watch as his eyes widen, and in the distance, I hear the sharp inhale of breath.

"Oh my, I'm so sorry." Kim stands abruptly and is walking over to me. Before I can even speak, she's pulling me into her arms.

They didn't know.

I let out a sigh of relief. I don't know what I would have done if they had known she was sick again and didn't tell me.

"Is that why she . . . ?" She starts to say didn't show up, but I nod against her. I don't want to talk about the time wasted with my mother, or the fact that her health is worse because she didn't address her illness at the first sign of symptoms. After going through this illness once before, it would be hard for me to believe she didn't know something was wrong.

I push away from Kim and head over to where my father is. He's leaning forward on the couch, his hand buried in his hair.

"Dad, I need to know how much you knew."

"I didn't know she was sick again," he whispers, obviously distraught by the news.

"But you knew the first time."

He looks at the ground, and I know the answer. I glance at Kim, looking to see how deep this is. Did she know too? By the tears pouring down her face, she also knew.

They both knew.

And it feels like the ground has been ripped out from under me. I feel like I'm being sucked into an abyss.

Like quicksand, I'm stuck, and the harder I pull to get out, the harder it is for me to hear or see anything other than the betrayal.

They let me believe she had abandoned me for all these years.

I lashed out about the pregnancy because I had thought I would be abandoned too.

In the background, I can hear them apologizing.

"River, let me explain."

"Explain what? That my life is a lie? That you knew she was sick the whole time?"

"She was getting treatment. You were so young and so emotional, and we didn't think you could handle it. When she went into remission, we didn't think it mattered."

I can hear their voices, but I just shake my head back and forth; I can't talk to them now. No. I can't. I need air. To breathe.

Without another word, I storm out of the house and down the beach to the private alcove.

The alcove where I made love to Grayson.

But more importantly, the alcove where my life changed.

Where I met Grayson Price for the first time.

The place where, unbeknownst to him, he saved my life.

My gaze focuses on the ocean, but the ripples of water blur in front of me due to the tears streaming down my face.

So clearly I remember that day.

My mother said we were going to visit my dad. Up until that point, she had never mentioned I had a father. I always assumed he had died. I mean, why else would we live the way we did, unless we had to.

We lived out of her car.

That's not to say we never had a house because we did. During my school years, my mother would take jobs as a yoga instructor in far-off places. By the age of twelve, I had lived everywhere. From Africa to Brazil.

But when the summer came, we would move out of wherever we resided and travel.

I had expected a far-off, exotic location, but this year, we ended up in New York. The Hamptons, to be exact.

My mother had been acting weird. So when she mentioned my father, I didn't know what to expect. She didn't speak when we approached. She just parked the car. Together we walked over to the front door of the large house.

I had never seen a house so large.

She knocked, and when no one answered, she rang the bell.

"This is your dad's house," she said as she took my hand and led me around the back.

"My dad?"

"Yes."

"But I thought . . . I thought he was dead," I admitted.

"No, he's not dead, River. But—" She started to say more, but then she pushed open a fence to a patio, and she led me up to where a party was in full effect.

Music was blaring, and people were swimming. Around the pool, people were laughing and drinking.

"Why are we here?" I asked. "Are we going to a party?"

I was so confused. My mother stopped her movements and looked down at me. "River." She paused and a look passed across her face. She looked sad, but I wasn't sure why.

"I have to go away."

"What do you mean go away?"

"I have to leave you here with your father."

"But he doesn't know me. You can't leave me." Tears formed in my eyes. "If I did something, if I need to be better . . ."

She shook her head. "Let's find him." But before we can take a step farther, a man approaches.

"This is your daughter," she said, and he looked at me and back at her.

"This isn't funny, Lily."

"It's not meant to be a joke, Tyler," she fired back, and he took her upper arm in his hand and led her away from the crowd. I followed.

"What are you doing here?" he whisper-shouted.

"This is your daughter, Tyler, and she needs to stay with you."

She was leaving me here. She was really leaving me here.

With a man I didn't know.

She was abandoning me.

My whole life, I was nothing more than a burden, and she decided she no longer wanted me.

"I don't understand," he said, lifting his hand and scrubbing at his face.

Over the thudding of my heart, I heard the words that would haunt me. That would make me leave the party and head toward the beach. That would lead me to a spot in the sand behind a dune.

Where no one could see me.

"I thought—" He looks from her to me. He doesn't have to say the words. I can tell from the way his eyes are round in shock. He never thought he was going to see me because he must have thought she would get rid of me . . .

Not only did my mom not want me, but my dad didn't want anything to do with me either.

A pain I had never felt spread through my body, and I felt like I was drowning. Like I couldn't breathe. His words keep repeating in my brain over and over again.

I thought.

I thought.

I thought.

He never wanted me.

I didn't stay to listen to the rest. Too afraid of what more he would say to bring down my world. Did he think I was being put up for adoption? Or was it more?

As they argued back and forth, I quietly walked away, numb to the hushed voices whispering and gossiping. Once I was away from the party, I ran and ran and ran.

The water lapped against the shore. Waves roll in. The undertow fierce. The weather wasn't one for swimming, but that doesn't mean I can't. I study the water and then look back at the house . . .

No one would know I was gone.

No one would suspect until it was too late.

It would be so easy . . .

My dad wanted me gone. My mother thought I was a burden.

No one would notice.

I moved to stand, my mind resolved to what I was about to do, and then I heard his voice, or maybe I felt his presence, but before I could put my foot in the water, he spoke.

"Should you be out here alone?" he asked, and I turned around. Fierce green eyes looked down at me. When I didn't answer, his jaw tightened, and he looked back at the house and then back down at me. "Are you okay?" he asked.

"Leave me alone," I responded. I didn't want him here. If he was here, I couldn't go into the water.

I couldn't disappear, and I knew he wasn't going anywhere.

"Want to talk about it?" he asked.

"I'm not supposed to talk to strangers," I fired back. I was also not supposed to be swimming alone in the ocean, probably. But the faster he left, the faster I could.

"I'm Grayson Price," he stated, lifting his hand out, "and you're Tyler Reed's daughter, right?"

How did he know?

"I'm your dad's friend." He paused and let out a long exhale. "And I was on the deck and heard your mother."

I still didn't speak.

"Oh, look," he said, and he moved closer to the water. He bent down and pulled something green out of the sand. "Do you know what this is?"

I shook my head.

"This is sea glass." He lifted it, and I see a tiny piece of a rock in his hand.

"It's a rock," I mumbled back. Clearly, this man was delusional.

"No. Look closer . . ." He stepped closer to me. "Here." He reached out his hand, and tentatively, I took it. Looking down, I saw that he was right. It wasn't a rock, and it wasn't glass either.

"This was once broken. It was once jagged and scarred. It was left alone by the sea, thrown away, but it didn't break. That's the thing about sea glass. It didn't break, and it didn't disappear. No, instead, over time, it was battered by the ocean, by the waves and sea, but it actually thrived. The edges smoothed out, and something that was once thrown away became something beautiful."

And for some reason, his words flowed over me. I looked down at my hand and then back up at the ocean.

I was the glass.

I was broken.

But maybe I could make something beautiful, too.

"Can I keep this?" I whispered.

"Yes . . . Now, let's go inside. I'll get you food."

The memory of that first time with Grayson has me holding the necklace against my skin with the sea glass I reformed and turned into a piece I have always carried with me.

I need to talk to Grayson.

CHAPTER THIRTY-EIGHT

Grayson

WHEN MY PHONE PINGS ONLY AN HOUR LATER, I'M shocked.

I didn't expect her to contact me.

Don't get me wrong, I'm happy. But still . . . what the fuck?

River: Come to the spot.

Me: Okay.

It doesn't take me long to drive over. I hadn't actually gone to the Hamptons house yet. I've been driving around trying to think. I'm not sure what to do about River. But right now, I push that out of my mind.

I need to put her needs first.

I find her sitting on the sand with her hands buried in it.

"Can I sit?" I ask from behind her, and she looks over her shoulder.

"Of course."

"What's going on?" I ask, and she looks toward the ocean.

"Do you know you saved me once?" Her voice is so low, I'm not sure I heard her correctly.

"What?"

"You saved me." Her voice is louder now, resolute. She truly believes this, yet I have no idea what she's talking about.

"I think you're confused."

"No." She shakes her head. "I'll never be confused about

that. It was here actually. In this exact spot. When I was twelve."

I shake my head.

"I was twelve, and it was the first time I had met my dad . . ." She looks up at me, unshed tears filling her eyes.

"I remember," I whisper but she shakes her head.

"No. You don't understand."

I take her hand in mine and kiss her knuckle. "Then tell me."

"I was lost. Broken. I didn't want to live." Her voice trembles and the tears fall. "I came out here, and I didn't think anyone would care."

My own heartbeat picks up as I realize what she is saying. I follow her gaze as she stares out at the harsh waves battering the shore. "I thought . . ." A sob breaks from her lips. I want to stop her from speaking, but I know I have to let her talk. We both have so much unsaid between us, but now is the time for me to listen.

"You were here. You spoke to me. You gave me this." She takes her hands away from where we touch and lifts it and un-clasps the necklace she has always worn. The one I have never asked about but always wondered what it was.

"It's sea glass," she says, and suddenly the memory crashes into my head like a thousand freight trains.

The sad little girl.

The sea glass.

I had always remembered meeting her that summer, but the details had been blurry, lost to the many memories of my life.

"You kept it?" I say.

"And every time I think I'm broken, I think of what you said. You saved me then, and you saved me now."

"What do you mean?"

"You gave me back my mother. I'm going to save her." I realize she's made up her mind about donating her marrow. "Thank you for saving me not once, but twice."

I nod, too choked up to speak.

"Thank you for listening."

"Always."

And I meant it. From the bottom of my heart, no matter what our future is. Whether we have a future or not, I'll always be there for River Reed.

If she'll let me.

When I leave River, I feel uneasy. I never knew about River's and my shared path. Sure, I remembered meeting her, but this moment that was so profound to her was just a blip in my memory.

The whole thing feels like fate.

She's held the sea glass all these years.

I saved her, and for some reason, I feel like she's saving me. I fell in love with her, something I didn't think was possible. I want to be with her too.

But is it selfish?

I grab my phone and call the one person who would know if it's selfish to be with her. To leave her. The phone rings three times before I hear her voice.

"Hello."

"Mother," I say.

"Grayson. I didn't expect to hear from you."

"I'm a pretty awful son for never calling."

"You call plenty." She laughs, a sound I love to hear. For a long time after my father's death, she was a shell of the woman I knew, but hearing her laughter now means so much.

"Once a week," I respond.

"And that's plenty."

"I should check in more."

"I understand, dear, you're out living your life."

"Hardly," I mutter under my breath.

"What's wrong, Grayson? I know something is bothering you."

"How do you know?"

"You're my son. It's my job to know."

"I'm scared," I admit.

"Oh, dear. Talk to me."

"Do you resent Dad?"

"What are you talking about?" she asks, confused.

"He died so young, leaving you alone. Do you resent him for leaving you?"

I hear her inhale and exhale. "I told this to your sister, and now I will tell you. I would rather live the rest of my life alone than not have had those years with your dad. I don't resent him nor would I ever. I loved him and still do. Being with your father was worth every minute of pain because he was my soul mate."

"But Dad died so young, and Grandfather—"

"What's this about, Grayson?"

I lean forward in my chair back in my apartment in the city and place my hand on my head. "I met someone, and well, she's much younger than me. I'm afraid . . ." I can't even say the words.

"You're afraid to love her. You're afraid to leave her."

"Yes."

"You can't compare yourself to your grandfather and your dad. Your grandfather smoked cigars and wasn't healthy. He didn't go to the doctor. The warning signs were there."

"But Dad—"

"Wasn't much better. He was under a lot of stress, he was unhealthy, and he, too, smoked for many years. You can't live your life in fear of death. You need to just live your life. Tomorrows aren't guaranteed. They aren't guaranteed for any of us, but you are not like them. You are healthy, and you listen to your body. Don't be afraid of the unknown. Don't look up and realize the years have passed, and you have missed it. Live life now. Love now."

CHAPTER THIRTY-NINE

River

NOW BACK AT MY PARENTS', I SIT QUIETLY ACROSS FROM them in the living room. My mind whirls around with all they said before, and the vision that is now before me.

I watch as my father holds his arm around her, and how she protectively strokes her stomach.

Although they look sad about what has happened to me, I can see the love they have. Not just for me, but also for the unborn baby. My sibling.

When I first heard the news, I didn't take it well. I was afraid of losing what I had. Afraid of the unknown because I felt abandoned.

But finding out the truth about my mother has shocked me to the core. With the knowledge I have now, I realize I was never left or abandoned, but that everything was done to protect me.

To love me.

Not just by my mom, but also by my dad and Kim.

They have always loved me, and nothing will change that.

They love me unconditionally, just as much as they love the baby in Kim's belly. Just as I will love the baby too.

Standing, I make my way over to them and sit beside Kim, and what I do next has her mouth opening wide and exhaling in surprise.

My hand rests on her stomach; it rests on the small round bump where my brother or sister is growing. I look up and find wet tears in Kim's eyes. She then rests her hands on mine, and my father rests on top of hers.

"Whatever happens, we will get through this together, as a family," my dad says. He's referring to my mother. To her health and what the future brings. But just as Kim and Dad would do anything for this baby, and me, I would do anything for my mother and them.

Because that's what you do for the ones you love.

The doctor's words ring in my ear over and over. I know what I have to do. I know it deep down in my bones. The same bones that will hopefully heal my mother.

I just hope we aren't too late.

I have spent my whole life resenting my mom when it wasn't her fault. Yes, she could have handled it better, but watching my dad care for the unborn baby so protectively in Kim's belly makes me realize that maybe parents do things they think will protect them.

A day later, I'm sitting beside my mother in her hospital room. It's time to break the news, and I hate feeling so nervous to have this conversation. This is good. It's what has to happen.

"I spoke to your doctor," I start. "I'm going to donate my bone barrow."

She blows out a harsh breath, averting her eyes. Her fingers twitch as though she's fighting some internal battle I'm not privy to.

"No, River. I couldn't ask—"

I hold my hand up to stop her. I knew this was going to be

an awkward conversation, but she has to understand that this is something I have to do. It's as much for me as it is for her.

"Stop, Mom. Let me talk," I beg.

She nods, giving me the go-ahead.

"For years, I resented you. At times, I even hated you. I didn't understand how you could've left me."

She sighs. "I never wanted to leave." Her voice is soft and childlike.

"I know that now, Mom," I whisper, taking her small fidgeting hand in mine. "But for years, I didn't. I have pushed so many people away for fear of being abandoned. But I'm ready to heal now. I'm ready to open myself up and not be afraid. This is a new start for me too."

A tear falls from her eye. "It kills me to think about how you felt all those years. I need to explain. *Please* let me explain."

It's my turn to nod. I think I need to hear what she has to say as much as she wants to tell me. We both need to heal.

"When you came into this world, I loved you so much. I never wanted you to feel pain, and at the time, that's all you would've felt with me around. I never thought my leaving would hurt you. I left for you," she sobs, and tears well in my own eyes, watching my mom crumple.

"In the end, I was wrong. Now I realize I was also being selfish. I didn't want to see your pain, so I left, and it wasn't what any mother should ever do."

"I forgive you, Mom."

Another sob catches in her throat, and it takes everything I have in me not to bawl with her. I want to cry for all the missed years. I want to cry for the broken woman in front of me. Mostly, I want to cry because I'm scared for her.

"Thank you," she finally says, pulling my gaze back to her.

"I don't deserve it, but I just want you to know that I believed I was doing what was best for you at the time. I don't deserve this gift."

"Mom—"

She shakes her head, lifting her own hand to stop me.

"I don't deserve your help, but I will take it. I want a chance to be the mom you deserve."

My tears cascade down my cheeks. I envision holidays, weekends, trips, everything we've never had, and I cry harder. I want that future too, and the fact that she wants it too makes me so happy.

"You already are."

She squeezes my hand, and I lean into her, giving her a light hug. It takes everything in me not to crush her to me.

I sit with her for some time in comfortable silence, praying that everything goes as planned, and we can have that future I believe we both want.

⎯⎯⎯◆⎯⎯⎯

The process to make sure I was a match took much longer than I expected. Cheek swabs and having my blood drawn was only part of it. Countless sessions and examination were conducted to make sure I was fully informed about the procedure. They wanted to make sure I understood the full scope of what would happen, and to be honest, my head spun at all the information thrown at me.

It's been a long four weeks since I decided to help my mom with this, and as much as I have thought about what it would be like, being here in the hospital is so much different. I'm not prepared for the onslaught of emotions that hit me as I'm finally led into the operating room. The truth is, I'm scared.

My mouth feels dry, and my heart hammers in my chest. From all the research I've done, I know that the procedure doesn't take long, and I will be under anesthesia for the process, but it doesn't stop my heart from thundering.

I inhale deeply.

To try to calm my racing heart, I think of my mother. I think of all the time I will have with her if this goes well. I think of all the memories we can make, and of all the charms I can add to my bracelet. This procedure will give us time. I keep repeating that to myself, and with each new pull of oxygen, the rapid pulse in my veins slows.

"Are you ready to help your mom?" the anesthesiologist asks.

I nod. That's why I'm here, to help my mom. There's calmness at that moment while I remember the purpose of today. I stare at the ceiling, knowing what comes next. A bright light above me flickers in my eyes, and panic starts to flare once more. The man dressed in scrubs stands beside where I'm lying down.

"All right, River. Count down for me, starting at five," he says.

I do what he asked, and the light above me dims until it finally goes dark.

When I wake, I'm in another room. Sunlight filters through the window next to me. I squint, not ready for the brightness.

"I'll take care of that," my father says from a chair beside me.

I hadn't seen him sitting there. He jumps up, shutting out the offending sun, and I smile at his thoughtfulness.

"Hi, Dad."

"How are you feeling?" he asks.

"A little sore, I guess. But okay."

He smiles.

"What you did was brave, River. I'm so proud of you."

My smile is lazy, a side effect of the anesthesia. I may have been under for a while, but I'm still exhausted.

"I'd do it for you too."

"I know you would, but let's hope you'll never have to."

Of course, I'll never have to. He'll have another son or daughter who can help him. A child that he actually wants. The thought hit me like a Mack truck. It's unfair, but some truths never leave us. He may love me, but he hasn't always wanted me. Not like he wants this baby.

I take a deep breath, needing to stop this train of thought. I'm tired and emotional, and now isn't the time.

"Are you all right? You look troubled?" he asks.

"I'm fine. Just tired."

Before he can say anything, a knock sounds at the door and Kim walks in.

"How are you doing, sweetheart?"

"Good. I didn't know you were here," I say with a small smile.

"I've been in the waiting room. I wanted to give you and your dad some time."

She looks at my dad. "Your phone has been ringing off the hook."

"Shit. That's probably my client. I'd better take that. I'll be back, okay?"

"That's fine. I'm going to close my eyes for a bit," I answer, ready to do just that.

"I'll stay with your dad until you're ready for visitors," Kim chimes in.

I smile at them both. "Thanks for coming. It means a lot."

"Of course," they both respond in unison, before exiting and leaving me to shut my eyes.

They haven't been gone for five minutes when I hear the door creak open and heavy steps sound.

"You're back already?" I force my eyes to open. But it's not my dad. It's Grayson.

"Hi." His voice is soft as he makes his way over to me.

"Hi." I barely croak out the words. I'm full of emotion seeing him standing there in my room while my dad is steps away. It's brave and stupid at the same time. "Do you know my dad is here?"

"I saw him leave. I waited until he left the waiting room to take a call. We have some time. I just wanted to make sure you're all right." He walks to the side of my bed, leaning over and kissing my lips gently.

"I'm glad you're here."

"You couldn't keep me away, River. Nobody can."

"My dad?" I raise my eyebrow in challenge.

"Not even him. Not today."

Butterflies take flight in my stomach as goose bumps break out over my body. If that isn't a declaration of love, I'm not sure what is. My feelings for him are so strong at that moment. My blood pulses and heart thumps against my chest. He came.

"Kiss me again," I order, and he delivers.

Both of his hands cradle my face as he kisses me tenderly, as though I'm porcelain and will break. I give as much as I can, despite my exhaustion. He's everything I need as we say everything through our joined lips. Nothing could ruin this moment.

CHAPTER FORTY

Grayson

My mouth moves over Rivers. I don't want to hurt her, but I can't stop kissing her. I want her to feel how much I need her. I'm so lost in her that I barely register the door to River's recovery room opening.

Time moves in slow motion. The footsteps grow heavy, and before I can even pull myself away, I know who's here.

River's hand clutches mine. My lips are still on her lips.

"What the fuck are you doing?" Tyler's voice confirms my fear.

Shit.

How was I so dumb to kiss her in public knowing full well her family could walk in at any moment?

I waited until they left, but the truth is, I didn't care.

I wanted to get caught.

I turn and watch as he stalks toward me, and next thing I realize, I'm being pulled by my collar away from River.

Tyler is in my face, teeth bared and a vein pulsing in his neck.

"Calm down," I say, trying to lift my hand to separate us.

"Calm down? Are you fucking kidding?" he shouts, still holding me. He pulls back and slings me against the wall.

It's not that he's bigger than me, but the shock of the situation has me faltering. Fuck.

Although I knew this was inevitable, I'm still at a loss of what to say.

"Say something, you bastard." He pushes me again. "Are you sleeping with my daughter?"

"Dad, stop, please," River shouts.

He ignores her pleas, and when I don't answer, he punches me in the face. I should lift my hand and stop the punch, but I don't.

I deserve this.

I fucked his daughter.

"She's a kid," he shouts again as he punches me again.

"Stop," River yells.

My eyes fly to hers to make sure she's all right.

"This is the last thing she needs," I bark at Tyler.

"Don't tell me what my kid needs," he seethes in return.

"She's not a kid."

I don't see the next blow coming.

Punch. "Yes. She is." *Punch.* "You sick fuck."

I'm still pinned, sweat and blood dripping from my face.

"Stop," River says again. Loud enough to make me push against his shoulders so he lets me go.

I go to her side, running my hand down her cheek and swiping away a tear that's fallen. I barely register the blood pooling on her sheet.

"I love your daughter," I say as I begin to wipe the blood on my face.

"How can you love her? You don't even know her."

"Don't know her?" My voice is louder, and I get in his face. He had the time to say his piece, and now it's mine. "I'm the one she cried to. I'm the one holding her hand. I'm the one she talked to about the decision to do this. Where the fuck were you?"

His eyes are wide, his chest rising and falling in a fast clip.

"So don't tell me I don't love your daughter," I shout again, this time pushing him back. "Because I do. And she might not have told me yet, but I'm pretty goddamn sure she loves me too."

He punches me again. This time, my mouth fills with the coppery taste of blood.

"Stop," she shouts again. Our bodies are then forcefully separated. Both of us are breathing heavily as I realize the hospital security has pulled us apart.

I know if I don't leave now, the police will come.

"I'm going to go," I say to River. "I'm here for you, when you need it."

She nods as tears fill her eyes.

CHAPTER FORTY-ONE

River

"WHAT THE HELL HAS HE DONE? DID HE TAKE ADVANTAGE of you?"

"Of course not, Dad."

My dad raises his hands to his head and cradles it.

"It's not what you think. He saved me. And I love him."

"You don't love him. He's old enough to be your dad."

"He's only fifteen years older than me. And don't tell me how I feel. I love him. He has been there. He has helped me. More than you know."

More than you can ever imagine.

"You don't know what you're talking about. You are obviously being taken advantage of."

"I'm twenty-one, Dad, not twelve. But even at twelve, Grayson had my back. Even when you didn't."

"What are you talking about?"

"I heard you . . ." I say. I never planned on saying this, but his treatment of Grayson has me firing it back.

"What do you mean?"

"I heard you tell my mom that you wanted her to take care of me . . ."

"I don't know what you are talking about."

"You wanted Mom to abort me."

"I-I . . ."

"I heard you . . ."

"I never said that. Never once since the day I found out about you have I ever regretted you. I have loved you since the first moment."

"Then why did you say it?"

"Did you hear me say those words?"

I look down toward my hands. *I thought. I thought. I thought.* "No," I whisper. Because now looking back, I realize I didn't. My young and sad heart had heard words that were never really there.

"I was young and dumb. When she told me she was pregnant, I was barely seventeen. I was still in high school. I told her I couldn't have a kid—" he stutters and stops. "But I didn't mean it. I didn't know yet what love was. When I saw you, I knew. Every day, I thank God your mother didn't listen to an asshole teen. I'm so sorry." Tears well in his eyes.

Forgiving my mom was one thing, but I need him to know I forgive him too.

I don't want the past to dictate my future.

I need to learn to forgive.

That's the lesson in all this.

"I know that, and I wanted to tell you I forgive you, and I hope you forgive me. I realized lately that the future isn't infinite. And I don't want to hold on to any more resentment. I want to move forward. I want to be happy, and the only way to be happy is to put the past behind me."

"So now what?" he asks.

"Trust me to know how I feel. Trust me to believe that my love for him and his love for me is true. Trust me enough and love me enough to want me to be happy. Because he's the one who saved me from making a mistake. He's the one who made me believe again. He's the one who gives me all I have ever been searching for. He's the one who gives me a home."

CHAPTER FORTY-TWO

Grayson

Tyler steps out into the hallway. I know I should have left, but I didn't. I heard everything.

"How much did you hear?" he grits, obviously trying to refrain from punching me again.

"Enough."

He nods.

"You love her?"

"More than my life. I have spent the past decade or more of my life counting down the days to my end. She makes me want to live. She makes me want to cherish every minute. She makes me want more."

After a moment, he dismisses me, turning to walk away. Then he stops and stares over his shoulder and looks at me. "Don't break her heart," he grits out.

"I won't."

Then he walks away. I'm not sure where this leaves us, or what this means for the future, but I will have to deal with it at a different time because right now River is my only priority.

I step into her room, and she looks at me by the door.

"Is it true?"

"You'll have to be more specific." I keep my poker face intact.

"Do you love me?"

"Yes, River. I love you. But I thought you already knew that." I smirk. "I thought it was obvious."

"Nothing with you is ever obvious."

"You are my whole world. I was scared to live because I was scared my time was limited. I was afraid to lose you, to leave you. My father died at fifty-seven . . . I was on the phone with him. I heard him take his last breath. I-I wasn't there. I wasn't able to save him, again."

"What do you mean again?"

"You always asked why I hated my grandparents' house."

"Because your grandfather died here, but it's more than that, isn't it?"

"It is."

"You can talk to me."

"I know . . . I was there the day my grandfather died. I couldn't save him. And I couldn't save my dad. They both died of a heart attack. My grandfather was only sixty-one. So you see this is why I wouldn't let you in."

"I don't understand. I mean, I understand your pain, but why would that affect us?"

"I always thought . . . I always thought I'd die young, following in their footsteps, so I pushed you away. You might have left first, but I gave you no choice."

"And now?"

"Now I want to try. I want to see where this goes. I want to be with you. So what will it be, River? Will you have me? Do you love me?"

"I have loved you since I was twelve. Obviously, I'll have you."

CHAPTER FORTY-THREE

River

INSTEAD OF GOING HOME OR TO MY PARENTS' APARTMENT, Grayson takes me back to his. He says he wants to take care of me. It's odd to rely on someone, but I trust him and now with everything from our past out in the open, I know that I can trust him to be there for me and not leave.

I'm lying in bed with my phone in my hand when Grayson walks in and tilts his head at me.

"What are you doing?" he asks. "You're supposed to be resting."

"I am." I gesture around me. "See? Bed."

He lifts his brow and shakes his head. "All I see is you playing on your phone."

"I'm not playing."

"Then what are you doing?"

When he asks the question, I realize that I never got around to telling him about my little side project. At first, I didn't want to ruin our trip, so I didn't mention it. Then I was so distracted with him, breaking up, and then my mom, that I still haven't told him.

I pat the bed next to me. "Come sit down and I can tell you."

His eyes widen in curiosity as he sits beside me, propping his back on the headboard.

I hold my phone out to him, accessing the Google drive where I saved all the files.

"I never told you this, and well, now it's a moot point, but I found some weird discrepancies in my dad's books."

He takes my phone and starts to thumb through the files. It's hard to see, but he's looking anyway.

"Why didn't you tell me?" he asks.

"Well . . . things got complicated," I say, looking at him, and he grimaces. He knows I'm talking about what happened with us.

Him pushing me away, and me walking away first.

He leans down and kisses my forehead. "Well, things aren't complicated now. So why don't you start from the beginning."

And I do.

I tell him about Larry.

The weird comment when I first started working for my father.

His odd behavior.

I finally tell him about the threat and the files I downloaded.

By the time I'm done, Grayson is reeling with anger. I'm not sure who he's madder at, Larry for being shady and potentially hurting my dad's business, or me for not coming to him in the first place.

Probably me, by the way he's pacing the room.

"I'm sorry I didn't tell you sooner," I say, trying to calm him.

But it doesn't seem to do anything as he continues to walk back and forth.

"Why didn't you?" he asks, clearly upset. "I could have helped." He sounds sad, and I imagine it's because he knows back then I didn't trust him enough.

"I'm sorry," I whisper again, and a tear falls down my cheek. He watches the liquid and then closes the distance between us to kneel down before me.

"No. I'm sorry." He swipes the tears. "I love you, River. And I never want you to think I won't be there." I nod as another tear slips out. He wipes that one too. "From now on, we do this together, okay? You are not alone. You will never be alone again." He leans up and places a kiss on my lips. "Come on, we have a lot of work to do if we are going to figure out what the fuck Larry has done."

CHAPTER FORTY-FOUR

Grayson

I PICK UP THE PHONE.

As much as I want to handle this on my own, I need Jax to help me.

The files River gave me were off, and there was no doubt that the scumbag was ripping off Tyler.

But Tyler hates me, and I don't really think he'll listen unless I march in there with some proof.

He'd listen to River, but I want to be there too. Make amends. Talk to him.

I understand he didn't want to speak to me after he found out about us, but we've given him time to come to terms with our relationship.

Weeks, actually.

The thing is, I'm not going anywhere. River is mine, but I know it upsets her.

It's time I figure out what's going on with Larry and talk to Tyler. Not for their sake—for hers.

I pick up my phone and dial.

"Bro, calling me after hours. To what do I owe the honor?" Jax laughs it off, but underneath, I hear a clip to his tone.

I deserve it. I never call him unless I need something— case in point, now.

"Jax, I need one more favor," I say, feeling like an asshole.

Because even though I have mentally decided to stop being a dick to my brother, I have yet to back up that plan.

"Okay . . ."

"Can you come over?"

"Sure." That's the thing about Jax. No matter what I do, he's always there for me. It's time I try harder with my kid brother.

It doesn't take long for him to get here, and before I know it, Jaxson is stepping off the elevator and into my apartment.

I lift a hand when he catches where I am, and he takes a seat on the couch and then cocks his head.

"So what brings me here?" he asks, arms crossed, head inclined down.

"I need a favor."

"Yeah. We've already been through this on the phone. Now is the time you tell me what kind of favor."

"I need you to look into someone."

"No shit," he deadpans. "That's the only reason you call. And now it's all the time, so why can't you just admit you like having me here."

"Of course, I like having you here. You're my brother." His eyes go wide at my words. He looks taken aback, but then he shakes his head and rights himself, dropping back down the facade of not caring.

"Now that we have that squared away, tell me who and why?"

"It's for Tyler." I lean forward and grab my drink that sits on the table, taking a swig of the scotch before placing it down.

"I'm listening."

"River brought me some files, and I need you to track the accounts."

"How soon?"

"Yesterday," I joke, and Jax stands up.

"On it," he replies as he makes his way to the elevator.

"Jax."

He stops his movement and turns back to look at me. "I'm sorry for being a crap brother."

"You were never a crap brother. Sure, you were a dick"—I laugh at his words—"but I know you mean well. Always."

"Do you want to grab a drink sometime?"

"Sure." He starts toward the elevator, again.

"I'll forward you everything once I have it," he says as the door opens. He steps in and then it closes.

As always, Jax came through, and surprisingly, it took him no time.

"This dude must be desperate," he says through the phone. I called him the minute I got the email to go over what he found.

"Why do you say that?"

"At first, he was just skimming off the top. The amount was so small it's almost untraceable, but over the past few years, it's got to be more. Within the past few months, it's like he's not even hiding it."

I nod to myself.

This is probably how River found out.

"So where's he transferring it?"

I expect him to say some fancy offshore account.

But apparently, the idiot has been doing this for so long, he's not worried anyone will catch him.

But when River did . . .

Maybe that's why he's got so brazen in the off chance she tells her dad. He's stockpiling.

Jax runs through everything, and with all the information in hand, I wait for River to get here so we can decide how to proceed. I'd understand if she wants to do this alone, but I want to be there.

It's around noon on Saturday when she finally shows up. With school and work, both of us are busy during the week. Normally, she'd stay over on Friday, but she had plans with her roommate.

When I hear the elevator ding, then open, and her footsteps, I shout that I'm in the bedroom.

She walks right in and finds me.

"Hey," I say, pulling her into my arms and kissing her.

I don't let the kiss deepen because I have to tell her what Jax found.

"Come on," I say, leading her to the kitchen.

"Want anything?" I ask, before starting.

"No. What did Jax say?"

I plop the papers I printed off the computer, and River starts going through them.

"Wow."

"I know."

"It's been going on for years. I just don't understand how Dad didn't know."

"I think with business not doing well, he just assumed that's why he was so low on funds. The worse it got, the more he was able to skim because your father was no longer thinking straight. Larry was with him since the beginning, so he wouldn't have thought—"

"No. He wouldn't," she agrees.

"How do you want to handle this?" I ask.

"We need to tell Dad first. Today. I don't want to wait."

We arrive at the apartment in the city twenty minutes later. With Tyler working so much and Kim's due date approaching, they are staying in the city until the baby comes. Plus, apparently, the hospitals are better here.

When we walk in the door, we find her parents in the living room. Kim is very pregnant now, the baby due sometime next month.

Tyler looks at his daughter and then the smile soon fades from his face as he takes me in.

"We need to talk to you," River says.

He looks back and forth between us and then stands. "Kim, rest. We'll be back in a minute."

"Are you sure?" she asks this to River, who then proceeds to walk over to her stepmom, touch her large belly lovingly, and smiles.

"Yeah. We're cool. Maybe we can order pizza when we're done."

Kim perks up to that. "I'd love that. Your dad too."

"Come with me," Tyler grits as he walks out of the room, and we follow him into his office.

We sit, our coats still on from the cold weather that has finally descended upon the city. Although they want River here, it's apparent my presence isn't welcome. I don't care. I'm here for her, not for me. I keep my face impassive as I place the folder in front of him.

"I know you don't approve. I know you don't trust me. But please, put your feelings aside and look at what we found."

His jaw tightens, but he does as I ask.

"What's this?" he asks as he reads.

"It's exactly what it looks like," I respond.

"Who is stealing from me?" His voice is gruff and angry.

"Larry," River says.

Tyler lifts his hands and buries them in his hair. "Is there anyone I can trust?"

River takes that moment to stand. "I'm going to leave you guys to talk." She knows it's time.

When we're alone, Tyler glares at me but doesn't speak, so I do.

"I'm not going to say I'm sorry," I start.

"Then why the fuck are you here?" he fires back.

"Let me speak," I respond, and when he goes to open his mouth, I shake my head. "I'm not going to say I'm sorry because I'm not. I love your daughter. She is my whole life. She is the meaning of my existence. So, no, I'm not going to apologize for loving her because I love her more than anything. But I will apologize for how I went about this. I was a dick. Not just to you, but also to the woman I love. I will always regret my actions, but I won't regret the result. Because she loves me too." I lean forward. "I'm not going anywhere, Ty. So we need to resolve this."

"I'm not sure I can do that," he responds, and I nod because I understand. I'm not sure I would forgive me if I were in his place.

"I can understand that, but it makes her sad, so you're going to have to fucking try." His eyes widen at my harshness. "I refuse for her to ever be unhappy, and this is making her unhappy. So if you need to punch me again, so be it. Beat the shit out of me, but when we walk out the door, we are cool."

When Tyler doesn't say anything for a minute, I think I played this wrong. But then I see his lip tip up. "Okay."

He stands and walks out the door.

With one word, I know everything will be okay.

EPILOGUE

Grayson

I'D LIKE TO SAY THINGS WERE BETTER BETWEEN TYLER AND me right away, but in truth, it took months. After we bombarded him, we played the parts we had to play for River, but eventually, things got back to normal.

The past few months have been busy, to say the least. Tyler took the information we provided to him, and within a few weeks, Larry was arrested for embezzlement.

Thanks to Jaxson, we had enough evidence to get him put away for a long time.

Now, with it finally behind us, I can do what I have wanted to do for months.

So here I am, in a room I never thought I would step foot in again, holding the box my grandfather showed me all those years ago.

It was a few months before he died in this very room that he handed me the ring. A ring that had been passed down through our family, and he wanted to give that ring to me.

"One day, you will meet a girl who reminds you of the ocean. She will draw you to her like an ocean wave, pull you in like a rip current, and consume you like tsunami waves crashing down on your heart. And when you meet her, you'll give her this." He had said this at the time and I hadn't known the truth to his words, but oh, how right he was. River Reed was all the things he had said and more. She taught me that with love you cannot be afraid. That living each day as if it's your last doesn't mean you have to do it alone. It's about enjoying and cherishing and loving all the moments until you take your last breath. It's about *living*.

———◦———

I find her sitting on the spot where she always sits.

Now that she's reminded me of the meaning behind this spot, I think it'll be the perfect location for what I'm about to do.

Tonight is the Reed's annual Fourth of July party, but most importantly, it's River's birthday.

The party is set to start in a few hours, but I knew River would be out here thinking.

A lot has changed since last year, more since the first time she came.

Her mother is here with us, and River now has a sister.

There is only one thing that would make today more perfect.

"You engraved my birthday on this charm."

"No." I shake my head.

"No, you didn't engrave my birthday? I'm confused."

"Yes, obviously, it's your birthday, but that's not why I had this charm made to add to your bracelet. I know that this isn't a location you visited with your mom on a happy time ten years ago, but I was hoping today, we could make it happy."

She continues to stare at me as I take her wrist in mine and attach the charm. "The date engraved is the day we turned this beach into a special moment in our lives because the date isn't just your birthday anymore."

"It's not?" she asks as she stares at the piece of metal I had made to look like the shoreline.

"It's not," I respond as I kneel in front of her on the sand.

Her eyes go wide, and her hand starts to tremble.

"No. That date also symbolizes the day I tell you I want to spend the rest of my life with you. The date I ask you"—I pull out a box from my back pocket and open it in front of her—"to be my wife."

When the tears start to flow down her face, I smile up at her. An action that was once hard for me, but that is only one of many fears River helped me overcome.

"Will you marry me?" I finally ask, and she throws her hands around my neck.

"Is that a yes?" I joke.

"Yes. Yes. Hell yes."

I pull away and lean down and take her mouth in mine.

"Thank fuck. Now let me put this on you and let's go celebrate."

With the ring now on her finger, we return to the house. The party hasn't started, but everyone who is important to us is here and ready to celebrate our future.

As soon as our feet hit the patio, Kim comes running up to us. In her arms is River's sister, Melody.

"Let me see," she says, and River extends her left hand. "It's gorgeous."

"It really is," River responds with a large smile spreading across her face as she looks down at the blue diamond that sits on her finger.

The diamond that looks like the ocean.

Our ocean.

My grandfather didn't know it at the time, but the stone was perfect for River.

"My turn." Lily steps up beside Kim and pulls her daughter into a hug. From where I'm standing, I can see River's eyes fill with unshed tears.

"Today is a dream come true," River whispers, and her mom hugs her tighter. It really is. Tyler is next to come over.

He comes up to me first. "Thank you," he says. "You make her happy, and that's all I could ever want." He steps forward, and I extend my hand, but he shakes it off and hugs me. It's only with one arm, but after everything, I'm still shocked.

Once everyone sees the ring, my family is next to approach. Mom is the first to throw her arms around us, followed by a smug looking Jax and then a pregnant Addison with her husband Oliver in tow.

This is what it means to live.

I look around the patio surrounding the pool, and then I look toward the beach. It all began here, but it won't end here. No, our future isn't written yet.

Like the river, it bends and flows. It adapts and grows, always moving forward. I needed River to show me that.

To teach me how to believe in a future, and now I do.

BY AVA HARRISON

Imperfect Truth

Through Her Eyes

trans·fer·ence

Illicit

Clandestine

Sordid

Explicit

ab·so·lu·tion

Deceit

ACKNOWLEDGMENTS

I want to thank my entire family. I love you all so much.

Thank you to my husband and my kids for always loving me. You guys are my heart!

Thank you to my Mom, Dad, Liz and Ralph for always believing in me, encouraging me and loving me!

Thank you to my in-laws for everything they do for me!

Thank you to all of my brothers and sisters!

Thank you to everyone that helped with Entice

    Lawrence Editing

    Jenny Sims

    My Brother's Editor

    Marla Esposito

    Champagne Formats

    Lori Jackson

    Hang Le

    Special Thanks to Livia Jamerlan for helping me with the content and plotting of Entice.

Thank you to Ryan Douglas for the most perfect image of Grayson EVER!

Thank you to Sebastian York, Virginia Rose and Lyric for bringing Entice to life on audio.

Thank you to Candi Kane PR

Thank you to my AMAZING ARC TEAM! You guys rock!

Thank you to my beta/test team.

Melissa: You're the best! Thank you for everything.

Leigh: Thank you for the endless talks and helping me make sure this book was perfect! I couldn't do it without you.

Parker: Thank you for everything you do for me.

Sarah: Your input and feedback is always amazing! Thank you!

Jessica, Christine, Azalia and Becca. Thank you for your wonderful and extremely helpful feedback.

Jill: Thank you for all your help.

Harloe: Thanks for kicking ass.

Mia: Thanks for always talking plot with me.

I want to thank ALL my friends for putting up with me while I wrote this book. Thank you!

To all of my author friends who listen to me complain and let me ask for advice, thank you!

To the ladies in the Ava Harrison Support Group, I couldn't have done this without your support!

Please consider joining my Facebook reader group Ava Harrison Support Group

Thanks to all the bloggers! Thanks for your excitement and love of books!

Last but certainly not least...

Thank you to the readers!
Thank you so much for taking this journey with me.

ABOUT THE AUTHOR

Ava Harrison is a *USA Today* and Amazon bestselling author. When she's not journaling her life, you can find her window shopping, cooking dinner for her family, or curled up on her couch reading a book.

Connect with Ava

Newsletter Sign Up: bit.ly/2fnQQ1n

Book + Main:
bookandmainbites.com/avaharrison

Facebook Author Page:
www.facebook.com/avaharrisonauthor

Facebook Reader Group: bit.ly/2e67NYi

Goodreads Author Page
www.goodreads.com/author/show/13857011.Ava_Harrison

Instagram:
www.instagram.com/avaharrisonauthor

BookBub:
www.bookbub.com/authors/ava-harrison

Amazon Author Page
amzn.to/2fnVJHFF

Made in the USA
Middletown, DE
26 July 2020